Chapter 1

Veronica
Ride a Cowboy

"Can we start boarding already? I could really use that first class mimosa right about now," Lizzy says impatiently, as we wait for the gate agent to start calling boarding zones.

"Hold your horses. Geez. I want to get on the plane and in our seats too," I say, trying not to think about how much flying stresses me out. Well, not flying per se, but the chaos before the flight really. It's always made me anxious. Who am I kidding? Almost everything makes me anxious. Packing my bags, getting to the airport hours ahead of time, parking shuttles, security lines, boarding, all of it just stressing me out.

And Lizzy knows I can't relax until the boarding door is closed and we're finally just along for the ride. And it being the day after Christmas, all of it is even more of an absolute madhouse. My anxiety levels are through the roof.

"I know it stresses you out, *Veronica,*" she says, raising her eyebrows in my direction. "Even with TSA Pre-check, you still insisted we get to the airport *four* hours early for a domestic flight. What gives girl? It's vacation. Just let go."

Ah Lizzy, sarcastic and sassy as always. I wish it were that simple to just *let go*.

"Ugh. I'm sorry. I know it's excessive, but that's me." I smile back at her, shrugging.

Sorry, not sorry, Lizzy. I've known Elizabeth Frank, Lizzy, since college at Miami Oxford, just over a decade ago by now, and we've worked together for the last two years at Fischer Industries, a manufacturer of consumer packaging. She should know what she signed up for by going on vacation with me. She read the two page itinerary I made for Collin and her after all, at least I hope so.

"It's fine, V. I've been looking forward to this ski trip so much though. I can't wait to get to Wyoming, have a couple girls nights, get a few cocktails, and find a hunky cowboy. Didn't you say there are some cool old cowboy bars there?" she asks with a mischievous grin.

For all of my anxious, neurotic, self-conscious tendencies, Lizzy is the opposite. A classically cute bubbly and flirtatious blonde. She's stunningly fit with a big smile and effortlessly outgoing, but recently went through a bad breakup.

"Well first, I thought you were swearing off dating for a while? And second, yes there are some cowboy bars there, but I don't think there are any real cowboys left in Jackson, Wyoming. Pretty sure it's just tourists and local ski bros there now." She registers my response, but looks undeterred as usual.

FULL SEND

On the Slopes
Book 1

Dakota Forest

DAKOTA FOREST
AUTHOR

ISBN: 979-8-218-53453-0

Cover designed by Ivanna Nashkolna

Edited by H. Forest

Independently Published

https://www.instagram.com/dforestwrites/

https://www.DakotaForest.com

To my book girlies that just want a hunk of a mountain man to get lost in the woods with or bring you your third iced coffee of the day. He's out there somewhere. Just keep looking.

"Hmm. Well, I said I didn't want to date anyone for now. But if I can find a nice rugged cowboy, I wouldn't mind turning him into my own playground for a night. How's that song go again, save a horse, *ride a cowboy*?" She stares at me, eyebrows raised, with that same grin as she twirls her fist in the air like she's about to throw a lasso.

Oh boy. What did I get myself into by bringing her on this trip. I laugh out loud picturing Lizzy roaming the city, hunting the bars of downtown Jackson like a feral wolf, looking for her dream cowboy.

Looking at her, she could certainly have her pick. Even now with her casual travel day choice of black yoga pants, heathered gray crop hoodie showing a hint of her toned stomach, perfectly clean sneakers, and her hair pulled back into a ponytail, she looks like a smoke show. Like a Pinterest post about travel day looks. I've always been envious of how she can make even athleisure wear look that good.

"Oh what's so funny? You can't tell me you haven't thought of finding yourself a mountain man on all of your ski trips out to Jackson over the years?" She asks, knowing full well I'd love nothing more than a real, caring partner in my life.

"I mean… it's crossed my mind. But let's just focus on your cowboy first though," I say, my eyes drifting down to the dirty terrazzo floor of the airport terminal, a small feeling of despair creeping into my thoughts.

I've been hopelessly single for years, my anxiety driven, workaholic lifestyle cutting into my social and dating life, where my only recent romantic partners are the ones resting quietly in the drawer of my nightstand in black silk bags. I've wanted career success for so long, but I've started to question if it's worth the personal sacrifice.

My mind drifts off to thinking about the sad topic that is my love life, when I feel a buzz in my pocket.

Fuck, is that Jeff?

I pull my phone out, catching a glimpse at the notification on my work messenger app. Yep, it's my boss, Jeff. What does he want now? I look at my phone before putting it away. My momentary silence does not go unnoticed, unfortunately.

"Was that Jeff? What could *he* possibly want right now?" Lizzy asks cautiously, her voice nearly drowned out by the sounds of waiting passengers crowding the gate area.

"It's nothing. Just something for Earth SnaX and their new packaging line we're proposing. I'll get to it when we're on the plane." My answer is short. I'm ready to move on.

I dread thinking about work and Lizzy knows that, but sometimes it's hard to not talk about it, seeing as we work together and know so many of the same people. Lizzy has only been working at Fischer in Dayton, Ohio for a couple years, but I started thirteen years ago as a starry eyed intern with big dreams of a hot shot marketing career. And while I should consider myself lucky and successful, I don't know that I'll ever be happy with my job anymore.

I still remember when I picked marketing as my major over a decade ago. I had grand illusions of working as a successful professional in New York City for a big name company. Somewhere with exciting products that was far away from the doldrums of the Midwest, where I grew up. But all these years laters and I'm still here.

Ok. Stop it V. That's enough dwelling in the past.

It's vacation time.

The boarding door has now closed. Plea….

"About time," I mutter, an audible sigh escaping me as I tune out the flight attendants announcement that's still droning on in the background of the first class cabin. Lizzy silently nods in agreement. It's Thursday afternoon, New Year's Eve is in six days, and we're finally in our seats and off on our way for a much needed getaway.

"Well, we're in our seats and the door is closed. You know what that means. Vacation has officially started, Lizzy." I can feel myself finally exhale and relax.

I mean at this point everything is literally out of my control, I'm not the pilot after all. With all of our work travel, we have become spoiled with free drinks on our flights, even short ones like this connecting flight from Salt Lake City, Utah to Jackson, Wyoming, where we got upgraded to first class thanks to our frequent flyer status.

I know the door is closed and it's phones off time, but I still need to get this one last message out to Jeff, so he hopefully has enough for our presentation the week after next. Seriously does this guy ever take a break?! It's the day after Christmas dude!

Monday he told me I was being turned down for a promotion I've been gunning at for years, again. Now he's bugging me about Earth SnaX when I've had this trip planned all year? For fucks sake man.

Message sent. Ok, take a deep breath Veronica. Hopefully that's enough to buy a few days of peace and quiet.

Lizzy eyes me as I put my phone into airplane mode at last.

"So what'd he want for Earth SnaX anyways? Aren't they the snack bar company out in Oregon?" she asks. Although Lizzy and I both work at Fischer, she works in finance and only vaguely knows what I do on a day to day basis.

"Yeah… they're the healthy snack bar maker that we just picked up as a client. So that's his new pet topic that he can't stop bugging me about right now," I say, sighing as I slump into the comfortable first class seat. "We're pitching them some cool ideas for sustainable packaging. It's actually a fun project. I'm even starting to feel a bit invested in it."

"So when's the presentation again? Week after next?" Lizzy asks, sensing the slight change in my voice, knowing that I get excited about this project and working with them.

"Yep, while we're still in Wyoming. I'm a little anxious about the meeting happening while we're gone honestly," I say, my eyes dropping to my hands as I nervously fiddle with my headphones, trying to plug them in to the seat back in front of me.

A quick laugh escapes Lizzy's mouth. "Anxious? I love you, but you're always high strung. So what is it now? You put together a killer set of marketing collateral for their new wrappers and bulk boxes. So what's to worry about?"

I frown. "I don't know. I just have a feeling that Jeff's going to screw up the presentation and blame me or something. I wish it could have waited until I was back so I could just do it myself."

Lizzy seems to sense my apprehension as we continue to talk about work, trying to shift the conversation a bit.

"Well, I guess if we have to make all those work trips, frequent flyer status is a decent perk after all, V. I could get used to more first class upgrades," Lizzy says with her trademark eye roll.

I shrug, my heart not really in it.

"I guess you're right.. but that is *enough* talk about work. Come on, let's talk more about Jackson Hole. I'm dying to get back there finally." The words coming out more forcefully this time.

Lizzy drops her eyes, face a little pink, and a brief hint of guilt flashes across her face. I think she got the message.

Less work. More fun. Come on, let's go girl.

I have always been addicted to work, like my parents. My mom is a nurse, who worked mostly night shifts, while my dad is a regional sales manager for an industrial maintenance services provider. He is constantly traveling across the Midwest and Rust Belt visiting customers. While they were content to languish away in suburban Ohio, I wanted desperately to get away from home.

Unfortunately, life hasn't exactly played out the way I thought it would. Eighteen year old Veronica would ask present day, burnt out

Veronica, *What the actual fuck are you doing?* And she's right, I ask myself this more and more these days and struggle to come up with a good answer most of the time. I'm thirty four, and what do I have to show for it besides living in my hometown, working at a job that doesn't appreciate me, a job that I might actually be starting to hate?

While the work and the company wasn't exciting during my intern days, I got great experience and there was room to advance, or so I thought at the time. I also lived at home, close to campus, and saved money. It was the smart, sensible thing to do. By the book, according to the plan.

Practical Veronica always winning out over Fun Veronica.

After graduating, I stayed on as a full time Marketing Specialist, and things were going well the first few years. I got some small promotions early on, I was making good money, there really wasn't much to complain about. I kept busting my ass and putting in long hours. Just before my thirtieth birthday, I finally got to manage my own marketing team specializing in health and snack foods. It was all going according to plan at that point.

Fast forward five years, I've been passed over several times for a promotion to Marketing Director of North America, despite my outstanding performance reviews.

My path is seemingly blocked by out of touch old men, who probably should have retired years ago. What does a girl have to do to get past the good old boys club?

My boss, Jeff Flaherty, certainly isn't doing me any favors. He's a squirrel brained micromanager, who needles me about random, different topics out of the blue throughout the day on chat and by text.

Hello.

Hey.

Veronica.

What are you doing right now?

Where are you?

A constant barrage of single word messages or vague questions with zero context and no hint of what's next. I mean who does that?

Each erratic, unpredictable ping on my laptop or text message on my phone prompts a new rush of crippling anxiety and a mini panic attack. Sometimes I freeze and shut down, waiting for what's next. Other times I think I should cut him slack for being an old borderline Boomer that clearly didn't grow up with texting or DMs to learn modern day communication etiquette. Then I remember the near constant anxiety spiral he causes and think *hell no, do fucking better.*

Each year that goes by like this, my self doubt grows. I've given up so much while focusing on work, with practically no social life outside of my brother Collin, and Lizzy.

I look over to Lizzy. Shit. I've been zoned out too long. As if she's been reading my mind, she's eyeing me, a finger resting on her lips.

"So… a cowboy for me. But what about you V, what have you been *craving?*" she asks, raising her eyebrows as a grin takes shape.

The question is perfectly timed, but I'm still caught off guard and nearly choke on my water.

"Ughhhh. What?" I ask, still not sure what she's getting at.

"What do *you* want, V? It's vacation, we can have some fun out there, find some fuckboys or fuck *cow*boys. Is that a thing?" she says, looking up, holding her chin between her thumb and finger, pondering her own question. I notice the man in the row next to us shift awkwardly in his seat and cover his mouth, trying not to laugh at Lizzy's question.

"Lizzy. No, not happening. You know I don't have time for a dating life, and even if I did, have you seen the options out there? The dating pool is practically empty." I wipe my lips with the back of my hand, cleaning off the water I spit out.

"Oh come on. I know you want to find that special someone." She pushes, clearly enjoying how uncomfortable she's making me, as I try to sink further into the seat to hide.

"Nope, not doing this right now," I say, putting my hand up trying to move her off of this topic."Let's stay focused on finding your cowboy."

She's not wrong though. It's certainly not that I don't want to find someone, to find *love*. I would kill to find... *my person.*

A partner to come home to and enjoy dinner with after a long hard day. A companion to tell me everything is going be ok when I'm doom spiraling. A lover to hold me before bed, feeling their breath against the back of my neck as I drift off to sleep, and ok fine, do *other things* with. A man that looks at me like I'm the only person in their entire world. One that lights a fire deep inside me and makes the hair on my skin stand just by being near me.

I want that. I want all of it.

But dating is hard.

The apps, waiting for a text back, getting stood up, all of it just adds a layer of uncertainty to my life, one I'm not sure I can handle right now. It just doesn't feel worth it. Thinking about this now as I sit on the plane, I feel the tension growing in my face, the harbinger of possible tears in my near future.

No V, we are absolutely not doing this now. No crying on vacation.

"Well, I don't know about you, but I'm ready for two weeks off work and on the slopes. You sure you're ready for a real mountain?" I say with a wink. The question was rhetorical of course.

Lizzy is a great skier who's spent countless winters with her family in Aspen Valley, Utah. Is that the same as the steep chutes and powder at Jackson Hole, where Collin and I have been skiing since we could barely walk? No, but she can handle herself on the slopes.

"Ha. Very funny V. You know I'm always ready for a challenge. Besides, you'll be out in Aspen Valley with me in February, so you'll get to see for yourself if you think it's that easy of a mountain." Even after years of living with her in college, I still forget how she makes everything seem so easy and effortless.

If you could sum Lizzy up in two words, it would be *Always. On.* All smiles, ready for a night out, a spin class, dessert, an impromptu girls trip, you name it. She's always ready with a snarky come back prepared, like a grown version of a character from Mean Girls.

While I toiled away back home in Midwestern mid-level corporate purgatory, Lizzy did in fact get an internship at an exciting start-up on the west coast. She spent her first 4 years after college working there before moving home to Dayton. That shiny, exciting tech startup internship and early work on her résumé, combined with her firecracker personality, seemed to open up doors for her to climb the ladder faster. By the time she joined me at Fischer, she came in as a Director, albeit in our finance department.

It sucks, but it is what it is and I'm proud of her. She's an amazing friend and works hard for what she has.

I look over at Lizzy. Even on the short flight, she has a book out she started on the first connecting flight this morning. This one is called *Scorned and Spurred*. The bright orange and blue cover has clipart of a cowboy with his arms crossed watching a cute girl walk by.

I clear my throat, getting her attention. "Did you really bring cowboy smut for this trip, Lizzy?"

She looks up at me startled, then rolls her eyes at me exhaling. "Don't be such a prude, V. Just doing my homework, you know? I gotta get in the zone if I'm going to go cowboy hunting. You should take notes. You could use a little more excitement in your life."

I let out a little chuckle. "Yeah, I'm down for some excitement on the mountain too. The fresh crisp cool air, the beauty of the Tetons, a few nights out for drinks, maybe I'll even be your wing-*woman* while you hunt down that cowboy."

That last line gets a laugh out of her.

"I'm telling you, V. I'm gonna find a cowboy. Just watch me work," she says.

I can't help but shake my head and laugh. I'm starting to believe she'll pull it off when she's this serious.

"Geez. I didn't realize how ready I am for this trip. All of it, even catching up with Collin too," I say, winking at her.

Saying it out loud now, I'm starting to believe myself and actually looking forward to unplugging on this trip. I rarely take much time off, so this trip is a rare treat to get more than two weeks off at once. Thankfully, I was able to combine the week long holiday office closure, a little of this year's vacation time, and a week of next year's vacation time for the first week in January.

"Of course you are ready, V. You've practically planned the next two weeks down to the hour!" Lizzy scoffs.

Ok. She's pretty on point with that. I'm a fanatical planner. I get a sense of relief, of control over my life. It doesn't always work out, case in my point my life right now, but at least I feel prepared.

"And speaking of your brother, remind me again why Collin is going to be there with us?" Lizzy asks head recoiled back, raising her perfectly sculpted eyebrows.

I know she wanted this to be a girls trip, but it's Collin's condo too. I mean I get her hesitation still. Despite her being my best friend for over a decade, Collin and her have only met in passing a couple of times over the years. When we were in college, Collin was an hour away at the University of Cincinnati. Then when we graduated, she was on west coast while he stayed in Cincinnati. It just always seemed like they were ships passing in the night at the edges of my life.

I laugh, reminding her that Collin being at the condo will have its perks. "Just think of him as our house boy? Lighting the fireplace for us, taking out the trash, picking up carryout. You know, all the stuff we don't want to deal with on vacation."

We cackle together at the thought of it.

"Ok, V. I guess that'll be fine," she says with a smile and an eye roll as we're interrupted by the flight attendant with our mimosas.

"Just what I needed. Nothing gets the vacation started like a mimosa. Am I right?" I say, still smirking about Collin.

"Duh, girl. We're gonna need more of these on the trip for sure! I hope Collin has the condo stocked with OJ and Prosecco. Or is that off limits for him to buy too, and a liquor store run is already planned?" she asks, eyebrows raised looking down her nose at me.

"Lizzy Lizzy Lizzy…" I shake my head, a wide smirk on my face. "You're damn right I planned for that. There's a liquor store attached to the grocery store. One stop shopping."

"Fine by me. More time for drinks at this condo I've heard so much about," she says as she raises her glass in my direction.

"Vacation mode?" I raise my glass to hers.

"Vacation mode." She looks at me gleefully as we clink our glasses.

Chapter 2

Veronica
Twins

J ust like that, we've started our descent into Jackson. Even as a little girl, the landing approach on a clear day has never failed to take my breath away. The timelessly majestic Teton mountains, those jagged granite peaks, forever stretching towards the sky and so tantalizingly close, are visible to the west, just outside the windows of the plane. Over thirty years later and my reaction to this view still hasn't changed. Breathtaking.

I'm clearly not the only one that's impacted by these mountains, as I look over and see Lizzy. It's her first time coming to Jackson and it seems my description of the view was understated.

"They're just... beautiful. I haven't seen peaks like this before, not even back in Utah," Lizzy utters in quiet disbelief and amazement as she stares outside, her perfectly made up face practically glued to the window. "They look so close, like you could reach out and touch them if you wanted to."

Her childlike excitement brings a bit of warmth to my heart. I love seeing people happy about the same things that bring me joy. Like somehow if they weren't as excited as me, I'd have oversold it and let them down. It's also a rare treat seeing sass queen Lizzy let her guard down, overtaken by the sight in front of her. For once she's just absorbing it all.

A few moments later, we touch down and we're at our gate. We stand up as soon as the seatbelt light goes off.

Yes, we're those people.

Well at least I am, I'm ready to get off the plane and move on with the day. Even on such a short flight, it's been a long travel day and it feels great to stand up and stretch out.

"Gotta love a short connecting flight," Lizzy says, reaching into the overhead bin for her small carry-on bag.

"Then you're really going to like this small airport. They'll have the stairs up to the plane and we'll be at baggage claim in no time."

Just as I told Lizzy, we're off the plane in minutes, walking down the steps since the airport doesn't even have jet bridges. We're in what feels like a new world. I close my eyes and take a deep breath, feeling the cool crisp mountain air fill my lungs and chill my face. The mountain air brings a sense of calm over me that I haven't felt in ages.

It's good to be back here. My home away from home.

We make our way across the tarmac and through the iconic elk antler arch welcoming us to Jackson Hole, a replica of the arches found in the town square.

The airport is indeed small, although practically brand new. The way this place has changed over the last decade with the influx of money has been amazing to watch, albeit slightly disheartening as well for long time locals and visitors. A place that once felt like a secret - remote and off the beaten path - raw and original - has grown so much in recent years. But it's still special to me.

My happy place.

"Well look what the cat dragged in." A boisterous voice cuts through the hustle and bustle of the baggage claim area. There's Collin with a luggage cart, ready to go.

"Took you long enough," he says jokingly, tapping his toe and looking at his pretend watch. I could spot him a mile away. Any place feels like home when Collin is there with me, my biological other half.

"See, I told you there would be perks to having him here. Remember, house boy?" I jokingly nudge Lizzy with my forearm.

"Thanks for picking us up, Collin," Lizzy replies, charmingly as ever. No hint of the disappointment from before about this not being a girls trip. This is what I mean.

Always. On.

"Ohhhh… free mimosas?!" Lizzy squeals over her shoulder as she brushes past us making her way towards the Welcome Kiosk along the back wall of baggage claim and picking up a fresh mimosa.

To be fair to Collin though, he would insist this is actually still a girls trip. Collin, my *older* brother, by a measly twenty minutes, has been out as bisexual since the summer before his freshman year at the University of Cincinnati. So I get it, he wants to be included in all our girly shit and frankly I want him here too. But even if Collin might want us to think of this as a girls trip, he's anything but *girly*.

He has always been a classic troublemaker - always joking, always getting into something with his friends, especially his old friends out here. He played multiple sports through high school, and was always fiercely competitive with me on the slopes. It seemed like I was even getting dragged into whatever the boys were getting into back in those days. I can't really complain though. I think that's part of the reason I fell in love with skiing as much as I did and became driven to succeed in my career, or at least try to. I wanted so badly to keep up with the boys and even beat them when I could.

Collin was that way too, always wanting to impress our dad and it showed between his competitiveness and excellence in academics. I only realized after he came out that he thought he had even more reason to try and prove himself, even though he had nothing to prove.

He's tall, traditionally handsome, with wavy brown hair, a shorter cut version of my own, and a well manicured permanent five o'clock shadow. He's a gifted athlete and super intelligent. It was really just on our trips out here, visiting our grandparents that he got to unwind and be himself, finally out from under the eyes of our dad.

As for Lizzy's concerns about him joining our *girls trip*, she still raised the question if she should worry about my brother hitting on her, despite my initial reassurances.

Maybe it was a tongue in cheek joke or maybe it was a real concern of hers. She's not wrong to think men would want her. She would be an amazing catch and always has attractive men pining after her too. I mean she is single after breaking up with that prick

Johnathan too. They were together for years before she found out he was cheating on her this summer. Apparently, his frequent *work* trips were not so business related. So I totally get not wanting to deal with men for a bit after that.

But the thought of Collin being interested in Lizzy was enough to almost bring me to tears laughing. They are just not each other's type. Girly girl Lizzy, always put together in her cute matching yoga outfits or short dresses, with a full face of makeup and perfect hair, and Collin, my gay leaning bi brother with a thing for more masculine partners? As if!

At lunch last week, I tried to put her mind at ease.

> *"Lizzy, he'd be flattered, you're a catch," I cackled. "But for real, you wouldn't be his type even if he was still dating women. And as far as I know he's dated exclusively men for the last five or six years. Nevertheless, I assure you Collin will be on his best behavior. Well, with you at least."*

If anyone knows Collin's type besides him, it's me. Collin is my twin, a true mirror of myself in so many ways. I don't know where I'd be without him sometimes. Always there to vent to when work sucks. He's been my lifelong skiing buddy. He'll listen to me cry or when I complain about my love life, which has been helplessly dormant for years since my last serious boyfriend. I mean, again, who has time for that if you work a real job, workout, and want a full night's sleep?

Through it all though, over the years, Collin's been my rock. The one who can finish my sentences and read my thoughts.

I guess some things they say about twins really are true.

As Lizzy looks for our bags to arrive at baggage claim, I sneak a quick moment with him. Wrapping my arms around him and burying my head in his chest for a much needed hug. He holds me tight in his arms and it feels like I'm wrapped in a warm, comfy security blanket. After a few seconds, I break away looking back at him.

"Thanks for picking us up, *big brother,*" I tease, raising my eyebrows. He cracks that wide, familiar, comforting smile.

"Anytime, *lil sis.*" Ahh. This feels good. The *big bro, lil sis* routine has always been our little inside joke.

"You doing alright, V?" The tone was a bit more serious, maybe even a hint of concern. We talked on Christmas Day and he knows I got turned down for the promotion again.

"I'm good I guess, just the same old work BS. Just trying to get out of my own head. I'm glad I'm here now with you and Lizzy."

"Work still that bad?" he asks, a look of worry on his face.

I vent to Collin about everything. He's even asked why I haven't left Fischer years ago, maybe for a lateral move to start over somewhere else. And honestly, every time he asks, I can't really come up with a good reason for why not and I'm starting to agree with him.

But each time, that thought is followed up by doubt about what I could do now to change it? Could I just quit, take my hard earned savings, and completely start over? The thought of looking for a new job, the stress of interviewing, the waiting to maybe get a call back, all create a new wave of anxiety. I start wondering what could I have done differently? How the fuck did I get even here?

Maybe I'm just unlucky or cursed to be stuck in Ohio in corporate anonymity, rotting away.

As my thoughts start to spiral again, I remind myself that I can't just doom scroll through the snapshots of my life up to this point anymore. It's time to try and enjoy my well earned time off.

Back to the moment at hand, V.

No more pity party.

"Yep, same old same old at Fischer. Just happy to be back in Wyoming," I say, sighing a bit of relief as I look around the airport, admiring the floor to ceiling views of the mountains outside.

"Yeah. Well sis," he pauses for a moment, letting out an exasperated sigh before that big cheerful smile returns again. "I'm glad you're here too. But next time, can you maybe bring a cute single guy too? It's slim pickings out here in Wyoming for me."

Ah… There it is, always a witty joke lurking around the corner with him. I let out a short laugh and punch him in the shoulder. Oh Collin, you little shit.

"You know damn well if I had time to find a cute single man I'd be looking for myself first!"

He looks back at me, shaking his head, his eyes more serious this time. "Really sis, I've been pumped for this trip for awhile. It's been way too long since we were here together. I'm sure we'll have you cheered right up."

We look at each other and share a warm smile as Lizzy returns, two large duffels in tow.

"So um… bags are out. Maybe a little help here? And what'd I miss? Obviously something funny based on those laughs. This place is so small I could hear you two laughing all the way across baggage claim." She rolls her eyes and shakes her head looking at us.

"God you're definitely twins." She palms her face as she shakes her head.

Collin and I smile at each other. I start to respond but that boisterous reassuring voice chimes in.

"Well apparently, we were commiserating a bit too loudly about something we can all relate to, Lizzy. The lack of quality single men out there." Oh Collin. Yep, definitely twins.

"Oh yeah, Collin. I didn't tell you. Lizzy thinks she's going to find herself a hunky cowboy as her own plaything while we're here." I look at Lizzy, sticking my tongue out.

"Good one, V. Very funny," Lizzy huffs, like she's about to start pouting.

"Yeah, I hate to burst your bubble but your chances of finding one are about as good as winning the lottery," Collin teases.

"I see you are both comedic geniuses. Seems like this might be a nice girls trip after all," Lizzy says with a wink.

I look at Collin and Lizzy, all smiles. What a relief.

The vibes are good.

One less thing to stress myself out over.

Chapter 3

Veronica
Old Town

"So wait, I thought we were going to Jackson. What's Teton Village?" Lizzy asks, a confused look on her face as we reach the SUV. "Are you guys kidnapping me or something? I don't know if my dad will cough up the ransom money or not, but I want my cut if he does."

"I told you, Lizzy. The ski resort, *Jackson Hole*, is actually in the tiny town of Teton Village, fifteen minutes past the town of Jackson," I say, shaking my head as I hand my bag to Collin to throw in the back of the SUV.

"I swear, it's like we have this conversation every time we bring a new person out here," Collin says, shaking his head like me while closing the hatch of the cargo area.

The drive from the airport in the winter to Teton Village takes about thirty-five to forty minutes but goes right through scenic downtown Jackson, Wyoming so at least Lizzy gets a nice tour of that on our way.

Although there is a modest public transportation system connecting the airport, the town of Jackson, and Teton Village, we prefer having our own car for grocery runs, day trips, and because lugging our bags and skis on a bus is frankly a chore. This time is a bit different as it's the first time we've been out at the condo together since our Grandpa passed away, leaving the condo to Collin and me.

"So, how was the drive out here?" I ask Collin as we leave the airport parking lot.

"Not too bad. Twenty-four hours from Cincy but I stopped in Omaha for a night along the way to break it up," he says, eyes focused on the long straight road heading to Jackson."I left Sunday and got in Monday night."

"Remind me exactly what it is you do again, Collin?" Lizzy asks, looking out the window of the passenger seat at the mountains on our right.

"Online fitness coach and dietician. Pretty convenient when I want to work remote and come out here a few days early," he says.

"Oh, ok. That makes more sense. I thought you were a personal trainer and had to go to a gym or something. Didn't realize you did online stuff," she says, sounding surprised and disappointed. "Not sure why, but I was picturing you in some grey sweats spotting someone on their lifts or helping them with some deep stretching."

Collin and I both turn to Lizzy, mouths open.

"What? You can't tell me you haven't had the hot gym trainer fantasy before," she quips, arms crossed, letting out a huff and rolling her eyes at me. "Don't act like I'm the crazy one here."

I try to change the topic away from my brother in grey sweats, for my own sake. "So… How was Christmas, Collin? I know you were planning on spending it at the Chapman's place. Anything new there?" I notice him shift uncomfortably in the driver seat at my question.

We talked Christmas Day and I know Collin didn't mind missing Christmas at home. He has never been particularly close to our parents, part of the reason he stayed in Cincinnati after school instead of moving back home to Dayton.

"Actually it was great. I slept in until you called, then hung out with Chapman and his grandparents the rest of the day. His grandma made her meatloaf, which I was craving. Just an all around good day," he says, his tone more upbeat.

I'm glad he enjoyed Christmas for a change. He mostly came out to Wyoming early to help take care of some things around the condo, but I'm sure meeting up with our family friend, Tanner Chapman, and his grandparents was nice for him. Tanner's a local property manager that's been helping us take care of our condo since Grandpa passed away. Collin also brought our stash of wine and some goodies from home in his SUV, since the options in Wyoming can be a bit limited.

Between the airport and Jackson, we have a few minutes to take in more of the heart stopping views of the Teton Mountain Range. With the clear blue skies, Jackson Hole Ski Resort is clearly visible from the road into town out the passengers side windows.

"Holy shit," Lizzy blurts out, "you said this place was steep, but that's nuts."

"Told you, Lizzy. Jackson Hole is no joke." I can feel myself grinning as I make eye contact with Collin, the same thought clearly on his mind.

"So the condo is at the base of that, near that cluster of buildings?"

"Yep. About a fifteen minute walk from all the lifts," Collin adds.

I stare out the window when I hear a familiar song come on the radio.

"Collin, turn it up please?" I ask, watching his eyes in the rear view mirror.

"All these years and you still love this band. Don't tell me you still have a fan girl crush on Tommy Jacobs?" Collin chides.

"Oh fuck off, Collin," I snarl. "You know he's hot. I don't seem to remember you complaining when we went to all those Teal Tigers concerts in high school."

With one of my favorite songs now drowning out Collin and Lizzy, I gaze out the window at the mountains again. Even from the distance we're at you can clearly see the outlines of the ski slopes with little black dots that I know are skiers. Seeing them puts my mind right back into ski junkie mode, craving the rush from being on the mountain.

Chasing fresh snow or *freshies*. Waking up at the crack of dawn to be first in line for the chair lifts or *first chair*. Skiing in knee deep fluffy powder or *pow*. Wanting to be the first person to go down a run for the day with your skis leaving beautiful flowing brush strokes behind you or *first tracks*.

Sometimes I forget how much slang skiers use. None of it ever comes up in conversation back in the *real world* in Ohio. It's all flooding back now.

I sigh... I missed this.

On our left, before we reach town, is the sprawling National Elk Refuge. It's dotted with sleds chauffeuring tourists around to see the elk herds. Occasionally a wolf can even be spotted on the edges of the sanctuary, a reminder that this place is surrounded by total wilderness.

A few minutes later and we're passing through Jackson. Downtown or old town, was once a rustic small town with dirt roads, no traffic lights, and charming old western buildings. Our grandparents would tell us about how as recently as the eighties, the town still felt like a rural western town.

"Wow," Lizzy says, watching out the windows as Collin is still scanning the streets for a parking spot, "this place is so cute. Are all these old store fronts original?"

"Yep. Most of the facades are original. The stores in them have changed but the layout is pretty much how it's always been," I say, looking out the window at the row of shops we're passing, scanning for any new ones that might have opened since my last time in town.

"Hmmm. I think we need to stop in there later," Lizzy says, pointing up at a large neon sign. Oh boy.

Dotting the downtown landscape are a number of old saloons like the Silver Dollar Cowboy Bar and Horseshoe Saloon, sticking out above the rest of the shops with their old school neon signs. Lizzy is looking right at the cowboy bar. I'd expected her to be a bit more excited, but maybe the flight took more out of her than I expected.

"Oh we will, don't worry," Collin says smirking. "Just don't get your hopes on finding a cowboy there."

Lizzy huffs, folding her arms over her chest and glaring at Collin.

"You know, you should really see it at night, Lizzy. I remember as a kid our grandparents would take us out at night for dinner or to pick up pizza to take home. Collin and I would have our faces pressed against the window looking up at all the neon signs overhead. God I miss those days. It was almost like a year round Christmas light show," I say, reminiscing as I look out at the town square.

I can see Collin nod in agreement from the driver seat. "Yeah, some of them are pretty cool. Like the Cowboy Bar sign, it's animated and the cowboy is riding a bucking bronco."

It's not too hard to imagine what it would have looked like fifty years ago. Sure, the dirt roads have been replaced by nicely paved roads, traffic lights, and crosswalks, but the storefronts, saloons, and wooden boardwalks are all still here. Except now there's an abundance of high end boutiques, art galleries, and fancy restaurants instead of the old tack shops, gun stores, and feed shops.

Fortunately no high rises have gone in at least. The tallest buildings around town are four stories at most, preserving the views of the mountains surrounding downtown.

In the heart of it all though is still the old town square.

In the winter there's an ice rink in the center of it. Despite being touristy, our grandparents still taught us to skate there. In the summer it's a great place to enjoy a coffee and a pastry, and read a favorite book on a park bench.

Standing at each of the four corners of the square are the iconic elk antler arches, made from antlers collected by local Scout Troops from the elk refuge. At night, they're illuminated by countless strands of white Christmas lights. Even with all that's changed over the years, I've always thought the square was charming and romantic at night.

At this point, a coffee sounds great. But not just any coffee. I need the good stuff today. After we find a parking spot, we head straight to one of my favorite places to grab a casual bite to eat in town. It's not fancy, but I've been giddy all day waiting for this. One of my guilty pleasures, a treat for me when we're in town, are regular stops into Cowgirl Coffee, practically becoming a temporary regular. It's a charming little spot just off the old square, a perfect lunch to fuel up before going out shopping and showing Lizzy around.

My order hasn't changed in years. A large iced honey badger with oat milk, an extra shot of espresso, and a chorizo breakfast burrito. The honey badger, with its combination of cayenne espresso, cinnamon, honey, and oat milk might sound like a bit much, but to me it's the perfect combination. Cold yet spicy, sweet yet a bit savory. Paired with a breakfast burrito, it's my favorite winter breakfast, even though it's lunch today. *Mmmm.* I get chills of joy just thinking about it.

"V. I don't know how on earth you can walk around town when it's twenty degrees out and down an iced coffee like that," Lizzy chides after we grab our orders to go. "Either that coffee must be amazing or you must be a serial killer."

"You know Lizzy, someone once told me you can tell how dedicated someone is to the iced coffee life by whether or not they still drink them in the winter. Well I'm not just dedicated, I'm a diehard fan. This drink is my ride or die." No offense to Collin or Lizzy.

I'm not exaggerating. I think there have been days in the past here where I've had at least two or three of these throughout the day. I would kill for a place that could make these back in Ohio, a taste of *home* in the midwest.

As I'm enjoying my *iced* honey badger, my little bit of bliss is interrupted. There's a ping from my phone, the one I specifically set up for Jeff. I swear dude, it's the Thursday of Christmas break, our office is closed the whole week. What can you possibly need? I begrudgingly check my work messaging app, feeling the impending sense of doom creep into my psyche.

Nothing major. Okay breathe, V. He's just confirming another detail for the Earth SnaX presentation. I know this presentation by heart at this point. Slide for slide. Word for word. I swear at this rate, I should just do the presentation for him. Why should he get more of the credit for my work anyways? Calm down V, no need to spiral. Not even Jeff can take away the joy of a honey badger on a snowy morning in Jackson. I look out across the square, absorbing the views of the mountains and town around me, taking a deep breath of the cool morning air.

"Was that Jeff? What the hell could he want right now? That dude is *the worst*," Lizzy scoffs, a look of disgust on her face.

"Oh nothing, he's just confirming something else for Earth SnaX. No crisis, thankfully." I breathe an exaggerated sigh of relief and take another sip of my sweet and spicy drink.

"So what do you want to do next, Lizzy? You're the one who's never been here before." Collin has joined the conversation finally.

"Umm… shopping obviously? Isn't that what you do in ski towns?" She gestures as if she's strutting along carrying shopping bags in each arm. Lizzy's not wrong. That's what it feels like most tourists do and what most of Collin's friends on their first visit here want to do.

Collin and I take her for a stroll around the boardwalks surrounding the town square for a while, plodding along, our snow boots against the wooden planks sounding like something out of an old western movie.

I've always found the assortment of shops in ski towns and resorts to be amusing. It always seems to be a bizarre, confusing combination of touristy stuff like tacky t-shirt shops, souvenir shops, and cowboy boot or western wear stores, and then ultra high-end jewelry shops, rug stores, and art galleries.

Practical Veronica shakes her head in disgust. What a waste.

I've been saving my money like crazy for years, the idea of a safety net bringing a small amount of comfort to me. I think like many millennials, there's still residual trauma left over from the 2008 financial crisis, having interned through it and seeing the aftermath impact so many of my peers for so long, still playing catch up today. But a small, hopeful part of me clings to the idea that maybe one day I could abandon my life plan, quit my job, say fuck it, move somewhere I love, and start over. It's a fantasy I've tried to keep hidden deep in the recesses of my mind, but rears its head more and more these days.

As we work our way further along the boardwalks and store fronts, I look across the street towards the town square. At one corner under one of the arches, a young couple is standing there talking and laughing, coffees in hand. After a couple seconds of this, they share a quick kiss, press their foreheads and noses together, eyes closed, and then go along their way.

The charm of this place is overwhelming sometimes. I've always wondered if I'll ever have someone of my own that I can share this place with, making my own happy memories here. There are so many things here I want to show people and share with them to see their faces light up like mine. When do I get that, my person? I deserve happiness, don't I? I feel sad, angry, fearful, all at once.

Stop. Clear your head, V. Take a deep breath, a hopeful breath.

One day, maybe, one day.

After bouncing around town into a couple of souvenir shops and then window shopping a few others, Lizzy finally is looking for something specific.

"Alright guys, where's the best place to find locally made jewelry?" Ah there she is. Always looking for new things to compliment all of her cute, curated outfits.

Meanwhile most of my jewelry was left to me by my grandmother, including her gorgeous wedding ring and engagement ring. She always said she dreamed of me finding that *special somebody*, but these days that feels so far from reality. But I rarely buy myself anything nice. Practical Veronica says save money, don't buy it if you don't need it.

"You're asking the wrong person, Lizzy," I scoff. "You know I don't buy nice jewelry."

"Um, that doesn't mean you don't know where to look. You know this town like the back of your hand. Come on, don't hold out on your girl," Lizzy pouts, holding her hands out in a pleading gesture.

Collin steps in front of us. "I know just the spot. Let's go girls."

He pivots and is already walking away, waving with his hand to follow along. He leads us to a store just off the square, The Eclectic Elk. It's a quirky little shop, filled with goods from local artists and makers. Everything from jewelry, art prints to woven goods and other odds and ends.

After meandering around the store, I notice Lizzy has been lingering at one case a bit longer than the others.

"Hey, V! Come over here. You're going to love this."

Hmm. Wonder what she found. She knows I'm not much for jewelry.

As I reach her side and gaze down into the display case, I immediately know why she called me.

I admire the contents of the case, which is filled with some of the most beautiful chef's knives I've ever seen. Some have intricate Damascus steel blades with their beautiful color patterns and variations in striking contrast to each other. Damascus steel like this is difficult to make, no two blades truly alike. Each knife has a unique handle, some with colorful cast epoxy resin, polished walnut, or an elk antler, others inlaid with turquoise. Looking closer I see the handiwork of the blacksmith that made them, each of the blades indented with a small makers brand where the blade meets the hilt, a *T* and *C* overlaying each other inside of a horseshoe.

I do know exactly what these are. But these are much more refined than the last set I saw from this maker. Clearly he's been practicing.

Lizzy definitely knows me well, I love good knives in the kitchen.

"How have you never bought one of these before, V? Or do you have a set back home already?" she asks, eyebrow raised.

I'd love some of my own but before I can even get a word out, I realize Collin has snuck up behind us. His tall goofy ass is peering over our shoulders wrapping an arm around each of us.

"My buddy, Chap, makes those," he says beaming like a proud parent as he joins us in admiring the knives. "They're pretty badass."

Collin is right. These are the best knives I've ever used. I'd like a couple better sized for my hands to take home, but they're all amazing.

"We actually have a set tucked away back at the condo," he adds.

"Yeah. I haven't got a set from him yet. But hey speaking of your shadow, Collin, where is Tanner? I haven't seen him in years," I ask, still longingly gazing into the case.

Collin and Tanner Chapman have known each other since they could barely walk. They became best friends over the years, practically inseparable whenever we were in town visiting our grandparents. Tanner's family already lived here and our grandparents became close friends since the early seventies when ours bought the condo as a vacation home before retiring there years later. As his grandparents retired, they downsized into a condo in the same building.

Unlike us though, Tanner is a true local, born and raised in the shadows of the Tetons. His parents moved to Salt Lake City about a decade ago to be closer to his younger sister and brother, Grace and Clay, who are in Park City. Even after he lost his mom in an accident, his dad stayed there. Tanner lives in his grandparents old cabin, just down the road from Teton Village, where his grandparents condo and ours are. The cabin sits on what's left of their former ranch just off the banks of the Snake River on Moose Wilson Road. Most of the land has since been sold off, but they were able to keep the cabin and old barn for Tanner.

It's always been the same story with Tanner and Collin though. When Collin and I are in Jackson, it always seem like Tanner is lurking around somewhere waiting to go off on the next childish adventure with Collin, often with me in tow. We didn't see Grace and Clay as much, them being much younger than Tanner. When we would see them, I remember how fiercely protective Tanner was of them. But still, Tanner has always been every bit the jokester Collin is, but with an added level of self confidence. It always seemed like a paradox, someone so confident and unflappable, yet also able to seemingly make anything into a joke, never taking things seriously. At least that's how it always felt from the outside looking in.

"Chap's busy at his workshop but I'll probably catch him on the slopes tomorrow. He wants to do après at the condo tomorrow and then the Fox Saturday, anyways. Sound good, V?" says Collin.

"Yep, works. Lizzy has heard me hyping the infamous fox margs since we turned twenty-one!"

"Oof. Don't remind me of *that* night." Collin shudders at the memory of our twenty-first birthday night out, or more like the next day. I try to hold a laugh in just thinking about how hungover he was.

As we leave the shop, I'm still stunned thinking about Tanner's new knives in that case.

It's been at least five or so years since I visited Tanner's barn where his workshop is set up. Tanner's main gig for years has been as a property manager taking care of a handful of vacation homes and condos, with half of the barn set up for that. Plumbing and electrical tools, spare appliances, a snowblower, a plow for his truck, all things he needs to take care of those properties are right on site.

The other half though, that was reserved for his passion project.

Tanner's grandparents ranch wasn't particularly large and his grandfather still did side work as a blacksmith, namely for local farriers, forging horseshoes in a workshop in the back of the old barn. The old ranches in the area, and later the horseback riding outfits catering to tourists, supplied a modest stream of income on the side for the family, at least for a while.

Even as that side hustle eventually dried up by the time Tanner's grandfather retired, Tanner took an interest to blacksmithing and forging metal as a kid. After learning the fundamentals of the process to make horseshoes from his grandfather, he started to take an interest in tools and household items, namely hunting and kitchen knives.

Over the last few years, he's obviously become quite skilled at it, based on what's in the case at The Eclectic Elk. The knives he made for our grandparents years ago were great. Functional, durable, very utilitarian. But the ones in that case… they're something else.

They're absolutely stunning, a refined sense of artistry I didn't ever imagine Tanner being capable of honestly.

Chapter 4

Tanner
The Eclectic Elk

"I know Rex, another day with you by my side bud. How'd you ever get so lucky?" I look over to the passenger seat of my truck, looking right at Rex, no reaction as usual. He's in his usual spot by my side, his brown eyes staring ahead out the windshield at the snowy treelined road into town. "Jeez dude. Tough crowd." Still nothing. He just keeps looking straight ahead, watching as another plow truck drives past in the opposite direction. Maybe if I said *ball* or *outside* he'd do something, I mean he is a cattle dog after all.

All jokes aside, Rex is a great buddy and rides along with me most work days. Let's be real. He's with me almost any time I'm driving. Finally he looks at me before lying down in the seat, tucking his head between his paws. "You know I'm kidding bud. But it is another busy day."

Ain't that the truth. I'm barely keeping up with my schedule for the day and still haven't had lunch. I need to stop into the Eclectic Elk, grab something to eat, and get back to work at a couple properties later tonight. I already know I'm going to be crunched for time the next two weeks with my friends in town, so staying ahead of schedule would be ideal.

After finding a parking spot on the street outside the Eclectic Elk, I head into the old shop to make a delivery.

"Morning handsome!" I'm greeted with the familiar, excited voice of Giselle, the owner of the shop, before the door even closes behind me, jingling the little shop bells.

"Hey Giselle. Does Colt know you still call me that? If you're not careful someone might get the wrong idea," I say, winking at her before leaning in to give her a hug. Giselle and her husband, Colt, were my parent's best friends until my parents left town and moved to Salt Lake City almost a decade ago. Even now though, she goes into full mom mode when I stop in and still treats me like her own son.

"Yes. I do know," Colt calls out from the back room of the shop. "And hi Chap. Hope you had a nice Christmas."

I love stopping in here, as bittersweet as it is. Giselle and Colt are like family, some of the last I have in town after most of my actual family moved away. Even growing up I was friends with their son, Owen, until he moved away too. So while I love seeing them, it's still a reminder of how few of my friends and family are left in town. Honestly though, most places in town are like that now.

"Yep, it was a nice day. Collin was in town so I spent it with him and my grandparents," I say, loud enough for Colt in the back to hear. "Anyways, I'm here to drop off some more knives."

I feel unusually happy by how she excitedly opens the box, pulling the half dozen leather bundles out and laying them each on the counter. One by one she unrolls the bundles, revealing the knives in each of them.

"You came just at the right time. The Christmas rush and holiday shoppers were wiping out your case. I'm sure these won't last very long either." She pulls one of the longer chef's knives out from its bundle. Seeing the way she stares at the blade in front of her, mouth open, always brings a little warmth to my heart.

"You're too nice, Giselle. I'm glad business is doing great. I'm happy to keep making them and selling them here." I look back at the knives in front of her on the counter, thinking of the work that went into each one, what I was thinking about when I made them, a little piece of me left behind for their new owners.

"It's funny. You just missed your friends, the Perry kids. They were here less than an hour ago. They had some cute little blonde with them. The three of them couldn't stop looking at your knives and talking about them. Especially the Perry girl," she says matter of factly. I note how my body tenses and my breathing nearly stops at the mention of *her*. Knowing that she was just here, looking at my knives. Thank god Giselle is still looking down at the knives on the counter. Otherwise she'd notice the shade of red I turn at the mention of Collin's sister.

It's normally so easy for me to stay calm. My pulse is practically a flat line. But whenever I'm around her, it takes every ounce of my being to put on a steady face and act like I'm not a complete mess. For years, every time I'm around her my heart races and my mind is frantically trying to make sure I'm hiding how I feel about her from Collin. It takes everything out of me to make sure I don't look like I'm coming apart at the seams.

I snap myself back into reality, pretending not to be a hot mess inside. "Oh cool. Yeah, they're in town for a couple weeks. I'm sure you'll see them around. Anyways, I need to get going. I'll see you guys later."

I wave and turn quickly towards the door. Hurrying down the old wooden boardwalk to my truck, I can't help but think it's going to be a long couple of weeks if even hearing her mentioned gets to me like that. We're supposed to be hanging out, nearly every day. I hop into my truck, laying my head against the steering wheel groaning. I need to get my shit together.

Taking a second to clear my head, I look over at Rex curled up in the passenger seat. It's that moment my stomach chooses to grumble loudly, getting Rex to tilt his head at me curiously. "Yikes. Let's go get lunch, bud."

On my way back home, I stop into Cowgirl coffee to grab a sandwich and an afternoon pick me up. I'm glad to see another familiar face behind the counter. Looking around though, I notice it looks like she's the only one working out front.

"Hey Kelsey. How's it going today? Looking a little shorthanded back there."

She looks a little flustered, replying hastily while making a drink for another customer. "Yeah. We need to hire another barista. Stephen left for Boise."

Damnit. Stephen and I weren't close, but we were friendly. He grew up here and went to high school the same time as Grace and Clay. Every time I talk to someone, it feels like someone I know has moved away. There just aren't many born and raised locals left here anymore. By the time us locals graduate from high school, most of us have to leave because rent is sky high, the jobs are mostly service industry, and no one can afford to buy a place. So now most of the people I knew from high school, which I barely graduated from to begin with, are long gone.

"That sucks. I know it's getting hard to keep people around," I say, trying not to sound let down.

Kelsey slides my usual drink across the counter along with a premade sandwich. "Is what it is I guess. I'll see you around Chap."

I grab my order with an appreciative smile and leave with a wave, then head back to my truck. I need to get home to grab supplies for a couple properties that guests are checking into tonight before my plow run.

I eat my sandwich on the drive towards my cabin. Driving along, my mind keeps coming back to that feeling I got at the Eclectic Elk this morning though. The way I nearly panicked just thinking about seeing her. Nope. I definitely don't like that.

Fuck. I really do need to get my shit together.

Chapter 5

Veronica
Checking In

Before finally heading to the condo, we make the next stop on my itinerary - a trip to the supermarket and liquor store to stock up for the next few days. I'm not joking, this was on the plan I emailed to Lizzy and Collin for the next couple of weeks.

I need to grab a few specific things since I volunteered, well more like demanded, that I get to do most of the cooking on our nights in. Cooking has always been a passion of mine. Back in Ohio I rarely have the time to entertain and host dinners. Most of my favorite meals to cook are classic ski trip meals like chicken chili, Thai curry, and lasagna, which are meant for a large group and just don't work well to cook for one. That is unless I want leftovers for days. Sometimes it's just plain depressing.

At home, I largely end up spending my Sunday nights alone, making my schedule and meal prepping for the week. It's pretty healthy, saves time, and saves money. Practical Veronica wins out again. That's one of the reasons I've always enjoyed these trips. From the old days cooking in the kitchen with my Grandma to now, where I welcome the chance to stimulate my culinary curiosity and share that passion with the ones closest to me.

After stopping in town and hitting the grocery store, we're finally at the condo. It's nothing exciting or glamorous, a modest two bedroom, two bathroom split level unit built in the seventies with basically no updates since then. But it's ours, owned outright by our grandparents before leaving it to us instead of our dad, who had a strained relationship with them over his treatment of Collin and rarely ever visited them in Wyoming. Our grandparents were the most loving and supportive people, something we needed compared to our lives back home. But still, Collin and I now own this place, which is quite the accomplishment these days in Jackson.

The dated old building still has its subtle charm. A classic ski vacation condo styled on the outside like a Swiss chalet. We're greeted by the white stucco building with charming dark wooden spindles adorning the balconies and matching dark wooden accents along the eaves of the steeply pitched roof, capped off by a set of stone chimneys poking out of it.

We walk into the ground floor entrance and into the mudroom with its wood paneled walls, painted white now in a modest attempt to modernize the place, and drop our bags. Along the wall there's a bench that our Grandpa made for putting on ski boots, racks and hooks for skis, helmets, ski poles, and all of our other gear. In the corner there's a closet with a stacked washer and dryer and a hamper. It's great to be able to do laundry and not have to over pack for these longer trips.

Standing by the door, Lizzy squeezes past Collin and I frantically, looking for the bathroom.

"Thinking twice about all the mimosas now, aren't we Lizzy?" I tease.

Watching her run into the bathroom as we step out of her way, I palm my face and shake my head. That girl.

I make my way off the landing down the half flight of steps to the open floor plan dining and living area. The room has the same painted white, wood paneled walls, stretching all the way to the lofted ceilings twenty feet overhead. I go through the dining area and sprawl out on the oversized brown leather couch in the living room, facing the floor to ceiling stone fireplace.

Oh, that fireplace.

Seeing it brings warmth to my heart, even if we don't have a fire going yet. I can't help but smile at all the memories of holidays spent at the condo, sitting on the floor in front of the fireplace gleefully opening presents on Christmas morning. It feels great to be here as I sink into the comfy couch and think about the memories made here.

"Collin, you're in the bunk room right?" My voice carries across the condo as he comes in from the mudroom. Perks of an open floor plan.

"Yep. Already took the top bunk." Oh, Collin, just like the old days. Off of the landing is another short set of stairs going up to the other bathroom and two bedrooms, ours with twin bunk beds. Ugh. So many jokes about twins with twin bunk beds over the years.

"Great. We can let Lizzy have the other bedroom to herself. Would you mind dropping my bags in the bunk room with yours?" I ask, now draped over the armrest with my head resting on my crossed arms, observing him in the doorway at the top of the landing.

"Sure thing, my lady," he says with his best fake British accent, dipping his head and making an exaggerated curtsy. I guess he's now the house jester too.

It feels good to be here again with him though. The last few years, my busy work schedule hasn't allowed me to come at the same time as him. I did come out soon after Grandpa passed, but Collin wasn't able to that time. Being here together again just feels right, like home, more so than *home* with our parents back in Ohio.

"Well thank you, good sir," I reply, playing into his theatrics, my fake accent not nearly as convincing as his.

Lizzy emerges from the bathroom, a relieved look on her face.

"Well I don't know about you guys, but I could eat. Even with lunch in town, travel still takes a lot out of me. Tonight's curry, right?" She asks, looking back in my direction as she plops down at the dining room table.

"Yep. Thai green curry with chicken," I say, reminding them what the menu is for tonight. I swear these two don't listen sometimes and they're even worse together, which is a slightly terrifying development.

Thai green curry has always been one of my favorite dishes, especially on ski trips with others. A few quality ingredients go a long way to making it great. It's such a fun and surprisingly simple dish to cook.

Who am I kidding, when it comes to cooking nothing is simple or an afterthought with me. I literally planned out the dinners I was going to make for the nights we're staying in this week. I even brought my favorite brand of Thai curry paste and palm sugar for tonight in my checked luggage because the stuff at the grocery store is never as good. This is also why I wouldn't let Collin do my grocery shopping ahead of time and insisted on going today to pick my own ingredients.

I think a sense of control is one of the many reasons I love cooking. Maybe that's why it can calm me down on some of my worst days. Unlike my professional life where I can do everything according to plan and still get nothing rewarding out of it, with cooking, there is an immediate tangible result if I do things right. It feels calming to be in control of the outcome for a change.

Lizzy joins me in the kitchen. She's not the most helpful, especially in the cramped kitchen, but it's a welcome change from cooking at home, which normally means cooking alone.

"Don't just sit around and let us ladies do all the work, Collin. Go get the good knives out. How have you been using these knives we leave out for the renters the last few days? They're complete garbage," I call out from the kitchen to Collin, who's lounging in the living room.

"Hey, we're not all cooking gurus. A knife's a knife to me," Collin says on his way to the closet by the mudroom.

Ever since we started renting the condo when we're not here, we have kept a separate owner's closet with a lock. We don't keep too much in there, just things we don't want renters to have free reign of.

Collin is back in a minute handing them over before slinking back over to the couch, enjoying the fire that's blazing away now.

Good knives in hand, the rest of the prep work goes smoothly. Lizzy tries to help in the kitchen, but she's mostly there for moral support, glass of wine in hand. I do let her cut some of the veggies so she feels like she's making a contribution. After a while she takes note of the tool in her hand, looking at it as she flips her wrist over looking at each side of the blade.

"Wow. Collin's friend's knives really are nice. I mean they aren't as pretty as the ones back at the shop but even I can tell a difference." She looks over at Collin, rolling her eyes.

Yeah, Lizzy. That's why we keep them put away until we're here.

As I'm finishing up cutting the chicken, I notice Collin's box of protein bars on the counter. Ugh. My mind drifts back to work. Their packaging is terrible, all single use plastics, generic graphics. I think about Earth SnaX and feel a small sense of excitement, even pride, over what we have ready to propose for them. The presentation is just a little over a week away now and I still keep thinking about Jeff screwing it up somehow.

As my mind drifts off to the presentation and work emails, I'm brought back to reality as I feel a sharp pang in one of my fingers.

"Ah shit!" I yelp, realizing I nicked one of my fingers with the knife.

I drop it, and it clangs off the counter towards the floor. The razor sharp tip digs itself into the wooden floor, handle pointing back at me, landing precariously between my foot and Lizzy's. Shit that was close.

"V! You ok in there?" I see Collin rushing over, obvious concern on his face.

"Yeah, I'm fine. Nothing serious. Just go get the first aid kit," I say, holding my finger in a paper towel, applying pressure.

"Where's your head at girl? I've never seen you mess up in the kitchen. And you nearly took off one of my freshly manicured toes too!" Lizzy says, looking a bit frazzled as well.

"Sorry guys," I say as Collin returns with the first aid kit, "my mind drifted off to work for a bit and I guess I just zoned out."

At this point, my finger is bandaged and I can get my mind back on track to finish making dinner.

"Alright. This kitchen is too tiny and I don't want anyone losing a toe," I say, kicking Lizzy and Collin out.

They sit at the dining table like kids in timeout, still in view and conversation range, but no more need for their help in the small kitchen.

After combining the last of the ingredients in the pot for dinner, I'm finally able to take my glass of wine and sit near them on the couch in front of the fire. Sitting down with my feet up, I can relax while waiting on the curry. Should only be about thirty minutes or so with the heat simmering low.

The pain in my finger is now a dull ache drifting away.

We chat for a bit, thinking about the day shopping in town, and the day of skiing ahead of us tomorrow. Sitting here on the couch, catching up and bullshitting with Collin and Lizzy while they sit at the dining room table, I'm taken aback by the scene.

The way they're laughing and chatting, across from each other at the table, glasses of wine in hand. I know they're not a couple, but they look like one.

It reminds me of when Collin and I would be playing in the living room in front of the fire as kids. Our grandparents would enjoy a night cap, reminiscing about the day, their lives, sitting at that very same dining room table, in the same seats Collin and Lizzy are now. Smiling, laughing, just in love, no signs of it slowing down over the years.

God I want that.

It's amazing being here with Collin, and now Lizzy, but I want more. I want someone to cook with in the little kitchen. I want someone to stand on the balcony with, watching the sunrise. I want someone to sit in front of the fire with, holding me as we doze off after a long day on the slopes. I want someone to share this place with.

Their love seemed perfect and timeless. I remember Grandpa even had Grandma's engagement and wedding ring custom made for her because he always said nothing at any of the jewelry stores was worthy of his dream woman.

"Hey weirdo. What's up? You've been oddly quiet over there," Collin says as I snap back into the moment.

Shit. I've been daydreaming about finding love and staring off at Collin and Lizzy a bit too long I guess.

"Oh. Yeah sorry. I'm not sure where my head is at today." No lie there. Even though I feel a sense of relief and calm being here, my head is still all over the place.

"Uh oh. I know that look," Lizzy says, looking at me shaking her head. She's got a glass of wine in one hand, finger to her lips, and a wide grin forming. "You need to get laid, V. You're stressed the fuck out. Your head is a mess. You nearly just took off one of my damn toes."

"Eww, Lizzy. I'm right here," Collin says, covering his ears and shuddering. My face is already bright red as I cringe at this back and forth unfolding in front of me.

"Come on, Collin. Like... look at her? Don't you have some weird twin connection? You're probably the only one that knows her better than me." Lizzy gestures at me, hand outstretched, palm up, waving it as if telling him to look at whatever... *this*... is. "Tell me I'm wrong."

Ouch, Lizzy. She's not totally wrong though. It has been *a while* since I had any intimate encounters. After my last serious relationship ended years ago, I've been afraid to put myself back out there. Sometimes I debate what's worse, being alone or the fear of dating.

And it sucks, because fine, Lizzy is fucking right. I do have needs. I do like sex. No, I love it. But the idea of a random meaningless hookup, ick. I want it with someone that I feel a real connection with, someone that ignites sparks in me and makes my skin tingle. I want someone that I feel like I can trust too.

"Ugh… yeah… V. We love you, but she's got a point. You need to unwind," he says with a faint sigh followed by another small shudder, clearly trying to erase the thought from his mind.

Damn.

"Oh screw you guys. We are not having *this* conversation. Yes, I would love to have a partner. But no, I don't need to *get fucked.*"

"Oh yeah. We can put *get fucked* on your itinerary, right next to find Lizzy a cowboy." Collin laughs at his own joke, but Lizzy and I aren't as amused, collectively glaring back at him.

"Ok. That's harsh, Collin. But V, I mean come on… it certainly wouldn't hurt," Lizzy says with a wink, "just something to think about." She makes a quick kissy face at me, sassing me as always.

"Ugh. Enough already. Can we just not guys?" My patience is wearing thin now. "I get where you're coming from. But also, one night stands just aren't my thing. I don't want to just hook up with some rando. You know me better than that."

After rejoining them at the dining room table for another glass of wine, ok maybe a glass and a half after *that* conversation, it's time to take the curry off and serve it. I get up from the table and head over to the kitchen.

Opening the pot, I inhale deeply. Spicy and aromatic, a hint of sweetness from the coconut milk and palm sugar. It smells wonderful, perfect for a cozy low key dinner on a cold night like this. Looking outside the sliding glass doors along the back wall of the condo, snow is starting to fall steadily on the deck.

"Well, dinner is ready," I say with a sense of pride. "Alright *girls,* come grab a dish and serve yourself." I announce as I turn to the fridge, grabbing a bottle of Marlborough Sauvignon Blanc to replace the empty one at the table.

At last I can head to the dining room table, dish of curry in one hand, bottle of wine in the other.

We're all hungry and clearly thirsty. It's been a long day. Dinner smells and tastes amazing. Collin and Lizzy must feel the same way. I haven't heard a peep out of them since pouring their wine, as they dig in. I let out a sigh and a quiet content smile takes over my face as they enjoy dinner.

My brief moment of peace is interrupted though by another thought creeping into the back of my mind.

Maybe… they're right?

My head has been in a better space since we got here, but it's still a mess. Maybe I do need to *get some*. It's been forever since I've had a release, well one not from my own fingers or nightstand drawer partners. Fuck. I do want *that.*

Chapter 6

Tanner
Plow

Nights like this are pretty much my winter norm. My route usually starts in town with a few condo complexes and houses on the outskirts. Then I finish up around the mansions off Moose Wilson Road between downtown Jackson and Teton Village, not too far from my cabin. On the nights before big snow storms, I go out to pretreat their parking lots, long driveways and private access roads. I normally hit them again the next morning before the crack of dawn to plow them if needed too. Always with Rex by my side.

The roads out here get pretty sketchy. It sucks, but the town stops plowing after 9:00 PM and lowers the speed limit for safety. So if I can manage it, I don't like to be out later than I have to and I don't see much at night besides the occasional wandering moose or black fox.

It gets pretty lonely and is definitely a killer for my social life. Not that I really have one anyways.

Most of the transplants that have moved in are either fancy, big city types that are only here part of the year, old wealthy retirees, or some intolerable Silicon Valley tech bros whining about their stock options not vesting sooner, whatever the fuck that even means. It's harder and harder for a kid that grew up here, didn't go away to school, and has rancher grandparents to relate to anyone that's left in town.

Even my brother and sister left with my parents for the last years of high school, because they wanted to go to college in Salt Lake City. They were always way better students than I was. After graduating college, Grace stayed in the Salt Lake City area, getting a good job and able to afford her own place a couple years later. Clay wanted to stay too. He was in the middle of his competitive ski racing training and Park City was the perfect place for him to be. And my dad, well he wanted to stay with Clay and Grace after we lost mom.

I end up feeling like an outsider in the place I was born and raised. I've barely ever left this place my whole life. The farthest away I've ever been was down to Salt Lake City. I miss my friends and my family so much. I've even thought about leaving too, but my grandparents are still here, at least when they aren't staying with the rest of the family in Salt Lake. Plus I'm fortunate enough to have a place that's paid off. I feel like I owe it to the family to keep it.

Sometimes I just feel so alone, so depressed.

I get overwhelmed and I don't know who to talk to. No one ever asks how I am, they just see the happy face I put on, but that's just me trying to convince myself everything's ok. Even if I did talk to someone, I doubt they'd care or listen. Who would even notice if I was gone? If I moved to Salt Lake with the rest of my family or got hurt out on the mountain, would anybody here even notice?

Whatever, most of the time I'm fine. I have it easy, or at least that's what everyone thinks. *Oh Chap. It must be so fun and awesome doing whatever you want, whenever you want out in the mountains. Being carefree and adventurous all the time, never having to be serious. I'd kill to live that life.*

I know I shouldn't be complaining about my life, but it still bothers me that no one takes me seriously. It always feels like I'm that silly goofy boy to everyone around me. Like no one actually sees me.

They don't see that I work hard. I'm getting paid decent money to do my property management and plow work. Sure, I have plenty of time for skiing and toying around in my workshop on my knives on the side. And skiing has always been second nature to me and this job is pretty mind numbing. So the knives are a challenging, creative outlet to keep my mind working, and keep it from thinking about the people that I miss or shit that's bothering me.

But when I'm driving the plow, I have time to really dig into my thoughts, which can be good or bad depending on the night.

I've driven most of these roads a thousand times over the years being a local, so it doesn't really take much mental effort to do this part of the job. Most of the time I just get a hot honey badger from Cowgirl Coffee and listen to the radio. But now I'm looking forward to spending time tomorrow with my best friends, the Perry twins, since they're in town.

Man it's been forever since I've been with *both* of them together. Sure, I've seen Collin this week, and even plenty more over the last few years too. Sometimes he'll even call me while I'm out on my work runs at night since he stays up late just to shoot the shit and catch up. But fuck it's been years since I've seen *her*.

Driving from one giant house to the next, my windshield is pelted with snow as it falls faster and faster.

I keep reminding myself that if I get this shit done tonight, it'll be less work tomorrow morning plowing what's left on these driveways. Hopefully I can hit first chair. Should be a killer day on the mountain with this storm front coming in bringing *freshies*. Maybe hang out somewhere around the chutes off Sublette chair with Collin. Yeah that's the move, they've been holding some good snow lately.

Thinking of lining up for first chair and hunting fresh lines reminds me even more why I miss them so much. There are so few people left here that really get it.

This place is fucking special. Skiing is a gift. We don't own this place or these mountains, no matter where we were born or how much money we spend. These mountains are timeless, here long before us and long after we're six feet under.

The Perry twins get that. They respect it. I think they have a different appreciation for this place than everyone else. Even though they've been here a decent amount of time over the years, they know it can be taken away from them just like that, if their trip gets cancelled or work fucks up their schedule. They just get it, when you're here you have to take advantage of every precious second we have. Who knows when it'll be our last. I can't imagine staying weeks here and hopping on a plane, wondering when I'll ever be back like they have to.

They didn't come from some crazy wealthy family either like most of the people out here now. They were lucky as hell that their grandparents bought a place back here when this was still just a remote ranching town, a ski industry afterthought. And they recognize that. I think between spending time with my family and their grandparents part time, they appreciated just how unique this place was because they weren't here everyday. Meanwhile I spent my time looking forward to seeing them because I was already here. They spent their time looking forward to coming here. In some ways, they might even appreciate it more than I do.

Rex whimpers, getting my attention back to the task at hand. "Shit Rex, good catch." A stray elk wanders towards the edge of an access road to one of the neighborhoods I need to check on.

Trying to stay present is proving hard though, I keep thinking about tomorrow. Yeah... tomorrow. I get to catch up with the gang. Shit. I don't know if I'm ready for this. To see *her* again. Even if I freeze and panic just thinking about her like I did this morning.

"Too bad you can't join me on the slopes or at their condo tomorrow, bud. Would feel a lot better with you by my side. That'd be awfully nice." Looking over at Rex, still nothing.

I laugh to myself. Why do I think that's ever gonna change?

My mind drifts back to tomorrow. I wonder if she's single now. I'm always afraid to ask Collin about her dating life, that if I pry too much

I might tip my hand and show my feelings. Hopefully she's not with someone like her last boyfriend. I remember when she was out here, she was constantly glued to her phone, him texting and calling her 24/7 to check in, stressing her out. Collin would tell me stories about when that guy would finally pretend to care, he'd treat her like some delicate flower that needed to be handled with kid gloves. She doesn't need that, she needs someone to remind her that she can do anything.

That girl is fucking tough.

I've seen how she can hang with the boys. Skiing some of the toughest lines on the mountain, getting into trouble around town and at the bars, mostly because she was following Collin and me around for all our bullshit. I think that's why I remember how protective of Collin she was. She never tried to hide how much she cared about her brother and it was so easy to see how compassionate she was. She was just always watching out for us and it made me feel special too.

Now I wish she had someone that could remind her that she's a badass, especially when she just lets go of needing to control everything and has fun.

Thinking back to her skiing tough lines reminds me of my last memory of her. We were skiing together with Collin, her chasing us down Rendezvous Bowl after taking Big Red up. I remember that button nose, her radiant smile and a few strands of that brown hair were the only visible parts of her under the mirror tinted ski goggles, my reflection staring me back in her lenses.

She had swagger. She was confident. She was beautiful. No signs of being anxious, just living in the moment.

I just hope she's doing alright. Collin said work's been rough on her the last few years. I don't know why she kills herself like that in that office. She's too smart and creative for that. I know I couldn't do that.

I am looking forward to catching up with them together though. They're both so much happier when they're around each other, even more when they're here. It feels like I'm back with family when they're around, like this place is really home again.

She seemed like she was always happy back when we were kids, the three of us spending their winter ski trips together on the mountain and at the condo. On their spring and summer breaks, their grandpa would bring them over to the cabin and barn on the old ranch, back when we still had a horse corral big enough to let a horse out to ride.

That thought brings a warm feeling over me in this cold ass truck. I remember how she'd smile when Grandpa would let her ride that old pony of ours, Starlight. She could ride her for hours and never stop smiling and laughing. I hope she feels like that again one day.

Chapter 7

Veronica
Alta Zero

Our condo sits on the edges of Teton Village, 6,311 feet elevation at the base of Jackson Hole Resort. At that elevation, I have to remind myself, well probably Lizzy too now that I think about it, to stay hydrated. Altitude sickness is no joke, especially if we're drinking wine and cocktails the night before.

After a quick breakfast at the condo, we leave for the fifteen minute walk to the center of the village where we can start our first day on the slopes at the base area gondola. Being that it's only a short walk has always helped get first chair.

As we walk through the village, I'm reminded that this place is still special. It's not some fancy sprawling place like those mega resorts in Colorado owned by a giant corporation, but rather still owned by local families. We quickly make our way past the relatively small group of hotels, shops, bars, and restaurants. Sure it's gotten fancier over the years, but it's still quaint and charming.

After walking through snow covered paths on our way to the gondolas, we reach the center of it all, the beating heart of Jackson

Hole, the aerial tram, and its iconic clock tower. I still remember when the old tram and clock tower were taken down and upgraded with this current bigger and faster version. Not quite the same charm as the old one, but a functional improvement for sure. Known by locals as *Big Red*, it whisks a hundred or so diehard skiers and tourists high above the ground in its two fire engine red cars, each emblazoned with the white silhouette of a cowboy on a bucking bronco.

It stretches from the base of the resort to the top of the mountain at over ten-thousand feet, soaring above us. It's a breathtaking ride, whether you're going up to test your mettle on the steep chutes and bowls that define the mountain, or make the round trip to just enjoy views and grab some waffles at the cabin on top.

To this day, I still feel like a kid every time I ride it, my face glued to the windows taking in the views of the mountains and the valleys surrounding us on all sides.

We keep walking, gear in tow, to the area just past Big Red at the base of the resort, where there is another mix of gondolas and chair lifts. This is where we're starting today, going to a mid mountain area with more intermediate level terrain before venturing off to the more exciting parts of the slopes. Even though we're all advanced or better skiers, it's a good idea to give us at least one warm up run before hopping on the tram for our first day out this season. After all, we did have a few bottles of wine last night.

We're in the lift line for the main gondola in the center of the village, by 8:45 AM. Exactly as I planned for our first day on the slopes. Sorry, not sorry, Collin and Lizzy.

"Remind me why we need *first chair* again?" She clearly wanted more beauty sleep this morning, not that she needs it.

Lizzy, as expected, has shown up in a fashionable outfit, something I'd never wear. Slim and tailored white ski pants with black accents and gold zipper hardware, a matching jacket with a faux fur trimmed hood, and a glossy white helmet and pink goggles. To top it off, she has two strands of her perfect blonde hair sticking out and tucked up between her goggle strap and helmet, like little pigtails for ski girls or *slut strands.* Her outfit looks cute, but I can't imagine it's very warm. She does look perfect for Aspen Valley, I'll admit. But she stands out like a sore thumb here compared to the regulars, who are known for dressing for functionality with the harsh conditions in the Tetons.

She's in stark contrast to me, with my loose fitting waterproof shell pants and jacket, with no concern for matching colors or brands. In my case, orange pants and a teal jacket. I wear a small backpack with water to stay hydrated and extra layers if the weather shifts.

My *outfit* is complete with a matte black helmet, my mirrored goggles resting on the small brim until needed later. Not exactly the trendiest or most flattering attire, but it does the job. Practical Veronica wins here, keeping me warm and dry. Nothing worse than getting wet on the mountain.

Collin is in similar practical attire like me, black pants and a blue jacket, desert tan helmet and blue tinted goggles. After more than thirty years of skiing with me, he's a pro at getting ready early in the morning to get in the lift lines before the chairs spin at 9:00 AM. Lizzy keeping pace with us and being on time was an unexpected surprise. I'm glad to see she's a little more functional in the morning than our college days, albeit with the same snarky morning angst as ever.

"Oh boy, Lizzy," Collin says, shaking his head as we wait for the lifties to begin loading us onto the gondola. "I see you've never been skiing with V before. I learned a long time ago you're just along for the ride when you come out here with her. Besides, it's on her schedule she sent us for the next two weeks. *FIRST CHAIR*, in all caps, practically every morning."

"Very funny, Collin." I raise my eyebrows at him. But he's right. Whether it's a deep powder day or a bluebird day with freshly groomed corduroy runs, chasing first tracks has always been a therapeutic obsession for me. I can't control the mountain, but I can control when we get out there. I probably have my Grandpa to thank for this obsession, an old man that liked to *wake up before the moose* as he would say.

Our parents rarely came on our trips. They were always so busy that they would ship us off for the holidays, spring break, and chunks of summer break to spend with our grandparents.

Grandpa would wake us up at the crack of dawn to go skiing. Eventually I became so accustomed to it, I started waking up before him, coming down stairs and getting my ski gear together to make sure we got first chair, just like he always wanted. Every day here felt like Christmas, with breakfast by the fireplace with Collin and our grandparents and the mountain having a new surprise in store for us each morning.

The lift line has finally started moving and we walk over to the gondola cars, claiming the first one up.

Aspen Valley, where Lizzy is used to skiing, as bougie as it is, mostly has traditional chair lifts. They have just one rarely used gondola where the lifties load your skis on for you anyways. This is now painfully obvious with Lizzy. I load my skis into the rack on the gondola door and hop in the car, but Lizzy is still fumbling her skis until the liftie grabs them and loads at the last second.

"Yikes! Glad I don't have to do *that* every day," she huffs as she barely gets into the car before the doors start closing automatically. The brief look of panic on her face washing away.

The ride up gives me a chance to take in the view of the mountain and the valley below, a view that never gets old. We're ferried away from the base and up the mountain and a welcome sense of calm sneaks its way into me. I think about the day ahead and what the next two weeks have in store and feel a sense of optimism I haven't felt in ages. I swear, sometimes these gondola rides really are like therapy. Too bad skiing isn't cheaper.

After riding the gondola up towards the mid mountain area, we work our way across a cat track over to my favorite part of the mountain, where the Thunder and Sublette chairs are. Two chairs taking skiers to rocky cliff bands, steep chutes, tree filled gladed ridge lines, and several of the mountain's best powder filled bowls. This part of the mountain is special.

We get off of the chair lift for the first *real* run of the day, I'm not counting the warm up run off the gondola. No, we're going for something a bit more fun. A little more adventurous. The three of us make our way to a black diamond groomer, freshly surfaced the night before by the resorts grooming equipment. It's a steeply pitched run, but should be fun. After securing first chair this morning and beelining it over here from the gondola on the cat track, we're the first ones to get to it today.

Looking down the run, it's a perfect, glistening sheet of corduroy, not a single ski track having disturbed the manicured surface yet. This is why I insist on getting up early and making first chair. Being the first one to leave their tracks on the untouched snow is pure bliss.

We take off down the run and I'm hardly able to contain my joy, a smile gleaming over my face. Sure it's a black diamond run, but the steep pitch is perfect to rip turns on. As I sail down the mountain, I'm overtaken by all the sensations coming back. It's been nine or ten months since the last time I was on the slopes, but it's always been like riding a bike for me, my body never forgetting the movements needed to descend down the mountain.

The sound of the edges of my skis cutting into the snow with each arching turn, the cold air rushing across my face, all of it bringing something in me that's been dead back to life. It feels amazing to just let go and focus on my skis on the snow, the wind in my face, not a care about anything else in the world.

After a few laps, I've been impressed with Lizzy, who has held her own on some of the more difficult terrain. She's been keeping up on steep groomers, wide open bowls, and a couple treed glades. Time to start challenging her more I guess. We hop back on the Sublette chair, hoping to go do a little exploring before lunch.

After lunch, Collin texts Tanner and wants to peel off and get a few runs in with him.

"See you girls at the condo later, right?" Collin asks, ready to head off to find his friend.

"Yep, you got it. 5:00 or so work for you?" I don't know why I even ask. It's been the same routine forever.

"Should be fine. Tanner has to take care of something for work but he should be there a bit later with pizza. So I'll see you girls there." And with that, Collin heads down the slopes, off to find his shadow like countless days before.

"Where do you think they're heading?" Lizzy has been surprisingly quiet until now.

"Who knows. Probably off to do some dumb reckless shit." I shake my head, thinking about their past escapades.

Lizzy asks to see a bit more of the mountain, but I think from her subdued body language she's wearing out on me. We get a couple more runs in before eventually heading over to Sublette chair.

As we ride the chair up, I have my eyes down on my phone. As much as I want to, I can never fully get away from work. Remind me again why I even bother if I'm going to keep getting passed over for promotions? Shit. There's an email from Jeff about Earth SnaX.

Are you kidding me? It's Saturday! Half way through reading his email about his latest urgent need for their new products, I'm startled by Lizzy erupting with such a shrill, girlish scream she practically pops out of the chairlift.

"Oh my god! No way! What th- Look! V!" She's frantically pointing up ahead of the chairlifts in front of us.

I look up from my phone, spotting a skier perched precariously at the top of the ridge up ahead to our left. The edge of this ridge is made up of an area known as the *Alta Chutes*. Alta One, Two, and Three are narrow, steep, rocky chutes lined with tightly packed trees on either side. They're technical, challenging terrain for the best of skiers and are deservedly marked as double black diamonds or *experts only*. Further ahead on the left beyond One, Two, and Three is a roped off area, marked permanently as closed on the trail maps. It's a rats nest of rocks, trees, small cliffs, and scant pockets of snow to try and navigate through. That area contains the unmarked runs, Alta Zero and Negative, which are practically unnavigable to any skiers and boarders, and requires permission from Ski Patrol to even enter.

"Wha… ugh." I can't hide my eye roll even under my goggles as I see the skier in his old ratty tan ski pants and burnt red jacket drop into the rocky area. I already know what's next as he nails the top of the line through the narrow slivers of snow bound by cliffs and trees on either side, before coiling up his body to unleash a backflip ever so effortlessly off a granite outcropping. As he stomps the landing cleanly, he lets out a primal *yeeeewwwwww,* a practically involuntary exclamation of giddy skiers when everything is clicking and they're flat out feeling it.

Lizzy bursts out again, "Who do you think that was? They must be a crazy pro skier, right?! V, how can you just roll your eyes at that?"

I already know who it is though. That style, the body language, the palpable confidence, the simple ease and grace for doing such a challenging feat, not to mention the boyish grin he wore under his orange tinted goggles the whole time.

I let out an exasperated sigh. "Because that's *Tanner. Fucking. Chapman.*"

Sure enough, looking at the bottom of the run, there's Collin cheering him on. They might be in their thirties now, but these boys never change.

Chapter 8

Veronica
Abe Froman

When we get back to the condo after a day on the slopes, I'm glad I'm not on cooking duty and we're doing pizza. It's been a long day and I'm beat.

"Alright girls, time to relax. Hopefully Chap doesn't take too long picking up pizza." Collin calls out as he opens a bottle of red wine, three glasses lined up on the table.

As we change and unwind after a long day of skiing, Collin starts a fire and we take our wine to the coffee table in front of the fireplace. I'm taken back to the times here with our grandparents, watching Grandpa teach Collin to start the fire while I would make molasses cookies in the kitchen with Grandma.

Mom and dad were both always so busy with work, either traveling or working crazy long hours. Even before their divorce after we graduated college, on the rare occasions when our parents happened to actually be around, things weren't always great, especially for Collin. When he finally came out as bi, all dad could say was, *"Great, you like girls too, so you don't have to date guys."*

I cringe at the memory and how it gutted Collin. That's partly why he stayed down in Cincinnati after college. Or at least I think so. I totally get why he doesn't mind missing Christmas back home in Ohio.

My relationship with mom was always strained and still is. The constant questions about why don't I settle down with a nice man and start a family. The more she pushed, the more I'd think that maybe dad and her *settled* with each other, never actually being in *love*.

Sometimes I think that's why Collin and I have both struggled so much romantically over the years.

Shit. There's a lot to unpack here and vacation isn't the time or place to do it. There's a fire and I have a glass of wine to enjoy. Back to reality, V.

As I melt into the couch, I can feel the stress of the last few weeks at work drift away and I'm ready for the weeks here ahead. Nothing gets me out of my own head like being here with Collin, and now Lizzy.

I think about the days ahead on the slopes, and stare off into the fireplace from the couch, watching the flames dance and crackle. It's soothing, the way it brings back memories from the past, flooding my body and my soul with much needed warmth.

My wine induced, fireside daydreaming is interrupted when I hear the mudroom door open.

"Sup bro!" Collin's voice welcomes Tanner into the condo.

I drape myself over the back of the couch, looking back into the dining area to see Tanner and Collin starting to sit down at the dining room table, setting out the pizza.

"Hey there, Ronni. Been a while." His voice is deeper than I remember, a slight bit raspy too, but relaxed as always.

Ugh. *Ronni*. That old nickname. No one has called me that in ages. In fact I think the last person to call me that was Tanner. He's right though. It has been a while, years actually. He's still Tanner, the boy I've known most of my life. He's sitting next to Collin, but his eyes are locked on me. Something about the way his eyes linger on me causes my pulse to quicken and my cheeks to grow warm.

On the surface he looks the same. Obviously tall and well built. But up close it's even clearer how broad he is, muscles straining his long sleeve t-shirt. His shaggy golden brown hair is tousled and sticking out from all sides of his black flat bill hat, his signature après ski look unchanged after all these years. His eyes are still a striking shade of green, his tanned skin drawn tight over his high cheekbones, the same scruffy but short beard trying to hide the sharp line of his square jaw and finished off with a thick mustache.

Looking down, the tattoos on his hands are still there, the once crisp black edges dulled from years of working with his hands and countless days in the sun. I can still make out the letters on his knuckles saying *FULL SEND.* Whenever we'd come out to visit after high school, it seemed like I could always spot a new tattoo on him. I still remember when he got his first one the summer after we graduated high school.

It's a jagged little line on the inside of his wrist, the stylized silhouette of the Teton mountains celebrating skiing Corbett's earlier that year.

All of it is so familiar, but he does look *different*. The corners of his eyes with faint crinkles, his shaggy hair and scruffy beard with stray grays. Maybe older? More mature? Definitely not a boy anymore. Either way, it's nice to see a familiar, welcome face.

I pry myself off the couch, my legs still barking at me after the day on the slopes, and walk towards the dining area.

"It has been a while. Glad to finally have a chance to catch up, *Tanner.*" I linger on his name, Tanner. No one calls him Tanner except his grandparents, everyone else calling him Chapman or simply Chap. See, I can play along too, Tanner.

"Ah. Glad to see you remember my name, *Ronni*. I didn't forget yours either." A sly grin grows across his face as he locks his eyes on mine longer than I'm used to, the crinkles around his eyes deepening. It feels like he's staring deep inside me, searching for something. I can feel myself shift awkwardly, my thighs clenching, my mind wondering what he's looking for. It's like I'm exposed and laid bare to him. Huh. Well that's… new.

I try to regain my composure, remembering what I was doing before he walked in.

"So Lizzy, this is Tanner, Collin's *bestie.*" I flick my eyebrows at Tanner, teasing him before watching as Lizzy eyes Tanner. She clearly noticed where my attention was just lingering.

"Nice to meet you, Tanner." She looks at Tanner, eyeing him with mild curiosity. Maybe she really is taking a break from boys for now.

"So what'd you bring us tonight, *Tanner?*" I ask, eyeing the boxes of pizza on the table.

"Oh just the classics from Big Red's." He shrugs his broad shoulders in one of his trademark, calm indifferent gestures.

"Tell me you got the Flyin' Hawaiian. Spicy and pineapple? Count me in as always." Collin's eyes are wide as he opens the first box, now seated at the dining room table with Lizzy, passing out plates.

"Yep. I know you'd never let me forget." Tanner eyes me with a smirk and tilts his chin up as he slides a box of pizza towards me at the other end of the table. "And for you, *Ronni.*"

I cock my head, giving him a curious look before opening the box. I grin wildly at its contents. A sausage pizza, with fresh chopped basil and extra balsamic drizzle spread across the top, one of Big Red's signature pizzas.

"You remembered my Abe Froman, with the extra balsamic drizzle? I can't believe you remembered!" I look to Tanner, a grin of appreciation still on my face. I can feel the slightest bit of heat and color hit my cheeks. I don't know why, but it feels good that he remembered something about me like this. One of those times where the thought really does count.

And if I'm not mistaken, I think I might have caught a throat bob and hint of blush in him too. A rare brief glimpse past his armor.

Whatever it was, it was short lived as he turned his attention back to Collin, talking about the day on the slopes.

Collin and Lizzy open another bottle of wine while Tanner grabs his own beer from the fridge.

We're all hungry and clearly thirsty. It's been a long day. Tanner is sitting quietly at the end of the table, his green eyes seemingly catching my gaze whenever I happen to look his way.

"So Lizzy, my boy Chap here is the knife maker," Collin says proudly between bites. "We'll be seeing him around the next couple weeks."

"Alright, *Chap*," she says before rolling her eyes and looking at me. "There goes our girls trip, V."

A snort of laughter escapes my mouth and I put down my wine.

"Don't worry, Lizzy," I say, looking back at Collin and Tanner, "Tanner here means we'll be seeing less of Collin I'm sure. He's always been his damn shadow."

After grabbing another slice of pizza, I notice Tanner's been awfully quiet for a change. "So Tanner, it looks like you're still up to your usual shit, and dragging Collin along with you."

"Huh?" He says, looking momentarily confused while Collin snorts a laugh.

"Looks like she caught you dude." Collin says between bites of pizza.

"Oh come on. That was pretty slick over on Alta Zero after lunch."
I think I caught him off guard. For just a moment, there's the slightest hint of blush in his cheeks above his scruff.

"Oh, that backflip. Yeah…" He shrugs. "Didn't think anyone was watching besides Collin, honestly. The line looked good when we first took Sublette up. So I checked with my Patrol buddies at the top to make sure it was ok to duck the rope and hit it. The landing was so clean. It felt great to just send it. Totally worth it. Were you ladies on the chair or something?" He says this as if it was just a regular occurrence, the same expression and demeanor you'd expect of someone who was giving you the time of day. So matter of fact. So calm.

Can he be serious? *Oh that backflip*? Didn't think anyone was looking as you hit one of the hardest lines on the mountain? One that requires permission from ski patrol to even try it, right under the chairlift for everyone to see? And you don't just hit it, but throw a backflip in for fun?

The memories of Collin and Tanner's shenanigans come flooding back. I just can't with him sometimes. He acts like it's no big deal at all, like it's skiing the bunny hill at the base of the mountain or something.

This is what I've never understood with him. It's not that he's outwardly cocky or arrogant. No. Sure he can be loud, rowdy, and fun. But his confidence shows through in how calm and steady he is. How he can treat death defying acts as just part of everyday life, completely unfazed by them. It almost feels like an act to anyone who hasn't seen him like this before. How can he think something so crazy is just... *normal*? I'd kill to just have one tenth of his confidence.

Clearly, Lizzy isn't buying it though. Oh boy, I can see her eyebrow arching.

"So then why hit a line and drop a flip in it like that *Chap,* if you don't even care about putting on a show for an audience? You're not just trying to impress some cute ski bunny or your buddy Collin here?" Ah Lizzy, my snarky sidekick.

Tanner has a puzzled look on his face, his eyes dropping to the table for a moment. I wonder what he has to say about this. After a few seconds of contemplation, Tanner finally looks back up, right in my direction, emerald eyes peering through me again.

Seriously. What is with him and the eye contact today?

"Not really trying to pick someone up out on the slopes." He lets out a small huff and continues. "But as far as hitting tough lines goes, skiing for me isn't about what anyone else thinks. I don't care about what someone thinks of my form or being seen at some fancy resort in some cute outfit."

He breaks eye contact with me to glare at Lizzy briefly before returning to me.

Ouch dude. I can feel that burn from here as Lizzy sneers back at him, her eyes shooting daggers. Sorry girl, he's not wrong. I get it. Skiing is about how it makes me feel. I don't do it for someone else.

Tanner continues his answer, unfazed. "Sometimes it's just about having fun and pushing yourself to grow. That's what I love about skiing here. The mountain is in charge, the weather changing it every day, and sometimes even within the day. We're just along for the ride, never actually in control of it. So if a line looks good and is speaking to me, I'll take it when I can get it. Who knows when I'll ever get the chance to hit it like that again. Sometimes you just gotta take a deep breath and *send it*."

The question might have come from Lizzy. And yes, that dig was definitely meant for her. But Tanner's gaze practically never left my eyes the entire time he answered her question. Was he really talking about skiing? It feels like he's talking right to me.

It was a great answer. I couldn't agree more, even if I don't ski the same crazy lines as him all the time. The freedom and ability to let go on the mountain is something I totally understand. But hearing a serious and heartfelt answer from him is certainly jarring. Maybe he has matured.

Lizzy rolls her eyes and scoffs. "You ski bros. What does *send it* even mean?"

Tanner looks wounded, like his way of life has been insulted.

"I got it. Sometimes you just gotta stop overthinking it, say fuck it and let go of it all. Just do it. *Send it.*" What was that? I can't believe those words just came out of my mouth like that. Tanner looks back at me, a sense of approval on his face. I don't know if that's because I came to his defense or agreed with him, but he seems satisfied. He leans back in his chair, arms crossed, nodding his head in agreement, eyes still locked on mine.

And that's how the rest of the night goes. Tanner and Collin talking about past exploits. Lizzy interjecting with occasional jabs, albeit in good fun. Or at least I hope so. And maybe I'm just seeing things, but I might appreciate the extra glances and smirks from Tanner. Either way, all of it feels like home again, the condo coming to life with the laughs of those closest to me.

Chapter 9

Tanner
Déjà Vu

"Maybe another warm up run would have been a good idea." Lizzy looks back at Ronni, Collin, and me, standing above the narrow Tower Three Chute. Why do I always feel like I'm standing at the edge of a cliff with Ronni?

All of us are tired after staying up too late at the condo last night after pizza. Ronni was right though. Lizzy is a good skier, but maybe a double black diamond experts only run like Tower Three Chute wasn't the best idea to dive into after an easy warm up run.

"Relax, Lizzy. You got this." The way Ronni's coaching Lizzy, smiling and laughing, trying to put her friend at ease, it's so endearing.

"What's wrong, Lizzy? Little bit steeper than Aspen Valley, eh?" Collin on the other hand. Well, he's an ass as usual. "Probably should have had an extra coffee to get ready for this."

"Oh fuck off, Collin." Ronni snarls, sticking her tongue out at her brother with Lizzy quickly matching her. I snort a laugh, shaking my head watching the three of them. "It's really not that bad, Lizzy. A few quick turns and you just need to watch it when you get down to that choke point by the big rock. Once you squeeze through there, you're home free. Just watch me."

I watch as Ronni jumps down into the run, calm, confident, and carefree. I could watch her like this all day. The way she glides down the run, the ends of her braids flowing behind her in the wind. I feel the heat creeping up my neck and a wide grin forming on my face.

"Damn, a little déjà vu. Right, Chap?" Fuck. I snap myself out of my trance, looking back over to Collin. I swear, I don't know how he hasn't picked up on my feelings for Ronni over the years.

I let out a short laugh. "Yeah, she's something man. Always making us look like little bitches."

I look back to Lizzy. "See. It's not that bad. You good? If you want, you can go ahead and we'll wait back to make sure you get down ok."

Lizzy eyes me a bit cautiously before looking down the run, finding Ronni a hundred yards down or so waving at her. "Sure, Chap. Thanks."

She takes the run a bit more slowly and less gracefully than Ronni, but she still nails it. When she reaches Ronni, they give each other fist bumps before turning back to us.

"You're turn, bro. Gonna outdo your sister?" I ask as Collin looks up at me, letting out a long sigh.

"That's a tall order man. See you down there." He chuckles before I pat him on the back, still giving him shit right before he goes down the run.

"Saving the best for last as always, I see," I yell at him as he skis away.

After Collin gets down the run, I size up my line. The big VW Bug sized rock right at the choke point has a nice packed down mound of snow on it and the landing zone looks soft after watching the other three hit the run.

Maybe I could…

Yep.

The entrance to the run goes smooth. My first few turns barely take any effort. I line up to go to the choke point of the chute, heading straight for the big snow covered rock. I look up just briefly and catch Collin and Ronni giving me a puzzled look before their eyes go wide. I even catch Ronni start to shake her head.

I gauge my speed perfectly. The snow on top of the big rock is just firm enough for me to pop off of as I leave the ground, turning into a 360 degree rotation, watching the world spin around me.

I come down hard, but still in control. The snow in the landing wasn't quite as soft as I expected, but good enough. I ski over to Collin, my heart pounding and pushing adrenaline through my veins. Nailing a landing like that always makes me feel so good, so alive.

"Nice, Chap. You still got your moves," Collin says, reaching towards me to bump my gloved fist.

I pull up my neck warmer to help wipe the snow off my goggles. "If you say so. I was starting to feel like I'm getting too old for this shit."

"Well, if that's you feeling old, I'd take that any day. Now, come on. Let's get back to the chairlift and get another run in." He turns to Ronni, who is still just shaking her head, her goggles resting on the brim of her helmet.

"What? I told Collin we were saving the best for last." I shrug, raising my gloves hands towards them. Lizzy meanwhile is back to giving me the same death glare from last night.

Fuck me. I do not envy the guy that ever tries to date her. "Was that a sick enough line for you, Lizzy?"

Lizzy rolls her eyes before looking down to fiddle with her gloves.

Ronni looks back to me though, a sheepish grin on her face. "It was pretty good, *Tanner*. But maybe next time work on your landing a bit. Looks like you hit it a little hard there and got sloppy." She dips her chin and smiles at me and winks before pulling her goggles back down.

I feel butterflies in my stomach as she turns away, my breath hitching. The way she gets to me so easily always startles me. It's like she's always been able to see me, the real me, and she can poke and prod around in my head to push my buttons.

Hitting a big ski run? Sure, no problem.

But her just smiling at me or batting her eyes? Still all these years later, it's enough to make me feel like a silly teenage boy again.

Collin turns and starts skiing back down the mountain towards the lift. We end up in line for the old two person chairlift. Looks like I'll be riding with Collin.

After hopping on, Collin grabs a snack bar from his backpack. "Want one? I have extras." He looks to me, holding a bar out.

"Sure. Thanks bud." I say, taking my gloves off before grabbing it from him.

"No problem. Glad I'm back out here on the slopes with you though. I missed this." Collin looks forward, chewing as we ride the lift up the mountain.

"Same man. I wish you guys were out here more often like the old days. It's pretty boring without you guys here," I reply, sighing and hanging my head. I find myself looking down at the slopes below us, thinking about all the fun times I've had here with him, Ronni, even Clay and Grace. I do miss those days.

"Boring?" Collin asks, turning towards me with a surprised look on his face. "You can't tell me this place is ever boring, especially for you. You got everything you want man. The slopes, river to kayak, mountain biking. Even your workshop is awesome. How could you ever get bored?"

I muster a halfhearted laugh. I never know how to explain to anyone, much less to Collin, that I feel so alone most of the time.

And he's right. I love this place. It's amazing. But it's not the same without someone to share it with. And everywhere I go, something always brings back memories of all the people that aren't here with me any more. Everyone that's moved away or stopped coming to town.

"I guess you're right. It's still pretty great here," I say, shrugging my shoulders.

My eyes drift out over the scenery around us, settling on where the granite peaks of the mountains meet the horizon. As the silence lingers between us, I can feel Collin's gaze on me.

"You good bud?" he finally asks, nudging my shoulder with a fist.

I stay quiet, dwelling on that question. I know he's my best friend. I should feel like I can open up to him. But it just feels selfish to complain. Everyone's got their own shit to deal with, why should I be any different? It never helps. I remember the last time I truly vented a decade ago. It didn't change anything though. It hurt so much to open myself up for once and be so let down.

I let out a long sigh. "Yeah. Yeah, man. I'm good. Just a little tired. Still catching my breath from that last run. Come on. Let's find another good run!" I put on my best smile, hiding my feelings again before punching Collin back on his thigh. "You might beat me in the gym, but I'm still going to kick your ass out here."

Collin snorts a puff of air before giving me a sidelong glance and dropping the topic, seemingly satisfied with my answer. And why wouldn't he be? He doesn't have any reason to think I'm anything but fine.

Leaning into the padded backrest of the chair lift, I look down at the snack in my hand and see the tattoo on my wrist. It's the one I got right after I turned 18, right after I skied Jackson Hole's toughest run for the first time nearly fifteen years ago. The corner of my mouth ticks up into a genuine, warm smile at the thought of that day.

Fifteen Years Earlier

Some things never get old. Waiting here at the top of the mountain in the cold winter air, the wind is whipping flurries around the three of us like we're in a snow globe. We're standing at the top of a *slope*, ok maybe more of a cliff, with our ski tips dangling precariously over the edge. Nope, this feeling definitely never gets old.

I look over at Collin and Ronni. He's still griping with her about how steep this run is.

"Come on, lil sis." He points down into Corbett's with both hands, raising his palms up as if we can't see just how steep and gnarly the chute is, bound by imposing granite cliffs on either side. "This shit is crazy. There's a reason we've never skied it, Veronica. Even my bro here hasn't hit it yet!"

I'll give him that. Corbett's Couloir is Jackson Hole's iconic run, always on the list of the scariest ski runs in the country. Plus being right in front of the aerial tram's path, there's an audience if you end up falling and biting it. They're in town for President's Day Weekend before they head back to their parents in Ohio. We've talked about doing this for years and we finally get a chance to do it with perfect weather and conditions while they're here on a break.

I soak in the moment with them. Collin's still arguing, trying to back out. But *Ronni*. She's palming her face, shaking her head while strands of her long brown hair are blowing in the wind. They're always so competitive and egging each other on. She's trying not to laugh at her brother and it's fucking adorable.

She turns in my direction, sending me a heart melting smile before glancing back to her brother.

"Oh come on, it's not that bad. We've definitely skied worse." She elbows him before glancing back at me, flashing a soft but confident grin as she tilts her chin up. "Tell him, Tanner."

I'm glad most of my face is covered by my neck warmer and goggles, because I can't hide the shade of red my cheeks turn whenever she says my name or smiles at me.

"Ronni's right, bro. We're all gonna do it eventually. So quit being a little bitch and just send it." I say, shrugging. He hems and haws, still unconvinced.

I start to gather myself, lining up to hit the tricky line. It's a near vertical drop for about fifteen feet, bound by granite cliff walls on either side requiring two pinpoint turns, before it opens up into a more manageable, but still super steep, pitch. I haven't hit it before, but the three of us always said we'd do it together before we graduated high school. It's our senior year and they might only make it out one more time before the end of the season. So yeah, today's the day. Let's fucking send it.

I look back over at the twins to check in with them one last time before heading down the chute. Collin is still shaking his head. I've always been able to read his body language. Right now I can tell he's not entirely sold on this run, even if he's more than skilled enough for it. "Come on, bro. You got this. You'll be fine. Let's hit it!"

"Ugh. Yeah. You're right. I'll be ok. You want to go first though?" He looks at me, hoping I'll show him the way and give him a confidence boost.

His sister groans and lets out a huff.

"Seriously, quit being so lame. Do you need a girl to show you how it's done?" I watch as one side of her lips pulls up into what I think is a sly mischievous grin, her way of saying *watch me*. And I'm pretty sure she's shooting me a wink under her tinted goggles. "Later *bros*!"

She clicks her ski poles together twice and before I can respond or even laugh, she drops down into the chute and I feel my heart skip a beat. She nails each of the tight turns effortlessly and confidently. I watch as she descends further down the steep pitch, her long hair flowing beautifully behind her in the wind. She skis off, taking my heart with her and I don't even care.

It's hers. She can keep it.

Forever.

Chapter 10

Veronica
A Little Taste

Lizzy takes a bite of her snack bar as we ride up the two person chair for one of the last runs of the afternoon. Really? How many pocket snacks does she have stashed away?

After getting her legs under her on Tower Three Chute this morning, I'm pleased at how she's settled in well and been crushing some of Jackson's more difficult terrain. She's definitely earned her Frisky Fox Spicy Margs tonight.

"So what's Chap's deal, anyways?" Lizzy barely even looks up from her snack bar, catching me off guard at the casualness of her question.

"What do you mean?" I ask, with what I assume is a puzzled look plastered over my face. "He's Tanner. Just a good old friend."

"What I mean, Veronica, is what's his *deal*?" She sighs audibly over the wind of the mountain air. "He's hot, like a real hunk of a rugged ass man. Not some whiny boy back home in the office in Ohio in khakis and a polo."

She looks up from her snack bar, her goggles hiding most of her expression. "You're telling me you've *never* been interested in him?

Not even a little tempted to dip your hand into the cookie jar? Not even a little taste?"

I groan in exasperation. Even when she swears off dating or finding a man, it still somehow comes back to this, even if it's at my expense.

"No, Lizzy." I find myself pausing much longer than I had expected, waiting for some retort or quip from her. The silence lets me think about her question more though.

Why have I never looked at Tanner that way? He was always cute, maybe a bit awkward and lanky when he was younger. But he was always Collin's best friend too. It always just felt like there was this invisible line between us that neither of us would cross. I've just known him forever and kind of assumed he'd always just be here, a good friend we'd see when we're in town.

I let out a breath it feels like I was holding way too long. "Ok. I mean yeah, Tanner glowed the fuck up, Lizzy. But I'm not his type."

Lizzy snorts a very unflattering laugh. "Not his type? V. He was looking at you practically every chance he got last night."

I furrow my brows and look at her. Ok, yeah. She noticed that too? That is a new thing with him, or at least one I've never noticed. I was starting to think I was a bit crazy. "He's always been hyper-protective of Collin and me. So it's not that weird for him. We just haven't seen each other in a long time."

She finishes the last bite of her snack bar, fitting in words while still chewing. "Well V, if he's not into you, what is his type then? He might not be a cowboy, but I'd take a ride on that mustang."

If I was drinking, I would have spit out whatever was in my mouth or choked on it. "I swear to God Lizzy. You can't help yourself, can you?" I shake my head in disbelief and roll my eyes under my goggles. "You know what? Go for it. You might be in luck. Allegedly his type is blonde, attractive ski girls. Basically you, Lizzy. Shoot your shot."

I groan again at the thought and immediately regret my words. This should be interesting.

Chapter 11

Veronica
Frisky Fox

It was another great day on the slopes. Another day to recharge what I felt like was missing in me, a sense of adventure and belonging in a place that makes me feel whole.

After dropping our ski gear off at the condo and changing, Lizzy and I head back to the village to meet the boys at the bar. I changed into some comfy leggings, decent boots for walking, a cowl knit sweater, and rebraided my hair before throwing on a beanie.

Lizzy is always on, as usual. She threw on some thick wool tights, but also put on a cute short black sweater dress. A perfect ski-lodge look.

Walking into the bar, I'm hit with all the memories of past nights spent here. We snag a high top right next to the bar on the first floor. At this time of day, the après crowd is rolling in and the place is electric.

A band is warming up on the stage in the corner, but they're drowned out by everyone in the bar talking about their highlights of the beautiful day. The latecomers now are heading upstairs to the second floor bar overlooking us. I smile looking up there at the balcony, laughing at the life size stuffed moose hanging from the ceiling, pulling a sled.

If you came to the Frisky Fox without knowing the history of it, your first reaction would be that it was the result of a cliché attempt at making a Wyoming ski dive bar, a theme park caricature. Sure it gives off that vibe, with its wood paneled walls covered in taxidermied animals, old skis, antique tin signs, and other knick knacks.

Except for the fact that it's the real genuine article, having been here since the sixties. Oddly enough, it started out as an admittedly unusual combination of an opera house, spaghetti restaurant, and saloon. These days it's known for killer après ski food, steaks, and margaritas.

God those margs are dangerously good.

Collin and I have been coming here, more often than not with Tanner, since we turned twenty - one. It's a staple for us anytime we're in town, regardless of the time of year.

"Spicy margs, right? I've been told that's the drink here," Lizzy says practically shouting over the noise looking for confirmation, as if we haven't been talking about this all week.

"Yep. That's it. Grab me one too. I got next round. Thanks, girl."

While Lizzy goes up to the bar, I look down at my phone to check the time. It's 4:15 but I wanted to get here early and grab a table before it's too crowded. Plus I can grab a drink with Lizzy before the boys show up.

Before I can even put my phone away, I feel it buzz in my hand. I swear if this is Jeff *again* today. Oh, that's… weird. It's not Jeff, but an email from Cindy at Earth SnaX, my main client contact there. She normally goes through Jeff, but does occasionally come straight to me for some things.

My anxiety starts to race.

Why is she reaching out directly? They're based in Oregon, so it's not that unusual for me to hear from them later in my work day with the three hour time difference. But it's the Saturday after Christmas. What could she want?

Ok, my anxiety is going to get the better of me. If I don't check this, I'm going to be consumed by wondering what she wants.

> *Hi Veronica!*
>
> *First off, this is not urgent, so I hope you don't see this message until you're back from your well earned vacation! Jealous you're out skiing, I'm more of a Colorado girl, but I've heard Jackson Hole is amazing.*
>
> *When you're back, I'd like to set up time to get your input on some ideas, unrelated to the upcoming presentation. Looking forward to hearing all about the slopes and catching up!*
>
> *Cindy*
> *Cynthia Peters*
> *SVP, Product Branding and Marketing*
> *Earth SnaX*

I exhale, realizing I was holding my breath. No idea what that's about, but glad it's nothing urgent though. Not that I'm going to let anything derail tonight. I've been waiting for a Spicy Fox Marg since I booked the flight out here.

When I look up from my phone, I'm surprised by someone standing at the table. And not a pleasant surprise.

"Hi there. Haven't seen you around here before," says the guy standing opposite me. "Name's Dustin."

Just what I needed. Some random guy trying to hit on me.

"Hi." I say, wanting this conversation to end as soon as possible. Can Lizzy please get back here already?

He leans onto the table, clearly not sensing my lack of interest in a conversation with a stranger. "Can I get you a drink?"

This guy screams *Tech Bro Chad*. Perfectly clean cut. Way too put together for après ski drinks. I bet he didn't even hit the slopes today. He's probably the type to take a one hour ski lesson and call it a day.

"No thanks. Just waiting on my brother and friends." I wish this guy would just take the hint and move on to wherever his gaggle of bros is.

While I roll my eyes as dramatically as I can to try and continue to show my disinterest, his eyes shift from me and grow wide with what looks like terror. Before I can turn to see what he's looking at, I feel a hand run across my back and rest on my waist.

"There you are, babe. I've been looking for you." That deep raspy voice. I calmly look down at the tattooed hand resting on my hip before looking back up to Tanner, smiling eagerly.

I'm 5'9" and Collin is tall at 6'1". And right now, Tanner is towering over me. Last night I only really saw him sitting at the table. But standing next to him now, this close, jeez. What is he like 6'4" or something? I can see why Tech Bro Chad here is intimidated and I definitely don't mind it.

"Hey sweetheart." I bat my eyes and put a hand on his chest, playing along with his little show to drive off this bro. "Where are my brother and Lizzy?"

Tanner tilts his head towards the bar before pulling me in close to him. "They're up at the bar grabbing drinks. They should be back soon."

At that, Dustin finally tucks his tail and leaves our table.

"Thanks, Tanner. Appreciate that. You know you're pretty good at playing big sexy boyfriend," I say appreciatively.

His face goes an unmistakable shade of red at those words and there's an awkward, yes definitely awkward, moment of silence lingering between us. His hand is still on my side and I'm still leaning against him, somehow in no rush to leave this spot.

He slowly levels a grin at me that stops just before it reaches those fierce green eyes, piercing into me and searching for something like last night.

Ok. Lizzy is right. I definitely wasn't imagining that last night. But what's up with him?

"Um hey guys. Here's your drink, V. But-," Lizzy startles both of us and Tanner quickly pulls his hand away. "But what's going on here?"

She waggles her finger back and forth between us questioningly.

"Tanner was just saving me from some obnoxious tech bro." Lizzy eyes me curiously before shrugging her shoulders. "Thanks again for the drink, Lizzy."

Tanner finally takes off his jacket and hangs it on the hooks under the table. And. Oh. My.

I knew he had put on muscle after seeing him last night, but the long sleeve shirt hid *a lot*. He's now wearing a black Jackson Hole t-shirt that's straining at the seams to hold back his thick arms and broad chest. The once trim, lanky boy from years past is bigger, broader, and more rugged than I remembered. Certainly looks like he's made from granite, cut from the mountains themselves.

And I can see the other tattoos, including one I've never seen before on his forearm. It's a chef's knife wrapped in roses on his forearm. There's something I can't quite make out reflecting back in the blade between the roses.

Yes, he's definitely grown into a man. How on earth is he always single? He's definitely a catch now, if he wasn't before.

Lizzy moves to Tanner's other side after handing me my drink. "Well, *Chap*," she says, popping her lips and batting her eyes. "If you're done playing V's fake boyfriend for the night, how about playing my real boy toy?"

I nearly spit out my drink and quickly cover my mouth to hide a laugh. Damn. Well I guess Lizzy is definitely shooting her shot.

I notice Tanner momentarily tensing before feigning a laugh and leaning against our high top table. "Very funny, Lizzy. I'm flattered. But I think my night is pretty booked with work after I leave here."

Lizzy leans closer to him, running her finger over the salted rim of her margarita before bringing her finger to her lips. "Alright. Your loss." She flicks her hair over her shoulder and turns back to me. "Oh and V. Collin said he was getting a twenty-one special or something at the bar, whatever that is."

I groan and palm my face. "Oh no. Not again." I mutter. "Why did you leave him unsupervised, Tanner?"

Tanner's smile is back as he laughs at my reaction. "I figured it'd be fun. He rarely gets to let his hair down and let loose like he does here."

"Fair enough. But you're carrying him home if he gets too wild." I point my finger at him. "I know I don't have to remind you about *that night*."

"Oh god. I hope he's better behaved than that tonight," Tanner says laughing, showing off his dimples and that perfect smile. He certainly is handsome.

And I'm clearly not the only one to notice. Lizzy has inched closer to Tanner, angling towards him.

"So, Chap. Nice moves out there on Tower Three today." Lizzy's words bring us back from the memory of our wild nights here before. "Have you skied that line like that before?"

I watch as Lizzy eyes Tanner a bit more mischievously than last night. Clearly she wants to take her shot at him after our earlier conversation on the lift.

Tanner has a bewildered look on his face. Or maybe it's more mild irritation? I watch, almost giggling as he seems to struggle to answer Lizzy's question.

"Oh. Tower Three. Yeah. I've done that before." he says, putting on a less than enthusiastic smile.

I can see she's intrigued by this hunk of a man in front of us. Oh, Lizzy. I thought she was only looking for a cowboy to have a fling with right now? Tanner isn't her cowboy, but maybe he's rugged enough for her after all.

But Tanner isn't having any of it. She keeps trying to get his attention back, batting her long lashes, hunting for a topic he's interested in. But he keeps changing the topic or checking in on me with that deep, lingering stare from the night before, as he politely shows just enough interest in Lizzy's conversation.

Hmm. What's up with that?

Better dive back into the fray and save Lizzy from herself.

"So yeah, uhhh, first chair tomorrow, right?" I try to diffuse the brewing tension, looking at Tanner and then Lizzy, already knowing the answer.

Where is Collin? He's left me alone with these two way too long.

"We know you wouldn't have it any other way, Ronni. So 8:30 AM outside the tram center?" Tanner looks at Lizzy briefly before returning back to me.

"Sure, Tanner. That'll work," I say.

As we talk more about the plan for first chair tomorrow, Collin has reappeared bearing gifts. I groan when I see what he's holding.

"Ladies and gentlemen, I'd like to reintroduce you to our old friends or maybe frenemies, tequila shots. Let's fucking go!" Collin passes them around the table. We each grab our glass and raise them for a toast.

"To old friends in new places and to new friends in old places!" Collin is always a great toast maker.

We all down our shots, grimacing over the cheap tequila. Oh yeah, the memories of prior nights here are coming back now.

"Oh and I forgot, they brought friends!" Collin reveals a tray with another round of shots on the table behind him. He's on a roll. It's good to see him this happy and back with his best friend though.

I love seeing Collin in his element like this. He's always been a social butterfly. Actually, more like a social chameleon, able to blend in with different groups and mingle as if he belonged anywhere and everywhere at once. He was a great high school athlete and was good friends with a lot of the jocks back then, laughing at teenage boy jokes like they were the greatest thing ever. But at the same time, he'd come hang with my girlfriends and me after getting home from practice, sitting down and instantly entering our debate over who Blair is going to end up with after the latest episode of *Gossip Girl.* Here though in Wyoming, with us, it feels like the real honest Collin. No blending in, just authentic, relaxed Collin.

This routine of shots and margs goes on for another hour and a half. Lizzy is surprisingly holding her own with Collin, maybe even outdoing him. Collin is a mess as usual. Lizzy and him are on the other side of the table now, gossiping away about some nonsense they saw on social media, scrolling through their phones, comparing feeds. I'm thrilled, yet somehow equally terrified, that they're becoming fast friends. I'm not sure I can handle that much snark and sass in my life.

I check in on Tanner. He's still been uncharacteristically quiet compared to the brash boy from my childhood. And last night everyone was so tired and hungry, we still didn't get the chance to talk much.

"So what else is new, Tanner? No girlfriend, as usual. Still hitting big lines when you aren't taking care of rich people's houses I see."

"Well, Ronni," he's entirely focused on me now. "Looks like you can see right through me as always. Single, yes. Big lines, sure if you say so."

When he doesn't add any more, I move to a friendlier topic.

"So, making any special knives right now?"

"Actually yeah. I made some here and there for the Eclectic Elk and some of my grandparent's friends and I'm working on a few more. But I've got one I've been working on for a while. Something special for the owner of a property I manage." A dreamy smile takes over his face. I can tell he really loves working on these knives.

"Oh really? What's special about it? I used the set you gave us for the condo last night. Still the best knives I've ever used by the way, even if my finger got caught up in some friendly fire." I hold up my bandaged finger tip to show him the damage.

"Ouch. Sorry about that," he says, wincing as if he's responsible for the cut from the other night. "Well, the new one is a classic K-Tip chef's knife but with a type of Damascus steel I haven't tried before. Honestly can't say much else about it, haven't decided exactly where I want to go with it yet and not sure if it'll work out."

He shrugs and breaks eye contact. "We'll see where it goes. But I think it just might end up being my favorite when I'm done with it, if I get it to work out anyways."

He takes a drink of his water before bringing his eyes back to mine. "What about you? Still single and still at the cubicle farm back home?"

I can't hide my reaction, I stare in disbelief, my mouth open. Did he really just say that? I mean he's not wrong but that still stings.

"Looks like you can see right through me too, I guess," I say. I turn to talk to Lizzy and Collin, when I feel a strong hand grab my wrist stopping me.

"Hey. I'm sorry, Ronni. Didn't mean it that way." His eyes are remorseful, looking like his words pained him as much as they did me, even if they are true. "I'm glad you're here though. It's good to see you guys together at the same time. Even though I live here, this place just feels more like home when both of you are around."

His hand is still lingering on my wrist, his thumb gently running over the back of my hand. The feeling of his touch is electric, like his skin is on fire. I don't know if it's the margs, his deep voice, or the feeling of his hand on my wrist, but suddenly I'm not irritated with him anymore.

"Don't sweat it. You're right though, it does feel good to be back. This place is home, even if we aren't always here." He nods in agreement before letting go of my wrist.

"So what else is new?" I ask, my mind still thinking about that electric touch as I touch the place his thumb was just rubbing. "Your grandparents still live upstairs from us, I know. Still driving that minty clean old truck?"

An unexpected smile and look of excitement takes over his face, the remorse in his eyes gone and replaced with a boyish sparkle.

"Actually yes, I still have mom's old truck but it's mostly just for plow work at this point. Still though, I keep it just how she loved it. I finally bit the bullet and got a sweet Sprinter van and decked it out for early morning ski days. It's pretty slick. Cozy bed for Rex and me, plenty of room for gear, little stove for making breakfast. Probably take it down to Salt Lake and Park City some time to visit Clay and Grace. If you lived out here, I'd totally see you owning one."

"You don't have to sell me. Sounds amazing. All of it." Damn. What I'd give to live in this fairy tale of a place like him. I wish I could just let go like that, live completely in the moment, embrace the ski bum life and take off to go where I want when I want.

"Yeah. It sure is. You know, I missed this. It's good to have you guys back."

We look at each other, both exhaling, enjoying the moment of calm thinking about the magic of this place.

The town, the mountain, the village, the times shared with loved ones. As I take it all in, I realize this might be exactly what I needed to recharge myself from my life back home and the office, or as Tanner would now say, the cubicle farm. My brother, old friends, even older friends. My favorite places. My favorite flavors and comfort foods.

I realize Tanner has the same contented look on his face.

I break the silence. "Want another drink, Tanner? I'm buying." I noticed he hasn't had any from the last couple of rounds.

"Nah, I'm good. I gotta drive home tonight. Forecast is looking like a big snow day. Gotta wake up early and plow a couple driveways in the morning before I can meet you at the slopes. Want me to bring a coffee for you? Iced honey badger, oat milk, extra shot, right?"

My jaw hangs open as a quiet stunned look engulfs my face.

How the hell did he remember that?

The pizza last night was one thing. We've been ordering that since we were teens. But I don't think I've had a coffee with this guy in four or five years and somehow he knows my favorite drink from the local coffee shop in town. I guess he has a good memory? How 'bout that.

My face still scrunched in disbelief that Tanner remembers my old coffee order.

"Um yeah actually, that's exactly it. Thank you. On another note, I think we might want to think about cashing out and heading home." I shift my eyes over to Collin and Lizzy. Collin is sitting down now, elbow on the table, head resting on his hand. Shit he might be about to pass out.

"Yep. There's our boy. Geez, some things never change." He notices Collin too apparently. But it's never been truer as we erupt in laughter.

I mean really, Tanner is right. Here we are over a decade later and we're going to have to carry Collin home just like our twenty-first birthday all over again. I'm still an anxious mess, now with the added stress of trying to salvage my stalled career. Tanner is… well Tanner, I guess. Maybe a smidge more mature but who knows what's really going on in that head under that hat.

Can things really stay the same like this forever with the three of us?

"You're right about that. It's our twenty-first birthday at the Fox all over again. Will Collin ever be able to handle more than a round of drinks?"

"Doubt it Ronni. I think he's actually getting worse at this. Didn't even think that was possible."

Chapter 12

Tanner
I Liked That Shirt

"Ronni, it's fine, really. I can carry Collin. He's still got a little gas in the tank. Well I hope so anyways."

Oh, my boy Collin. You really fucked up, *again*. When are you ever gonna learn? Hardly our first shit show at the Fox, I guess bud, but damn if you don't go all out. At least this time Ronni is with me as we leave the Fox and make our way back to their condo.

"So how you feeling there, *big brother*?" Ronni chimes in, smirking and giggling like a mad woman looking back at Collin while she walks side by side with Lizzy. He's hanging on my shoulder, my arm helping support him as he stumbles back to their condo. She already knows the answer though. He feels like shit. She's just taunting him for fun.

Well played, Ronni.

It's so good to see her like this though, smiling, laughing, happy. Yes, *happy*. It's been years since I last saw her at all and back then she was with that fucking tool. I think he managed to make her even more anxious than she usually is, constantly putting more and more on her plate. I never want her to be unhappy or alone, but I'm just glad she's not with him now. Thinking about it now though, I can already feel a familiar tinge of jealousy well up inside me.

"I'll... be fine, lil sis," mumbles Collin with his head hanging down hiding his face. There's my boy, looks like we have a pulse. "I just... need... to get..."

Oh god damnit. Seriously, again bro?

I watch while he throws up on the ground in front of us. Nope, there's more. He throws up again, his head still down, but this time facing me. With my jacket open, it covers my shirt.

Well fuck, I actually like this shirt.

"You alright, Tanner?" Ronni asks as she comes back to us, joining me in helping hold up her brother, my dumbass best friend.

I look over at her, taking in her face. Her skin glowing under the washed out moonlight, her subtle but high cheekbones framed by her long brown hair in matching braids sticking out of her beanie, her cute little button nose a bit red from the freezing air. Her soft, full lips open as if she's about to say more, her delicate eyebrows raised over her big gold flecked hazel eyes, which are looking back at me with a look of genuine concern.

"Yeah, I'll be fine. Let's just get him home." My answer is short. This is definitely not how I planned the night going.

It's a fifteen minute walk back, but with him like this now... yeah, it's probably going to take three times as long.

I could carry him home alone and let the girls get back to the condo, but Ronni now insists on helping, unable to ever hide how much she cares about her brother.

It's always been that way. Ronni, the voice of reason, behind the scenes keeping an eye on Collin and me when we'd be out doing god knows what.

At least tonight there's an added bonus from us having to carry him back though. I get to spend an extra thirty minutes with Ronni tonight, even if Lizzy is chatting away with her and I'm wearing Collin's second hand tequila shots and margaritas. Just glad he was drinking on an empty stomach. At least I can hear her voice, her laugh, and see that smile.

Walking back, our arms are wrapped under Collin's shoulders, Ronni on his left, me on his right. I'm bearing most of his weight since he can barely walk. I can just feel her arm brushing against mine and her fingers settling on to my bicep. It might just be in my head, but it feels like she's letting them linger there.

It sends shivers through me. I know I'm not showing it, but being this close to her again after all these years is like exposing a raw nerve. All my senses are heightened. I feel my heart racing again. Even in the cool night air, I'm sweating, but not just because I'm carrying her brother home. No. It's that familiar feeling I get every time I'm around her. Like I'm unraveling from the inside out.

I've had a crush on this girl for years, but always at a distance. She would only be in town a week or so here and there, seemingly always with Collin around. The times she would occasionally come to town without him, she was either dating someone like that douchebag years ago, spending time with her grandparents, or I'd be too afraid to see her without the excuse of Collin being around. On top of that, she's successful and has a career in Ohio now.

Why would she ever be interested in me?

I barely graduated high school. I live in Wyoming. I drive a snowplow and fix stuff at rental properties. It never felt right to try, like there was never an opening for me. I always settled for admiring her from arms length.

I think part of me even sabotaged my own attempts at dating and relationships. The idea of being with someone else while Ronni existed in the same world hurts. The times I would try to date, I found myself going towards blondes, or anyone that didn't remind me of Ronni, knowing my heart wouldn't be in it if I was thinking of her.

Even here at home in Wyoming, going to certain places in town would be a painful reminder that she's not here and a glimmer of hope that maybe she'll be back one day. Every time, I'd wonder if I still have a chance with *her*, this gorgeous, sweet, funny, caring but anxious girl?

Damn. Collin is moving his head around again. He better not have more in there… Ok, false alarm.

"I swear, if he throws up again," I look at Ronni and Lizzy shaking my head, "I'm going to make him do my laundry by hand tomorrow."

Lizzy snorts a laugh. "Sounds like a fair punishment to me."

"I just can't get over it," Ronni says, laughing back at Lizzy. "It really is like our twenty-first birthday all over again."

Something about that laugh and her smile always gets to me. I don't know why, but she's always made me feel so alive. Every day around her feels that way.

Alive.

Sometimes I think that's why I do all this shit - the backflips, the cliff drops, all of it. Just to feel alive, to feel something, like I did when she was around more back then. It's better than staying home in silence, depressed as shit, with no one to talk to.

I steal a glance at Ronni while her and Lizzy chat about the day. She's smiling. That beautiful fucking smile has never changed. It warms my heart to see her laughing with Lizzy. My eyes peer over my shoulder behind Collin over to Ronni's backside. Watching her walk, I see her ass is still perfectly perky as ever. It looks amazing in her yoga pants, which are also showing off her impossibly long but toned legs. Fuck she's hot.

After taking *that* in for a minute, I'm back to reality, listening to Lizzy and Ronni talk about their plans for the coming year, clearly avoiding talk about the office though. I knew work always stressed her out, but Collin told me the last few years had been pretty brutal for her. I'm glad she feels relaxed here. I know I do, more so with her here.

Maybe this time is the opening I've been waiting for. I don't know when I'll get another chance to see her again, let alone when we're both single. Maybe this is actually my last shot.

Yep. Fuck it.

I'm just along for the ride in this crazy life. It's time to feel something again.

Take a deep breath. You got this, Chap.

Chapter 13

Veronica
The Mudroom

Tanner and I amazingly manage to get Collin home in one piece. I mean if we're being honest, he clearly did most of the work, but I'm still claiming my participation trophy after helping them stumble along. That should have only been a fifteen minute walk but somehow turned into a forty-five minute drunken hot mess.

"Night guys. It's way past my bedtime. Good luck with him. Deuces!" Lizzy struts past us, cocking her head to the side, holding two fingers up, as she heads into the condo. She stops just inside the door from the mudroom into the unit, looking back at Tanner.

"Oh. And *Chap.* I'll leave my door open if you change your mind." She grins at him, blowing a kiss before she turns and heads up to her bedroom, leaving the three of us behind in the mudroom. I look at Collin, he's slumped against the wall, already passed out on the bench. And now he's snoring like a chainsaw. Cool cool. So it's just Tanner and me now.

Tanner chuckles and shakes his head side to side, looking back at me, one side of his mouth forming the hint of a smile. "She is something."

"That is one way to describe her," I say, leaning against the wall by the bench, next to Collin. "I thought she was your type though?"

"No," he says, with an unusually curt tone. "She's nowhere near my type. But hey. Do you mind if I throw this in your laundry, Ronni?" he asks, tugging his shirt away from his chest, highlighting Collin's handiwork from the night.

A puff of laughter escapes my lips. "Sure, Tanner. That's fine. Hamper is behind you, next to the washer."

He turns away from me, taking his jacket and hat off, hanging them on the wall hooks. Slowly, he reaches his long, sinewy arms behind him, pulling his shirt over his head revealing the ropey muscles of his defined back. Wow, he's even more muscular than I thought at the bar when the shirt was still on. I don't think I can remember the last time I saw Tanner without a shirt, probably some summer swimming with Collin and him at the river. He's certainly easy on the eyes now.

But instead of tossing his shirt into the hamper, he tosses it right into the washer. He grabs the hamper and dumps in my laundry too. Oh no. Did he just see my thongs in there? I feel my face flush at the thought of him seeing all my dirty underwear. Still, weirdly thoughtful of Tanner to do that. He definitely didn't have to.

As he's tossing in a pod, he asks, "So Ronni, where do you want this piece of work tonight?" while tipping his chin towards Collin.

"Great question," I say with an exasperated sigh. "He took the top bunk so that's probably not a great idea now. How about the couch? I don't think our troublemaker can do much damage from there."

I notice another newer tattoo on his chest that I haven't seen before, but I can't make out what it is before he turns back towards Collin.

"Works for me." Without the slightest hint of strain or effort, he wraps his arms around Collin and lifts him off of the bench, throwing him over his shoulder.

Wow. How on earth is he this superhuman strong? Wait, could he have carried him home alone?

He heads into the condo and his stride looks entirely effortless even with Collin draped over his shoulder. As muscular as he is, he still moves fluidly, not like a lumbering giant, but gracefully, almost like a hockey player gliding on ice, a hint of power lurking beneath.

He heads down the few stairs over to the couch in the living room, flopping Collin down like a rag doll. All of those muscles on full display working harmoniously in unison, putting on quite the show.

I kick my snow boots off in the mudroom and follow behind them. I grab a blanket from the basket next to the couch and tuck in Collin. He's going to be hating life tomorrow. I'm ruthless when it comes to herding people around in the morning to get first chair and I certainly won't be cutting him any slack. I mean come on, I sent him the agenda for the next two weeks. He should have known not to go so hard tonight.

"Looks like my work here is done." Tanner laughs, giving a little two fingered salute, clicking his tongue in his cheek, as he heads back to the mudroom to leave. I follow behind to walk him out and lock up, feeling myself let out a long yawn.

It was a full day on the mountain followed by a long happy hour turned hot mess express. I'm ready to get in bed and finally get some sleep.

As we reach the door leaving the mudroom, Tanner pauses before turning back to me. Something has been off about him tonight, all evening actually, besides the obvious that he's now shirtless. What's with all of the eye contact he's been making with me tonight? And letting his hand linger on my wrist. It's like there's a hint of vulnerability beyond all that bravado. Even last night I remember him blushing, something I've hardly ever seen him do.

Something is clearly on his mind. But what? Tanner has it easy, living the good life here in Jackson, far from the stressful realities us in the real world face. Is he worried about Collin maybe? No, that can't be it, a night like this is hardly a new thing for those two. I doubt it's work. What the hell could he possibly be worried about?

"You alright, Tanner? You've been awfully quiet the whole walk back. And what's with all the eye contact lately?"

We're practically face to face leaning against the door frame. God. For all the years I've known him I've only ever thought of him as Collin's childhood best friend. Sure we spent time together and he was always cute. But he was just a close family friend.

Now though. Damn if he doesn't have the body of a man. I definitely don't remember all of… *this.*

My eyes scan his body, taking in the piece of living art standing in front of me. A body of rugged and striking muscle. Now I can make out the new tattoo on his chest hidden by the curls of his chest hair. It's a tiger head, its mouth open showing its teeth. But instead of orange and black, it's stripes are teal and black. His chest hair trails down his abs to his waist. His flat, toned lower abs on full display, defined by his raised hip bones on either side and one pulsing vein trailing down under his belt line, highlighting that V.

Wow. If I stare any longer I'm going to start drooling.

Shit. Too late.

I'm snapped out of my trance by a quick low whistle.

"Yoo-hoo, my eyes are up here," he says with a hushed laugh and a wink, after catching me practically eyefucking him. I can't hide my embarrassment as my face goes flush and I turn red. "But, yes. I'm fine, Ronni. It's just been a long day." I can hear the tension building in his deep, raspy voice, as it nearly cracks.

Tanner leans further into the doorframe from the mudroom. His arms stretching overhead, his broad shoulders filling out the doorway. This man towers over me, and I'm not short. There's something primal about his presence, something dangerous yet alluring.

Standing like this, I can see just how well built the rest of his upper body is. His biceps and triceps are stretched out yet flexed, his powerful forearms and hands gripping the door frame, the veins in those gorgeous arms peeking through his tanned skin. From here, I can make out the rest of the detail of the chef's knife on his forearm. The blade is wrapped in roses and vines, but peering through the gaps, reflecting back in the blade are a woman's beautiful eyes. They're a subtle hazel color, almost like my own.

I still can't take my eyes off his hands though and the way he's gripping the door. He could grip me like that with those large hands. What the hell, V. Pull yourself together and snap out of it.

"Yeah, you're right. It's been a long night. It sure has been good to see you though." I'm trying to regain my composure, but it's futile. I turn red again as I immediately realize what I just said. Good to *see you!?* Who says that after just getting caught ogling their brother's best friend?

What is wrong with me tonight? Maybe it's the altitude or all those spicy margs. Or maybe it's the insanely built specimen of a man inches from me.

He lets out a little chuckle as he catches my embarrassment. That smile, those dimples. Have they always been there all these years too?

"Well, I ought to get going." The words come out of his mouth, but his body isn't following his own command. We're still face to face. Something is still off with him, an emotion I've never seen in the decades I've known him or at least one I've never noticed before.

What. Is. It?

"You sure you're alright, Tanner?" I inch closer and put my hand on his side to offer some reassurance, feeling his bare skin. God those muscles. I can feel him stiffen at my touch.

Wait… am I having this effect on him? Could I be throwing the unflappable Tanner Chapman off his game?

Standing this close to him with my hand on his side, I can't help but notice that something about him is timeless. His face, his features, all of it unashamedly rugged and masculine. Like if we went back in time a hundred years to rural frontier Wyoming, he'd stand out just as much as he does today.

I feel my eyebrow beginning to arch as my hand lingers on his side. I glance down at my hand, just above his jeans. Dear god, even this man's legs are jacked, his quads outlined through his faded blue jeans.

He reaches toward me, the back of his hand brushing my cheekbone as he tucks a strand of my hair back behind my ear. The sensation of his warm, callused skin on me gives me goosebumps up and down my arms and over the nape of my neck. He's so close I'm overwhelmed by his scent. It's like being near a stream running with clean fresh melted snow, pine needles all around, but still masculine with hints of oak and earthy leather.

God damn everything about him like this is so overtly sensual.

His eyes break contact with mine and he looks down at the ground for just a second. The ever present confidence of Tanner Chapman is briefly replaced with a look of boyish nervousness as he bites his lower lip and exhales in a whisper.

Is that... doubt in his face? This man, so ever confident, ever so calm, is doubting himself?

Could it *really* be because of me?

Before I could finish that thought, those piercing green eyes fix back on me, his lids low and heavy. There's a hungry force behind them now. I can hear his breath become heavy and watch his teeth dig into his lower lip. He leans forward, tilting my head up towards his face, his lips closing the final inches between us. My hand is still glued to his side as he lowers his other hand from the doorframe and rests it on my hip.

Our lips meet. He opens his mouth just enough for me to feel his breath heavy on my lips before he closes in again, ever so slightly biting my lower lip. Our mouths open, his tongue slides along mine, inviting me to kiss him back. I can't resist. I push my tongue into his mouth, slanting mine to feel all of his mouth against mine.

My legs are trembling. Urges I haven't felt in ages all flooding out of me at once. My hand drifts to his belt line, a finger hooking just inside the waistband of his underwear, which is peaking out from his jeans. Without his shirt on, I'm tantalizingly close to his abs, and *more*.

He leans against me, pinning me to the door frame, one hand on my waist, the other cupping the nape of my neck, fingers running over my braids. I lean my body back into his, pressing my hips into him, feeling the muscles in his legs and the fly of his jeans through my leggings. I wrap one of my legs around him, trying to pull him even further into me. It's so overwhelming and so fucking hot I let out the softest whimper into his waiting mouth.

My hands drift all over him, starving to feel every inch of his bare muscular body. Somehow despite that chilly walk home, his skin is still warm to the touch, practically blazing. The heat his body gives off matches the desire growing inside me, sending sparks through me and making my skin tingle.

Fuck.

Sparks.

Tingling skin.

For just a second my mind drifts to the thought of his shirt that was covering this masterpiece of a body, now in my laundry rubbing all over my thongs.

Something stirs deep inside me. My heart is pounding.

Who is this Tanner? I want *more*. I want to feel him even closer. I want to lean in harder and keep kissing him back, exploring his rock hard body.

Before I can even start to fully let go of myself, he pulls his mouth away, with the faintest tug on my lower lip. He rests his forehead on mine for a second, his breathing labored and hot on my lips.

His deep, lustful voice breaks the silence. "I'll be fine, Ronni. I'm really glad you're here. Good night. I hope I'll be *seeing more of you* tomorrow."

Shit. I forgot I even asked him a question.

He stands back, eyeing me hungrily.

"Oh, and Ronni. The eye contact? That's because you have pretty eyes and I like looking at them." A grin takes over his face exposing his dimples behind his scruff. He grabs his hat and jacket off the hook, and leans back to plant one more gentle peck on my cheek. And just like that his sense of joy, and a replenished look of assuredness is back on his face. He turns and starts to walk back out to the condo parking lot where his slate gray Sprinter van is parked.

"Now try and get some rest. First chair tomorrow, you know the drill. 8:30 AM, Tram Center. I'll still grab your coffee. Going to need some stamina to make it through another full day." His voice cuts through the frosty air from across the parking lot, a mischievous smirk on his face and that boyish laugh.

There he is again, the Tanner I know, and then… this other Tanner, I haven't seen before. I watch him climb into the driver seat, still shirtless even though it's below freezing out.

He pulls out of the lot and I bury my face into my palms. I can feel my stomach and my heart fighting over which one can do the most gymnastics inside me right now.

What on earth was that…

Vulnerability? Self doubt? All of those beautiful hard muscles? That kiss?! Then just calmly walking away?

Tanner. *Fucking*. Chapman.

What the actual fuck!?

And what about me? Staring him down, touching his bare skin, drooling over him, grinding myself into him.

Where did all of that come from? And why am I so turned on right now?

Chapter 14

Tanner
Full Send

I drive home while the radio in my Sprinter van is on in the background, not even registering what's playing. Jesus. Fucking. Christ. Did I really do *that*? Years of wanting Ronni and now… *now* is when I finally decide to go after her?

I palm my face, shaking my head. I can feel the shit eating grin plastered on my face. I definitely did it. I sent it. I really did kiss her.

That kiss though. The way she stared me down, grinding herself into me. The feeling of her tongue in my mouth. And she didn't slap me or pull away. She leaned back in for *more*.

Yep, totally worth it.

I still feel a sense of panic as it dawns on me that I guess it's all or nothing now. My cards are on the table. I find Ronni first thing tomorrow morning and either go for it all or apologize and hope I didn't fuck up everything else. I'm already bringing her coffee. It'll either be a peace offering or a promise now.

Ugh, can I just get home already. It's only a fifteen minute drive but feels like an eternity now. I want to be back at the cabin, sit down on my couch, grab a beer, and take a breath. I really just kissed the girl I've been in love with for years. My best friend's twin sister. A family friend. Fuckin' hell.

What if Collin finds out? Doubt she's gonna tell him tonight, he's still blacked out on their couch. But tomorrow? I don't know what I'd do if I ruined my friendship with him, much less both of them. I'd really be alone then.

As I pull into my driveway, the feeling of dread is partly replaced with something else. Something foreign. A sense of hope, optimism, a spark that's been missing. Maybe I really can land the woman of my dreams?

The feelings I've hidden for years all come rushing back like an avalanche and I can feel myself getting swept up in it. I've tried so hard for years to hide how much I've wanted her. My immature behavior, the jokes, the attitude, the shenanigans with Collin. All of it a crudely built, but surprisingly effective, shield meant to hide my feelings for her and my depression from everyone around me. That's all out the window now. She's seen through a crack in that decades old wall I've kept up and I can't hide it any more.

Shit. I don't want to hide it now.

She's the one that could see through it finally. I keep going back to her words.

You sure you're alright, Tanner?

Ok, sure. She was the source of what was on my mind all night. Yeah. But she still saw through me, saw *me*. And she cared enough to ask if I was ok and then to ask again, not just drop it. Not like everyone else. *Oh it's just Chap being Chap. Nothing's ever wrong with him.*

God damn I feel alive again, my steady and calm heart now pounding like crazy in my chest. I want this so bad. I can feel it throughout my body. Literally, my whole body.

I've been replaying that kiss over and over in my head. The fire burning in me thinking about the feeling of her finger tip creeping into my jeans, her grinding up on me in those yoga pants, the thoughts getting louder and louder in my head the entire way home.

Great. It was hot as fuck but now my dick is fucking *hard*, throbbing and pushing against the button fly of my jeans so much it's starting to hurt. I can practically hear my molars grinding.

Calm the fuck down. You've got work to do here bud.

As I park and shut the door behind me, I close my eyes and take a deep breath. I open them before letting out a long exhale, watching my breath ripple away from me in the cold dark air.

Damn. It's good to feel alive again. I could get used to this feeling.

As I walk in the cabin, I'm greeted by Rex, excited as always. Maybe even a bit more pep in his step, like he can read my mind. Or maybe I've just been talking to him for way too long now. Who cares? Even for an old boy, he still has that Aussie Cattle Dog burst of excitement every time I come home.

"Hey buddy. Good to *see you* too." I can hardly contain my laughter, getting a puzzled head tilt from Rex. Yeah, that really happened. She really said that. I think about how flush she got after I caught her eyeing me. The girl I've wanted for years really undressed me with her eyes. Well, I was already half undressed but still. Maybe I do have a chance after all.

Alright, I need to get shit done if I'm going to hit first chair tomorrow with them and make the best of this spot I put myself in.

A beer sounds great right about now. I grab a yellow jacket from the fridge then I drop onto the couch and open my laptop, sitting a bit awkwardly with the *situation* in my pants.

Ugh. I need to focus and my dick is not helping.

I'm quickly joined by Rex who curls up in his usual spot by my side, quietly judging me for withholding attention.

"I know bud, dad's got to work for a bit so I can spend time with Ronni tomorrow. We'll go play before bed." He doesn't look convinced, but lowers his head onto the couch anyways.

Fortunately being a property manager is pretty easy when you're handy and have free time. I need to check my schedule tomorrow for any check ins or check outs coming up that I need to handle on top of plowing at dawn. Tomorrow is Sunday and those are normally pretty easy, with most people checking in earlier in the week.

I take a quick look at my schedule portal. Ok, schedule's clear. Lucky me, I guess.

Maybe the cards are going to fall my way after all.

As I finally start to calm down from the excitement of the last hour, I close my laptop and look for the tv remote on the coffee table.

God, the coffee table is a mess. Shit, my whole cabin is a mess. I look around the place… yep. A single guy definitely lives here. Thank god no one is coming over.

The coffee table is littered with dirty ski base layers, random topographic backcountry maps, a set of touring bindings I need to clean, fix, and remount and other bullshit. Let's not even get started with my kitchen counter and dining room table. When was the last time I even used that to eat at?

I need to clean this place up. I can't imagine what a girl would think if I actually brought someone home. As I start cleaning, I find my nail clipper and file on the coffee table buried under my wool long johns. Huh that's where that was. I could use a nail trim. Put that on my *shit to get done list* tonight, I guess. Ah, there's the remote. How'd that even get under my throw pillow?

I look over at Rex. "Was that you?" No reaction from him. "Sure bud… play it cool like that. I'm watching you," I say as I look down my nose towards him, pointing a finger at him like I know he's responsible.

It's a moment like this where I would normally head out to my workshop with Rex and toil away on a knife. Most nights, it would be exactly what I need to clear my head. But tonight, I'm just tired and my head won't be in it. The ones I'm working on now are a bit crazy, a ten inch k-tip chef's knife with a Damascus steel blade and matching petty knife.

I haven't tried this particular combo of metals before though. I'm using the same typical high carbon steel I've been using lately, but trying some salvaged milder steel I found around the barn as the second part of the Damascus mix. My first attempt at forging this into something good enough for a blade went nowhere, but I think I have an idea on how to make it work now. Either way, I'll get back to it soon enough.

While I try to wind down, I grab another beer from the fridge and turn on the TV for a bit to check the weather forecast. Looking like snow again.

Hell yes. I could use a powder day.

The thought of being knee deep in pow, bobbing along through the turns down a steep bowl, chasing Ronni. Ok, well maybe she's chasing me but that's not the point. The thought of a ski day like that after tonight sends fire through my skin, my heart racing.

Fuck it feels good to… feel *this* again.

I click off the TV and head towards the door with my beer.

"Ok, Rex. Let's go bud." I grab Rex's ball and crack the door. Rex leaps off the couch, eager to start our nightly routine.

For the last few years, waiting for the times Collin comes to town, Rex has practically been my best friend. Sure I know people in town and see my grandparents, but it just gets lonely here. Rex is the best sidekick I could ask for. Always there. Always happy to see me. You just have to love dogs.

"Alright boy. Go!" I toss the ball towards the barn. Fucking dogs I think as I laugh out loud into the cold night air. I could watch Rex sprint across the path in the snow covered ground he's worn out forever.

Playing toss with Rex, beer in hand, watching my breath in the frosty night, is exactly what I need to refocus on what went down tonight and what's ahead for me.

I've buried this hope, this dream, in me for so long. The idea of making a plan to make it come true is a startling, but oddly grounding feeling. Something that, for years, was just a dream is now a real, actionable thing. I just can't believe I'm here right now. These feelings deep inside me are scary as fuck.

Hope, happiness, optimism, but also the fear of losing all of it.

But still, there's a chance I can do this and get to have what I've wanted for so many years. My skin tingles at the thought, goosebumps up and down my arms, hair standing.

I take a deep breath. Ok. Girl of your dreams, Chap. Let's make it fucking happen.

Full send.

.

Chapter 15

Veronica
Thunderous Explosions

I wake up to an all too familiar, yet comforting sound in Teton Village. The distant, thunderous explosions of Ski Patrol's avalanche control work. To some tourists and those unaccustomed to life near avalanche terrain, the sounds might be unsettling and frightening. Others might even mistake it for fireworks or thunder.

But for me, the sound of explosives high in the mountains brings a sense of excitement. The harbinger of a powder day and fresh deep snow on the slopes. This is something I crave, something I look forward to with wide eyed excitement when I hear these sounds in the morning.

Looks like the weather forecast was right. I start to think about the prospect of a day hitting steep and deep powder lines, a true treat for any Jackson Hole diehard.

Before I get anywhere with that train of thought, my mind is taken somewhere else, a different kind of excitement.

Are you kidding me? I'm *turned on*? How in the — Tanner. Oh my god.

The thoughts come racing back. Those abs. Those arms. That kiss! It was all a blur, but a steamy one that's clearly been in my dreams. I think about how I was eyefucking Tanner the night before, running my hands all over his body, grinding myself into him, his tongue in my mouth teasing mine.

Yes. I'm definitely turned on.

I bury my face into my pillow, biting it while letting out a desperate, muffled moan. *FUCK*. Is Collin still in bed above me? Wait, no. He slept on the couch last night. Thank god.

On cue I hear Collin and Lizzy distantly chatting away. I roll myself out of bed, trying to ignore that I'm wet right now and don't have the time to give myself a desperately needed release. Nope. Certainly didn't include that on my morning itinerary for this trip.

I don't know what last night was. It was certainly hot. Like *really hot*, but what the actual fuck. Kissing Tanner Chapman? I can't even begin to process that right now.

To the back burner of my anxiety list it goes. Alright, V. Let's get this show on the road. Can't waste a powder day on the slopes.

Lizzy and Collin are probably expecting breakfast right now, if they haven't made themselves anything yet and we've got a full day planned for us.

It's 7:00 AM now, so we've got a little over an hour before we need to leave the condo. A quick breakfast will have to do.

"Morning, *lil sis*," Collin says, from the dining room table as I walk down the landing towards Lizzy and him, "surprised we got up before you."

"Yeah well what can I say, even the best planners get off track every now and then." I mean yeah, no lie there. I wasn't expecting to have *dreams* about your best friend all night and wake up grinding myself into the bed, Collin.

"So what's for breakfast, Chef V?" Lizzy asks, always hangry. I don't know how a girl that small and fit can eat like she does. Seriously.

"I'm thinking bacon, egg, and everything bagel sandwiches. Should be quick. Work for you guys?" They both nod in approval, sipping their coffees.

"Coffee, V?" Collin asks.

"No, I'm good. Thanks though," I say, remembering I'm supposed to have a coffee waiting for me from Tanner later on.

Fuck, Tanner. Those eyes, those abs, those lips… Nope, no time to think about that. Got to focus on breakfast and feeding these two.

After a quick breakfast, we head over to the mudroom to gear up for the day on the slopes. All of the memories of that kiss come back again and I struggle to focus on getting ready for the day of skiing. I finally remember Tanner ran the washer last night, so I open it up to swap the laundry over to the dryer. While I'm moving laundry over, Tanner's black shirt with the faded red bronco on it falls out, prompting another flashback to the night before.

"What's that, V? Looks a little big for you," Collin asks, noticing the men's shirt in my hands now.

"Oh this?" My mind snaps back from the image in my head of those chiseled abs and ripped arms in the doorway, the shirt in my hands concealing them only the night before. "You really don't remember, do you? This is Tanner's. He had to wash it last night after you hurled your tequila and margs on him during the walk home."

"Oh… My bad. Sorry, V. I wondered how I ended up on the couch."

I snort a short laugh. "That was Tanner. He fireman carried you over there and dropped you like a sack of potatoes." How could I forget that image? Tanner picking up Collin like it was nothing, his muscles putting on a private show just for me to see.

Yikes. I need to snap out of this and get on with the day.

After getting ready, we make it over to the Tram Center by 8:30 to meet Tanner. He's already there, my coffee in hand, waiting for us.

Collin sees the coffee, a clear cup with my iced honey badger. "What gives, Chap? No coffee for me?"

Tanner lets out a smug laugh. "Well dude, you were practically blacked out last night at the Fox when I asked if she wanted one. Can't take your order if you can't talk."

"Well I didn't get one either, Collin. Don't feel too bad," Lizzy says as she frowns at Tanner, still seemingly holding a grudge from the night before at the Fox.

He looks in my direction, extending my drink towards me. "Here, Ronni. Just as you ordered."

Our eyes meet as I take the cup from him in my bare ungloved hand, our fingers brushing each other. Even with his bare hand holding my iced coffee in the cold winter air, I still feel that fiery skin, and a spark of electricity flows through my body. All of the sensations of last night rush back into my body. As if he can sense it too, a subtle grin takes hold of one side of his lips, his dimple peaking out for me to see.

"Thanks for the horny badger." Fuck my life. Ugh… "I mean honey badger, thanks for the *honey badger*, Tanner," I say as I feel my face turning a shade of red brighter than the tram cars running overhead.

How has he wormed his way into my head this badly after one kiss? I can't even talk straight.

See you.

Horny Badger.

Fuck me.

Collin and Lizzy let out a chorus of laughter. Even Tanner practically chokes on his own coffee. I let out a groan. It's going to be a long fucking day if my brain is going to be like this.

The four of us take the chairlift up for our first run of the day, me on the far end next to Tanner with Collin and Lizzy on the other end.

Great. The last thing I'm ready for is to be this close to him. Or maybe it's exactly what I want? Even through the layers of our ski gear, feeling his burly body against my side on the lift is enough to bring back a flash of heat thinking of last night. I feel myself squirm in my seat remembering his touch and that kiss.

Collin and Lizzy are chatting about Tower Three Chute from the other day, while Tanner laughs and tells Lizzy she handled it great for the first time. I don't miss that his gloved hand ends up resting on my thigh, something that the others don't seem to notice. Maybe he's thinking about last night too? And I don't mind it.

No. I don't mind it all, weirdly enough.

But I want to talk to him, alone.

Ok. Maybe a little more than talk.

Chapter 16

Veronica
Cut Loose a Little

Skiing with Tanner has always been *intense*. Collin and I know practically every square inch of this mountain. But with Tanner, it's like the mountain and him are one. At first, it might feel like he has a severe case of squirrel brain. He skis powerfully, almost violently, but can stop at a moments notice to suddenly change course, flashing a glance back at you over his shoulder to make sure you're still with him before he drops down into a chute or trees on the side of the run.

It's not indecision or forgetfulness, but instead an eery sixth sense that runs through him, the mountain talking to him, his mind taking in the weather, the wind, the sun exposure. All of it guiding him to hidden stashes of fresh snow or untracked lines still waiting to be skied, like a wolf hunting its prey. Animalistic and raw. Once you learn to read his body language and anticipate his turns and stops, it's utterly thrilling and heart pounding. I've always appreciated the way he skied because he's just so *good*.

But now the thoughts of that kiss last night and the spark at his touch this morning are racing through my mind, and it's... It's fucking hot.

He's completely going for it on the slopes and we're just tagging along for the ride only knowing the destination is going to be worth it. I've always enjoyed it, the feeling of letting someone else, someone you trust, be in control. Not having to think about what's next, just living in the moment. But now, it's him and all I want to do is keep up with him, watch him, and chase that spark from last night.

After letting Tanner play guide for the morning, we head back towards the base of the mountain. Lizzy wants to opt for a long, mellow groomer run to take a gondola back up to the mid-mountain restaurant for an early lunch.

Unsurprisingly, a very hungover Collin and gondola-virgin Lizzy are a hot mess trying to load onto a gondola today. While Tanner and I manage to get our skis in the rack and settle onto the benches, Collin and Lizzy are still bumbling and fumbling around as the doors to our car close and we're whisked away up the mountain. We can't help but laugh as Collin and Lizzy end up on the car following ours.

A few seconds pass and then I realize he's stopped laughing. I look over, his hooded gaze already waiting for me. It's just the two of us, alone, in the small gondola. I guess I'm going to get the moment alone with him I was thinking about earlier. The one I've been both dreading, yet craving since last night. Well obviously my body wanted it if this morning was any clue. But what's happening here? Are we going to talk about it or just pretend like it didn't happen? Either way, after that kiss last night, fuck that damn kiss, I'm now alone, face to face with Tanner. I can feel Horny Veronica inside me start to wake up again from this morning.

Tanner can sense it too. At least I think so? He's always been so hard to read in the past.

He's already taken off his gloves and helmet, setting them neatly on the bench beside him. He leans across the gondola car and gives me a sweet, delicate, slow kiss.

My heart flutters and my eyes close. His hand cups my cheek, his thumb running over my lower lip. The feeling of his touch kicks the embers of the fire he lit in me from the night before, sending sparks flying inside me. My own skin feels like it's burning now, matching his. But he starts to pull his head away and it's torture. All of it is just enough to leave me needing more as my head leans forward trying to follow his.

"Tanner. About last night. It was-." I try to find the words for all of this, but he's already one step ahead of me.

"I'm glad I'm not the only one that was thinking about last night," he says, that deep and confident but hushed tone sending shivers through me. He's sporting a devilish grin and those dimples peer through his beard. "It really is good to *see you.*"

God those dimples aren't fair.

"No. I definitely thought about it. But why did you just stop and leave?" I can barely keep eye contact with him, the lust in his eyes palpable and cutting right into me.

His grin turns almost feral. "Because with the way you were grinding into me last night, the way your hands were roaming over me, there was no way I was going to be able to stop. And I wanted to do so many things with you last night."

My mouth goes dry, thinking back to how good it felt to run my hands over his body. "Oh yeah? What did you want to do first?"

He hums with amusement through his grin. "Well, I could tell you. Or since we're alone now, I could give you a little tease. Because I think you and I both wanted more last night. And I think you *really* need to start enjoying your trip. Cut loose a little. So maybe I can help with that, help you relax and have some fun, if you'll let me."

I feel a growing want between my legs, the sensation from this morning is back in full force, raging in me. He slowly lowers himself on to his knees in the gondola, his hands running up my thighs.

Is he… is he going to unbutton my pants? I can barely process what's happening.

"Tanner?" I say with a muted voice as I exhale deeply, trying to catch my breath.

Really, is this actually happening? As if I wasn't stressed enough about life, now I have this sexy man I've known most of my life trying to go down on me in a gondola. I mean fuck, he's hot and I want it. But really?! This, here, and *now*? My anxiety skyrockets as my mind races.

Now I have a new internal struggle. Practical Veronica and Horny Veronica who have *very* competing needs.

"Tanner. There's no way. You're insane! This is barely a ten minute lift ride. We canno-." Before I can finish that sentence he looks into my eyes, cutting right through my layers and layers of stress and doubt. He puts his finger up to my lips and gestures *shhhh*.

"It's going to be ok, Ronni. Don't you trust me?" His confidence is there as always, but something is different. Something more serious, no, *lustful*, is behind his eyes now. Shit. Those beautiful green eyes. How have I never noticed them before? Something about them grounds me, pulling away the curtains of anxiety clouding my mind.

Back to the moment. Focus, V. Yes, I do trust him. I've known Tanner for years and for as silly and unserious as he can be, he was always reliable. But *this*?

"Yes, I do but this is-," I start to say before he cuts me off again.

"Then can I?" He asks looking into my eyes then back down between my legs and back at me raising his eyebrows, letting his eyes finish his question.

Fuck. There's that look in those eyes again.

My mind goes back to the thought of skiing just mere moments ago, trusting this man with our lives leading us across the mountain. Looking into his eyes now, it's like he's pouring his own confidence into me, sharing as much of it as I need.

After all, I did wake up fingering my clit, my pussy soaking wet this morning just at the thought of those abs and *that kiss*. Fuck it. Maybe he's right and I do deserve to feel good and relax for once.

"Ok, Tanner. Yes."

By the time the last syllable escapes my mouth he already has my pants and base layers down to my ski boots. There isn't enough time to take off everything and get my ski boots off. He pulls me to the edge of the gondola bench, effortlessly throws my legs over his head with those strong, muscular, sculpted from granite arms. His face is lost in between my legs.

Thank god I remembered to get a wax before we came. I was thinking we might end up in a hot tub for a night or two, but I definitely wasn't anticipating this scenario.

First, he just kisses my body, right above my aching clit, which now desperately wants to feel his tongue. As if he was in my head, his next kiss lands squarely on my swollen pleasure spot. That little bit of touch is enough to make my legs and pussy clench. I moan desperately, not having been touched like this in ages. He doesn't pull away after his next kiss, instead letting his tongue start to work on me.

"Oh god. Please don't fucking stop." I'm practically panting now, squirming, wanting more as he runs his tongue back and forth over my clit.

"I wasn't planning on it," he says with a quick laugh and what I assume would be that ever present grin. If I could actually see his mouth that is. But he already has it back to work as I look down at him, only able to see his shaggy messy golden brown hair. I run my fingers through his tousled locks and he lets out a small moan of approval. I can feel the sound reverberating in my clit. The feeling of his scruffy beard between my legs only adds to the overwhelming sensations coursing through me.

His mouth is wide open, his lips pressed firmly against my wetness, all of it. His tongue dances back and forth slowly, tauntingly from my clit to the outer edges of my pussy, teasing both just enough to bring me closer to the release I was craving this morning, but also leaving me wanting more. So much more.

God this is really happening. It's been so long since I've been touched by someone other than myself and now I'm watching this insanely built, gorgeous man on his knees for *me*.

Just as the thought of wanting more entered my mind, I realize his strong hands are in motion. It's like he's slipped himself into my mind, reading my thoughts. His left hand works its way under my jacket and long sleeve wool shirt, stopping when he reaches my unlined sports bra. His hand rests over my breast, cupping it while his fingers teases my hard bud through the fabric of the sports bra.

Before I could even acknowledge him, he's already started again. He manages to slide his hand under my bra and now I feel his scorching skin against my breast as he teases my hard nipple even more with a slight tug.

"Fuck," he murmurs as he comes up for a moment of air, "your tits feel even more amazing than I imagined."

With one hand teasing my nipple, the tip of his tongue is now focused solely on my desperately aching clit. I let out a loud moan, grateful that no one can see us or hear us through the tinted windows, the nearest car at least a hundred feet in either direction.

"God, Tanner. Yes. Your tongue. It's. So. Good." I can barely get the words out, practically stuttering. I feel just how eager he is with his spit running down from his tongue through my slit to my already wet pussy.

"Shit," I moan, barely able to think, grabbing his hair and pulling him harder against me. "You're going to make me come if you kee-," I start to say before I feel a new sensation.

Tanner now gently starts to tease my dripping wet pussy with a finger. First, he touches the inner lips of my pussy with just his fingertip, all the while his tongue continues to push me closer and closer, flicking up and down my clit. He slides his finger in me further before firmly, gently curling it in a *come hither* motion on my inner walls.

For a brief moment my thoughts are broken by an interloping sound, the whirring of the car passing a lift tower.

Shit. How much longer do we have? Are we going to be able to-?

My thoughts are taken right back to the beautiful, skillfully tongued man between my legs eating me out like he's been starving for my body.

"Fuck," I moan as he gently works another finger inside me, filling and stretching me even more. I can feel his strong hands work his fingers up to his palm, his last knuckles teasing the edges of my opening. This whole time his tongue hasn't stopped and I feel a sense of tension come over my body, the kind that comes right before…

Oh my god, yes. I'm getting close. So fucking close.

"Tanner…," I whimper. "Please. I want to come." I'm so ready for this. It feels so good. My body keeps tensing and coiling up, ready to let go.

"Good. I want you to come so bad. Please. Come for me," he says, his words muffled by my own wetness still in his mouth.

I thrust myself further into his mouth as I lace my fingers into his hair and pull it, pressing his face into my body. I hear a moan come from his mouth, as I push myself against him harder, rocking my hips forward. His moan is one of the hottest things I've ever heard and it's enough to almost push me over the edge.

"It feels so good." He gently sucks on my clit while flicking his tongue across it even faster while his strong, thick fingers still massage the inner depths of my pussy. I shudder, squeezing his head between my thighs to keep him exactly where I need him.

My body starts to shake as I come. Desperate to hold on to something, anything, I run my hands back through his hair, grabbing tightly.

"Oh. Fuck. Yes." I moan as I feel a world of stress leave me, my body still shaking, and a wave of heat comes over me. I arch against the gondola bench.

I look around me, my vision blurred, but I still manage to take in the views from the lightly tinted gondola, admiring the mountains surrounding us, while the wave of euphoria takes hold of me and I ride out the orgasm.

When was the last time I came like that? Have I ever even come like that?

While I'm reveling in the feelings running through me, Tanner ever so casually sits up with a look of pure satisfaction on his face. He leans over, giving me a quick kiss on the lips. He leans back down, helping me pull my pants up, kissing my thighs before they're covered and buttons me, tucking my shirt back into them.

"Tanner… that was… *something*."

The words feel like they're coming from someone else, like I'm floating here in the gondola watching the whole scene, still in disbelief that it really just happened. My heart is pounding. My head is a frazzled mess of racing thoughts and emotions.

"You're welcome. Now, can you start enjoying your trip? You aren't in town often enough and I like seeing that smile," he says with his usual grin as he looks up, wiping off a bit of sweat, spit, and maybe even some of my arousal that are all glistening in his scruff and mustache. He sits back down on the bench opposite me in the gondola, grabbing his gloves and helmet.

Suddenly there's the louder, telltale clanging and whirring noise and I realize we are pulling into the upper gondola station to unload.

"Holy shit, Tanner. You are insane! We had what, maybe an extra forty seconds? We could have been seen. Were you even paying attention to where we were?"

He looks at me with his usual grin back on his face, and winks before shrugging his shoulders.

"I wasn't worried. We're fifty plus feet above the slopes, the windows are sort of tinted, and the nearest people are in the cars way ahead of us and behind us. Besides, I knew you were going to finish on time."

I feel my jaw drop. This fucking man. Is there anything that shakes that confidence or makes him worry?

Just as we reach the upper gondola station, he reaches a hand to help me start getting out of the car.

Oh no. My legs are completely jello. I could maybe walk if I wasn't wearing heavy ski boots, but now I'm riding the struggle bus.

"Don't worry. You got this," he says, as if he knew what I was thinking. As the door opens, I stumble off the gondola like a baby deer. He catches me and still manages to grab my skis from the rack on the door. A world of emotions and physical euphoria are taking over me now, just as we see Collin and Lizzy's gondola car arriving.

"Alright. Let's act normal. We gotta have lunch with your brother and Lizzy." He looks over at me, giving me a little upward flick of his eyebrows, before the calm and cool expression takes back over his face. Just casual as can be.

What. The. Fuck?

Chapter 17

Veronica
Glowing

Just as soon as I manage to get off the gondola and gain some vague sense of my bearings, Lizzy and Collin are unloading off the next gondola car. How the hell am I supposed to get through lunch with the four of us? Tanner really said *act normal,* as if nothing happened.

I just got tongued down, fingered, and given the most body shaking orgasm of my life, in a gondola. From Tanner. Fucking. Chapman.

We all toss our skis on the rack outside the Rendezvous Lodge, before heading to the cafeteria upstairs.

Shit. My legs are still jello.

Was it worth it to let him go down on me like that? Dumb thought, V. Yes, yes it was. God I haven't come like that in forever, maybe not ever actually.

Now my legs are dead. That's not going to help me on the two flights of stairs up to the dining room in ski boots, much less the rest of the day on the slopes.

Collin and Lizzy have already raced ahead to find a table in the old cafeteria. Tanner is lagging behind, but I see him gaining ground as I reach the first flight of stairs. My knees tremble watching him come up to my side on the stairs. That man just gave me the orgasm of my life on a ski gondola. Out of nowhere.

"Need a boost, Ronni? Looks like you're struggling with these stairs." He says as he wraps one of those strong arms around my waist, locking eyes with me, then motioning up the stairs with his gaze. With his arm wrapped around my waist, bearing the weight of my spent body, we make our way up the stairs, which is surprisingly comforting.

What is going on here between us?

As we near the top of the second flight of stairs, he drops his arm back to his side, looking at me with a sly wink before making his way over to the table where Collin and Lizzy are waiting.

I don't think they saw me with Tanner's arm draped around me. Thank god.

We reach the table and I'm ready to sit back down. My legs need a break and I plop down onto the bench with a thud as Tanner slides onto the bench next to Collin, across from me. I can still feel the wetness between my legs as I try to focus on what's next, lunch with Collin, Lizzy, and *Tanner*.

"Remind me why we're getting cafeteria food? Ski lodge food sucks," Lizzy scoffs.

"Well, they have a captive audience, Lizzy. Not many options. Sorry it's not up to your Aspen Valley standards," Collin says, clearly teasing Lizzy.

I finally open my mouth, doing my best to follow Tanner's sage advice and *act normal*.

"I could definitely use some food. I'm famished. It's been a quad burning morning on the slopes with Tanner leading the way. Speaking of tired legs, would you mind grabbing my lunch while you're up Tanner?" I look back to him, still not sure of what's happening or what to expect next from this man.

"Sure, Ronni. I'm good on food but I'll grab yours. I could use a drink though. Got a bit of a dry mouth. What can I grab you from the counter?"

"Chili in a bread bowl and a red Powerade. Thanks, Tanner!"

Are you serious? Taunting me right now? I start thinking about his mouth though. I'd blush if I wasn't still already flush from that gondola ride.

I swear though, if men have anything, it's… *The. Fucking. Audacity.*

As the three of them go up to get lunch while I man our spot at the table, I finally exhale and put my face in the palm of my hands, elbows up on the table. What the fuck, V? That was hot, but really, what the fuck is happening?

Tanner is the first one to get back, sliding my lunch across the table to me on a cafeteria tray.

"Hey there, you should eat up. Long day ahead of us." I look at him, a soft smile exposes his dimples through his scruffy beard. It's unreal how he can go from smoking hot rugged man to charmingly sweet and cute like this.

"Thanks, Tanner." I want to say more, but Lizzy and Collin are already getting back to the table as he sits down.

Digging into our lunches, we reminisce about last night at the Fox.

"Wait, I had how many tequila shots?" Collin asks, a horrified look on his face.

"Um like, at least four or five. And that doesn't even include the margs, Collin," Lizzy says, taking alternating air shots with her hands to remind Collin what he looked like last night.

"Fuck me. I guess one of those nights every decade is fine. Glad that one's out of my system," he says.

"Yeah sure, Collin," Tanner says, his deep voice sending chills to my core. "Next time can you just aim away from my shirt when you drink too much?"

Well played, Tanner.

"So V, what's for dinner tonight?" Lizzy asks, looking my way. I swear it always comes back to food with her.

"Oh, right. Dinner. I was going to make chicken tacos. It's already marinating back in the fridge." That will definitely make my night simpler.

As lunch goes on, I realize my thoughts have slowed down. My mind isn't racing from one idea to the next. I'm sitting here taking in the conversation with everyone, oddly relaxed.

Can this post orgasm bliss continue forever please? I guess I really did need that.

My phone buzzes in my pocket, interrupting my blissful moment. I guess that question is answered. Seriously?!

As I pull my phone from the chest pocket of my jacket to take a peak at what on earth it could be this time, I feel my heart stop.

It's Tanner.

> *Tanner: Just wanted to let you know you're glowing right now. You look amazing. Glad to see that smile.*
>
> *PS - I still can't get over how good you taste.*

I look across the table at him, but he's looking right at Collin, as they're chatting about always keeping your ski tips pointed down hill. His fingers, *those fingers*, are resting just inside his lower lip, his mouth slightly open.

Is he… fucking tasting me?

"I swear, V. If that's Jeff, I'm going to personally beat his ass when we're back in the office. That dude needs a sanity check."

Lizzy's words startle me as I realize I've been staring at Tanner too long.

"Oh no, it's not Jeff. Just one of those targeted ads from signing up for an email and text list. It's crazy how fast they send those, like they're reading your mind," I say, hoping my babbling is enough to get her off the trail.

"Alright. So what's left for the day? We skiing with the boys or just us this afternoon?" I'm torn. All I can think about is Tanner right now and the thought of being close to him for the afternoon sounds frighteningly good. But I feel like I need to spend some girl time with Lizzy after all.

"I'm down for a run with the boys before splitting off for some girl time. We'll see them for drinks and dinner back at the condo." Practical V is going to win this one.

After lunch, I still feel shockingly good though, my mind keeps going back to the gondola. That was so intense. So hot. My mind starts to think about Tanner in the mudroom and the magic of his mouth just now, when Collin interrupts.

"So remind me when we need to be back at the condo, V?" Collin asks from the other end of the table. At least he remembered there is a plan for the day this time.

"Lizzy and I will hit a run with you before some girl time on the slopes. Meet back at the condo around 5:00 for drinks and dinner. Sound good?"

"Perfect, V. Tanner and I will see you girls then," Collin says as he stands up, putting his hand on Tanner's shoulder. "Come on, Chap. Let's grab our skis and meet them outside."

As I watch them walk away, towards the stairs at the end of the cafeteria, I'm still taken aback by how tall and rugged Tanner looks next to Collin. His broad shoulders and chest, his athletic build, all still noticeable even through his loose ski jacket. With Collin busy looking ahead, Tanner looks over his shoulder, winking back at me.

Fuck my life. Just when I thought everything was dull and boring, apparently I'm into Tanner Chapman now.

Chapter 18

Tanner
Dinner is Served

I t's been a long day of skiing, but we're finally back at the Perry twin's condo. Perfect timing. I could use an après ski drink right about now. My nerves are fried, my adrenaline running full tilt all day and not just from hitting jumps off cliffs. It was a killer day on the slopes for sure. Fresh powder, hit some fun lines with the twins and Lizzy.

And oh yeah, I got to make the woman of my dreams come on a gondola.

That was *fucking crazy hot*.

My dick's been throbbing all day just thinking about how wet she was and how her legs wrapped around my head while she came. The way she pulled me into her by my hair.

Time to hold that thought and try to act normal though. I'm sitting at their dinner table with Collin and Lizzy while Ronni is in the kitchen. At least the table is my friend here, giving me a little coverage while I try to hide the bulge in my jeans.

"No way, Chap. Not buying it. There's absolutely no way you'd enter a skijoring contest. You're a crazy son of a bitch, but I don't believe you." Collin looks at me, completely doubting my level of seriousness.

"Um. Does someone want to tell me what *skijoring* is?" Lizzy looks confused like we're talking about video games or something.

"Oh god, Lizzy. You fucked up. He's never gonna shut up now. Tanner has been talking about this for *years*," says Ronni from the kitchen. I love it when she remembers things about me from the past. Little reminders that maybe I wasn't as invisible as I felt for all those years. I look back to Lizzy.

"Ok, Lizzy. They probably don't do this in Park City or Aspen Valley, so that's a fair question." I'm trying to be nice, but she's still scowling at me. Damn. What's it going to take to make her accept that I'm not into her? Anyways."So yeah, skijoring. Basically combine a rodeo and park skiing. They build a course through town, covering the roads with snow and build ramps and jumps. Then the skiers grab a water ski handle that's tied to a horse and a cowboy pulls the skier through the course fast enough for the skier to hit the jumps, racing through town. It's fucking gnarly."

Lizzy looks at me, surprisingly interested. "Cowboys you said? I think I could get on board."

"You're in luck, Lizzy. There's always one in town the weekend after New Year's Day. We should be able to go to it this year," Ronni says from the kitchen.

I look over towards Ronni from the table, still in the kitchen as Collin and Lizzy start talking about cowboys. She's changed into some black yoga pants and a red tank top showing the criss crossed straps of her sports bra over her toned back, her long legs and perky butt perfectly outlined. She looks at me, her smiling face framed by her hair that's still in a pair of long braids. She has one of my knives in hand as she gets ready to start cutting onions and cilantro. She looks relaxed, at ease. I can only hope in some way I've helped with that.

With the urges in my jeans under control, for the moment anyways, I head to the kitchen to grab a beer from the fridge.

Ok, let's be real. I just want to be close to her again while Collin and Lizzy are distracted talking about cowboys.

The kitchen is tiny, barely enough room for two people to stand in, let alone cook together. The fridge is opposite the counter she's working at and I have no choice but to bump into her as I squeeze by. The front of my jeans brushes against her ass, sending shivers through me and my dick fucking twitches hard.

"Oh, sorry, Ronni. Tight squeeze in here." My dick twitches again at the thought of her tight pussy squeezing my fingers earlier today. Fuck I need to get my shit under control. I still have to make it through dinner with everyone.

"No worries, Tanner." She says, a wry smile on her face as I grab a beer from the fridge. Fuck, she's thinking about it too.

"All good in here? Happy to lend a *hand*." I'm sure she's got it under control, but still I would do anything to have an excuse to stay this close to her.

"Nope. All good. You've done *more* than enough with those hands today, Tanner." There's a subtle sultry shift in the tone of her voice. We're side by side in front of the counter now, me standing between her and the others in the dining room.

"Well I'm glad you're having a good trip, Ronni. Let me know if you need a hand with anything."

"Don't worry, I will. Lord knows those two aren't gonna help," she says, shaking her head.

"Hey we heard that, V. Very funny," Lizzy chimes in from the dining table.

As I turn to head back to the dining table, my body blocking their view of Ronni, I feel a hand press against the back of my shoulder. It runs down the sleeve of my t-shirt before it reaches my skin.

Fuck me. I stop dead in my tracks.

When her finger reaches my skin, she delicately runs her finger nail down the back of my arm. I feel the hairs on my neck standing, chills running through me. Her touch cuts through me to my core.

I manage to pull myself away and head back to the table, beer in hand. I carefully sit back down, adjusting myself under the table the first chance I get when Collin and Lizzy look back to Ronni in the kitchen.

With that situated, I look back towards the kitchen. She's back to work, dicing the cooked chicken now. I love watching people use my knives, but with her it's something else. I know she loves cooking and appreciates them. Watching the way she deftly handles them in her hands, nimbly cutting away, brings back the memories of the hours I spent making each one and makes them all worth it.

"Chap, settle this debate for us. Lizzy thinks there are still real cowboys crawling all over the bars in Jackson. Can you tell her she's crazy?" Collin looks at me, shifting my attention away from Ronni.

"Ok, Lizzy. Here's the deal. This place is fuckin' expensive to live in. The only working ranches left in town raise bougie ass fancy wagyu cattle and have a small handful of cowboys." I'm now fully invested in this. I can't wait to watch this fancy resort girl try to pick up a cowboy in town. This is gonna be fun to watch.

"Alright, Chapman. It sounds like there's a *but* the way you said that." Lizzy eyes me curiously. Collin is also now watching me closely, clearly interested as well.

"Right, so there are some but you're gonna have to fight the local girls for them. Good luck with that, I know that's a fight even I wouldn't want to pick. Those girls are fuckin' mean. Now, your best bet is the rodeo when it's in town, but that's only in the summer. Since it's winter, maybe the skijoring event. Those bring the guys from the towns further out where the real cowboys are."

Collin and Lizzy are both grinning now, hooked on my every word. Oh man. The nights with them the rest of their trip are gonna be fun to watch.

My *how to catch a cowboy guide* for Collin and Lizzy is interrupted by Ronni, bringing food to the table. Everything looks and smells amazing. Chipotle marinated chicken, fresh sliced jalapeños, diced onions, cilantro, fresh cooked tortillas. This is way better than I ever eat at home.

She's always been so good at cooking, so natural at hosting people. The table is covered in a spread that looks like something even my grandma, always ready to serve you more food than you need, would approve of.

I've always wondered why she wouldn't do this for a living. With the huge mansions, wealthy tourists, and second home owners throwing parties, there's always a demand for private chefs in town. She'd be so natural at it and be her own boss. I've never seen anything she can't do when she puts her mind to it.

"Dinner is served. There's more beer in the fridge and here's a fresh bottle of wine. Dig in," she says, sitting down beside me, Collin and Lizzy opposite us at the table.

"Damn, V. Everything looks great," Lizzy says, "Thanks again girl."

"Hey, I'm just ready to eat. It's been a day," Ronni says, taking a sip of wine.

The dining table is small and we're only a foot or so apart. Being this close to her after having my tongue inside her this morning, while sneaking around my best friend is such an unexpected rush. I don't think I'm the only one that feels this way.

She takes an extra second or two to place a napkin in her lap and while her hand is under the table, she drags her finger nail carefully up my leg over my jeans, before placing it back on her wine glass on the table. I take a deep breath, practically shuddering.

God. She's having as much fun with this as I am. Well two can play at that game.

"Hey Ronni. You remember that concert we saw at the spring festival back in high school? The time you guys came for the season closing over spring break?" I look to her, one side of my mouth quirking up.

She glances to me, pondering my question as her wine glass rests on her lower lip. "Yeah. I do. That was a fun night. What made you think about it? That was ages ago."

"When I was driving this morning, I heard a song from one of those bands on the radio. I can't remember their name though. I swear, it's been on the tip of my *tongue* all day." I watch as my words have the desired effect and her eyes go wide for just a second as hints of pink creeps onto her face. Under the table I can feel her fingers dig into my knee and I try to hold back a laugh. But she quickly gathers herself and I doubt Collin or Lizzy noticed anything.

"I'll have to think about that, Tanner. It has been a while." She grabs the bottle of wine in the middle of the table and turns to Lizzy as she refills her glass. "So, Lizzy. Did you have a favorite run the last couple days?"

"Hmm… I'd have to say Laramie Bowl. Great pitch, awesome snow coverage, protected from the wind. Definitely fun with today's powder." Lizzy says before inhaling another bite of her food.

Damn, Ronni's right, that girl can put down food. Where does it even go?

"Nice choice, Lizzy. We'll keep that in mind tomorrow. Time to really show you around now that you've got your ski legs under you." Ronni's all smiles tonight. She definitely wasn't this happy the last time I saw her. I'm loving every second of this.

I watch as she takes a sip of wine, a small drop of it runs down her lip. She takes her finger tip, with her manicured pink nails, wiping off her lips before putting it back in her mouth.

Fuck me. My dick is straining against the fly of my jeans under the table again. I can't imagine what those lips would feel like around *me*.

Chapter 19

Veronica
Dessert

"Hey guys, does anyone want ice cream? I've been craving it," Lizzy asks from the kitchen after inspecting the status of the freezer and lack of sweets. I swear that girl has a bottomless stomach, always room for dessert.

"You read my mind, girl." Collin chimes in from the dining table, sitting across from me. "We could walk to the bodega in the village and grab a couple pints. You game?"

"You didn't have to ask! Let's skedaddle. Anyone else want to join?" Lizzy replies.

Finally, here's my chance. I lie as best as I can.

"I'm stuffed and can barely get off this chair. I think I'm going to hang back and work on cleaning up here. Grab a flavor with peanut butter though, if they have it!"

"Sure thing, V. How 'bout you Chap?" Lizzy asks as she looks over at him. He's been comfortably lounging on the oversized brown leather couch opposite the fireplace since dinner, still sipping on a beer. He looks so natural, so relaxed like that. Why can't I ever be like him? Can he really be this calm after today, the gondola and lunch?

"I'm good, Lizzy. I'm gonna stay back and help Ronni clean," he says.

Is he thinking the same thing as me? He can't be.

"Alright, losers," Collin teases. "We'll see you guys in a bit." He and Lizzy make their way up the few steps to the mudroom and toss on their jackets.

Just like that, they're gone.

Ok. No time to waste. Not everyone has the confidence of Tanner Chapman.

I set my wine glass down on the dining room table. I think I have the upper hand this time. I've wanted to touch him, to feel him ever since the gondola, before lunch. The thought of his strong hands and the way his mouth brought so much unexpected pleasure to me has been running through my mind all day. Tanner is still nursing a beer on the couch, watching the fire roar. I head towards him, standing right in front of him, practically straddling him.

Is this a power pose? I hope so.

He looks up, a smirk on his face, beer in hand.

"Well you look like you're in a better mood, Ronni. What's new?"

Are you fucking kidding me? He knows the answer. That fucking tongue of yours working magic on me is what's new. There's that grin. That confidence. But now it's combined with those lustful green eyes from the gondola just hours ago. Has he been waiting for this moment too?

"I never got the chance to thank you for that treat on the gondola, *Tanner*." I'm trying to match his confidence, but can anyone really do that? He squirms and shifts a bit in his seat. Can I really catch him off guard? I lean forward, putting my knee on the couch between his legs and a hand on either side of his shoulders on the back of the couch.

I'm shocked at just how much I want him. The tension in the room is only faintly cut by the crackling of the fire behind me.

I kiss him. A quick gentle touch of the lips, biting his lower lip before slowly pulling away. Staring into his eyes, I get the same electric feeling as this morning.

"What are you thinking?" he asks, mouth wide open in anticipation.

I lower myself down to my knees on the carpet between the couch and coffee table, with the fireplace behind me. He can't be expecting this, can he? I mean I'm barely expecting this myself. He shifts restlessly again, just the slightest bit of stiffness appearing in his body. Question answered, I think.

I slide my hands over his jeans slowly up to his hips. You cannot be serious. His thighs are so damn muscular. There isn't a spot on this man's body that isn't chiseled and rock hard. I stop my hands just at his belt line, leaving my fingertips just inside of his jeans. Maybe he remembers that feeling from our kiss in the mudroom.

My fingers linger there for what feels like an eternity before my right hand is on the move again, inching closer and closer to the fly of his jeans, dangling a finger just inside the buttons, excited at the prospect of what is waiting for me beneath.

"Is *this* ok?" I look up at him, my eyes begging for a yes.

His eyes look at me longingly, with the slightest hint of desperation as he nods in approval. Oh the feeling of being desired, something I haven't felt in ages. I cup him over his jeans for a tease, for both of us. Even through his jeans, he's so fucking hard, pressing against the fly. Well I guess I might have caught his mind off guard, but definitely not his body.

"Are you *sure* it's ok?" I ask again, smiling and raising my eyebrows as I lock eyes with him, taunting him. Maybe I can match some of his confidence after all.

He nods yes again in earnest, more desperation in those beautiful green eyes, biting his lip. I start unbuttoning his jeans, eager to get to him. A spark of excitement coursing through me, the fireplace behind me, thinking about the gift I'm about to open for myself.

Before I can even get to the last button, I press one hand against his lower abs. I feel my body shudder when I touch those muscles. I slide it further down under his boxer briefs and grab his dick. Jesus, it's throbbing. Its girth fills my hand. I can practically feel his heartbeat through it.

I realize I'm wet, craving to have what's in my hand buried inside me. God, where have I been hiding this part of me? His fingers this morning were such a satisfying tease, but now I'm this close to the real thing and it's all I want.

My mind starts doing the mental math of how long we have alone. It's only a 15 minute walk each way to the bodega and back.

Fuck me. No time for that.

"Come closer." I curl my finger at him, wrapping my arms around his waist, bringing him to the edge of the couch. It feels so good to hold him. I slide my hands up his back under his shirt, finally getting to touch all of the muscles I saw last night.

I slide his jeans and boxer briefs down to his ankles, getting a full look at what's in store for me. His thick, lengthy cock is so hard, standing ready for me. It's practically twitching with each of his heartbeats as the blood pulses through his veins, a single eager drip already running down the tip of it.

The Tanner I've known for years is certainly *all man.*

I look back at him after admiring his cock.

With him on the edge of the couch, my wanting mouth is now only inches from his dick. God, his fucking big cock would feel so good inside of me and all I want to do is climb in his lap and ride him. But having him in my mouth will have to do for now.

"Have you been this hard since our little ride earlier?" I ask, raising my eyebrows again in my best attempt at a sultry taunt. I mean it's been awhile, my game is off.

The thought of him being on edge all day because of me makes me so horny, if it's even possible to get hornier at this point.

Still holding on to his waist I lean forward and give the head a little kiss. I slowly lick the tip with a flick of my tongue all while keeping my eyes locked onto his. I can feel his body shudder, only heightening my own excitement.

"I've been this hard since I kissed you last night and you were grinding up on me," he stammers with that deep raspy voice, barely able to get the words out.

Fuck. That's even hotter. He's been trying to hide *this* all day today?

My heart is pounding. Tanner's dick is in my face and my arms are still wrapped around him. It's a race against time, again.

I can hear the crackle of the fire behind me. It's getting steamy in here with the fireplace to my back, but it's not just that. The fire there is overshadowed by something new, the flames of desire for him roaring inside of me. As I lock eyes with him again, his cock inches from my face, I can see the flicker of the fireplace reflecting in his eyes.

I move my hands and take off my tank top, revealing the sports bra from skiing earlier. My nipples are peaked and showing through, my braided ski pigtails hanging in front of them. Clearly it's enough for him though as I watch him practically salivate looking at my chest.

I lean forward again, this time putting one hand around the base of him tightly, a thumb rubbing his balls. He's nicely manicured down there, which is a pleasant surprise given his otherwise scruffy and tousled look. He moans as I squeeze him, feeling even more blood rush to his cock.

"Fuck, Ronni. I-" He cuts himself off and hisses sharply as I put the tip of his cock in my mouth, gently holding it there and teasing him with the tip of my tongue.

God, I'm starting to drool again. It seems like every time I look at him I can't help myself. I let some of my spit run down his shaft. With the tip of him in my mouth, I start stroking his length in my hand. The sound of my spit working his dick in my hand is making me so fucking wet.

If only we had more time.

I start working my mouth up and down him slowly, my tongue feeling every inch of the veins of his cock.

I can feel him flexing his ass, pushing his hips and his dick in and out of my mouth in rhythm with the motion of me sucking him. His right hand rests on his knee, squeezing tightly, flinching, as I move my mouth further and further down his cock with each motion. When I finally reach the base, my tongue reaches further giving his tight balls a quick tease. I think I surprised both of us by taking all of his length in my spit filled throat and mouth. Tanner writhes and lets out a raspy moan of approval.

He lets out a low groan. "Ronni. Don't stop." He grins as he puts his other hand on my shoulder, grabbing one of my pigtails and gently, but firmly, cupping the back of my head just above my nape.

Hearing him like this, so raw, his guard completely down, only hastens my resolve to make this man let go. I keep taking his length in my mouth, but at a faster pace, my tongue still teasing his shaft with each stroke. I cup his balls in one hand, my thumb massaging the base of his throbbing cock. My other hand grabs his hand on his thigh and he squeezes mine tighter and tighter. His grip is so strong that the jagged lines tattooed on his wrist are distorted by the pulsing veins in his forearm.

"Please. I want to come in your mouth so fucking bad. Ple-" I keep my pace but now focus solely on the tip of his cock, swirling my tongue over it, and the upper part of his shaft.

"Fuck. I'm gonna come." He grunts and moans completely untethered, gripping my braided hair even tighter.

He convulses, his whole body flexing and shaking. I take in the view of his lower abs and quads harder and sexier than ever as he lets go in my mouth. I realize sucking him off has turned me on almost as much as the release he gave me earlier. With him still in my mouth, I swallow and slowly, tauntingly work my mouth off of him. I give his throbbing tip another quick kiss as I sit up facing him now. Looking back up at him grinning, I admire the stunning, now spent, man on the couch in front of me with a sense of accomplishment coming over me.

After quickly regaining his composure, he looks down at his watch.

"At least fifteen minutes before they're back. Shit you're good." He lets out an amused sigh. "That was... that was amazing." He leans forward, his hand cupping the side of my face and kisses me on my lips. His tongue, *oh that fucking tongue,* sneaking just inside my open mouth.

"Damn. Here I was hoping to beat your time." I smirk, reveling in my work at making this man lose himself completely.

Really, who am I right now? As I stand up to put my tank top back on, it dawns on me that he's right. We have a decent bit of time before the others are back.

Are we going to talk about this? Whatever *this* is?

"So… Tanner." I nervously stand beside the couch. My finger tips are digging into my lower lip.

"Are we uhh… we going to talk about whatever it is that we're doing?" I gesture with my hand back and forth between us.

He slides his pants up, buttoning them, not moving from the couch. A quiet look of concern on his face, as if he was anticipating this question.

"Sure," he starts, his voice low and cautious, "but I'm going to tell you something. The *only* thing I care about right now is seeing you happy. I'm glad we're having fun together. But me getting to enjoy what's happening is just an added bonus." He smirks, before continuing. "I know you're anxious, a lot. I know you get stressed. I know you worry. This is your vacation though. A time to unwind, and that's all I want to help you do. I want you to be happy. To feel good. To let go."

His words catch me by surprise, a quiet stunned look on my face. That's certainly not what I expected. Tanner has always been about as straightforward as they come. He's never one to beat around the bush.

Is this really all about me? No, not about me.

For me?

"So what? No feelings, no emotions? We're just having fun? Where is this all coming from?" I ask, trying to wrap my head around what he just said.

The look of concern is back on his face and he clearly takes his time to consider his next words carefully.

"Come here," he says, seated back on the couch, patting the cushion beside him.

I sit back down, unsure of what to expect. There's something comforting, intoxicating even, about being this close to him. Before I even realize it, I'm resting my head on his shoulder. His hand finds mine, that fiery skin sending shockwaves through me at every touch.

"You're right, Ronni. This isn't coming out of nowhere, at least for me. I always thought you were untouchable, my best friend's sister. Someone I could look at from a distance but never have. Never deserve." I lift my head and look up, only to catch his gaze locked on our hands. "So I'd be lying if I said there are no feelings and no emotions. But this isn't about me. I just want *you* to be happy, to feel good, to laugh and smile for a change."

I don't know if it's the altitude or the drinks with dinner, but my head is swirling. The thought of Tanner, the childhood friend turned into this specimen of a man, having hidden feelings for me. Not just having feelings for me though, but caring this much about my wellbeing.

"Tanner. This is," I let out a long breath, "I don't even know what to say."

He tilts my head toward his face, planting a soft kiss on my lips, his eyes fixing on mine.

"You don't have to say anything. We don't have to label this, Ronni. There aren't any expectations. Let's just keep having fun." His eyes don't leave mine for a second, but they're gentler now.

Maybe Lizzy and Collin were right. Maybe I do need *this.* And he isn't some rando, he's one of my oldest friends. Someone I can trust.

"So, friends with benefits?" I ask.

"More like… an old friend with benefits, if you insist on labeling it. But it's whatever you want. I'm all yours, however you'll have me. *My body is yours,* Ronni. Obviously it's working based on how at ease you've been today. You haven't stopped smiling since lunch." He trails off as his familiar grin is back and his eyes keep peering right into me, pleading for me to want this with him.

A small breathy chuckle escapes my mouth as I turn red, blushing at the way this man made me feel on the gondola today. He's right though. I've felt more *alive* for the last 24 hours in a way I don't think I ever have before.

"Well, you're right about that. Can't argue with you there. So what are you saying? Just *send it* and and see where this takes us?"

He lets out an all too familiar boyish laugh before planting another kiss on my lips, holding my hand tighter.

"You're starting to sound like me. I think you said it better than I could, because that's exactly what I'm thinking. We're just along for the ride. Let's just enjoy this and see where it goes, ok?"

He takes his other hand, running it over my braids, sending shivers through me as he plants another comforting kiss on my forehead.

My head is spinning. The idea of a fling with Tanner with no preset expectations seems insane.

No, it *is* insane.

Completely unplanned, no agenda, no itinerary. Tanner said *my body is yours* and I kind of like the sound of that.

"Ok, Tanner. Screw it. I'm along for this ride with you."

Chapter 20

Veronica
Mudroom, Part 2

W hat am I getting myself into? I should be anxious right now, but I'm not. This is so unlike me.

But the idea of a man this incredibly gorgeous, one that I trust, telling me his body is *mine* to use as my own playground... is insanely hot to say the least. He would definitely be an upgrade over the toys in my nightstand.

Somehow my anxiety is replaced with excited anticipation. Sitting next to Tanner on the couch in the front of the fireplace is so oddly comforting that I can't help but feel grounded in the moment here and now.

"I don't know about riding *along with me,* but I definitely wouldn't mind you *riding* me." His words come unexpectedly, his deep, raspy voice, now lustful.

Yes, excited anticipation is an understatement. I look back into his eyes. Fuck, he's so hot. I feel my body clench.

"Too bad they're going to be back any minute," he continues, a hint of disappointment in his voice. Me too, Tanner, me too. The thought of riding his cock that was just in my mouth is frighteningly enticing.

"Speaking of them, are we saying anything or…?" I ask, palms up, shrugging my shoulders.

"Oh, fucking hell no. I know Collin almost as well as you, but when it comes to this, I have no fucking clue how he'll react," he says as a terrified look takes over that calm and confident face. I can't help but laugh at his brutal honesty and terrified look. "What's so damn funny, Ronni?"

"In all the years I've known you, I don't think I've ever seen you scared of anything. It's an interesting look for you." I tease, my wry smile taunting him. His expression softens, his trademark calmness returning.

"Very funny. But on that note, what's on your plan for tomorrow, Ronni? I'm assuming you have dinner planned out."

"Let's see." I trail off, pretending to flip through my imaginary paper planner. "Tomorrow was going to be carryout from Momo Hut. Why, what are you thinking?"

I look at him, a sly smirk on his face. He's clearly got something in mind.

"So the owner of one of the places I manage is out of town most of the time, and he's actually pretty chill. He has a guesthouse with a hot tub he lets me use when I feel like it, as long as he's not in town. Would you be down to bring the carryout over to the guesthouse and the four of us can have a night in a private hot tub? It's actually walking distance from here, just a couple streets over." His expression shifts. He looks genuinely excited, eagerly awaiting my response.

"I mean it sounds awesome. But you're telling me this guy doesn't mind you using his hot tub or guesthouse? It's the holidays, doesn't he have renters?" After a few days of skiing, a night at a hot tub does sound great though and I'm sure it would be an easy sell to Collin and Lizzy.

A snort of laughter escapes that beautiful face.

"Let's just say this guy isn't worried about rental income. He's loaded. You'll have a great time. Trust me. Besides, there's something I want to show you there." He's all smiles again, looking excited at the prospect of surprising me.

"Is that some kind of euphemism, Tanner?" I tease, flicking one of my braids over my shoulder.

"Maybe? Is that a yes though? You still haven't answered my question," he says, his voice lustful and raspy again as his eyes lower.

"Ok, yes. Let me bring it up to Collin and Lizzy and you can finish selling it."

"Perfect. Sounds like a plan," he says as he leans toward me, slanting his mouth and pressing his lips to mine. I savor the moment of this hot kiss, his tongue gliding hungrily along all the right spots in my mouth.

Shit. We both pull back at the sound of keys in the mudroom door.

Tanner shifts back and sits on the other side of the couch, legs crossed, his face immediately regaining his calm expression.

"Go over to the table, Ronni. Act like you're cleaning." He smiles, reminding me of why we stayed behind in the first place.

Fuck, he's good.

Collin and Lizzy come in the mudroom door, pints of ice cream in hand, seconds after I reach the dining room table.

"Howdy guys. We hit the jackpot," Collin says, as they each hold up two pints of ice cream.

"One pint for each of us!" Lizzy says, giddy for dessert.

"Did they have any peanut butter flavors?" I ask. Come on, I still want an actual dessert.

"Yep, coming at ya." I look up at Collin, pint of ice cream already flying through the air at me, landing squarely in my hands.

"Nice catch, Ronni. What about me, bro?" Tanner asks. I choke down a laugh. You sir, already had your treat.

"How could I ever forget, Chap? Plain old vanilla, as always. You really gotta spice things up sometime, bro," Collin says, tossing a pint towards Tanner. I hold in another laugh, thinking if only Collin knew.

"So, Collin. Lizzy. I was talking to Tanner about tomorrow night. Before you ask, it's a carryout night on our itinerary." I glare at them, enjoying that I cut off their joke before it could happen. "Instead of carryout here, Tanner says he's got a guesthouse with a private hot tub we can use. He said it's only a couple streets over and walkable. How's that sound?"

Collin and Lizzy look at each other for a moment before looking back at me.

"Hell yeah! Sounds dope," Collin says, never one to turn down a good time.

"Hmm. What's the deal with this mystery guesthouse? Are we going to get kicked out for crashing a hot tub or have to avoid renters at the main house?" Lizzy has a skeptical look on her face.

Tanner gets up, heading to the kitchen for spoons. "Well. I told Ronni, TJ ain't exactly hurting for money. He doesn't even rent the house the eight or nine months of the year he isn't here. Definitely a property manager's dream."

"Alright. I guess it does sound fun. And I did bring a swimsuit. Let's do it," she says.

"Awesome. Should be a great night. Dinner in the guesthouse and drinks in the hot tub." Tanner eats a spoonful of ice cream, stealing a glance in my direction. "Besides, Ronni's gotta see this dude's kitchen. It's absolutely insane. Might give her some ideas."

"Alright, alright," I say. "Now you're talking my language. So let's meet here after skiing tomorrow, change, and head over there? Collin? Can you and Lizzy plan on going into town to grab the carryout?"

"Sure V, we can do that. I know you'll be anxious all day if we don't have tomorrow planned out for you," he says, looking at Lizzy, rolling his eyes about my overzealous, anxiety reducing, need for plans.

"Thanks, big bro," I say, enjoying the unintended benefit of needing to plan things out. I'll get rid of Collin and Lizzy for an hour or so tomorrow so I can have some alone time with Tanner. I look at Tanner, a subtle grin on his face, approving of my machinations.

"Sweet," Tanner says, clapping his hands together once, "sounds like a solid day."

The night wears on, everyone devouring their ice cream, gathering on the couch and floor around the coffee table in front of the fire. Tanner nurses the same beer he's had for a while, since he's driving home later. Collin and Lizzy are nearing the end of a bottle of wine, hopefully their last for the night.

"So, ski day tomorrow, 8:30 AM at the tram center again. Meet at the condo after the slopes. Then carryout and hot tub at this dude TJ's guesthouse?" Collin asks, as his eyes are starting to droop.

"Come on, Collin." Lizzy glares back at him. "V's gone over the plan for tomorrow at least three times tonight alone. Get with the program dude."

"So, is that a yes?" He shrugs, palms up, looking for confirmation.

"Yes, Collin. That's the plan," I say, amused at how he always has to be reminded.

"Sweet. Hey, Chap," he says, his eyes briefly more alert, "if you're grabbing coffee tomorrow, can you get me a hot Cowboy Cubano? You know, since you left me hanging this morning."

"Sure, bro. Since you're conscious tonight and remembered to order, I'll grab one," he says, before looking at Lizzy, "How 'bout you Lizzy? Happy to get your order too."

A small smile graces her face, perhaps accepting the peace offering.

"If you're offering, Chap, I'll take a horny badger," she says with a mischievous smirk. Tanner palms his face, shaking his head. She winks at me then rolls her eyes and more seriously says, "I'll take a small flat white. Thanks!"

"Alright," Collin says, standing up from the couch, yawning with arms outstretched over his head, "I'm off to bed. See y'all tomorrow." And like that, he's off to the bunkroom.

"Yeah. I'm beat. Goodnight guys," Lizzy says, leaving right behind Collin.

"Well, looks like it's just us again." Tanner's expression has changed back to the sultry, lustful man from the gondola. His gaze intensifying.

"Yeah. Funny how that keeps happening." I arch one eyebrow, a sheepish grin forming at the corner of my mouth.

"Almost like someone planned it, if I didn't know any better." There's a fire in his eyes now. I realize the feelings of desire raging between my legs while he was in my mouth are back. As if he can read my mind, he leans in, kissing my cheek, his warm breath on my skin sends my heart racing.

"Come with me." His words are short, but direct in that low, commanding voice. My body follows him instinctively, his words putting a spell on me, as we head to the mudroom.

Fuck. What is he thinking now?

"Close the door behind you." He looks at me, a fierce determination behind the emerald green gems in his eyes.

"Um… What are you planning on?" My chest is pounding, back in this mudroom, alone, with him. I now know full well what this incredibly hot man is capable of doing to me.

"I want my shirt back," he says, his voice low, hushed, and raspy. "This one's a bit sweaty after today."

His hands go towards the waist of his jeans before he takes off the faded blue t-shirt he's wearing. His abs with that vein running prominently towards his waistline, his chest, all of his incredible muscles are on display again in the same room where this all started twenty-four hours ago. But this time, I greedily stare him down, taking in the stunning sight in front of me. Forget eyefucking, I want so much more and I'm not going to be shy about showing it.

He reaches for the dryer, opening the door. His long arms stretch out as he looks for his black t-shirt from the night before. I blush as he pulls out one of my thongs first, a small black one, holding it up to look at. He looks back at me, twirling it around one of his fingers, a bemused look on his face.

"I like this, but I'd like it more if I was pulling it off of you with my teeth." I didn't think a man rummaging through my laundry could turn me on, but here we are, and it's doing it for me. I feel my thighs clench and notice how wet I still am from sucking him off before.

I flush for a moment, before stepping towards him up on my toes to whisper in his ear, my voice sultry.

"I think I'd like that too."

He reaches back into the dryer, finally pulling out his black t-shirt and hanging it on one of the wall hooks. He takes a step toward me, pulling me closer, his hands on my waist, thumbs caressing my hip bones.

"Now. Do you think you can be a good girl, and be quiet for me?" His gaze lowers to mine before he kisses my forehead. His hand drops from my waist and cups the needy parts of me between my legs over my yoga pants.

I look into his eyes and nod, my breath heavy.

"Good," he says, as his hand drifts back to my waist before sliding down into the front of my leggings.

He pins me back against the wall, his other hand gripping my ass, supporting me, as he starts to tease my aching clit. The way he holds me in his strong hands creating so much pleasure, so fast, is overwhelming.

My mind briefly drifts to a mental image of Tanner, shirtless, in his workshop. I think of his muscles glistening in sweat while he works over a hot fire. The same skilled hands working on me now gripping his tools and pounding hot metal.

I'm brought back to the moment with him by his scent. It's everywhere and fills every breath I take. Earthy leather and that fresh pine. God, he smells like the forest, the mountains, and his ranch.

I wrap one leg around his, pulling him closer to me, opening myself more as his hand explores my clit and teases my lips, already so wet in anticipation of his touch.

"I had a feeling you might be ready for more. Looks like I was right. You are so fucking wet." He slides his fingers up and down my slit, lingering on my opening and clit. I moan at the touch, grabbing his shoulders tightly.

"No," he tsks, slowly. "I said you have to be a good girl for me and be quiet. If you keep that up, I'll have to stop and that won't be fun for either of us now, will it?"

His voice is intoxicating, sending me closer to the edge. I've never been called a *good girl* before nor have I wanted to be called one. But now it's fucking hot coming from Tanner. I thrust my clit and pussy back into his hand, desperate to get another release from him. He senses my eagerness.

"Don't worry, we're going to get you there," he says.

He slides two fingers in me, making the same motion as he did earlier on the gondola. He takes his thumb and massages my clit.

I feel a knot of tension forming, deep and low, that's going to let go any second. How can he get me there this fucking fast?

He drops his head to my neck, kissing my bare skin, before whispering, "You're about to come for me, aren't you?" he asks, pumping his fingers deeper into me.

His warm breath on my neck, his words, his hand, all send me into the abyss as I come. Hard and fast. I shudder, pressing my pussy into his hand, driving his fingers further in me, my arms wrapping around him, feeling the heat of his muscular body.

I let out a moan, and quickly the hand that was cupping my ass covers my mouth.

"Shhh, Ronni. Can't wake them up." He grins, reveling in his handiwork at making me come again. My spent body slouching forward into him. He drops his hand down to my throat, just under my jaw. He grips me gently, but firmly enough that I can still feel how strong he is, sending another rush of energy through me. My eyes linger on the ink on his forearm, feeling like my own eyes are staring back into my soul. He leans forward, kissing my open and waiting mouth, a long exhale escaping me, muffled by his lips.

"Fuck, Tanner," I whisper as he pulls away. "I could get used to this kind of treatment."

He lets out a short, hushed laugh, before leaning towards me and whispering in my ear.

"I told you, Ronni. My body is *yours*. Use me however you want. You just have to be a good girl and ask."

Those words send chills through me and I shudder again, his hand still holding me in my yoga pants.

"Be careful what you offer up, Tanner. I know what I want." I lean into his hand, pressing my sensitive clit into his palm. My voice is raspy and sultry and I think it has the effect I want. "And I'm not afraid to ask."

He grins with a sense of accomplishment over delivering me another orgasm, but also a sense of amusement in his eyes at my words. He leans down toward my ear. "I like the sound of that."

I bite my lip and smile up at him.

Begrudgingly, he pulls his hand out of my pants with a deep exhale. He brings his hand to his mouth and *licks his finger tips*. "God you taste so fucking good."

My cheeks instantly heat. He is something else. That's for sure.

He pulls his shirt off the hook and puts it on, ending my free peepshow.

"Well, I really do have to get going," he laments, "but I'll be *seeing you* tomorrow."

I palm my face and try to contain my embarrassed laughter. "Oh fuck, Tanner. Are you gonna let me live that down?"

He stands in the doorway, a low hum escaping his familiar confident grin.

"Probably not. We'll see. Now get some rest, Ronni." He leans back to me, leaving a gentle kiss on my waiting lips.

I admire the view as he leaves, heading to his van in the parking lot, just like last night.

My body is drained, but not the way it has been from years of overworking myself and stress. This is from pure pleasure and release, all thanks to Tanner.

I really don't think I've ever felt this way, this satisfied, this happy.

Maybe he's right. Maybe I should just say *fuck it, let's send it*, more often.

Can it really be that simple?

Chapter 21

Tanner
Bang One Out

"Come on, Rex. Let's go. Time to work." We walk through the cold night air over to the barn. I wanted to work on this pair of knives the other night, but my head just wasn't in it. Tonight though, there's a sense of relief in me, a sense of calm, and I can think of nothing more I want to do.

Well… almost nothing anyways.

I would have definitely liked more time with Ronni, especially if we were alone.

It's fine though. I needed to work on this. This is the second time I've tried this particular steel combination. I rushed, working angrily, and screwed it up the first time. I wasted all of those hours making the last set of billets, the layered blanks of steel, that get turned into blades. I had to make another set, but now I'm almost out of the steel I salvaged for one of the two layers. I better not mess it up again.

The process for making these blades is long and can be pretty frustrating some times. First, there's picking the right combination of steels to use. Then it takes hours and hours to weld layers upon layers of the two steels together to make a billet. It's definitely the mind numbing part of the process. For these knives, I had to melt down the old steel I found around the barn and cast it into a shape that I was able to make into the layered billet.

After making a new set, I finally get to have some fun. That's what I'm doing tonight. The fun part. I let out an audible laugh that overshadows the sound of the flames from the blazing hot furnace.

Fun.

Fuck yeah, I definitely had some fun tonight. Well, all day really.

My body feels like it's on fire. It feels electric. And it's not the two thousand degree furnace I'm standing in front of. The images, the sounds, the feelings. The memory of the whole day is flooding back through me. Ronni pulling my hair to bring my face into her while she wrapped her legs around me while she came. The feeling of cupping the back of her head and tugging her braids while her lips worked on my dick. Her hushed little moans and whimpers while I fingered her in the mudroom. All of these things I've only barely let myself dream of happening today. It's everything I've ever imagined and so much more.

Fuck me. This is intense. I need to clear my head if I'm going to bang one out tonight.

Normally when I work on knives, especially the forging part, it's when I'm depressed, thinking about how alone it feels here sometimes. Other times when I'm angry, my mind shifts that depression into a feeling of unfairness. For some obvious reason, banging and pounding hunks of red hot steel for hours gets all of that out of my system.

A release.

I look back at the furnace, the larger of the two blanks is an intense shade of red, ready to be worked. I pull it out by the temporary handle and put it in the forge press. I start hammering the red hot block of metal over and over until it's nearly a quarter the thickness it started, then fold it over on itself before hammering more.

When the metal starts to drop below its working temperature, I place it in the furnace again to get it back to that shade of blazing red. I'll do this for hours and hours, creating layer after layer of thin, hardened, forge welded steel to get something good enough to turn into a finished knife eventually.

While I wait for the steel to get back to the right temperature, I look over at Rex. He's somehow sleeping on his bed in the corner of the barn despite all the noise I'm making. A smile forms on my now sweaty, dirty face. I've always been jealous of his ability to just sleep, anywhere, any time.

There's an eerie silence in the workshop while I wait for the steel to reheat. Normally by now, my heartbeat is pounding and my breathing is labored. But something is different tonight.

The anger, the sadness, the rage that normally fuels me are gone, replaced by something so different. A sense of calmness, a clear mind.

Normally, I try to do anything to distract myself from how much I miss my old friends and family. How much I miss having Ronni in my life. I've tried dating but never felt a real connection to any of them, always comparing them to her. It always felt like my brain was a chaotic mess, the sound of radio static.

Tonight though, my head is crystal clear.

I realize I've been working slow. Steady and focused. The emotions that have clouded and filled my head for so long are gone. At least for now.

All I can think about is *her*.

The feeling of her touch, her lips, the sight of her smile, and the sound of her laugh.

But now, instead of a distant memory, like looking at a piece of art in a museum I can't touch, it's real.

"Fuck."

I say the word out loud, breaking the silence in the barn.

Is this what it feels like to feel whole? To be happy?

Chapter 22

Veronica
Marmot

Another day, another mudroom induced morning of waking up aching between my legs. I can physically feel how much my body wants to be with Tanner. Somehow in less than thirty-six hours, this part of me has gone from an afterthought and the butt of Collin and Lizzy's joke, to completely alive. Longing not just to be touched, but for *his* touch.

I can hear Collin and Lizzy in the dining room, and this time I don't even care that I'm running a little behind on my own schedule.

I reach between my legs and give myself the slightest tease, savoring just how much my body wants him. For the first time that I can remember in years, I'm not thinking of giving myself a release, but instead of waiting to be with him again. Craving him to take my body where it needs to go, where I want it to go. The thought of denying myself pleasure now, while waiting for the next stolen moment with him, is wildly thrilling. I grab my phone, sending Tanner a text.

> *Me: It's the second day I've woken up wet thinking about you. I'd take care of these needs if I wasn't going to see you later. ;) XOXO.*

I'm startled as I see three dots appear, Tanner texting me back almost immediately.

Tanner: Mmmm. Save that thought for later. Horny Badger.

I palm my face, muffling a small giggle. I'm really never going to live that down. Hearing it from him though, like that, I almost love the nickname.

I edge myself a bit longer before finally getting out of bed. After getting dressed, I find Collin and Lizzy downstairs. It's almost 7:30 in the morning and it's another ski day. To my pleasant surprise, they're ok with another quick breakfast today.

"So, V. What's up? Grandpa's lessons on getting up at the crack of dawn seem to be wearing off." Collin calls from the dining room table. "I can't remember the last time I got up before you and now it's been two days in a row," he boasts before biting into his bagel sandwich.

He's not wrong to wonder. It's very atypical for me, but for once, I sort of don't care. I make up a half truth that's hopefully good enough to not raise their suspicions.

"You know, I'm honestly just a bit more relaxed. I didn't hear from Jeff at all yesterday, I'm enjoying the time on the slopes, and I'm just having fun." Ok, so maybe a bit more than a half truth.

"I like this version of you, girl. I'm ready to see you let your hair down tonight a bit too, enjoy the hot tub, not have to worry about dinner." Lizzy eyes me curiously, already grabbing a second bagel for another sandwich.

"What can I say? I'm at ease and feel at home in the mountains, I guess?" I shrug, looking back at both of them.

Checking my watch, it's nearly 8:00 AM. Damn, we need to get going.

"Alright guys, time to take this show on the road. Tanner's meeting us with coffees at the Tram Center in half an hour, remember? And it's a fifteen minute walk so…"

"Ahh there she is, good ol' V," Lizzy says, smirking at Collin.

"Damn. I was just starting to like the new sleeping-in-V," Colin chides, dipping his chin in agreement.

I'm pleased when we get to the Tram Center at 8:30 AM on the dot. As we walk up, I can practically feel my heart in my throat as I see Tanner standing there waiting, coffees in hand again. His now seemingly unmistakeable, imposing presence sends a wave of excitement through me, wondering what he has in store for me today. Instead of being a nervous wreck, consumed by uncertainty, I feel shockingly alive, wondering what the day will bring.

Tanner looks my way. He's already got his helmet on, goggles resting on the brim of it. He wears a subdued grin, as he hands my coffee to me in his bare, ungloved hand, the one with *SEND* tattooed across the knuckles. This time I let my hand linger a bit longer on his as I take my drink from him, relishing in feeling our fingers touch.

"Thanks again, Tanner. I could get used to slope-side coffee service," I say politely, trying to play it as cool as I can. That is as cool as I can while I'm secretly doing whatever *this* is with my brother's best friend.

"No problem, Horny Badger," Tanner says, grinning ear to ear. My face goes a shade of red that would give Big Red a run for its money. I'd be furious at him right now if it weren't for those addicting green eyes and irresistible dimples.

Oh, and the orgasms.

Definitely those.

Collin and Lizzy predictably can't control their laughter at my expense either. Jokes on you guys, I don't see you getting any out here.

"Damn Chap, I don't think we can ever let her live that down. Good one, bro," Collin says, punching Tanner's shoulder, as he grabs his coffee.

"You know, I think I'm starting to warm up to you. Well played. I might need to hold that nickname back to use against her sometime," Lizzy says, taking her coffee and nodding at Tanner in approval.

Well, I guess that's one way to throw them off our tail, Tanner. Well played, indeed.

"Alright guys, very funny," I say. "Now can we get in line for the gondola? And don't miss the car this time. Ok, Lizzy?"

"Damn. I guess Chill V was short lived this morning, Collin." She looks at him, shaking her head.

The morning goes on like this on each of our lift rides, with friendly banter and jokes. Collin and Tanner are doing their usual thing, talking about what ski runs look good today, what bars we should hit for New

Year's Eve tomorrow, and just being themselves. Lizzy and I spend most of our chair rides gossiping about our mutual college friends back home and their lives. I still can't believe Lizzy's old crush Ivan is playing minor league hockey in Cincinnati.

It's been a beautiful ski day to this point. The sky is a stunning shade of brilliant blue, without a cloud to be seen for miles. It's in perfect contrast to the granite mountains and the endless white snow covered slopes.

A truly picture perfect bluebird day.

Without fresh snow overnight, we stick to the groomer runs except for a couple excursions off the side where Tanner manages to score us some stashes of untracked powder from the days before. As we get closer to lunch time, we head down to Marmot chair, an old and very slow two person chairlift that goes up to the mid-mountain lodge where we'll get lunch again today.

Tanner is the first to get in line for the chair, the fastest one down the run as usual. At the last second, I zoom past Collin and Lizzy to get in line for the chair with Tanner, taking the first one up. As we get on and we're moving along, I look back at them, sticking my tongue out and making jazz hands at them.

"Snooze you lose! We'll see you at the top!" I yell back at them on the chair behind us, catching my breath from racing to get past them in line.

I've been dying all morning for just a few seconds alone with Tanner. Not sorry guys.

"I was hoping you'd do that." Tanner's reassuring, deep voice immediately gets my attention back and away from them, now solidly out of earshot.

"So… what's the plan today, Tanner?" I look into his eyes, placing my hand on his. Our bodies are shielding us from the view of Collin and Lizzy on the chair way behind us, not that they could see anyways.

"Plan? That's your department, Ronni," he says with a smirk.

"Very funny. But really, no crazy plans for the chairlift?" I ask, knowing the answer is *no* as we aren't hidden inside of a tinted glass gondola, but still somehow hoping he has something in mind.

"Nope. I just wanted to sit next to you. Talk and enjoy the day."

I look into his eyes, taking in his smile, those dimples. Ugh. I just don't know how I've never seen this before, all these years I've known him. He's fucking gorgeous, a timelessly beautiful man. And I think he's obsessed with me.

"Alright. So, carryout and hot tub tonight? Should be fun." That gets me a sly grin with an uncharacteristic look of caution in his eyes. No, not caution. Maybe fear? It's still so new to me to see anything other than quiet calm and confidence in Tanner, but I feel like I'm becoming a quick study.

"I'm actually both excited and incredibly terrified," he says, lowering his gaze to our hands on his thigh, squeezing mine tighter.

Damn, I was right on with that one. *Terrified.* I guess I am a quick study in the emotions of Tanner Chapman.

"What?" I let out a laugh. "Why? What on earth do you have to be terrified about?"

"Fine. I'll tell you, but no more laughing, alright?" He looks genuinely embarrassed for some reason.

"Promise," I say, my curiosity now piqued.

"Ok. So do you remember your twenty-first?" He asks, the look of caution still in his eyes.

"Umm yeah, how could we forget that?" I try to contain my laughter. Seriously, how could I forget. We talk about that night every time we're out here, and Collin and I still talk about it back in Ohio.

"Well, what about the day after? Do you remember that?" His face is still oddly serious.

My mind drift backs. The river? I do remember that day. We were so hungover, but it was a beautiful day, just the three of us. I don't remember anything out of the ordinary about it though. Just a laidback day swimming in the sun, out behind his cabin.

"Yeah, we were all swimming at the river. Why?" I'm trying to contain the eager curiosity. Why this day so many years ago? Why is it triggering him like this? I'm dying to know what has Tanner running through shades of embarrassment and caution.

"Ok. Good. You do remember. Well, for all these years I can never get the image of how fucking sexy you were that day out of my mind. Your bare stomach, your shorts hanging off your hips. Your nipples were showing through your Teal Tigers crop top you were wearing all summer. That image has been burned into my brain for years and would come back any time I hear their songs." He finally looks back at me, the caution in his eyes now replaced with desire.

Fuck. He's been this into me for that long? I can barely remember what I was wearing that day. It's actually kind of hot hearing him describe it this way. The way he remembers everything, every little detail like he has a little Veronica library in his brain.

"Damn. Good memory. But you'll get to see me in a little bikini tonight. So why are you terrified?" I'm still curious, obviously.

"Because I had a raging hard on all day and I was terrified that you or Collin would notice," he says, shifting awkwardly on the chairlift, clearly uncomfortable.

"Ohhhhhhh. Now, that's why you sent us to go get the truck while you were still in the water, isn't it?" I look back at him, the look of caution has faded completely.

"Yeah. Exactly," he says, the look of desire and confidence in full control of his expression now. "And now I'm excited that you're going to look just as fucking good tonight and I'm terrified that I'm going to have to hide my hard cock from Collin and Lizzy all night in a cramped hot tub."

He looks into my eyes. I can practically feel how much he wants me right now. I squeeze his hand and lower my voice.

"I guess it's my turn to have images of you burned into my mind. Remember, I woke up wet the last two mornings, just thinking of you." My voice is hushed and slow, clearly having the impact I wanted. I feel him shudder and squeeze his thighs together.

"Careful now, Tanner. Don't get yourself too worked up. Don't want you having to hide *that* at lunch too."

"Fuck me." His voice is muted and raspy, practically a groan. "It's going to be a long day and night, isn't it?"

I hope so.

Chapter 23

Veronica
Loaded

"**H**oly shit, Chap," Lizzy says, practically shouting, "you weren't fucking kidding. TJ must be *loaded*."

The four of us stand in the driveway of TJ's house, taking in the mammoth mansion in front of us. It's lit in the dark by the well placed landscape lighting. It's only a couple streets over from the condo, but this street is made up of much newer, more modern homes that back directly up to the slopes.

The house is slung low to the ground, an angular roof extending from above the garage all the way to the far end, where floor to ceiling glass gives a peek into the main open living space. Despite its modern design with glass, exposed metal beams, and timber accents, it's nestled delicately into the trees and blends into the scenery surprisingly well. Lizzy is right, TJ must do well for himself.

"Yeah," Tanner trails off, breaking the silence, "so managing these properties, I've learned there are rich people and then there are *rich* people. Normally, rich people might be able to buy a second home, but they need to rent it out sometimes to afford it. But the *really rich,* they can buy a place like this for ten million dollars and let it simply sit empty most of the year until they need to use it here and there or let their friends crash. TJ is certainly the latter."

"Damn, dude. This place is sick," Collin says, "ever been to any parties here?"

Tanner laughs. "No, not really. I've been around a few times when he's had people over but TJ isn't much of a party animal."

"So back to our plan. Where's the guesthouse, Tanner?" I ask.

"Oh yeah. My bad. When you guys get back, just go through that gate next to the garage on the right. You'll go past the main house and see the hot tub. The guesthouse living room opens right up to the hot tub. Can't miss it," he says.

"Alright cool. Lizzy and I will go pick up the food. Order's under your name, right, V?" Collin looks back to me for confirmation, with a thumbs up gesture.

"Yep. You got it. Want to pick up some ice cream while you're out?" I suggest, pressing my hands together, bouncing up and down pleading. Collin laughs. "Lizzy and I were already planning on it. Same flavors as before, I assume?"

I nod in approval, sensing that I might be about to get the moment I've been hoping for all day. A moment alone with Tanner. I feel my body ache in anticipation of being alone, with him, and having more than a few minutes.

"Cool. See y'all in an hour or so," Collin says, as he turns to head towards his SUV.

"Later losers," Lizzy scoffs, "don't have too much fun without us."

After watching them turn the corner and out of sight, I move to Tanner, grasping his hand and intertwining his fingers with mine. His hands are so large and rugged that mine just get lost in them. A wave of relief comes over me as I'm finally able to touch him after playing cat and mouse all day, hiding from Collin and Lizzy.

"So, I was told there's a kitchen I have to see," I say, looking up into his eyes, grinning with anticipation.

He lets out a low hum. "Be patient, Ronni. Wanted to show you the guesthouse first."

I'm so tired of patience. All I've wanted today was to be close to him.

"Fine," I grumble, "if you insist."

As we enter the guesthouse, I'm in awe. It's modern and sleek like the main house and impeccably decorated, as if it was used for the latest Crate and Barrel catalog.

"So... I think we've got what, just under an hour?" The lustful look is back in Tanner's eyes. It's been less than two days now and I'm already addicted to that look in his endless green eyes.

I step towards him, he's so tall that I'm eye level with his collarbone and I have to crane my neck to meet his eyes.

"I seem to remember you saying your body was *mine* to use as I please?"

He nods, a low growl escaping his mouth before his lips are pressed into mine, his tongue offering just a tease as it lingers in my mouth.

"This way," he says, his voice low, leading me by my hand to the guesthouse's main bedroom. I'm barely able to contain my eagerness. I can feel the desire about to erupt within me. Things that have been buried so deep inside for years, are all flooding back, all thanks to this man.

As we head to the bedroom, he pulls a few condoms from his jean pockets. The gesture is reassuring.

"Actually, I meant to ask," I say, "I have an IUD and I haven't exactly been with anyone in ages so…"

"It's been a while for me too, but I always get tested and I'm fine," he says.

With that out of the way, I follow him to the bed. He hops in and sits back against the headboard. I take my t-shirt off while on my knees on the edge of the bed in front of him, revealing my small black triangle bikini top.

He takes his turn to ogle me for a change. Looking at my bare stomach up past my breasts, my nipples hard and showing through my bikini, until he meets my eyes.

"Fuck," he says looking at me, his voice labored with his heavy breathing, "take that top off."

"Like this?" My voice is sultry. I undo the ties and let it fall to the bed, my fingertips hiding my nipples from view and yet still teasing myself. He groans in approval as he strips off his shirt. The sight of him shirtless, propped against the headboard, his unnaturally perfect abs and pecs waiting for me to touch, only fuels my need for him.

But now his eyes are fixed on my ribs.

"That. When did you get *that*?" He points at the side of my breast, looking at the small tattoo of the outline of the Teton mountains on my upper ribs, matching the one on his and Collin's wrists.

"I've had it for years. I got it the summer I turned eighteen, the same year we skied Corbett's." I smirk thinking back to when I got it. "I didn't quite have your confidence to put it on my wrist or hands, so I put it somewhere not everyone would see it."

"I'm glad I'm getting to see it. I like it on you. But then again I like everything about you." His brows lower over his eyes and he curls his finger slowly at me. "Now come here."

Fuck. My knees are shaking in giddy anticipation.

I've felt his tongue do wonders on my clit and pussy. I've had every magnificent inch of him in my mouth. But the feeling of desire to have his cock buried in me is overwhelming.

"Fine. But take your pants off," I demand with a smirk, pointing at his jeans.

He eagerly obliges, throwing them to the floor beside the bed. I straddle him, grinding myself against his erection. Even through his boxer briefs and my sweatpants, I can feel how needy his cock is, sending a shiver through me I feel to my core. There's a look of desperation and longing in his eyes, matching my own needs.

I lean forward, my mouth to his ear. His heavy, warm breath against my skin is intoxicating. "Fuck me, Tanner. I want to use your body," I whisper.

"I thought you'd never ask," he says, his devilish grin reappearing. He wraps his muscular arms around me before flipping me on my back, him now on top of me.

"So can I take your pants off?" he asks slyly. I nod.

He looks down at me, his gaze lingering on my hard nipples. I can feel the desire deep in his eyes, realizing this is the first time he's seen my bare chest. Looking into his eyes, it's like I can see how much he's wanted this moment since that day on the river, over a decade ago. He's savoring it, his mouth barely open, biting his lower lip. I can feel his cock brushing against the inside of my thigh, twitching with each beat of his heart.

He leans down to me, kissing me on the lips before cupping my breasts, giving each nipple a delicate kiss, teasing them with his tongue. His mouth lingers over my tattoo, placing an extra kiss there.

He works his way down my stomach, kissing me along the way. With each kiss I can feel his mustache brush against my skin sending shivers through me while he slide my sweats off. As he takes them off, he stops for a second, smiling.

"I see you remembered something else I like," he says, his eyes looking at my small black thong he pulled from the dryer last night, before sliding it down and tossing it to the side.

"Please, Tanner. I want to feel you," I plead, looking into his gaze.

He leans back down, planting a kiss just above my swollen, ready clit.

"I just wanted to make sure you were ready for me," he says, before his mouth is on me again. He runs his tongue along my pussy before landing on my clit. A spasm runs through me as I arch my back, my shoulders and ass pressing into the bed.

"Fuck, Tanner," I moan, "the way your tongue knows exactly what I want is so hot."

"Does that mean you're ready for me?" he asks, his mouth still mere inches from my wet aching pussy. I can feel his breath on me, he's so close.

I nod, hurriedly this time, desperate to feel him. He comes up to me, his face now meeting mine as he takes off his boxers. He kisses me as he slides his pulsing cock up and down my wet slit, tormenting me. I push myself into him, pressing my clit against his dick. I let out a needy whimper and grab his shoulders.

He pulls back from me, holding his length in his hand, touching the head of his cock to my wetness, before notching the tip just on the edges of my opening. I look into his eyes, they're smoldering, showing the same sense of need I feel.

He brings his lips to mine, as he eases into me. I can tell he's holding back though, admiring his tight flexed muscles. At first, he braces himself, giving me just the tip.

I've seen it, held it, and had every inch of it in my mouth but my aching body is still shocked to feel it inside of me. I gasp, my pussy clenching and gripping him tighter. He goes slowly, letting me fully enjoy his size. With each thrust, he goes deeper and deeper. His cock fills me and stretches me like I've never felt before. The feeling of it bare with nothing between us, my hot wet center against every inch of him, is so intense.

"Fuck, Ronni," his breathing is labored, "you're so fucking tight and wet."

"Oh god, Tanner," I whimper, "please, I want all of it. Give me all of it!"

He growls as he leans back, looking at me with unfiltered lust in his eyes. With his cock seemingly already in me to its base, he wraps his hands under my thighs, pushing my legs back towards me. I gasp as he thrusts into me again, my pussy barely able to take every throbbing inch of him.

I run one hand along his scruffy jaw, the other splayed across his back, unable to resist clawing him with my nails digging into his skin, feeling the muscle beneath.

With each powerful, nearly overwhelming thrust of him, I feel myself getting closer and closer to letting go of the tension building inside me. I wrap my legs around him, never wanting to let this man go.

"Please, don't fucking stop, Tanner."

Chapter 24

Tanner
Enjoying the View

I shudder as she wraps her legs around me, pulling me further into her tight, wet pussy. God fucking damnit, this woman is going to make me lose myself. I can't get enough of the sight of her beneath me on the bed. Aching for me. I have her knees pinned back in my hands and I'm staring down at her perky tits and hard pink nipples. I watch her pussy taking every inch of me bare. I'm buried in her and the feeling of my cock in her with nothing in between us is fucking incredible. I'm practically drooling at the sight and it's almost enough to bring me to the edge with her.

No. Fuck that. Over the edge.

She's going to pull me completely over the edge in an avalanche of pleasure.

I stare into her hazel eyes, the soft gentle expression normally there is gone. The gold flecks in them now a shimmering look of passion and desire. With each push deep inside her, she moans and whimpers and I can't fucking get enough of it.

I push, she makes a sound.

I thrust, she gasps.

I rock my hips into her, she swears at me to keep going.

It's so fucking hot. She's so fucking hot.

I've dreamed about fucking her for years. My deepest sexual desires and fantasies revolving around her.

But now, she *wants* me. She *needs* me. The satisfaction of her wanting me is everything.

She's taking every throbbing inch of me and it's more than I could have ever imagined. Now that I've *tasted* her like this, I haven't even come yet and I already know I could never feel alive without this in my life anymore.

Without *her* in my life.

I lean back again. Enjoying the view while keeping myself deep inside her. I look into her eyes, taking one hand to start rubbing her clit with my thumb. She writhes as I play with her clit and thrust slowly, bottoming my cock out in her. The sight of my shaft covered in her glistening arousal with each thrust is driving me mad.

Fuck me, I can feel my eyes roll back in my head. It's unreal how good she feels around me.

Yep. I've died and fucking gone to heaven.

"Fuck, Tanner," she says, nearly gasping, "I'm so fucking close."

"Good. Be my good fucking girl," I growl. "Keep fucking taking me, just like that. Your little pussy feels amazing."

She looks up at me, her lips parted as her eyes start glazing over.

"Please, just like that. Don't you dare fucking stop," she says, running her nails along my back.

I look down at her, thinking about how close she is. A hum of pleasure rumbles out of me. "I was hoping you'd say that."

Jesus Christ. It's taking every bit of me to not lose it right now.

I can feel her walls tightening around my cock and I just want to let go in her. I steady my breath, focusing on what I really want. I want her to come so fucking hard and see stars while I'm buried deep inside of her.

She mews somewhere between agony and ecstasy, squirming around me. I can feel her nails digging deeper into my shoulders now and it sends a shiver through me.

This woman. She's fucking something else.

Chapter 25

Veronica
Evergreen Forest

With each tortuous push of Tanner's cock deep inside me and his thumb now teasing my clit, I can feel myself getting closer and closer. He fills every bit of me in a way I never knew I needed. My body starts to tense as I push myself up into his length and hand, craving a release.

He hums back to me. "Can you be a good girl and come for me? I can tell you want it."

I nod, biting my lower lip. My body shaking with each breath, his voice speaking to my core.

He leans forward, his elbows now pressing against the tops of my shoulders, his broad chest caging me in. My legs fall to his side and I wrap them around his waist, pulling him even further into me. His lips brush my forehead, my mouth now on his neck and collarbone. My hands are on his back again, digging in with each thrust of his hips into me. With his body like this, the base of his shaft is rubbing my clit each time he pushes into me and it feels so fucking good.

His pace quickens and I can feel the knot of tension in me start to completely unravel. His hands run through my hair, holding tightly. I bury my face in his neck, moaning in ecstasy.

"That's right. Let go and come for me." His husky voice pushes me over the edge.

The orgasm that takes over me is more intense than the others he's given me. My pussy clenching every inch of him as his cock fills me entirely. I melt into his arms, my head pressed against his hard muscular chest, my skin loving the warmth of his body. I can feel his heart pounding as his pace now becomes more erratic, more feral. Each push of his hips into me is more intense as he chases his own release. I can feel his body tighten, his ass clenching and flexing as he starts to lose control. I feel each twitch of his bare cock as he comes deep inside me.

He tilts my face towards his, craning his neck to kiss me, our mouths both open as we catch our breath.

I look into his eyes. I could get lost in them forever, like staring into an endless evergreen forest.

"Ronni," he says, still breathing heavily, "that was amazing. *You're* amazing."

He leans back, his cock still deep in me. I rock my hips toward him, wanting to savor the feeling of fullness he gives me as long as I can. I run my fingers through his chest hair, my hand lingering over the tiger head.

"Interesting choice with the teal stripes. I didn't know you were a fan, Tanner." I look up at him as he lets out a low chuckle, that I can feel all the way through his cock into my center.

"I may listen to them every now and then." He grins at me slyly, like he's hiding a secret.

After getting out of bed and grabbing me a warm damp towel, he stops short of the bed. He looks at me with a smile on his face, his eyes running up my legs and stopping as our eyes meet. The way he looks at me melts my heart and I can feel a smile spreading across my own face.

"I love seeing you smile. You know that, right?" he says, catching me by surprise, a quick giggle getting out before I can regain my composure.

"Um, I can tell. You're always looking at my face every time I look over at you. You're kind of intense." I smirk, winking at him.

"That's because I'm serious, Ronni. I hate seeing you upset. I'm glad you're having a good time. I hope your trip is going according to your plan so far," he says, coming back to the edge of the bed. He sits down next to me, running his hand through my hair. His presence is somehow both exhilarating and comforting, getting me to live in the moment but also feel like everything is going to be ok.

Like I can just be me. Be myself.

"You know, I don't actually *like* planning," I blurt out.

He laughs, caught off guard by my seemingly random outburst, one I'm emboldened to make with how comfortable I am around him.

"Oh really? It always seemed like your favorite thing," he says. His expression changes when he senses that I wasn't joking.

"No. I hate it actually. It takes all of the fun out of everything. I want to be more spontaneous, to live in the moment. But not knowing what's next, it's terrifying. Planning is just a feeble attempt to cope with my anxiety. At least with planning, I can try to prepare myself and not be scared of what's next. But it feels like I'm missing out on so much in life living this way." I feel a look of worry starting to form on my face.

He eyes me carefully, his hand still running through my hair.

"Remember what I asked you before on the gondola, Ronni? *Do you trust me?*"

I nod, unsure of where he's going with this.

"Yes. I do."

"Then let me help you. I get it, life's scary. But it's easier when you have people around you that you trust. It might sound backwards, but let someone you trust take that burden of planning off your plate and trust them to surprise you in a way you'll like. You can trust Collin and Lizzy, I would. Know that they are there for you and will keep you safe." With a raised eyebrow, he continues. "You trusted me to surprise you on the gondola, remember?"

Shit. I can't argue with him. It's still so jarring to see Tanner so sensitive though. So serious.

I lean towards him, holding his scruffy face with one hand, pressing my lips to his.

"Trust isn't always easy. But I'll try, Tanner. Thank you," I say, my eyes flutter shut as I press my forehead to his.

He stands back up, a fresh idea on his face.

"Hey," he says, his ragged, deep voice breaking the silence, "we have like 15 minutes before they're back. I told you I wanted you to see this kitchen."

"Oh. You were serious? I thought that was just a clever ruse." I look at him, enjoying the sight of him shirtless, only having put his jeans back on. He laughs. "Unintended benefit, Ronni."

He turns to get dressed and I gasp.

"Oh, fuck."

"What?" he asks, looking back at me terrified. "What's wrong?"

"Your back," I cover my mouth, seeing I was a little too aggressive with my nails. "You look like you got clawed by a raccoon."

"Don't worry," he snorts. "I'll come up with something."

After getting dressed, we walk hand in hand back to the main house until we reach the kitchen.

I'm stunned. Tanner was right. The kitchen is incredible, like something out of an architecture magazine. I wander the enormous kitchen as Tanner leans against the refrigerator at the end of the room. It's modern like the exterior of the house, with matte black countertops and sleek oak cabinets. In the center, there's a massive island with waterfall counters and an oversized Italian range. I run my fingers over the ornate knobs on the eight burner range, picturing the meals I could prepare here. As I reach the end of the counter, heading towards the dining area, I notice a knife block with familiar handles. TJ must be a fan of Tanner's work as well.

As I look into the open dining area, something else on the wall catches my eye. There's a ten foot by ten foot painting of a tall, slender man with blonde hair. He's holding a microphone up, singing, facing an unseen crowd not in the painting. His face is so familiar though.

Wait. It can't be.

It's Tommy Jacob. The singer from Teal Tigers. This dude, TJ, must be a huge fan.

Wait. Fuck. TJ.

"Tanner, is this fucking Tommy Jacob's house?" I whip around to look at him, he's already grinning as wide of a smile as that face can fit.

"Told you I had a surprise for you. Now you've been in his kitchen and fucked in his guesthouse. Something nice to think about the next time you listen to him." He laughs, clearly amused that his surprise worked.

My jaw is hanging wide open. "How did you know? How did you remember I love Teal Tigers?" I ask, incredulous that he could think of this the same way he remembered my coffee order after all these years.

He walks closer, pressing his body into me as I lean against the edge of the dining room table, the painting still visible over his shoulder.

"I told you, Ronni," his voice husky and low again, "I've thought about you in *that* t-shirt for years. Hard to forget."

He cups my ass, pulling me closer to him as he kisses me gently, tugging my lower lip as he pulls away.

"So, Tanner," I look him in the eyes with a smirk, "time to *act normal* again?"

"If we must," he growls. "Let's go, I guess."

After heading back to the guesthouse, we hear the footsteps outside of Collin and Lizzy coming back with the carryout. I can just hear them mumbling something about finding Lizzy a cowboy together.

Dinner is quick, standing around the island in the still impressively large kitchen of the guesthouse. Not quite the monstrosity of the main house kitchen, but it still dwarfs our condo's kitchen or even mine back at my house in Ohio.

While we're standing around, the boys are talking about TJ, now everyone realizing that it's Tommy Jacob's house that we're at. Lizzy seems less interested though, her eyes fixed on me.

"Ok, Lizzy. You're starting to creep me out," I say, putting my plate of dumplings down on the counter. "Why are you staring at me?"

There's a soft but still mischievous smile on her face as she eyes me up and down.

"You've been all smiles since lunch yesterday. I rarely get to see you this relaxed. You're practically glowing. It's a good look for you," she says skeptically.

I blush a little, not quite sure how to handle the compliment. *Yes, Lizzy. Three orgasms in the last day and a half will do that to you.*

Nope. Not saying that.

"If you say so, I guess." That seems like a more appropriate answer.

"Seriously, V. It's good seeing you like this. Tanner even changed your sacred itinerary yesterday from a lazy night at the condo to a fun dinner here with a hot tub. You didn't even bat an eye at the change," she says.

I think about it for a second. She's right. It does feel good to just go with what the day brings, especially when Tanner is leading the way. I should do this more often.

"Yeah, I guess this place really brings out the best in me. Just feels so good to be here," I say, shrugging my shoulders trying not to give away any hints of my exploits with Tanner over the last two days. Oh Lizzy, if you only knew girl.

My gaze shifts over to Collin and Tanner. Tanner is looking away from me, but he must have heard Lizzy. I see the signs of a smile forming on the one side of his face I can see, one of his dimples now clearly noticeable through his beard.

Those dimples. My heart flutters.

I still don't know exactly what we're doing together. Yes, we're having fun. Yes, he has feelings for me. I know we aren't labeling it yet.

Normally, this kind of uncertainty in my life would make me spiral and panic. But I'm eerily calm and at peace, for now at least. I don't know what's next, but I know I don't want this feeling to stop.

Chapter 26

Veronica
Hot Tub

"So yeah, TJ's pretty boring actually," Tanner says, looking at Lizzy.

She huffs in disappointment, holding her plastic wine glass above the bubbling water of the hot tub.

"Damn, I was really hoping you had some crazy rockstar stories."

"Hate to burst your bubble," Tanner says, shaking his head, "but yeah, he's boring. Comes out here a couple times each winter to ski. Tries to make it out in the summer and fly fish a bit, not much else. Oh, and he does really like to cook too."

"Yeah, no shit," I say. "That kitchen is insane. Glad someone is using it."

I look at Tanner, sitting in the opposite corner of the hot tub directly across from me, Collin and Lizzy in the others. His chest and shoulders are still above the water and the view is incredible. I would kill to just be able to go across the hot tub and curl into his lap.

"So, Chap," Collin says, cracking open a new beer, "is this the coolest place you manage?"

"It's pretty cool," Tanner says, "but not the coolest. There's a guy with a dozen or so acres along the Snake on an old ranch. He built a new house, pretty similar to this, but the land is amazing. Fishing access, places to ride horses, insane views of the mountains. It's perfect."

Watching Tanner talk about this place is charming in its own way. I doubt he even realizes it, but when he describes the mountain, the river, the land, his entire demeanor changes. His voice is softer, his eyes sparkle, his dimples show while an involuntary smile takes over his face. It's like he's letting his guard down and giving you a glimpse into what really makes him tick. I've always known he loved Jackson and the Tetons, but hearing the way he knows the this place, it's like he's talking about a close family member or loved one, or even himself.

"So, Chap. You said your dog gave you those scratches? What is he, a fucking wolf?" Lizzy asks, still eyeing Tanner.

He laughs, almost choking on his beer. "Rex is a cattle dog, but he packs a punch. I was sleeping on the couch last night and he curled up on my back, until a moose outside startled him. The little shit ripped my back up good when he jumped off to go bark at the door."

Lizzy seems to accept that answer, but her eyes still linger on his bare chest above the waterline with a mix of skepticism and lust.

Tanner takes note of Lizzy's gaze before drying his hands on a towel and grabbing his phone, laughing as he types something out.

"Well guys, TJ says hi and he hopes we're enjoying the place. Wishes he were here," Tanner says.

"Damn, look at you. Texting famous celebrities," Collin says, lifting his beer to cheers Tanner.

My phone's on silent, but I see my screen light up with a notification. I wait a minute before grabbing my phone to check. It's a message from Tanner.

> *Tanner: Thinking of you, maybe a little too much. Got a bit of a Teal Tiger crop top situation again… ;)*

My heart skips a beat, thinking about the way he ruined me tonight before dinner, leaving my body craving more. I reply, before putting my phone away.

> *Me: Thinking of you and your situation too… XOXO*

Getting my mind back to the moment, I change the subject to something more predictable.

"Collin? Lizzy?" I start. "Do you guys remember the plan for tomorrow?"

"Ugh, V. Just when I'm starting to think you're being less… *you*… you go and bring up the itinerary," Lizzy scoffs before taking another sip of wine.

Collin laughs, looking back at me.

"Why don't you go ahead and pretend we forgot and walk us through it again? We know you'll feel better if you do."

I guess I am that predictable. I think back to what I told Tanner just before dinner, that I want to be more spontaneous. I think about how he's right, I can relax and trust him. I can trust Collin and Lizzy too.

"Alright. Fine then. If you want me to be less *me,* let's say screw it. What do you guys want to do tomorrow?" I ask, glaring at both of them, my eyebrows raised. I smirk before my eyes meet Tanner's, who nods and grins in approval. Geez. That did feel good.

Lizzy is the first to wipe the surprised look off her face and quickly gets a giddy look. "Well I know what I want. After we go skiing, let's go out for dinner and then I can finally look for a cowboy at one of those cool old bars downtown."

Collin nods to Lizzy, clinking his beer to her glass. "Now that's a good plan."

Tanner laughs and runs his fingers through his wet hair.

"Sorry, Ronni," he says, trying to hide his disappointment. "I have to work in the morning so I won't see y'all on the slopes. I'll catch up with you at the bars later though. Where're we going first?"

I look over to Lizzy.

"Since this is Lizzy's first time here and she's hell bent on finding a cowboy," I say, rolling my eyes, "I figured we'd start at the Silver Dollar Cowboy Bar. Sound good to you guys?"

"Oh hell yeah, V," Collin says, looking over to Tanner. "You ready to check in on our old friend, Tanner? I hope he's still there."

Tanner lets out a chuckle and reaches over to Collin, giving him a jab in the shoulder with his fist still holding his beer.

"I hope so, bud. Been a while since we've checked in on him."

"Umm… someone care to fill me in?" Lizzy asks, annoyed she's missing out on an inside joke. A look of excitement then takes over her face. "Wait, is your old friend a cowboy?!"

I roll my eyes, shaking my head thinking about Collin and Tanner. All these years and they still have to do this same old shit. I sigh.

"You'll see, Lizzy. I told you these boys never change," I groan.

Chapter 27

Tanner
Horny Badger

"Come on bud, let's go." I watch Rex sprint from the barn towards the truck kicking snow up behind him. He wiggles around excitedly waiting for me to get there. I'm not too far behind him, carrying the box of knives I finished up the other day. I need to drop these off at the Eclectic Elk. They open at 9:00AM, which gave me just enough time after my plow run this morning to come home for breakfast, let Rex out for a round of fetch, and to grab the knives.

It's just another typical work day for me, especially with the fresh snow coming in last night that needed to get plowed first thing this morning. I've still got plenty I need to get done today, but at least I'm getting an early start. And I get to hang out with Collin, Ronni, and Lizzy later tonight. Ok, so maybe it's not such a typical day for me. Yeah, the last few days have been anything but typical. That's for sure.

It still feels surreal. This thing between Ronni and me right now. It's consuming every minute of my thoughts. I could barely sleep last night replaying the time we had by ourselves at the guesthouse. I'd be happy to just let myself get lost in those memories. But I do actually have to get shit done today, especially if I want to see her later.

Driving into town, I realize I'm still a bit groggy. Maybe it was staying up all night at TJ's hot tub or maybe it was being up early for work, but I definitely need another coffee. Pulling into the drive thru at Cowgirl Coffee on my way, I'm greeted by Kelsey, who usually works the morning shift, at the window.

"Morning Chap. Working or skiing today?" she asks, smiling as always.

I lean out the window of the truck, drumming my finger tips on the door, clicking my tongue. "Work unfortunately. Busy day. But I should be back on the slopes tomorrow."

She shrugs. "Bummer. Should be awesome out there today. So what are you having today?"

"The usual. Large hot horny badger, please." Oh fuck me. Now I'm saying it by mistake too. I feel my face heat and go bright red as Kelsey laughs. "I mean honey badger. Large. Hot. Honey. Badger."

"Sure thing, Chap." She shakes her head, still grinning as she goes to make my drink.

With my coffee in hand, I finally get to town. I park off the square by one of the new buildings going in. I still can't believe we have to keep building these here. It's one of the subsidized housing units local businesses chipped in on together to keep workers around locally instead of an hour away in nearby towns on the other side of the mountain pass. Just another daily reminder of all my old friends and locals that had to leave.

Walking into the Eclectic Elk, the box of knives tucked into the crook of my elbow, I'm reminded of one of the reasons I do love Jackson so much. Sure, it sells a lot of stuff for tourists. But the walls are covered in so many things made by locals, people that still fight to stay here and make things that show what this place is about.

I see Giselle behind the counter, clearly amused by me staring at one of the paintings on the wall. It shows a brightly colored wolf standing on the edge of a creek. I'd love one of them, not that I have any place big enough or nice enough to hang it.

"I love that one too. Her work's some of my favorite," she says with a familiar friendly smile.

"Yeah. She always paints cool stuff and I love her style." I keep looking at the painting, admiring it. "She's the one who did that huge custom piece for Tommy Jacob's, right?"

"Sure is. So. How's the family doing, Chap?" She leans over the counter, elbows propping her head up on her hands framing her face.

"They're good. Meeting my grandparents for lunch later. I'll tell them you said hi. But on another note, I'm here to drop off these." I take a step towards the counter, placing the box on the counter in front of her.

She opens the box, taking out one of the knives. "Seriously. I can't believe we already sold the last round from a few days ago Tanner. I could sell every one you can make. If you went anywhere close to full time on these, you'd be going gangbusters." She places the knife down, looking at me. "Just think about it."

I smile back, halfheartedly. "Maybe. We'll see. You know that's not why I do it."

We've had this conversation so many times. I love making the knives. It's fun. It's an escape. I don't want to lose that part of it by turning it into a joyless business.

She laughs, shaking her head at me in a way that almost reminds me of my mom. "Fair enough. But you know I'm always going to ask."

"I know. Anyways, I need to stop at Gloria's before I pick up lunch for my grandparents. I'll see you in about a week to drop off a couple more knives." I make my way towards the door back outside, before turning back. "And tell Colt I said hi and have a Happy New Year!"

"Same Chap. See you around," she says as I walk out.

I make another stop to drop off a knife for a customer and pick up pizza before heading over to Teton Village with Rex. It's been a productive morning and for the first time in a while, one that just feels optimistic.

I look at the picture in the corner of my dash, the one of mom and me the day she gave me this truck. God she loved this thing. I still can't believe she gave it to me when I graduated high school. But feeling optimistic for a change, happy about everything, all I can think about is how much I want to talk about this with her, if she was here. There's so much I wish I could tell her.

I park in the lot outside the condo building, noticing Collin's SUV parked next to my grandparents. It's always felt like such a lucky, happy coincidence that our grandparents all met decades ago and then ended up living in the same building.

I walk up the stairs past the Perry's unit, thinking about the killer day they're hopefully having on the slopes. I'm definitely looking forward to seeing them later tonight. That's for sure.

"Hey Grandma," I say, walking into the condo. "You and Grandpa ready for pizza? I brought Big Reds."

She comes over and takes the pizza from me, handing it to Grandpa before giving me a big hug. "Oh sweetie. How was your morning?" She pulls away from the hug, but not before making me lean down so she can kiss me on the cheek.

"Fine Grandma. Busy with work. Plowed, dropped off some knives at the Elk, and grabbed a coffee before getting pizza and coming over."

Grandpa pats me on the shoulder with one of his big bear paw sized hands. "Come on, Tanner. Enough chit chat. Let's sit down and eat. I'm starving. Nancy can talk your ear off at the table."

The three of us sit down while Rex curls up in his usual spot on the couch in front of the fireplace. We catch up on the week over pizza. Grandma seems to have an endless list of questions about the Perry twins and what we're all going to be up to while they're in town. But for once, they're a welcome topic. They're in town and things are going well. Really well.

"I just can't wait to see Veronica and meet her friend Lizzy. You're going to make sure they come over for dinner one night, right?" She has an excited look on her face. I know they're gone a lot of the time visiting the rest of the family in Salt Lake, but I am glad they're here for days like this.

"Yes. I will make sure she comes over. But if you keep asking about Ronni, I think Collin's feelings are going to get hurt. You know he loves his status as your favorite Perry twin," I say with a wink.

"Oh. Collin's not my favorite. I just tell him that because I know it makes him happy," she says.

I laugh. "What? That's what you've always said though, even when he's not around. Why isn't he your favorite?"

I watch as Grandma smiles and shares a knowing look with Grandpa before he sighs and grins back at her.

"Oh Tanner. Your Grandma's favorite has always been Veronica because we know she's your favorite."

I inhale sharply, holding my breath. A very unwelcome, unfamiliar feeling of panic sinks in. Grandma laughs, seeing the terrified look on my face before placing her hand over mine on the table.

"Honey. We've always known. The way you've always looked at her. The way you talk about her. The way you smile when she's around." Somehow her words make me relax just enough to finally exhale.

"How do you know that?" I ask, still a bit terrified that they've apparently known for god knows how long.

"Tanner," Grandpa starts, "you might be able to fool Collin and Veronica. You might be able to even fool yourself. But believe me, we've known for years."

Well that's unsettling. I guess I've been a lot worse at hiding my feelings than I thought. But that doesn't change the fact I've wanted to hide my feelings from everyone.

I think back to talking with Collin on the chair the other day. I was this close to opening up to him. This close to telling him how lonely I've been lately and how down I've felt. Fuck it. Let's give this a shot. They already can see right through me apparently.

"Alright. Well since you two know everything, maybe I'll share something else. But you have to promise me that you will not share this with anyone. Dad, Clay, Grace and especially not Collin or Ronni's friend Lizzy. Can you do that?"

Grandpa straightens in his chair. "We'll make that promise. But you know the Chapman's rule about promises."

I close my eyes and sigh deeply. "Yes Grandpa. I know. We're as good as our word and if we make a promise-."

He cuts me off before I can finish.

"If we make a promise, we'll keep it or die trying."

"Good. Well, I think Ronni and I might be more than friends now. I don't what we are exactly, but we're-." This time it's Grandma that cuts me off.

"Sweetie. You don't need to tell us. All we want to know is if you're both happy?" She smiles at me the way only a grandmother could.

"I think we are. Yes, we definitely are right now. I just... don't know where it's going. I just know I never want it to end." The wave of relief from saying that out loud finally, even to my grandparents, is instant. Geez. That felt good.

Chapter 28

Veronica
Little Bitch Bear

Today was surprisingly uneventful on the slopes. After calling it an early day and taking a much needed afternoon nap, we head to downtown Jackson to meet up with Tanner. I borrow Lizzy's black sweater dress since I didn't pack anything particularly exciting for the trip. I mean come on, I wasn't planning on any of this to happen. No where on my itinerary was there a line for *finding an impossibly handsome and sexy friend with benefits that wants to make me come every chance he gets.* A man that I'm pretty sure gets off on just watching me smile. But now, part of me just wants to look good for a night on the town, another part of me wants to look good for Tanner. Even now, his confidence is oozing into me and I feel amazing tonight.

Tonight should be fun. A night out for drinks with Collin, Lizzy, and Tanner. But there's a sinking feeling in my gut. It's New Year's Eve, and downtown Jackson is so romantic, and I have a man here that I think I might be starting to have feelings for.

No. One that I definitely have feelings for.

I can't stop thinking about him every second. The way he makes my body feel is unreal. But the way my mind is clear when I'm with him is frighteningly welcome. But I can't act on it, and have to settle for these little stolen moments with him.

Lizzy and Collin unsurprisingly both look fantastic. Lizzy is wearing a silver sequined nineteen-twenties styled cocktail dress with white cowboy boots. Collin is wearing slimming blue jeans, a nice white shirt, and a well tailored blue plaid blazer.

When we get to the bar, I'm flooded with nostalgia. Much like the Frisky Fox, it would be easy to come into this place and think it's a cheesy tourist trap. But it's been here since the thirties and remains authentic.

The first thing that jumps out is the size of the place. Running down the right hand side is an obscenely long bar. The counter is lined with thousands of old silver dollar coins covered in epoxy, like they're floating in a sea of black. They were originally put there as a way to lure in visitors wanting to see them, and the trick still works today.

Behind the bar is a collection of old timey mirrors with bull horns above them. In front of the bar are some of the coolest bar stools I've ever seen, made out of old saddles that tourists pretend to live out there cowboy dreams on. The theme continues through the rest of the bar with wood paneled walls on all sides, wooden log support beams running down the middle of the room, and a collection of Old West artifacts throughout.

As I look down the long bar, I see Tanner. Even with his back to us, it's easy to pick out his tall, broad frame while he talks to two bartenders. Seeing him now, I'm reminded of the sinking feeling in my stomach this morning when we got to the Tram Center and Tanner wasn't there waiting for us with coffees in hand. It's startling how much I have already gotten used to Tanner being there in the morning, a grounding presence to start my day.

We head his way and he turns around to greet us. As he looks at me, I stop in my tracks, looking at him from the ground up. He's wearing a pair of clean brown Chelsea boots, a pair of perfectly faded jeans, a brown leather belt with a large western belt buckle, and a white and blue western shirt with pearl snap buttons. But his face, I can't stop staring at it.

"Damn, Chap!" Collin shouts as he brushes past me and bear hugs Tanner. "You clean up well. I can't remember the last time I saw you without a beard. What's the occasion, bro?"

"New year, new me I guess," he says looking at Lizzy before landing on me. "Gotta start the new year off right."

"Looking *fine*, Chap," Lizzy says, with a whistle as she eyes him.

"It's a good look for you, Tanner," I say, giving him a forearm to the ribs. "Didn't realize you could clean up like that when you're not in ski gear."

I think I played that subtly enough. But he's right. Definitely a new Tanner. I didn't think he could look any better but fuck me, he sure can. His once scruffy beard is now shaved down to a near perfect five o'clock shadow, but his mustache is still full, just a bit more neatly trimmed. His chiseled jaw now that much more visible and it's practically criminal how easy it is for him to flash his dimples without his beard. I can already feel sensations deep inside me rearing their head again.

As my eyes meet his, I realize he was doing the same to me, his eyes starting on my legs. I can feel my face start to go pink, blushing at his gaze. I'm a fair bit taller than Lizzy, so the dress shows more of my legs than I'm used to and he definitely took notice.

A man clearing his throat interrupts our moment. "Ladies and gents, what are you having tonight?"

We all turn to the two bartenders Tanner was talking with before we arrived, now eyeing us with exhausted looks.

"Guys. This is Benjamin and Alexis. They work here, but also over at another dive I'm at most of the time. So please, be nice to them. I have to see them even when you're not in town," Tanner says, looking down his nose at us as if to say *behave please*.

"We'll make it easy on you," Collin says, "four yellow jackets, please."

As Collin waits for our beers, I look back to Lizzy and Tanner. "So Tanner, get all of your work in this morning?" I ask.

"Yeah, started at the crack of dawn as usual," he says, "but I finished plowing early and dropped off some knives with Rex downtown before lunch with my grandparents. Even got a little work in on the other knife project. Starting to go well I think. How 'bout you guys, good day so far?"

"Pretty good, Chap," Lizzy chimes in. "Easy ski day and a nice afternoon nap. Got plenty of beauty sleep in too."

Lizzy has hopped onto one of the barstools next to Collin, her bare legs on display as she looks at Tanner. Collin turns away from the bar, beers in hand now.

"Alright guys, I just wanted to say there's no one else I'd rather be celebrating the new year with than you guys," he says, raising his stubby beer bottle as we all bring ours in. "Now, cheers to us and whatever fortune the new year brings!"

After taking a sip of our drinks, Tanner looks at me with a smirk.

"Hey, Ronni," Tanner says, "want to go check out the jukebox? I could use your musical taste."

"Sure, I bet we can find something worthwhile. See you guys in a sec," I say, looking back at Collin and Lizzy.

As we reach the jukebox, I look back toward the bar. I see Collin and Lizzy, now talking to a very handsome cowboy, sandwiched between them. He looks younger than her, but that's her type. Tall, muscular, dark hair, a five o'clock shadow covering his square jaw as he smiles wildly. She's never been shy about finding herself a boy toy. Lizzy is running her finger down his chest over his shirt while Collin talks to him, playing wingman for her.

Hah! Maybe Lizzy will find a cowboy to ride after all.

"Looks like they're a bit distracted finally," Tanner says, looking down at me before tilting my chin towards him, giving me a soft kiss. His touch sends shivers through me, bringing back all the memories my body has of him.

"I missed you this morning. I was getting used to my lift line coffees," I say, smirking up at him.

He laughs, his sparkling eyes looking down at me. "You know if you lived here, I would gladly make that into an everyday thing for you."

"I wish. But some of us have to live in the real world." As I say this, a small frown crosses his face and he looks toward the ground.

"The real world… You know, it's not all fun and games here, Ronni. It's not always the fairy tale you think it is," he says, the frown still trying to take over his face.

"What do you mean, Tanner? It's me, you don't have to bottle it up," I ask, holding his hand tightly, lacing my fingers through his.

"It gets lonely here. Most of my old friends are gone, my parents left, and you guys aren't here very often any more. It's just… I feel alone most of the time. Sometimes I just feel…," he says, hanging his head, looking at our hands now.

I feel a knot growing in my stomach. I've always thought of Tanner as this invincible, brash, happy go lucky person. But seeing him this vulnerable now, like how he was that first night in the mudroom, thinking of him being alone, feeling isolated here… it guts me.

"Tanner." I squeeze his hand tighter. "I don't know what's happening with us yet or where it will go, but I can tell you one thing. Collin and I will always be here for you. Call us, text us, but please, just talk to us. Open up. You're never alone."

"Hey. I'm opening up now, aren't I?" he says this with his characteristically smug look back after I let go of his hand.

"True. That's a start. But talk to someone else too. Like your grandparents. They're in town a decent amount," I say, noting the surprised and then almost guilty expression.

"It's funny you mention that. I might have opened up to them today," he says, still wearing the same expression.

"Why do I get the sense I'm not going to be thrilled about this?" I furrow my brows looking at him sternly.

"Well we were talking about you guys being in town and one thing lead to another and yeah. I might have let it slip that something is going on between us." He shrugs, his hands raised and palms out turned.

I stand in silence. On one hand, I'm thrilled he opened up to them. On the other hand, I'm terrified about what they know.

"I know. I'm sorry. I should have asked you. It just felt like I needed to get that off my chest and it was such a relief." As he says this, I can see his body visibly relax. "Please don't be mad?"

I rest my head back on his chest, hugging him tightly again. "I'm not mad, Tanner. But if we tell anyone else, can I be the one to do it?"

"Deal," he says, planting a kiss on top of my head.

I wriggle out of his hug and peak toward the bar, seeing Collin and Lizzy still with the cowboy. With the coast clear, I lean forward, holding him closely, feeling his chest on my cheek, listening to his heart pound. Until that moment is interrupted by a buzz in my pocket.

I slide my phone out, checking the notifications. Lizzy texted me saying she's got news. I assume that's about the cowboy I just saw her with. But something else catches my eye. There are three new notifications on my office messenger app, all from Jeff. I just checked it this morning. It's a holiday. Really, can he be serious? I open the first two, both questions about Earth SnaX I've already told him the answer to a dozen times at least. I just can't catch a break from work, even on vacation.

I sigh and feel that familiar sense of dread come back over me. As if he could sense it too, I feel Tanner pull away from me, the warmth of his chest gone.

"Hey. It's my turn to ask what's wrong?" He looks down at me, a look of caution in those green eyes.

"It's just work. I don't get it. It just seems like I can never do enough for this guy, no matter how much I prepare and how hard I work." I lean back against his chest, loving the feeling of being in his arms.

"I don't know why you let it bother you so much. You should find something you actually enjoy. You could do anything you set your mind to. I mean it," he says, resting his head on mine.

I laugh into his chest. "Remember, Tanner. Real world. Some of us have careers we want to keep building. What was it you said again? It's not all fun and games here anyways?"

I note how his body tenses at my response. "Sorry. I just… don't like seeing how it upsets you."

I pull back from his embrace. "It's fine. Don't worry about it," I say, hand gesturing back towards the jukebox. "Now, how about something a bit more uplifting?"

"Ok. We can have some more fun, but you have to promise me to stop looking at your work email and messages so much while you're here. Deal?"

I groan in exasperation. "Fine. If it keeps that smile on your face and I can keep seeing those dimples, sure. I will try to ignore my phone more. You're right. It's my vacation after all."

"Good," he says, now looking back up, his beautiful ear to ear smile returning, "Now how about we play some tunes?"

I move past him to the jukebox. It's an old fashioned one that still has the hand placed paper labels for each song. I spot a familiar one, pointing it out to Tanner.

"That one."

He looks down and smiles.

"Why did I even ask… I should have already known," he says shaking his head, as he puts a quarter in and keys in the song.

"It's too bad they haven't released anything new in years. Since you're such good friends with TJ, tell him to write a new song." I nudge him playfully with my elbow.

"I'll be sure to pass that along," he says with a laugh.

I smile as the Teal Tigers' song starts in the background, thinking about how many times I've listened to this song and now thinking about the night I shared with Tanner at TJ's guesthouse. But there's a small part of me that's sad hearing it, thinking about how much I'd love to dance out on the floor with Tanner, in the open, not afraid to be seen.

I glance back over to the bar, now only seeing Lizzy talking to the cowboy. Shit. Where's Collin? Did he see anything? Tanner senses my anxiety, seemingly reading my mind.

"Relax. I'll find Collin. I'm pretty sure I know where he is," he says. "Go have fun with Lizzy for a bit. We'll catch up with you."

I walk over to the bar, right as Lizzy waves to the cowboy walking away from her.

"Damn girl," I say nodding my head at her in approval. "When you put your mind to it, you get shit done. I didn't think you'd find a real cowboy in this town, but looks like you did."

She looks at me, a sly grin on her face. "Well… he's cute. That's for sure. I did get his number, so we'll see."

I'm startled when I hear a familiar voice all the way across the bar over the noise of the crowd.

"Bull shit dude, I totally could." Ugh. It's Collin.

"Come on, Lizzy. Let's go check on them. They found their *old friend*."

Sure enough, as we walk to the other side of the main room by the stairs going down to the bathroom, we find Collin and Tanner in front of a large glass display case.

Since we've been old enough to drink and first came here, Tanner and Collin have mocked this taxidermied bear standing on its hind legs in the display case. The legend, well actually verified truth, is that a hunting guide came across this bear unexpectedly and was attacked. In the ensuing struggle, he managed to kill the bear with his bare hands.

So every time we've been in this bar over the last decade, Collin and Tanner inevitably insist that they could have killed it with *their* bare hands, like the story goes. It's not the biggest Grizzly bear, standing just a bit taller than me, but for fucks sake, it's a god damn Grizzly bear.

Now Collin, I have my doubts. Sorry, big bro. But, Tanner? Woof, I've seen that man's body and the strength within it. I'm not putting anything out of his abilities.

"Um, is this your *old friend*?" Lizzy asks with a confused look, bringing my attention back to the spectacle in front of me.

"Well, more like frenemy," Collin says. "I still think I could take it."

"No way, dude," Tanner says, punching Collin in the shoulder, "you're too small. I bet I could though. I could totally take down Little Bitch Bear."

"See, Lizzy," I interrupt, "they've been arguing for years, insisting that they could kill this bear with their bare hands."

"Really?" she asks, eyeing Tanner now. "I'd watch that fight."

"Whatever, V. I still think I could take it," Collin says. "It's still just Little Bitch Bear."

As I stand here, watching Tanner and Collin continue to carry out this insane argument, I can't help but smile and feel a familiar sense of joy watching this scene.

Collin is happy, enjoying the night out with his best friend. Lizzy manifested herself a cowboy, wherever that ends up going. And Tanner…

Tanner continues to surprise me. One second he's his old boyish, confident self with Collin, convinced he could kill Little Bitch Bear. The same Tanner that gave me an unexpected earth shattering orgasm on a gondola. The Tanner that has shown little glimpses of vulnerability. The same Tanner that puts me at ease, letting me feel like the best version of myself I've been in ages.

Oh. Fuck.

Am I… falling in love with Tanner?

Chapter 29

Veronica
Twin Powers

After leaving the bar, our newly bonded posse walks across Cache Street to the town square. Lizzy is still enamored with the charm of downtown Jackson, insisting on seeing all of the old western storefronts and wooden boardwalks. The scene is made all the more beautiful by the sparkling white Christmas lights wrapped around the trees and elk antler arches in the town square. A steady snowfall completes the picturesque evening.

Lizzy and Collin lead the way, with Collin in much better shape than the last time he left a bar. Even after the tour on Friday, she still wants the full history lesson of downtown Jackson.

They've become fast friends, a wonderful platonic dynamic duo. Walking behind them, I can just hear Lizzy asking Collin if he wants to come out to Aspen Valley with us in February. I'm still not sure what to make of them though. Their sarcastic, snarky personalities seem to be melding into my own personal bully, always ready to taunt or tease me.

"So Lizzy, you think I could take that bear or are you like V?" Collin asks her, holding his fists up and flexing his arms.

"I don't know, it's a pretty small bear. But V's right, it's still a fucking bear," she guffaws before taking a sip of her beer she smuggled out of the bar.

"Ugh. You guys suck," Collin scoffs.

"Maybe you should train a little harder in the gym, bro. Put those personal trainer skills to use on yourself," Tanner says. "Pack on a few pounds of muscle and you might finally convince me you could take down Little Bitch Bear."

Collin turns his back toward us, rolling his eyes.

"Very funny, Chap," he says, before turning his attention back to the sidewalk in front of him. He leads us through the center of the town square past the ice rink towards one of the arches on the opposite corner.

"So, what's the plan tomorrow again?" Lizzy asks, looking back to me.

Before I can even answer, Tanner's deep voice cuts through the cool night air.

"8:30 Tram Center, I'll bring coffees. We can get a full ski day in while everyone is hungover and have the slopes practically to ourselves all morning. Then figure out something for dinner. That sound good to you guys?"

Lizzy and Collin both shrug their shoulders and nod.

Tanner looks to me next. It's more or less what I had originally planned, but still. It's nice not to have everyone looking to me for my plan all the time. It sucks feeling like people are always on edge around me, treading lightly. Like if they go against my plan, I'll be an anxious mess. It's not like I want to be like this all the time. I don't want to *have* to be in control.

"Yeah, Tanner. Sounds perfect," I say. "We can see how everyone's doing around lunch time and play dinner by ear."

"Awesome," he says smiling, "and sometime this week, we need to get dinner with Grandma. She's been dying to see you guys."

"I could definitely use some more Grandma Chapman in my life. Christmas Day wasn't enough. Ugh those cookies and her chicken pot pies. So good. Sign me up, Chap." Collin is practically drooling by the time he finishes talking. Shoot, even I'm hungry now thinking about her cooking.

"Definitely, Tanner. Count me in," I say.

"You know me guys. I'm always happy to put down some food," Lizzy says, shrugging her shoulders. "Now, can we keep walking? It's cold as shit here."

As Lizzy and Collin start walking down the winding sidewalk through the square, I cozy up to Tanner. I let my hand brush his while we walk side by side.

"Thanks, Tanner," I whisper.

He looks at me, a puzzled expression on his face. "For what?"

"For making the plans for tomorrow. It drives me nuts when everyone always looks to me for what they're *allowed* to do. Like somehow, I have to approve everything. It's a reminder that I do struggle with anxiety. Just because planning helps my anxiety doesn't mean *I actually like it.*"

"Oh. Well, thank you for letting me know. I'll be sure to do it again." He smiles for a second before looking ahead at Collin and Lizzy. Hearing him say this, I know he'll do this again too. It's like if I say something or ask for something one time, it's lodged in his memory forever.

We walk through the square, still cautiously lagging behind Collin and Lizzy. We reach one of the elk antler arches, glistening with white Christmas lights. I feel Tanner's hand slowly grab mine, holding it tightly. I look up at him, his beautiful smile, those piercing green eyes staring into me, stripping away my layers of anxiety and self doubt, planting me firmly in the here and now.

I feel at peace in a way I can't remember. I deserve this. I don't care if Collin or Lizzy sees. I still don't know what this is or where it's going, but I do know this is the best I've felt about life, *about myself,* in ages. I'm going to enjoy every second of my time with this man because who knows when I'll feel like this again.

Time to be more like him.

Send it, V.

I lean forward, standing on my tippy toes to reach his face. I pull him towards me, one hand on his lower back, one cupping his softly stubbled face. Our lips meet and it feels like time stops.

He kisses me back, his lips longing for me. He pulls me in closer now, one hand on my hips and the other on my nape. I begrudgingly pull away, our foreheads still pressed together. I can feel his warm breath on me in the cold night air. I'm close enough to feel his heart pounding in his chest, like mine.

"Tanner, I think I'm falling for you," I say, practically whispering to him.

"Well, Ronni," he says, his deep voice lowered, matching my whisper, "I started falling for you years ago and now I finally feel like my feet are on the ground here with you."

The magical moment is interrupted by Collin's familiar presence as he clears his throat with exaggerated *ahem.*

Fuck. Whatever. I'm ready for it. I deserve what I have with Tanner right now. Not even Collin can take that away.

I look at Tanner, his face is much more concerned. I know he was dreading this moment.

"Well?" Collin's voice is low, darker than usual. He looks at us, his wide eyes taking in the picture. Lizzy is next to him, but she's easy to read. Her jaw is dropped, but only for a moment as it turns into a wide grin as she starts to nod her head in approval. But Collin, his face is still blank.

Shit. What is he thinking?

My twin powers aren't kicking in. I have no sense of what is going through his mind.

Chapter 30

Tanner
Captain

Collin's expression is blank. Between kissing Ronni, and the way Collin and Lizzy are staring at us now, I can feel my heart trying to jump out of my fucking chest. He's practically a brother to me, but I can't read his face right now. I swallow, but can't make the knot in my throat go away.

"Celebrating the New Year a bit early, aren't we?" Collin asks, finally breaking the silence.

"Collin. I swear. We wanted to-," I start to talk before he bursts out laughing. I look to Ronni, the terrified expression on her face is gone. She's now eyeing Collin with suspicion, one eye squinting and an eyebrow raised.

Collin finally manages to stop laughing long enough to talk.

"Oh man, I had you guys. You should have seen your faces," he says, still bent over at the waist, hands on knees as he starts laughing again. Lizzy now joins him, cackling maniacally.

"Um. What?" I ask, still not sure what the fuck is happening. Is he mad? Does he think this is a joke? Ronni looks at me, clearly wondering the same thing.

"Dude. You're my best friend, practically my brother. V, you're my literal twin sister. You guys think you could sneak around sharing little grins and winks for days without me figuring it out? That's fucking cute." He takes a deep breath before exhaling. I think he finally got the laughing out of his system.

"Well, I didn't know," Lizzy says, interrupting Collin while he revels in scaring the shit out of us for what felt like forever.

"You little fucking shit, Collin," Ronni says. "That's not cool."

"Oh I beg to differ," he snorts. "The look on your faces was totally worth it."

"So, to be clear, you're not mad?" I ask, finally able to exhale.

Collin straightens up, walking towards Ronni and me, putting a hand on both of our shoulders.

"Not at all guys," he says, bringing both of us in for a hug, "not at all."

He pulls back, looking at us both now.

"But I swear to god, don't fucking hurt each other." His face is serious, pointing a finger at me, then Ronni. We both nod.

"Alright, I'm all for this. But can we carry on now? I still want to see the rest of town and stop for ice cream." The three of us turn towards Lizzy, clearly unashamed at interrupting the moment.

"What? I'm cold and about to get hangry. Let's go. We got all week for touchy feely shit guys." She waves for us to follow.

"You really want ice cream in this cold ass weather?" Collin looks back to Lizzy, waiting for an answer.

She huffs. "I guess I'm sort of like V with her iced coffee obsession. Maybe she's not that crazy after all."

"Alright, alright," I say, holding Ronni's hand walking past Collin and out in front of Lizzy, "if you guys want ice cream, let us lead the way."

Well, that went better than I expected.

We walk through town, Ronni and I hand in hand, her head on my shoulder. I have to admit, it does feel better not hiding from Collin and Lizzy. I'm just glad I don't have to worry about him now. It's such an incredible relief.

After getting cones, we sit outside the ice cream parlor on a pair of benches. We're on one of the boardwalks, opposite the town square.

"Jeez, this ice cream is great but I'm exhausted now. Roll me away and throw me in bed please," Lizzy says, trying not to nod off on the bench with Collin.

"Yeah, it's been a long night and I didn't even have any tequila shots at the bar. I'm ready to sleep," he says.

"We are so lame guys, we're all getting old. You realize that, right?" Lizzy looks at all of us, still enjoying her ice cream in a waffle cone.

Everyone looks at each other, sighing in acknowledgement.

Ugh, she's spot on. Even I'm tired. I've been up since the crack of dawn working and the nerves from worrying about Collin's reaction are taking a toll on me tonight.

"Alright, let's call an Uber to get back to the condo. I'm ready to get a solid night's sleep," Collin says, getting up from the bench.

Ronni and I stand up. I grab her hands, pulling her in for a hug.

"See you tomorrow, horny badger," I say smirking. She's still not amused by my nickname, but I fucking love it. She blushes even more now that Collin and Lizzy know about us. I want her to come home with me so bad tonight. I want to spend the night with her, waking up to her by my side in the morning, starting a bright new year together.

"Seriously, I'm right here guys," Collin says, his brow furrowed as he looks at us.

"Sorry, Collin." I look down at the ground.

"Gotcha again," he says, now smiling. "Seriously, stop trying to hide. I'll admit though, it was adorable for a bit. If you guys want to stay up and ring in the new year together at Tanner's place, go for it. It doesn't bother me."

I look at Ronni, a bit surprised but also totally happy about it. She nods, a smile growing on her face before she rests her head back on my chest.

"Thanks, Collin," I say nodding. "How about instead of 8:30 Tram Center, we'll see y'all at the condo around 7:30? I'll bring coffees and pastries."

"Sounds perfect to me," Lizzy says, yawning and shuffling her feet. She's clearly ready for bed.

"Awesome," Ronni says. "Happy New Year guys. We'll see you in the morning."

"Happy New Year to you too, lovebirds," Collin says. "Love you both."

After Collin and Lizzy catch an Uber back home, Ronni and I head back to the truck to go back to my place. The whole ride back, I can't take my eyes off her, holding her hand for the entire fifteen minute drive.

"That went surprisingly well," she says, exhaling a much needed sigh of relief.

I chuckle. "You have no idea how terrified I was, Ronni. I've played that moment out in my head hundreds of times over the years and never once did it go *that* way."

"Are you telling me you were afraid of Collin?" she asks, sitting up straight now, eyebrows raised. "You can't tell me the unflappable Tanner Chapman is afraid of my brother? The same Collin that bitched out on Corbett's and wouldn't go down until both of us did? The same Collin that would obviously lose to Little Bitch Bear?"

I can feel myself frowning. I hate talking about my feelings. I try to bury this so much and hide it, but with her it's like she can just tell what's going on in my head. I keep thinking about the mudroom, and she knew something was off with me that night. It's like... I actually want to tell her everything that's going on in my head now, to stop hiding my fears and problems.

"I wasn't afraid of Collin, that's not it. I've been afraid of losing him for years." Ugh it feels surprisingly good to say that out loud.

"Why would you lose him, Tanner? Because of me?" She's looking at me with a surprised expression on her face. She grabs my hand again and the warmth from her touch makes me want to keep sharing everything.

"Because Ronni, I've had feelings for you as long as I can remember. But Collin's my best friend. And every time I think about you and wanting to try and tell you how I feel, to make something happen, my mind immediately goes to what happens if it goes wrong, if Collin ends up hating me, if I lose both of you. I've been so afraid of that for years. And every time I think of that, of feeling even more alone, I just... I just shut down and want to turn off my thoughts, to drown out the pain somehow."

Fuck me. I've never said that out loud to anyone.

Today is a day for firsts apparently. First, opening up to my grandparents about this. Now, opening up to her even more.

I look over at her in the passenger seat. There's a look of sadness in her sparkling hazel eyes, but also one of understanding and compassion.

"Tanner," she says softly, still holding my hand, "thank you for telling me that. It's ok to talk. It's ok to let it out. Please. Keep doing this. You can always talk to me, to Collin. You know that, right? Maybe you should start taking your own advice more, just *send it* and tell people what's bothering you. Also, I'm pretty sure it would take more than trying to be serious and date me to make Collin hate you."

She laughs after the last bit.

"Are you saying... we're dating then?" I ask, as we pull into the driveway, eyeing her carefully.

She laughs before leaning forward to give me a kiss.

"Fuck it," she says, "yes, we're dating."

I can feel myself grinning ear to ear as I lean towards her to kiss her. Her mouth opens to greet mine. God it feels so good, to feel her tongue slide along mine, hearing her breathe so close to me.

But maybe she's also right. Maybe I do need to start opening up and talking more about what's bothering me. It was ok today with my grandparents. Nothing bad happened. If anything it felt like a relief to be vulnerable. I've always been so willing to take physical risks on the mountain, on the river, in the backcountry, and with other dumb stunts. I've always been ok with those risks, accepting them and thinking the best case will still play out. But when it comes to emotional risks, being vulnerable, I've always just shut down and been unwilling to take them, fearing the worst case.

Maybe it won't always be like it was a decade ago with mom.

And with Ronni now, I was so wrapped up in my head about Collin getting mad or upset about me being into Ronni that I was absolutely unwilling to risk it. I assumed the worst was always going to happen, that I'd end up with neither of them in my life. I never once let myself think that everything would be ok. I never once thought that Collin wouldn't care or maybe even be happy that we were interested in each other. And after tonight, the way he reacted so well, I can't help but think I should have done this years ago. Maybe if I had taken the risk then, I could have had so much more time with her.

I look back over at her in the passenger seat, still smiling at me, her hand on my thigh. If opening up means more times like these with her, then I will fucking try to keep doing it.

"Come on, let's get inside. Someone wants to see you." I gesture towards the cabin with my head.

As we walk in, Rex is there and practically jumps into Ronni's arms.

"Well hey there, Captain! It's been a while. Are you still the bestest boy?!"

She gets down on her knees, scratching him behind both ears giggling the whole time.

"Captain? You remembered his full name, Captain Rex?" My jaw drops. I can't fucking believe she remembered that.

I actually might be a bit jealous at how much of her attention he's getting.

"You seriously think I forgot his name was Captain Rex? Did you forget how many times I watched those movies and cartoons with you and Collin, even when you guys were in your twenties?" She looks at me, rolling her eyes.

Yep. She's perfect.

Chapter 31

Veronica
Without a Clock

I forgot how much fun it was having a dog around the house. They're always happy to see you, always just living in the moment. I've considered getting one, but I never thought it would be fair to a dog with the long hours I work.

I play with Rex for a few minutes while Tanner heads towards the kitchen to get Rex's dinner.

"Come on, boy. Time to eat. You'll have plenty of time to play with Ronni later," he says, as if Rex is a person understanding every word.

It's funny listening to the way he talks to Rex. He looks right at him and they even make eye contact. These two clearly have full conversations when it's just them around. I laugh at the thought.

"What's so funny?" Tanner asks, eyeing me suspiciously while he leans against the kitchen island. "Never seen a guy talk to his dog before?"

"Nope, not like that at least," I say, sitting on the barstool next to him. "I get the feeling you guys have lots of conversations."

I watch as his eyes drift to the ground, wringing his hands awkwardly.

"Yeah," his tone more serious now. "I know I'm talking to myself, but I do vent to him. It sounds crazy but it helps me work through things."

"It's not crazy, Tanner. I get it," I say, taking his hand in mine. "It's not easy opening up."

I look up at him, one side of his mouth trying to pull up to smile. I feel like I'm getting a glimpse into a part of him he's been concealing for years, something I'm not supposed to see. It's endearing, but heart wrenching to think that he's been hiding so many feelings for so long.

I let go of his hands and reach up to hold his face, wanting to put him at ease. With his beard trimmed down now, I can feel the lines of his face. My fingers run over his jaw and cheekbones. He's still the goofy, silly cute Tanner I've always known, but like this I can't help but appreciate all the little details I've taken for granted and the way he's aged.

His eyes close at my touch, his mouth opening and I can feel his warm breath on my wrist, the sensation hitting me all the way down to my needy pleasure points. My finger lingers on his dimple, my thumb on his lips, running across the edges of his now neatly trimmed mustache.

"Ronni," he says, his voice low and husky, "It's getting late. Want to get to bed?"

"Mmm. I was hoping you'd say that," leaning forward to whisper playfully in his ear. "I want what's mine."

"Oh yeah, what's that?" His husky voice in my ear, I can feel his breath now on the nape of my neck, making the hairs on it stand up as I inhale sharply.

"You said your body is *mine*, remember?" My hand is on his chest now and I can feel his pulse quicken at my words.

"Finally, I get you without a clock. I hope you're fucking ready for me," he says, practically growling at me.

"Why don't you see how ready I already am for you?" Our eyes meet before mine look down to my fingers, now twisting the hem of my dress, inching it up my legs, baiting him to touch me.

He groans at my words and at the sight of the dress inching up my thighs. He leans into me on the barstool and I can feel his need for me as he presses his body into mine, feeling him through his jeans. Knowing how much this gorgeous, selfless man worships me sends chills through my body.

He starts kissing my neck, just below my ear, his lips making my shoulders roll back and my back arch. I run my hands under his shirt and pop the pearl snap buttons open, desperate to take it off and feel his burning skin. His shirt now unbuttoned, he pulls it off, letting it fall to the ground.

Fuck me, I don't think I'll ever get tired of seeing his bare chest and shoulders or those perfect abs. I can feel my own growing need between my legs. Without prompting, I feel Tanner pull away from my neck and I watch as he slowly drops to his knees. He looks up at me longingly, pure fire in his eyes. He runs his hands up my legs and under my dress, the worn calluses of his strong rugged hands teasing my skin, making it tingle across my body. His hands stop when his fingers reach the band of my lacy black panties.

He slides them down my legs before cupping my ass in his hands, pulling me to the edge of the bar stool. His hands move up to my hips and his thumbs linger on my hip bones. I'm squirming, my body begging for more of his touch. He's torturing me, kissing the inside of my thighs, but not going further. Looking down and seeing his shaggy golden brown hair between my legs knowing what he can do to me is pure torment, my body tense in anticipation.

"Tanner." My voice is a breathy plea.

Sensing my want, he rests his head on my thigh, his stubble teasing my skin, and he looks up at me. His beautiful green eyes make my heart skip a beat, as I run my hand through his tousled hair.

"I've wanted to taste you every fucking minute since the gondola," he says, a wry grin on his face. His words cause me to squirm more, my calves wrapping around his body now, my swollen clit and wet pussy desperate for him. "And knowing this perfect pussy gets this wet for me makes it so much better."

"Then taste me. Please," I whimper. "Do it."

He groans in approval at my permission. His eyes move down between my legs and he licks his lips before his mouth is back on me. He's not the only one that's been craving this moment. I've wanted this since the gondola too, wanting to feel his tongue on me, inside of me.

"Oh. Oh my god." The words barely escape my mouth as I moan, running my fingers through his hair pulling his head towards me.

His tongue lingers on my clit, taunting me, making me want so much more. He sucks my clit with his tongue caressing it before finally running his tongue down to my wet opening, pressing it into me, tasting me.

He opens his mouth wider, groaning against me as he presses his tongue further and further inside me. I grab his hair tighter at the sensation as I close my eyes, my legs still pulling him to me.

"Please, Tanner. Fuck me," I say, desperate to feel more of him inside me again, the teasing from his mouth too much. "I want to feel your cock in me again."

I can feel him groan against my clit, teasing me even more before he stands up.

"I was hoping you'd say that. I want to make your tight little pussy *mine*," he growls at me, making my entire body clench in anticipation.

I feel his arms wrap around me, grabbing my ass, lifting me off the bar stool and bringing me to him. I wrap my legs around him, feeling his hardness through his jeans, my bare skin right against him.

He carries me to the bedroom, lying me down on the edge of the bed. I rest on my elbows, looking at him standing at the foot of the bed, his bare chest heaving with each lustful breath. The desire in his eyes is completely exposed.

"Make me *yours*," I say, curling my finger at him. "Take off those jeans and fuck me."

Without hesitation, he takes them off and is standing there now in nothing but his black boxer briefs, his erection straining against the fabric.

He steps toward me, leaning over me just enough that I can feel it against my wet, aching center. "I like seeing you bossy. It's so god damn sexy."

He grins and starts to pull off my dress, leaving me in just the black bralette, my hard nipples shamelessly showing through.

He leans back over me, kissing my neck, his hands running down the backs of my thighs. He presses himself against me though his boxers, the urge to feel him inside of me is driving me mad. The devilish grin on his face says he knows exactly what he's doing.

"Take them off, Tanner. Now," I demand, my voice in tatters. "I want to feel you. All of you."

"Anything for you, *bossy* girl," he says. With one hand, he slides them off, never taking his eyes off mine. He leans back over me, now sliding his cock through my slickness, teasing me again.

Fuck. The need to feel him is overwhelming.

Sensing my urgency, he notches the tip of his cock at my opening before grabbing my ankles and resting them on his broad shoulders.

I look up at him, his rugged body coiled and ready to ravage me. The fire burning behind his emerald green eyes tells me I'm in for a long night of passion.

And I'm ready for it. I can feel my entire body tingle with anticipation at the thought of spending a whole night with him. No sneaking around. No rushing to finish.

Just us.

Chapter 32

Tanner
For Me

This woman is so fucking hot, so beautiful, it's not even fair. I don't stand a chance of lasting very long. My eyes want to take in every bit of the sight in front of me. It drives me mad how she can look this insanely good. My cock is throbbing in my fist, her ankles on my shoulders.

My mind is spinning and I can't make up my damn mind about what I want to do to her next. There isn't enough time in the world to do everything I want with her. I want all of her. Every single little bit of her.

I want to be in her mouth, feeling her pouty lips wrap around my cock.

I want to be in her tight little pussy, feeling the way it grabs me when she comes on me.

I want to jerk off on her. Fuck, it's taking every ounce of self control I have to not jerk off and come all over her perfect perky tits, even if she's still wearing that little bralette.

No, I want us to savor every last second of this. Slowly, I slide my finger down her flat toned stomach, past her belly button, across her clit, leaving my fingertip right on her opening. My finger is now right next to the head of my cock, torturously teasing both of us. I watch her shudder as I tease her with my finger.

"Please, Tanner. Stop teasing me and fuck me. Now," she demands, her voice wanting. Her eyes show her need, but also her confidence. She knows what she wants and now she's practically demanding it and I fucking love it.

This... this is my Ronni.

She's so wet and ready for me, putting my self control to the test again. My finger dips into her and I bring it to my own lips, savoring her desire as I look into those beautiful hazel eyes. "Mmm. I love that *this* is for me."

She bites her lower lip, pressing them together to hide a smile, nodding at me desperately. I ease myself into her, shuddering at how tightly she grips the head of my cock as she lets out the softest whimper.

"Fuck," I growl, "your little pussy is so god damn good."

I run my hands up and down her legs, the sight of them up on my shoulders practically enough to make me lose control in her.

My next thrust is a little bit deeper, but I'm not ready to totally let go.

Not yet.

No, I want every second of this I can get.

Chapter 33

Veronica
Shattered

I can tell he's holding back. Even his first gentle thrust sends a shockwave through me. The feeling of his thick cock back inside me bringing me so close to an orgasm, my back arching against the bed. His next thrusts are harder and deeper. His hands are on my thighs pulling my body into him each time as he finally buries himself in me to the hilt, his balls slapping against me with each thrust.

"Fuck. You're so fucking deep," I moan, my hands grasping for his ribs to feel his hard body.

"Your pussy takes all of me so fucking well," he says, grinning as he keeps pounding me.

His words drive me mad, the want, the need in them. The way he looks at me stirs something inside me that I feel all the way through my clit and pussy, making me clench around him, only increasing the intense sensation of pleasure. I can feel what's becoming a welcome and familiar sensation start to build in my core, the need to come thanks to this man.

"Please, don't you dare fucking stop," I say locking eyes with him. A glassy look in his eyes starts to take hold.

"I'm not stopping until I leave you shattered on my cock, Ronni," he says, his deep raspy voice pushing me closer and closer.

He leans over me now, bringing his knees on to the bed. He grips my legs behind my knees, pushing them further back, his cock somehow impossibly deeper in me with each push of his hips.

I run my hands over his chest, gripping his chest hair, watching my nails digging into the muscular flesh, desperate to brace myself for the orgasm that I know is about to rock me.

He dips his head down, letting me feel his heavy exhales on my forehead.

"Let go. Come for me," he says, his voice deep but fraying as his breathing quickens. He gets his wish as I feel my body shatter.

Holy shit.

No toys, no fingering my clit, just his hard cock bringing me here, convulsing and melting into his body, pure ecstasy running through every fiber of my being.

Where did this man fucking come from?

Chapter 34

Tanner
Cowgirl

Fuck me. I'm going to fucking lose it. The walls of her dripping wet pussy flutter and grab my cock as she writhes and moans through her orgasm, calling out my name. It's the hottest, most intense thing I've ever felt in my life.

I keep pounding her, but I can feel myself letting go. My vision is starting to blur.

"Come for me, Tanner," she screams, clenching me even tighter inside her, digging her nails into me. "Make me fucking yours."

I let go, making one last deep thrust to the hilt as I can feel myself draining into her. My throbbing, pulsing cock held tightly by her. I can feel her tighten again, as if she wants me to stay buried in her like this forever. I wouldn't mind that. I could just live in this moment. Her hands rest on my back, her nails now just barely digging into me as she softly kisses my neck.

Yep. I could stay here forever.

"God damnit, Ronni," I say, my head turned towards her, kissing her hair, "you're unreal."

I slowly roll off of her, admiring the view of her flush, sweaty body. Her nipples taunting me through the bralette I somehow left on. Our bodies are pressed against each other as we lay on our sides.

"You aren't too shabby yourself," she says, batting her lashes and flashing that intoxicatingly soft smile. Her hazel eyes cut right to my heart.

Fuck, I love this woman. I've always known that, but now it's so real. Something I feel through my entire body.

I run a finger down her cheek, holding her chin between it and my thumb. Her mouth is so sexy. I think about how good it looked wrapped around my dick the other night. I can already feel myself start to get hard again, desperate for more of her.

She hums softly, pressing her thigh against me. "Did you not get enough?" Her voice is now low and sultry.

"I could never get enough of you. Ever." I pull her against me, kissing her forehead.

"Good," she says, pushing me away and onto my back.

Before I realize it, she's on top of me. Grinning down at me with her long brown hair over her shoulders, dangling in front of her breasts.

"It's my turn to make you *mine*," she purrs, grinning as she reaches for her bralette, pulling it over her head and flinging it on the floor.

Fuck me. I'm definitely hard again.

I can feel her dripping wet pussy pressed against my shaft, my own release running down her thigh. But I'm aching just as bad as her. I raise my hips, straining to grind myself against her, hungry to be back inside her.

I look up at her, admiring her perky tits, her pink nipples raised. I run my fingers up to them, cupping them in my hands. She holds her hands over mine for a second before looking at me, her beautiful smile turning mischievous. She grabs my wrists, pushing my hands back down to the pillow on either side of my head, holding them there. Her tits are inches from my face and all I want to do is put them in my mouth.

"Now, now," she tsks playfully, her voice impossibly seductive, "it's my turn to make you lose control."

Jesus Christ. Where did this come from? Nope. I don't even care. I'm fucking into it.

She cranes her neck so she can reach my lips, biting and tugging the lower one. I groan at how much I want her to put my aching dick back in her. She starts to slide her slick, wet slit up and down my shaft. With each rock of her hips, I know she's teasing her clit and it makes me want her so bad.

"Fucking hell, Ronni. I need you so bad, all of you." My voice is broken and I'm barely able to get the words out.

"Tell me what you need," she says, emphasizing each word before she leans down over my face, running her hard nipples over my cheeks, making me shudder. She lets go of my wrists and works down my chest, kissing my abs, before stopping just above my pulsing cock.

Her eyes are on fire, filled with ravenous desire. "I said tell me what you need."

I look down at her, my mouth gaping as I take in the unashamedly sexy, confident woman of my dreams. Literally, the woman of my teenage wet dreams. "You. I need you. I need to be in you." My voice is practically breaking when she takes her eyes off of mine and lowers her mouth onto my cock. She swirls her tongue over the head of my cock before slowly running her mouth down my length, her cheeks hollowing as she sucks me, hard. I nearly fucking shatter, slamming my head back into the pillow.

"Jesus fucking Christ, Ronni." My breathing is labored.

She looks back up at me, my cock slipping from her mouth with a popping sound as she momentarily takes mercy on me, lacing the fingers of her hands through mine as she rises up to straddle me again.

"What Tanner, did you like that?" She looks down at me as she grabs my wrists again, pinning them back behind my head.

She lets go with one hand and raises herself up just enough to grab my cock with her hand, notching my tip just at her dripping wet entrance.

My whole body shakes as I nod, grinning ear to ear.

"Now, I'm gonna ride you until we both come, ok?" she says, giving me the most playful bedroom eyes I could imagine.

"Fuck. Anything for you, good girl," I stammer, pressing my hips into her, desperate to feel her take every inch of me.

She leans forward, running her breasts over my face again as she slowly starts to work her wet pussy down me. With each rock of her hips, she takes more and more of me until she's finally taking all of it. I look down through her tits, between our bodies and watch as she rides up and down on me. It's so fucking hot, watching how she's grinding her clit on my shaft with each stroke, her wetness visible and shining on me.

"I'm... I'm not going to last very long if you keep that up," I say, breathing on her tits right in front of me.

"Good, I'm already so close. You fill me so good, Tanner," she whimpers between panting breaths. She picks up the pace, riding me harder and harder, her tits in my face driving me insane. She's still pinning my hands and I just want to grab those perky tits.

"Put them in your mouth. Tease them. Please, I'm so close. Suck on them. I know you want to," she says, watching my eyes glued to her breasts inches from my face. God damn, this girl is in my head, reading my thoughts.

My tongue grazes her nipples and she moans in approval. And fuck me, I'm losing it. I thrust into her, rocking hard trying to match the rhythm of her hips.

"Yes, fuck me. Pound my little pussy," she demands through gritted teeth.

Her words ruin me. My whole body flinching wildly under her as I come. I keep thrusting though, my cum mixed with her own arousal, dying to watch her let go again.

"I'm yours. You made me yours," I say, my voice tattered into shreds and raspy as fuck. She doesn't know it yet, not fully, but I've always been hers.

I can feel her walls clench around me at my voice, making me shudder again. She's bucking on top of me at a wilder and more frantic pace as she comes.

God damnit. I didn't think she could get hotter but fuck, she's a goddess riding me like this. She's so confident, so relaxed, but still so intense somehow. It feels like my worlds are colliding. It's like watching her let go on the mountain, the way she skis so confidently and relaxed, except now she's letting herself go on me and it's the best thing in the world.

She rides her orgasm out before collapsing onto me, releasing my hands. Both of us are drenched in sweat. I wrap my arms around her, cupping the back of her neck, leaning forward to kiss the top of her head.

"You are just full of surprises," I say.

"Glad you enjoyed that. I guess I have a little cowgirl in me that needed to get out. It's Wyoming after all," she says, raising her head to look up at me.

That's my good girl.

My cowgirl.

My little horny badger.

Chapter 35

Veronica
On the Slopes

Waking up in bed next to Tanner, I can feel the warmth of his body against me. Snuggled into the soft red plaid flannel sheets with him, Rex sleeping at the foot of the bed, it's somehow perfectly familiar and completely foreign all at once. It feels like I've always been here and the rest of my life before now has just been a dream. Like today, I'm waking up where my heart has always been.

I guess this is one way to start a new year.

My eyes linger on Tanner sleeping beside me. He's still bundled up under the covers, his arms crossed under his pillow. Everything about him is so timeless, rugged, and masculine. In this old cabin, it feels like we could be waking up on the Wyoming frontier a century ago.

My gaze wanders to his face. He was already gorgeous but seeing the details of his face now, with his beard nearly gone and mustache trimmed, I could get used to starting my day like this. Laying on my side facing him, I softly run my fingers across his face.

Every day since this man kissed me, my mind has been clear. At ease. Sure, I was a little worried about getting caught by Collin initially, but even that paled in comparison to the pleasure and comfort he brings me.

Yes. I'm definitely in love with Tanner. Fucking. Chapman. Am I crazy for falling this hard for someone this fast?

Maybe? I don't know.

It just feels so right. He's been a part of my life for so long. He just fits in. We're passionate about this place, skiing, and the happiness it brings us. We know each other's families. And now we know we have amazing chemistry together.

As my mind starts trying to imagine what a future with him could look like, my fingers tracing the line of his jaw, his head shifts and he lets out a contented low grunt. His eyes flutter open and a warm smile crosses his face as his green eyes meet mine. He unwinds his hands from under his pillow to cup my cheek, his hand matching mine.

"Am I dreaming? Or are you actually here, waking up with me in my bed?" He leans forward, planting a soft kiss on my lips.

"It sure feels like a dream, but nope, I'm definitely here in your bed," I say, my hands drifting down his side, resting on his hip.

He lets out another contented grunt.

"As much as I like the idea of a morning quickie, I think we're back on the clock, Ronni. Gotta get Collin and Lizzy coffees and some pastries as promised." As he says this, he wraps his leg over my hip, pulling our bodies together. In one quick movement, he's now on top of me, his hands pinning mine above my head, his powerful chest inches from my face.

"Later," his eyes say exactly what he has in mind, the corner of his mouth lifting, as he leans forward to whisper in my ear, "you're mine."

If you only knew Tanner, if you only knew. I'm falling head over heels for you so fast, so hard. I'm already yours.

We get to the condo a bit earlier than expected, coffees and pastries in hand for Collin and Lizzy. I know Collin took it surprisingly well that Tanner and I were together. No, not well, great actually. I hope a night to sleep on it hasn't changed things.

And Lizzy, well her expression gave her feelings away. Can't wait to talk with her about this. I'm sure she has a million questions already and I'm not sure I want to answer all of them.

As we walk into the condo from the mudroom, Collin and Lizzy are nowhere to be seen. Glad to see they're back to their usual selves, sleeping in after a night out.

"Tanner, can you go ahead and set out breakfast? I'll go get them up," I say, turning up towards the bedrooms from the landing.

As I turn, I run into an unexpected object.

No. Not an object.

A... a fucking cowboy?!

I take a step back to see the cowboy from the Silver Dollar Cowboy Bar the night before, hat in hand, walking out of Lizzy's room.

Fuck. She really did it. She bagged her cowboy!

"Pardon me, ma'am," he says with a thick draw as he heads toward the mudroom on his way out, nodding at Tanner.

Well I guess Lizzy must be up. Might as well start there. As I walk towards the main bedroom, Lizzy is coming out of the door and starting to close it. When she turns and faces me, her expression is unusually startled. I mean, I did just catch her cowboy on a walk of shame so I guess that checks out.

I smile, already wanting to hear all about how she pulled that off. As I reach the landing, I hear Collin's voice from inside the room.

"Hey, Lizzy, did he make it o-," he says, emerging from the bedroom behind Lizzy, freezing in place as he sees me in the hall. His eyes go wide and the color drains from his face.

"Uhh… morning, lil sis," he says, swallowing a lump in his throat.

Wait. What. The. Fuck. Did they…?

No. There's no fucking way!

"Guys. Seriously," my voice is loud and shocked, "what in the actual fuck?"

Tanner hears me from the kitchen and makes his way to us, stopping just short of the landing but still able to see the bedroom door.

"What's wrong?" he asks as he reaches me, stopping as he sees the scene in front of us. He pauses, eyeing them carefully. "Wait a second, did they?" He gestures between Collin and Lizzy with a smirk.

Lizzy is the first to address the elephant, well cowboy, in the room.

"Ugh. Oh my god you guys. Collin and I didn't fuck. We just shared the cowboy, ok?" she says as if their *whatever* was some trivial matter that didn't warrant acknowledgment or shock.

"Yeah. I mean… I guess it was more of a cowboy sandwich. We didn't touch ea-," Collin starts, before I cut him off.

"Nope. Nope. Nope," I say, extending a hand toward them, making a stop motion with my hand. "I haven't even finished my coffee yet. Just get dressed and come to the dining room."

I look back to Tanner who is trying his best to not burst into laughter, holding it in for my sake.

A few minutes later, Collin and then Lizzy join Tanner and me at the table in awkward silence, grabbing their coffees and a pastry.

"You guys have a good night ringing in the new year? Any fireworks?" Collin asks, winking before taking a bite of his croissant.

"Yeah, it was nice. Got to bed early," Tanner starts. "I'd ask about yours but-" he trails off, finally unable to contain his laughter. "Dude, this has to be at the top of your list of shenanigans and I wasn't even involved," he continues between his booming laughs. "But cowboys aren't really my thing. Now *cowgirls* on the other hand…" Tanner looks back at me and winks.

I roll my eyes at Tanner, his laughter stopping when he senses my lack of amusement. I mean… he's right though. I never would have thought that they would be just as wild of a duo as Collin and Tanner.

"I mean," I start, "just like… how?"

"Oh, don't be so surprised, V," Lizzy says defiantly. "I got his number at the bar and he texted me right after you two left us. He asked what we were up to the rest of the night."

She cocks her head to the side, shrugging.

"Yolo, I guess," she continues, before taking a bite of her chocolate croissant.

I palm my face, finally letting out a laugh I've been holding back. I can hear Collin and Lizzy exhale at my reaction, the tension in the room taken down a notch.

"Well, I don't know about you guys but I'm ready for the first chair of the new year. So can you two get ready and moving?" Tanner asks, eyeing Collin and Lizzy, still shaking his head and laughing.

Fortunately, the rest of the day is far less dramatic. After the morning's *happenings*, we get out on the slopes. As expected, the place feels empty, all the tourists and even locals sleeping in after a hard night of partying. I always love skiing the day of a holiday or after for this reason. It feels like we have the mountain entirely to ourselves, or at least until people sleep off their hangovers and come out later in the day.

After a couple mellow warm up runs, I realize I have a shadow today. I don't know if I'm skiing harder and faster or if Tanner is skiing slower, but he's been lagging behind me.

We all reach the next chair, Tanner and Collin sitting on the outside seats with Lizzy and I between them. As the lift takes us back up the mountain, I give Tanner a playful punch on the thigh with my mitten.

"So what's up, slow poke? You taking it easy today or am I actually kicking your ass?" I ask, trying to gauge his reaction through our goggles.

He snorts a laugh, "Nope, just decided I want to enjoy the view and watch my *girlfriend* shred a few runs."

Girlfriend. There's something about hearing that word from him, on the slopes here, that makes my heart melt and my body warm. I know we started this without labels, but it just feels so good now to be out in the open and acknowledge the feelings are clearly mutual.

"Bro, tone it down like two notches," Collin says from the far end of the chair, before letting out a laugh.

"Awww, you two are so cute," Lizzy says, with a mocking tone.

Ugh. I've had enough of the threesome buddies already today. Like they have room to judge after *their* night.

I place my hand on Tanner's thigh, resting my head on his shoulder. Even with heavy ski mittens and a helmet on, it feels good to be close to him. Nope, not even Collin and Lizzy's teasing can ruin this.

"So, what's next y'all?" Tanner asks. "You feel up for some tree runs? I was thinking we could head over to Grizzly Glade."

"That sounds perfect," I say before Collin and Lizzy can even respond. "Great thinking, *boyfriend*."

I watch Tanner closely, watching his mouth open wide as a completely unrestrained smile grows across his face, his dimples on display just under his goggles. His boyish excitement is unable to be contained.

"Ugh for fuck's sake, get a room you two," Lizzy scoffs.

I begrudgingly take my eyes off Tanner to look back her way, sticking my tongue out at her.

A few moments later, we hop off the chair and make our way over to Grizzly Glade. It's one of my favorite tree skiing areas on the mountain, a steep wide pitch littered with dense trees, boulders, and the occasional short cliff. It's challenging, but always fun. It does warrant skiing with a buddy close by though with the hazards present.

Even with the light snow from the night before, this area seemingly holds fresh fluffy snow from prior storms for days. I lead the way down the slope, darting between trees, avoiding rocks. I peak over my shoulder and can see the puffs of snow kicked into the air, meaning Tanner isn't too far behind.

As I make my way down, I'm caught off guard by an unexpectedly large mogul and I'm bucked up off the ground. I land awkwardly, taking a quick tumble and end up on my back. I'm momentarily disoriented, but I think I'm fine. I did fall hard enough that my skis came off and are on either side of me in the snow.

"Ronni!" Tanner yells from behind, his deep voice cutting through the trees. He's at my side in seconds, popping off his skis and getting down on his knees. He takes off his goggles, a frantic worried expression on his face. I pull my googles up to rest on the brim of my helmet, looking back at him.

"I'm fine, Tanner. I just got a little off balance," I say, reading his expression. There's a look of pure terror in his eyes. I prop myself up on my elbow, touching his face with my gloved hand.

"Tanner," I say softly, "I'm fine, really. Just help me up?"

I can see him finally exhale, his fears at ease. He lifts me up in his arms and I'm back on my feet.

"Sorry, I just…" he says, lowering his eyes, still breathing heavily. The way this man cares about me is heart meltingly palpable. I still can't fathom how he hid this for so long. Was I really so blind? And now that he's able to show it, wearing it all on his sleeve, I feel loved in a way I didn't think was possible.

"I know, Tanner." I place my hand back on his face, our eyes meeting.

"I love you," I whisper. The words shock me but they've never felt so right before. I lean forward to kiss him, my mouth open just enough to feel the heat of his breath on my lips. My hand is on his chest and he pulls back just enough to look down at me, his beautiful green eyes feel like they are looking deep into my soul.

"I love you too, Ronni," he whispers in his deep raspy voice. "I love you so fucking much."

He leans back towards me, our mouths meeting. This time I can feel the hunger in him, his mouth open and his tongue teasing mine. It's like decades of passion that's been brewing in him is flooding out, unleashed by the words he's wanted to hear and say for so long.

"Oh come on already," a familiar voice echoes through the woods from behind us. "Guys, I love you both, but seriously, baby steps here. Ease me into this a bit more."

We look back to see Collin and Lizzy further up the run, on top of a rocky outcropping, shaking their heads as they literally look down at us.

"I said get a room guys, not go hide in the woods!" Lizzy adds.

"You two really have a lot of room to talk right now," I shout, still holding Tanner.

The rest of the day goes on like this, openly enjoying being with Tanner, trading playful jabs with Collin and Lizzy. I feel like I'm living in a dream, a happy bubble.

When we're ready to head in for lunch, I end up with Lizzy on Marmot, the two person chair.

"Ok, first things first," I say as the old chair slowly takes us up towards the lodge, "I want zero details of *your* night with *my brother.* Zero. Got it?"

I look to her, she huffs crossing her arms.

"Fine, V," she says frowning, "can we at least talk about *you* then? I've gotten zero details since I found out about you and Tanner, freaking mountain man, Chapman last night. I'm dying for some girl talk here!"

"I guess that's fine," I say, feeling my cheeks flush. This is the first time I've talked about Tanner with anyone. It makes it all feel... so real.

"So, what's that mountain man like? Is *it* as big as the rest of him? Has he been giving you mind blowing orgasms every chance he gets?" Damn, Lizzy. You went right for it. This girl does not mess around.

"What makes you think I've even seen his dick?" I challenge.

"You expect me to believe you've been glowing this much and slept over at his house last night and not dipped your hand into the mountain man cookie jar?" she asks, eyebrows raised. "Because that's the only thing I can think of when *Miss I don't have time to date and I don't do one night stands* is now walking around calling this ski bro her *boyfriend*."

"Ok. That's fair. But first, he's not just some ski bro. And second, it's... proportional," I say, grinning wildly, "and he knows how to use it in all the right ways."

"Jesus," she mutters under her breath, "no wonder you've been so giddy the last few days."

She shimmies her shoulders. "So when was the first time you two fucked?" Ugh. Lizzy. Always direct.

"Remember when you and Collin couldn't get on the gondola in time and we rode separately?" I ask, biting my lower lip at the memory, practically feeling him between my legs again.

"Ugh. Don't turn this back on me," she pouts, before something clicks in her brain and her jaw drops. "Wait! Oh my god! Did you guys seriously fuck on the gondola?" she asks incredulously.

"Oh, god no! That would have been fucking crazy," I say, grabbing the bar on the chairlift. "But he went down on me and got me off just before the gondola ride ended. Like literal seconds before we met you two for lunch. Before he started, he said, and I quote, he wanted me t*o relax and enjoy my vacation.*"

Even through her goggles, I can sense the stunned look in her eyes matching her dropped jaw. "That's *fucking hot.* Like hotter than any of my book boyfriends. Or real life boyfriends for that matter. He sounds like a fucking keeper, V."

"I… I know." Admitting it out loud makes this all feel so real.

I spend the next few minutes filling her in on the rest of the sordid details. Last night after the bar, in front of the fireplace while they made the ice cream run, the mudroom kiss, the mudroom *again*, TJ's guesthouse. Ok. Wow. We have been busy

I think she might be actually impressed at just how much we were sneaking around and managed to squeeze in this past week.

"Damn," she says, letting out a sigh, "I think I like Horny Veronica. This is the happiest I've seen you in ages. But you're already calling him your boyfriend after just days. So is this, like, *serious*?"

My body tenses just a bit at the question. But I know in my heart the answer is yes. Although Tanner and I haven't openly talked about all the details that much, we know we've never felt this way before.

Do we love each other? Yes, as crazy as that sounds right now. Is there incredible chemistry? Um, hell yes. I think we'd do anything to make this work, but what would that even look like? Moving to Jackson, him going to Dayton, Ohio, or something else? I can't see this man living in Ohio, away from the mountains that are practically a part of his soul. And he'd be even further from his family.

Oddly, the thoughts and uncertainty don't make me anxious, just hopeful. It's like with him, I don't have to plan out every little detail. I can just trust him to be there for me and make me feel like everything will be ok. It finally feels like there's a light at the end of the miserable tunnel I've been stuck in for years. I know what's coming is bright, I just don't know what it is or how I'll get there.

"I'm going to take your silence as a yes. I can see your wheels turning, like you're clearly planning out all the scenarios to make this work." She knows me so well. "Love you, girl. I'm happy for you. You guys will figure it out," she continues, resting her hand on my knee. "So, does he have any brothers?"

I cackle at her question and how she can always pivot her tone on the fly. "Actually, he does have a younger brother, Clay. Definitely not your type though."

The lift is finally reaching the top and it's almost time to get lunch. But I keep going back to what she said.

He's a keeper.

Yes, he is. And now that he's all mine, I'm determined to figure out how to keep it that way.

Chapter 36

Tanner
Deep Breath

God damnit. Why am I sweating? Why am I this nervous? I've gone off cliffs on skis. I've bungee jumped. I've launched myself off bridges into rivers. Fuck, I finally made the leap and went after Ronni. Why am I this scared?

The last few days have been a blur, a smoking hot one, but a blur for sure. Ronni stayed over at my place again last night before spending the day in town with Collin and Lizzy, shopping again and taking a break from the slopes.

Probably my own fault, but I'm exhausted. I think we stayed up until 3:00 AM last night fucking again and again. Sex with her is otherworldly. The way she makes my body feel, the way she reads my mind and brings me over the edge, it's all so hot, so incredible. I think I could just spend the rest of my life like that, never leaving the cabin, just getting delivery for Gatorade and carryout.

It's probably not the worst thing that I got a few hours away from her today though. I finally took a nap and let my brain and dick recharge and got some work done.

I'm sure she enjoyed the day in town with her brother and Lizzy. I sort of feel bad that she's been spending so much of her time with me when Lizzy came out for a girls trip, but whatever. I can be selfish for once and I think Lizzy is actually ok with it, seeing how happy her best friend is for a change. Besides, they get to see each other every day in Ohio. And Collin and Lizzy have clearly bonded. I still can't get over that they not only found a cowboy, but one that goes both ways at that. Talking about finding a needle in a Wyoming haystack.

So now I'm standing at the door of their condo, a bouquet in my trembling fist. I can't remember a time I've been this terrified. I can practically hear my knees rattling.

Ok, Tanner. Take a deep breath. You're just picking up your *girlfriend* for our first real date. Mom would've killed me if I didn't bring flowers like a gentleman.

I knock on the door, waiting for what feels like an eternity for it to open.

"Oh shit. I'm never gonna let you live this down." Fuck me. I'm greeted by Collin's ever familiar laugh.

"Hey *lil sis*, your boyfriend's here for your first date!" He cackles, back into the condo.

I roll my eyes at him, "Did you really have to do that?"

"Yes. Yes, I did," he snorts as he pulls me into the mudroom, giving me a brotherly punch on the shoulder. "Now, come on in. She'll be down in a minute."

I've been in this condo hundreds, if not thousands of times over the years. But it feels so weird today as I sit in the dining room waiting on Ronni. It's Friday now, so it's been a few days since Collin and Lizzy found out about us.

I trimmed my hair and stubble up again. I'm wearing the same outfit as New Year's Eve. I'm cleaned up about as well as I know how. But I'm scared, excited too, but still scared.

Going on my first real date with Ronni. One on one, no hiding, no sneaking around. It's everything I've ever wanted but this still makes it feel so real and so fragile. I don't know what's next. I don't know how we'll make this work, but I know I'll do anything for her.

All of my thoughts are out the window when I see her come down to the dining room. She's got her hair back in some kind of double braid, her smile on full display. She's beaming. My heart and stomach clench. I can feel my dick twitch while my eyes drop down to her outfit. She's wearing a little black cocktail dress I've never seen her in before. I don't know if it's hers or Lizzy's but it fucking hits in all the right places, like it was made for her. The low neckline showing the perfect hint of her breasts. It's short and shows off her long legs, making me want to skip the date entirely and take her straight to my bed.

Our eyes meet and I feel my whole body relax finally.

"So where are you two lovebirds off to tonight?" Lizzy taunts us, barging in on the moment from the landing behind Ronni.

"It's a surprise. My favorite place downtown," I answer, my eyes never leaving Ronni's direction. Damn, I could look at her all day and never get tired of it.

Collin wraps his arm around my shoulder.

"Well, have fun you two. Don't do anything I wouldn't do," he says with a wink.

I walk over to Ronni, giving her a long, breathy kiss before grabbing her hand to walk out.

"Sure thing. So, no cowboys. Got it," I quip, pointing fingers back at Lizzy and Collin in the shape of a finger pistol, winking as we close the mudroom door behind us. I look at Ronni. "Are you sure we can even leave them unsupervised?"

Ronni rolls her eyes, laughing while she grabs her tote bag from the mudroom. We head out and hop in our Uber to downtown.

"Finally," she says, exhaling a deep breath before looking at me. "They've been teasing me all day."

I chuckle a bit, holding her hand.

"You look amazing by the way. I almost thought of taking you straight back to the cabin, but figured you might be hungry for actual food. So, are you excited?" I look into her hazel eyes, still feeling like none of this is real. How did I get this lucky?

"Yes, very excited," she says, giving me a kiss on the cheek, "but I'd be more excited if you would have told me where we were going so I could have looked at the menu."

"Hmmm. What did I ask you before? Do you trust me?"

She huffs, crossing her arms.

"Ugh. You know I do. But this is food, Tanner!"

"Well, you're just going to have to keep trusting me and go along for the ride I guess," I say, nudging her with my shoulder and smirking.

I wrap my arm around her, bringing her closer. She rests her head on my shoulder, grabbing my other hand lacing her fingers through mine.

I feel a buzz rumble between us, three quick pulses, interrupting the moment. Ronni nervously looks down at her clutch, resting between our legs on the seat of the Uber.

"Do you need to get that?" I ask with a chuckle.

She sighs and I can feel her shoulders tense. "I should. That's the alert I have for Jeff, my boss. If he's messaging or emailing me this late, it's probably something important."

I run the backs of my fingers over her cheek, tucking a stray strand of hair behind her ear. "It's fine if you need to. I just don't want that to ruin your night. I hate seeing the way you tense up when work is bothering you."

The corner of her mouth pulls into a half-hearted smile. The way I can tell she's upset about it, worrying about whatever her boss wants, kills me. They don't deserve to have someone like her working there if this is how they make her feel. I can feel my jaw tense and teeth grind at the thought of her feeling like that, all the time, back in Ohio.

"It's alright, Tanner. I'll check this one, but then my phone is off the rest of the night. I want to be here with you," she says, that half hearted smile growing into the soft, sweet one that I love.

"Works for me. Because I want to be here with you too, all of you," I say. After checking her phone, she leans her head back against my shoulder and I can feel both of us relax.

"I love you, Tanner," she whispers, "I've been looking forward to this all day."

"I love you too," I say, kissing the top of her head. She smells like her freshly shampooed hair, and I want to stay in this moment forever.

She watches our fingers and I can tell by the way she runs her thumb over the back of my hand something is on her mind.

"Ok, Ronni," I ask. "What's up?"

She looks back up at me, grinning ear to ear.

"Oh, nothing. Just wanted you to know you're not the only one with a surprise planned tonight," she says, still grinning devilishly.

"Oh really? Now, I'm curious."

"Too bad. You're going to have to wait. *Trust me.*" The look on her face both tortures and excites the shit out of me.

"Well played," I tease.

Damn it. What does she have planned?

Chapter 37

Veronica
Gloria's

Seeing Tanner this nervous for a date is somehow adorable and sexy all at once. I can tell how long he's dreamt of moments like this and the more they happen, the more I feel like I'm seeing parts of Tanner I never knew existed.

Were they always there and I just missed them?

Sure, the confident yet calm, brash boy, my brother's best friend, is still there. But under all of that there's a thoughtfulness to him, a compassionate side that I've never seen before. The way he remembers little details about me, the way he learns something new that I like or dislike and internalizes it, like it's a law he needs to live by to make me happy. It's so heartwarming, so genuine. The Tanner I always thought of as impulsive and reckless also relishes in planning surprises, going so far out of his way to find things to make me happy, wanting nothing in return, just my smile.

In the back of the Uber, I keep finding myself thinking that I want more. I want more of all of this, more time with him.

"Tanner, would you ever want to ski somewhere else? Like not Jackson Hole?" When I look at him, he's giving me a puzzled look as his lips press together in a sheepish smile.

"Why Ronni, Jackson Hole too easy for you now? Or don't tell me Lizzy got to you and you want to go somewhere fancy like Aspen Valley?" His confident, almost cocky tone is back.

"No, not that. I'm just thinking that it could be fun. Go somewhere new, challenge ourselves a bit. I think it'd be cool to do some exploring, together." I hold his hand tightly as I say *together*. I think I'd say yes to about anything now if it meant that we'd be together. "And who knows, maybe get me out of my comfort zone a little. Go snow storm chasing in your van."

His smile widens as his eyes study my expression before he finally answers me.

"I'd go anywhere with you, Ronni. But if you want to ski somewhere new, I'd love to go check out Alta and Snowbird in Utah. I've never been and I've heard their steeps are every bit as gnarly as here. And we could visit Grace and Clay. I know they'd love to see you." I can see a familiar expression on his face, the one I've seen so many times over the years. The one of excitement he gets when he's about to jump off a cliff or plan some crazy new challenge. "You're right. We could even take the van down with Rex. Tailgate at the mountain for breakfast. It'd be awesome."

A few minutes later, the Uber drops us off on a side street a few blocks away from the town square. Tanner walks us to a quaint little old house, covered in snow with white string lights sparkling along the roof line. Painted on the glass of the front door in gold outlined black letters is a name, *Gloria's*.

"Can you just tell me what kind of food it is already, please?" I look at Tanner, holding my hands together, pleading.

"Nope," he smirks, shrugging his shoulders, "still gotta trust me."

"Fine," I huff, crossing my arms, doing my best impersonation of Lizzy, "but if I don't like it, no surprise for you later."

That gets an eyebrow raise out of him, even a momentary look of panic. See, I can play your game too, Tanner.

As we step into the restaurant, the hostess greets Tanner, while she checks the reservation list. She grabs his shoulder and lets her hand linger there for what seems like a few seconds too many. Clearly, he's been here before if it's his favorite restaurant and it seems like she knows him.

"So what's the occasion?" she asks, eyeing me dismissively.

As if he could sense my annoyance with her, he wraps his arm around my waist, his fingers tracing the top of my ass. He leans over to kiss me on top of my head, his other hand running the back of a finger across my cheek as his eyes hold my gaze longingly. All of it a display meant to show her that he's mine and I love every second of it.

"Date night with my girlfriend," he says, not bothering to look back at the hostess.

"Oh," she says, a brief flush in her cheeks, "well, let's get you to your table. I see the chef made a note to give you his favorite table right in the window."

"Thank you for that," I whisper, looking up at him as she leads us to the table.

"Any time, horny badger," he says smirking. Fine, he can call me that any time as long as he keeps looking at me like that.

We sit down and finally I get to see the menu. And shit, it's perfect.

All Italian, all seasonal dishes with local ingredients. Pasta courses, meat courses, salad courses, all of it sounds amazing. I'm practically drooling over the menu. I put it down for a second to look at him, a familiar smug and confident look on his face.

"I take it you like the menu," he says, one eyebrow raised as the flickering light of the candle on the table casts dancing shadows over his tattooed knuckles. He slowly runs his callused fingertip over the rim of the water glass, making it sing. Somehow even that's sexy with him. Is there anything he can't do with his strong rugged hands?

"It's perfect. I just don't know how to pick what I want," I say with a short laugh.

"Well, I come and hang at the bar fairly often. So I've tried most of the dishes. Let's just get a bunch of the ones you want to try, share it all, and take the rest back for leftovers."

Looking across the table, I can't help but think how I've been missing out on him, on this, for so long. It's like he's the last piece of the puzzle I've been trying so hard to finish but couldn't find, only to realize I've been holding it in my hand the entire time.

Our waiter comes for our order, another local that clearly knows Tanner.

"Hey Chap, how you doing? Find any killer stashes lately?" He looks at me, a hint of amusement and a small nod of approval to Tanner. I'll take it. Better than the looks I got from the hostess.

"Been good, Bodi. Enjoying the week with my girl here," he says, smiling wholeheartedly at me, his own words making the smile genuine. "Found some good lines in Grizzly and Alta Zero the last week or so. Dying to get into the backcountry soon though."

Something is off with his tone, though. Two weeks ago, I would have thought nothing of it. But the more he opens up to me, I know what it is now. It's this little bit of pain, like he's so used to putting on a facade to the people around him. Talking so casually and confidently about big bold feats was his way to hide and bury his feelings, his depression about being alone, to make everyone think he's fine.

I reach across the table, holding his hand in mine. I want to tell him everything will be ok, that he doesn't have to do that anymore. I want him to know he can always open up to me.

It's a whirlwind of dish after dish. Beautiful handmade pastas, grilled and sautéed vegetable sides, locally raised beef, elk, and fresh caught trout from the Snake River. Each course coming with a new wine pairing. By the end of dinner, we're full and I'm probably a bit on the tipsy side. I think even Tanner is, his deep laugh more relaxed and infectious than ever.

It's a good thing we took an Uber. As much as I normally don't like getting dressed up for a fancy night out and dealing with rides, I was right in trusting Tanner. It's going to be worth it tonight after this dinner.

I think about how right now I have everything I want, but my thoughts start to creep back to my talk with Lizzy the other day on the chairlift. She was so confident that we'll make this work, but how? I can't imagine a world where I could ask him to leave this place, where he was born and raised, where he's so at ease and has access to everything he wants, *except me*. But I know if I did ask, he would jump and say yes, without hesitation. It just doesn't seem fair to ask that of him.

I see the look in his eyes change, as if he could feel my own thoughts drifting away from this moment.

"Hey," his voice is low and direct, "do you want to get out of here? The night's still young. We can go back to the cabin, just enjoy the time alone."

I see the corner of his mouth attempt to raise, trying to get my mind off of my prior train of thought.

"Can we at least see the dessert menu? Maybe get one to go? If it's as good as everything else, I'd kick myself for skipping it," I say, making puppy dog eyes at him, resting my chin on my hands, trying to say everything is fine.

His smile is back, sensing my change in mood, and he lets out a puff of laughter.

"Sure, Ronni," he says. "Anything you want."

He pauses for a moment, the corner of his mouth lifting into that sly look that I've learned means he thinks he knows something I don't.

"Ok. I know that look. Out with it." I demand.

A quiet chuckle escapes his mouth. "You know, if you like this menu so much, I can get you the recipes for anything on it."

There's a hint of amusement in his voice, like he enjoys taking his time, teasing me to get to the point. But I'm curious. I loved everything we had tonight and my culinary curiosity is piqued by the thought of trying to make these dishes at home.

"Why would they share them with you?" I look at him, raising an eyebrow, feigning mock skepticism.

He tilts his chin towards the open kitchen. "Look closely at the back wall, above the prep counter."

I look over to the kitchen across the restaurant. The back wall of the kitchen is floor to ceiling white subway tiles with black grout. Featured prominently above the counter is a long magnetic knife holder, with about a dozen or so knives of different styles. Chef's knives, slicers, cleavers, santokus. Even from here though I notice that they're all Damascus steel blades.

I look back to Tanner. He's still smirking, a dimple on one side peeking through his light stubble. "The chef got his first one from the Eclectic Elk and asked Giselle how to get more custom ones. Ever since then, I've been making whatever he wants. So I'm pretty sure I could get you a recipe or two."

I can't help but shake my head. "You just keep surprising me."

After dessert, which was totally worth it, I need all of my will power not to fall asleep on the ride back. I'm exhausted, but still eager to get to the cabin and enjoy every minute I can with Tanner.

Back at the cabin, we let Rex out. Tanner tosses the ball for him while we stand by the door, talking about our favorite dishes from dinner and which ones I think I could make on my own. I remember when my grandparents had a dog and I forgot how soothing and calming it can be to play with them. All of this with him just feels so natural. I could definitely get used to this nightly routine.

Finally we go back inside and curl up on the couch, watching the weather report to see what the ski day tomorrow has in store. We're meeting Collin and Lizzy for the normal morning routine, but then they're coming back here for dinner. I was planning to cook but Tanner insists on helping. And truthfully, I'm excited. I never get to cook with anyone, much less the man of my dreams.

Watching the local news, I rest my head on Tanner's shoulder. Although Tanner smiles every time I look up at him, something is still off. The normal intense look in his green eyes dulled ever so slightly.

"Ok," I say, rubbing the back of his hand with my thumbs. "What's up? You've been too quiet since we've been back here."

I can feel his body tense as he holds his breath. Clearly, I was right. It blows my mind how I can read him so well now. It's like ever since I realized he has such strong feelings for me, every other little thing about him clicked into place and makes sense now. He leans over, resting his head on top of mine. He sighs and his body relaxes.

"I'm worried about what's next for us." he starts. "This last week has been the best time of my life. I don't want to ever lose this feeling, to lose you."

My heart stops. I should have been prepared for this, I knew it was coming too. But it still stings to hear it, to think about it.

"Tanner," I say, tilting his face up to look at me, "I love you. I don't know what's next either. But I know this is real and I know we have time. We've got another week before I leave. Let's just keep enjoying this."

"I know," he starts, looking like he's swallowing a lump in his throat. "I'm just so afraid of feeling like I used to. Alone."

The knot in my stomach hurts just thinking about him feeling like that again. He's right. We should talk about this.

"Hey," I say, grabbing his hand. "You're right. Let's talk. We don't have to figure this all out right now, tonight, but let's start. I get five weeks of vacation a year, plus holidays. I'm already going to Aspen Valley next month with Lizzy and then I'm coming out here again in early March for a long weekend ski trip."

My mind is momentarily back in planning mode, running through every scenario to be with him in the near future.

"You could come down to Utah when I'm there next month for a few days and then I'll stretch out the March trip, work remote a few days, and take an extra day off. That'll get me a week and a half out here, *with you.* I promise I will use all my time off to get out here and spend as much time with you as I can. I'll work remote and stretch out holidays. I know it's not a lot, but it's a start until we can figure out a better long term plan. I just want you to know I'm serious about this. I know we can do anything if we work together. I'm serious Tanner, I love you. Just please, trust me."

I can feel him exhale deeply at my last words. *Trust me.* I think if anything, the idea of trusting me puts him at ease, the same way trusting him puts me at ease. I can see the hard lines of his face soften. He cups my cheek, kissing me on the forehead.

"Thanks. That sounds perfect. I love you too and I do trust you," he says, pressing our foreheads together. "I promise I'll always fight for this. I'm just sorry it took me so long to tell you how I felt."

"You never have to apologize, Tanner. I'm just finally glad you shot your shot and told me how you feel," I say, leaping to my feet now that he's finally relaxed again. "Now, as much as I like hanging with you on the couch, I'm going to get into my PJs. I'll be right back."

I kiss him before running back to the bedroom to change, Rex on my heels following me.

Looking in the mirror, I do a little twirl, I think even I agree that it's pretty hot. I can't believe I packed one of these.

Here goes nothing.

"Oh Tanner," I call from the bedroom door. "Ready for your surprise?"

He looks away from the TV towards me, his face practically going white as his jaw drops. He looks like he's seen a ghost.

"Fuck," he murmurs. "That's… a surprise alright."

I slowly saunter towards him, wearing low cut flannel pajama shorts riding just under my hip bones. But he's not looking there. He's looking at the hint of my breasts showing from underneath my Teal Tigers crop top. His expression changes as I get closer, his eyes filling with the most intense look of desire.

"Where did you get that? How?" His expression is still stunned, but the hunger in his eyes is intense as his teeth tug on his lower lip.

"It's not the same one, but I've always liked sleeping in these shirts. I've had them for years and they're so worn and soft,' I say, climbing onto his lap and draping my arms around his neck. "But I cropped this one, just for you."

His eyes run up and down me, savoring every bit of my body. I swear, I don't think I could ever get tired of being looked at like this by him. So much desire, so much longing.

"You're something, Ronni," he says, before leaning forward to kiss me, his fingertips tracing my skin just under my breasts, as if he wants to tease himself a bit longer.

To my surprise, he brings us both down onto the couch, now spooning me. He props his head up behind mine on his hand. His other hand cupping my breast under my crop top, my hard bud pressing into his callused palm. His finger tips run slowly over the skin of my other breast. I can feel that he's hard against my ass, but he's not acting on it.

I almost feel let down that he's not furiously trying to undress me and fuck me. That is until I feel his chest relax as he exhales, starting to say something behind me.

"You know, I've wanted *everything* with you, Ronni. Sleeping with you, dates with you, kissing, all of it. But with all the nights I've spent alone on this couch, I haven't dreamt of anything more than spending a night out with you and falling asleep here with you in my arms."

God damnit. Even when he's trying to be sweet and gentle, it's almost too much. Just when I think I can't love him more, he does something like this, so wholesome. My heart feels like it's going to explode.

I can feel a tear starting to form in one of my eyes before he leans forward, his lips gently leaving a kiss on the top of my head.

"I love you, Ronni," he says soft but low. "Thank you for the surprise. It's perfect, just like you."

Chapter 38

Veronica
Grandma's Boy

I guess it's my turn to be nervous about seeing someone I've known my whole life. Ugh. Well played, Tanner. I now know exactly how he felt. Why is it so different tonight? It's just Sunday dinner with the Chapmans.

I finish getting ready with Lizzy at our condo, trying to look nice but not over do it for a Sunday family dinner with my boyfriend's grandparents. Geez. That still feels weird to say, but in a good way. Like what's even the right level of looking good for this?

"Damn," Lizzy says, shaking her head, one side of her mouth pulled tight and up. "Haven't you known these people since you were like… old enough to walk? I thought they already love you guys like their own kids?"

I glare at her while she's sharing the vanity with me, fixing her own hair. Lizzy has been oddly optimistic and supportive of me being with Tanner. Even last night, the four of us had dinner at Tanner's cabin and she joked about how I already looked at home in his kitchen making dinner. She even told me how she could picture me living with him out here. I mean that sounds amazing, but hold your horses cowgirl.

"Yes, but I was also never dating their oldest, ok let's be real, favorite, grandson before."

She rests a hand on my shoulder. "It's going to be fine, V. If anything, they'll be thrilled about how happy you both are."

It's funny, I've walked up the stairs outside of our condo to the Chapman's unit hundreds of times. But today it just feels different, heading up with Collin and Lizzy to my *boyfriend's* family's place for dinner.

Before I can knock on the door, Grandma Chapman pulls it open.

"Oh my goodness," her sweet voice practically sings. "Come here, Veronica. It's been too long."

In an instant I'm sucked into a deep hug that feels like home, like my own Grandma's, before I can even react. God, do all the Chapmans give the biggest, most heartwarming bear hugs like this? Shit. Maybe Tanner really could take down Little Bitch Bear.

"It's good to see you too, Nan," I say, patting her back. "It has been way too long."

"Come on in everyone," she says, waving Collin and Lizzy into their unit, still holding me in her arms for what feels like an eternal hug. "Tanner's at the table with Samuel. Dinner is almost ready."

"Oh girl, she *really* loves you now." I look back at Collin, rolling my eyes at the smug look on his face. He's enjoying all of this way too much.

"Jealous you're not the favorite Perry twin anymore, *big bro*?" I taunt, sticking my tongue out at him.

He pulls a hand to his chest, mocking me with a fake gasp. "I don't even think dating Tanner would put you up above me, *lil sis*."

Reaching the table, I see Tanner sitting with his Grandpa.

His Grandpa is gesturing with his hand like he's swinging a hammer and I think I hear Tanner mention the horse barn. I assume they're talking about his workshop and blacksmithing, but they stop talking as soon as we get near the table.

Tanner is wearing that familiar heart melting smile as I walk towards him. He stands up, wrapping his arms around my waist, giving me a kiss on the forehead.

"Hey Ronni," he says, his voice low.

"Oh aren't they just the cutest thing you've ever seen?" We look over to Grandma Chapman, now standing behind her husband, clutching his shoulders as they both watch us.

I can feel my face turn bright red, still not used to everyone I know looking at us as a couple. I turn to Tanner for some reassurance, only to see the unflappable man I'm in love with blushing like a little boy. I feel the edges of my lips curl up as our eyes meet, knowing I'm not in this awkwardness alone.

"Your grandparents would just be so tickled if they were here to see you like this." Grandma Chapman is still looking at us, holding her husband tighter. I feel a lump in my throat at the thought of our grandparents and how much I miss them. But she's right, they would have been thrilled about this and that brings a smile to my face.

"Oh Nancy. Go easy on them," Grandpa Chapman says, his voice deep and eerily similar to Tanner's. "Now go ahead and grab a seat, kids. She'll have dinner out soon." I look at him differently now though, seeing the same square jaw, deep green eyes, and masculine features as Tanner. I find myself thinking that if Tanner ages like that… lucky me.

Woah. I'm thinking about *a future* with Tanner. That's new, but it's not even scary.

"Nan, that chicken pot pie smells as good as ever. V is a good cook, but I've been craving your cooking since Christmas," Collin says, sitting at the far end of the table, since his usual spot next to Tanner is now occupied by me.

"And you're still as sweet as ever, Collin," she calls from the kitchen.

The condo layout is similar to ours, just a second floor unit laid out in a mirror image. I watch from the dining table, admiring the way Nan makes use of the same small kitchen as ours downstairs. She always makes these great family meals, just like my Grandma would. I get why they were such good friends, always wanting to take care of their grandkids, enjoying the mountain together, having big family meals like this.

As she's getting ready to serve, Tanner gets up from the table heading towards her in the kitchen.

"Hey Grandma, let me give you a hand."

I can't help but smile watching him in the kitchen. He towers over his Grandma but looks like a little kid the way he asks what she needs help with and follows her every word. I catch him looking my way. He briefly melts into the boy I remember from our childhood, blushing as she whispers something to him before he comes back to the dining room, putting the dish of baked Mac and Cheese on the table.

I watch him, waiting for him to look back at me, a teasing grin already on my face. "I forgot how much of a grandma's boy you are."

He blushes again. "Hey, we all have our flaws."

"I didn't say it was a flaw." I hold his hand under the table. "It's kind of cute."

Nan comes in from the kitchen, setting the chicken pot pie in the center of the table.

"Alright, dig in kids," she says, before sitting down on the other side of Tanner.

"Thanks again for having us over, Mrs. Chapman. Everything looks great," Lizzy says, eyeing the spread in front of her. We told her to save room for tonight so she had a light lunch and I can tell by the way she's looking at the pot pie, she's on the verge of going full hangry on us.

"So how much longer are you in town, Veronica?" Grandpa Chapman asks, eyeing me as he brings a forkful to his mouth.

"Oh, Lizzy and I are here until Friday," I say. There's an awkward pause after my answer and I know why he asked. I can feel the inevitable follow up question coming.

So what are you and Tanner going to do? Please don't hurt our boy. Long distance?

We still don't know exactly what we're going to do yet, but I know I love him and we will work this out. In what feels like a new normal for me with Tanner, I find myself trying to be more like him, in the best way. I've been embracing being here in the moment and not trying to stress out over planning every little detail.

"Oh my god, Mrs. Chapman. This pot pie is so good," Lizzy says, sparing me the awkwardness. "My mom never made anything like this growing up. I'm going to need your recipe."

Thanks for coming to the rescue, Lizzy.

I look over to her and she winks at me. I'm almost laughing at the thought of Mrs. Frank cooking a pot pie. I don't think she's cooked a meal for us as long as I've known Lizzy.

The rest of dinner is uneventful, but still a welcome night with the Chapmans. It reminds me so much of the nights where Collin, Tanner, and I would be with all of our grandparents and his younger siblings.

I miss those days.

After dinner, the four of us head back to our condo and say goodbye to Collin and Lizzy before heading back to Tanner's for the night.

"So, your grandparents look like they're doing great." It's more of a statement than a question but he still answers.

"Yeah, not much has changed with them. Glad they're here in town as much as they are. I usually park in their lot when I ski and stop by after hitting the slopes most days."

"It's nice you get to spend so much time with them," I say, watching the snow falling on the road in front of us. I know the falling snow means Tanner has to be up early as well, meaning we'll probably go get coffees together. The thought makes me smile. I love getting to enjoy these small *normal* moments together, a glimpse into his every day life.

"It is, but they're not here as much as you'd think. With Grace, Clay, and my dad down in Salt Lake, they go stay with them half of the time." He pauses, something clearly eating at him. "I've actually thought of moving down there to be closer to the family all year."

"Really? I can't picture you anywhere but here, but I can imagine that'd be nice to be closer to them. It definitely wouldn't feel as lonely as it does here sometimes. Why haven't you done it?" I look at him, but his eyes stay focused on the road ahead. I can see the tension in his face though, his jaw tight.

"I think… part of me has always known that if I left, the odds of seeing you again would be so low. It's not like you would ever have a reason to visit me *there*. In a way, leaving here would be like I was giving up on you, saying goodbye to you."

I reach for his hand, trying to give him some level of comfort while I fight back the tears welling in my eyes. The idea that I've been so much a part of his life for all these years just keeps eating at me. I wish I had known years ago.

"Well I'm glad you stayed, Tanner. I can't imagine this place without you. I'm glad you didn't give up on me. I'll never give up on you. I love you."

"Love you too, Ronni." I can see the expression on his face relax as we pull into the driveway, my words seeming to put him at ease. If I could go back in time, I would do anything to have more of him in my life, knowing how deeply he loves me.

As we get out of the truck and walk towards the cabin, I rush in front of him, blocking his way to the door.

"Tanner." I rest my hands on his hips, looking up at him. "I mean it. I'm glad you stayed. I'm glad I'm here with you. I'm so happy you finally made your move and showed me how you felt. I don't think I can ever imagine this place without you anymore. I love you so fucking much."

I lean forward, standing on my toes to reach his face, desperate to kiss him. He slants his head, reaching down to me. Our lips meet, his mouth open and I can feel a low moan escape him. He pulls away from me, his hands holding my ribs. I watch his chest heave with each breath. He looks down at me, his eyes heavy. His lustful voice sends shivers through me.

"You know, you're fucking cute when you get all serious and in your power pose like this." He leans back down, planting another gentle kiss on my lips. "Cute and bossy."

When he stands there, looking down at me like this, with my back against the door, it's impossible to not feel just how imposing he is. He towers over me and when he's this close to me, his broad shoulders completely cage me into the doorway. I'm overwhelmed by his scent, the sound of his heart pounding, his raw masculine presence making my whole body buzz, sending electricity between my legs.

I rest my hands on his chest and start to stand back on my toes, wanting to kiss him. Sensing it, his rugged hands cup my ass and lift me up to him. My legs instinctually wrap around him and his body now pins me against the door. I wrap my arms around him, holding his shoulders as he kisses my neck, his breath heavy and steamy just under my ear.

"Why don't we take this inside?" His low voice escapes between muffled breaths and kisses.

"Please. Now." The words come out almost frantic between my panting breaths. The way Tanner has unlocked the craving for touch, the need for pleasure, and a physical connection with someone that was buried deep inside me is so liberating. I still can't get over how right, how perfect, our physical bond feels.

He opens the door with one hand, carrying me into the cabin with my legs and arms still wrapped around him tightly.

"What does my good girl want tonight?" he whispers into my ear as he carries me over to the bedroom. My pulse is racing, knowing that whatever I choose is going to be out of this world with him.

"I want your tongue. I want to feel it again." I kiss his neck, feeling my whole body tense when he growls in approval.

"Good choice, Ronni." He puts me down on the bed. His eyes run up and down me. He leans forward, his hands stopping at my waist, unbuttoning my jeans. He slides my shirt up, just under my breasts and runs a trail of kisses down my stomach, stopping just at the lacy blue fabric of my thong. His strong hands pull my panties and jeans down and he throws them to the other side of the bed.

The anticipation is pure torment. I can already feel my need pooling at my opening and pulsing through my clit.

He takes his shirt and jeans off, standing at the edge of the bed eyeing me. I can already see how hard his thick cock is, straining his black boxers. As much as I want his tongue on me, I need more.

"Tanner. I want to feel you. Let me touch… let me hold your cock while you eat me out."

He eyes me lustfully, his green eyes practically smoldering.

"Now that sounds fucking good, you needy little thing." He slides off his boxers and walks around the bed to my side. He climbs on to the bed, kneeling beside my head. His cock is only inches from my face when he leans down and takes off my shirt. He looks at my breasts, still covered by my bra, licking his lips before kissing just above the neckline. He works down my stomach to my aching clit, his chest now pressed against my hips.

He wraps his arms under my legs and cups my ass in his big hands, his strong fingers resting on my wet aching pussy, gently spreading me open. He plants a soft kiss on my clit before opening his mouth, sucking and licking it slowly. I feel my whole body clench and flex against the bed, except for my lower body pinned down by his broad chest.

My view laying here in his bed is one of the hottest things I've ever experienced. His throbbing cock is still right next to my face. I can see his muscular arms wrapping under my legs, his stubbled lower jaw open and flexed tight as he groans and licks my clit.

I grab his cock in my hand, holding it tightly. I can feel him moan into me as I rub the tip of him with my thumb before slowly working his thick, lengthy shaft in my hand. The pace of his tongue gets faster and he pushes harder as I keep fisting his thick cock.

It's so fucking hot the way our bodies are feeding off of each other's touch. Just when I start to pleasure him, he slides one of his fingers through my slick, wet lips to my pussy, teasing the opening. It sends a shiver through me and I flex my hips into him, desperate to feel more. My grip on his cock tightens and I know he feels it when he rocks his hips forward, practically fucking my hand. At the same time he slides his finger deeper into my dripping wet pussy.

I can already feel the tension growing in me, but I don't want this release yet. I want more. He's so fucking good at this.

"I need your cock in me, Tanner. I want it in my fucking mouth." He groans so loud in hungry approval against my clit, that the vibration sends a shudder through me and I can feel my pussy squeeze his finger tighter. He lifts his head for just a second.

"That's the fucking hottest thing you've said to me yet. My needy girl."

He lifts one leg over me and now he's straddling my face on his knees, his cock now within inches of my mouth. His mouth is already back to tormenting my clit when I pull him towards me, getting the tip of his cock in my mouth. His tight balls are right in front of my eyes and I can't help but squeeze them gently. It's so insanely hot to feel him in my mouth while he's eating me out like this.

I want to tell him how fucking close I am. With his cock in my mouth, the only way I can tell him is through the unspoken words of our bodies. My breathing, the way my pussy tightens on his finger, the way I work his cock harder and faster in my mouth when his tongue and fingers are hitting the perfect spot. The way I rock my hips forward, driving myself into his open mouth. All telling him I'm so close to letting go and to keep going.

I lean my head forward and take more of his length in my mouth, my tongue running along his shaft. He groans again, pushing his tongue against my clit and flicking it faster and faster. He rocks his hips towards my face, slowly easing his cock in and out of my mouth.

Jesus. He's fucking my mouth while he's licking my clit and fingering my pussy. Tanner's warm muscular body is spread across every inch of mine, holding me against the bed.

It's. So. Fucking. Hot.

The sensations, the touch, the sight, the sounds. They all send me completely over the edge. I can feel the orgasm coming and it's so overwhelming.

My pussy clenches his finger and I start to squeeze his head between my thighs. I know he can feel it too the way he groans again and starts to rock his hips faster. I moan and whimper as I come, but it's muffled by his cock in my mouth. He bucks his hips at the sensation and I open my mouth, letting him use it as he chases his own release. He comes deep in my throat while I'm still riding out my own orgasm. It's a perfect feeling, our bodies are so in sync.

I feel him rest his head on my thigh, slowly pulling his still throbbing length from my mouth, giving me a chance to swallow and catch my breath.

He rolls off of me onto his side, his head still resting on my thigh. He runs his fingers up my leg and over my stomach, resting his hand on my hip. He looks up at me, his eyes narrowed, and heavy, his mouth open catching his breath, but smiling. His mustache has a glint to it, his spit, sweat, and my wetness still there.

"You really can read my mind. That was so damn good. The way your mouth takes me. Fuck." He shudders. His low voice is labored and still recovering.

"It was pretty great for me too." I look back at him, my smirking face still flush. He sits up in the bed and lays back down beside me. I roll on my side, letting him spoon me, feeling his still hard length against my ass.

"Careful now, Ronni." He wraps his arm around mine, holding my hand against my chest. "Don't make me go for round two."

Chapter 39

Tanner
Deadline

While I'd love nothing more than to spend every minute with Ronni before she has to go back to Ohio, I can't blame her for wanting to spend the day with her brother and Lizzy at the spa. If anyone deserves the relaxation time, it's her. After all, Lizzy came out here to spend time with Ronni, they should have a fun day together. And taking Collin with them, now that Lizzy and him are a new dynamic duo, woof. They should be in for a *fun day*.

I'm also glad Lizzy has warmed up to me after the first couple days of angst when she realized I'm not into her. Definitely don't want Ronni's best friend on my bad side. And she's kind of scary and fierce.

I'll pick Ronni up later tonight at the start of my plow run. I've been looking forward to taking her with me on one of them for ages and it's finally happening tonight. Sure, Collin has come along on them from time to time over the years. Despite being twins though, Collin is not Ronni. No. Definitely not.

It seems like every spare minute I've had lately has either been on the slopes with Ronni and the gang or alone with Ronni, our bodies unable to be separated. A nice distraction, but still a distraction. So I do need this time to get some work done.

I've managed to get a handful of knives made for Giselle and now I can focus on my other project that's wrapping up. I normally don't work with deadlines when it comes to knife making. It's one of the things I love about making knives compared to being a property manager. I get to work at my own pace. But the property owner I'm making these for is important, and I'm on a bit of a time crunch. I've snuck in the time to get the blades pounded out, forged, and shaped. The edges are taking shape and ground now, and I should be able to finish them up today.

It's not just the knives I need to work on. It's me. I can feel myself becoming a mess, my heart being torn. I know what Ronni and I have is real, that we'll fight for it. But I'm still terrified of the unknown, of how we'll make everything work.

I can feel the dread creeping back in and that's the last thing I want right now. I don't want it to put a shadow over our last few days together on this trip of hers. She's been so happy here, not worried about her job, just living in the moment. I'd give anything to help her feel like that forever.

But could I ask her to move here and give up her career back in Ohio? Am I crazy for even thinking that again? This is so new and fragile but we talked about it, we're going to try and use whatever time we can to go back and forth. But still, I want more. My mind keeps going to the future, craving to know what our future will look like. I know she's worked hard for her career, even if it makes her miserable. I know that's a huge part of her life, her identity.

She has Collin and Lizzy back in Ohio. How could I ever ask her to be so far away from them? I know how hard it is to be away from your family, to feel isolated. If she's taught me anything recently, it's that I need to stop bottling things up, open up, and share my feelings. Even the bad ones. It's easy to share the good stuff, the fun happy things. But I need to take some emotional risks for once and share the rest too.

Being in my workshop, at least I can try to distract myself a bit. I need to get these blades etched in acid to show off the Damascus pattern and get them polished. Then I can mold their handles and finally finish them up.

Gloves on, I dip the nearly finished blades in the ferric acid. Leaving them there for a bit, I look over at Rex in the corner, happily oblivious and gnawing on a bone.

"You really got it made, dude." I look at him, shaking my head in amusement, jealous of how little he has to worry. No, how he *never* has to worry. Just mindlessly going through life, playing ball, eating, chewing a bone, and going on late night and early morning drives with me for work.

My peace and quiet is interrupted by my phone buzzing in my pocket. I take my gloves off and answer the call without bothering to see who it is, immediately regretting my decision when I hear that all too familiar grouchy and deep voice.

"Hey shithead. Heard you finally stopped being a little bitch." Clay's voice booms through the phone.

I let out a deep frustrated sigh, palming my face. Of course it's my brother.

"Oh for fuck's sake, who told you? And like you're one to talk. When was the last time you had a *girlfriend*?" I reply, not bothering to hide my irritation.

Clay lets out a low laugh. "Oh you know, just the Chapman family phone tree. Grandma called Grace, Grace texted Dad, and then he called me. And I'd have a girlfriend if Park City wasn't crawling in stuck up vacationing ski bunnies. You're lucky Ronni is cool as hell and is clearly insane enough to actually like *you*. But that's not why I'm really calling."

"I figured as much. What's up?" I look back to my workbench, still wondering why he actually called, other than to annoy me.

"I heard you're coming down to Park City next month with your new *girlfriend.* Figured we should try to hang out." Even over the phone, I can picture the smug look on his face.

"You know, you're kind of an intolerable asshole sometimes. But since you're my only brother, sure. Let's get together with Grace and Dad," I say, tapping my foot. "Sorry I haven't called lately. I've been so busy here with work and Collin and Ronni in town.

"It's all good, dude. Anyways, I gotta get back to work. Say hi to Ronni and Collin for me."

"Will do. Say hi to Grace and Dad for me," I say before hanging up the phone and putting my gloves back on.

Back to the task at hand, I pull the blades from the acid and rinse them off. Damn, they look amazing. The combo of old salvaged steel and new steel are making a crazy striped pattern of light and dark layers. The K-Tip blade shape is such a cool finishing touch.

After installing the handles and giving them a final quick polish, I take a moment to admire them. They've been a good distraction for the past month, but also somehow kept me focused on what I want.

I want her.

I've *always* wanted her.

Looking at the knife in my hand, I think back to my conversation the other day with Giselle. I really have gotten better at making these. This one's special. It's by far the best I've done and I think it might be better than the ones I used to look at in magazines and shops, dreaming I could make one day. Maybe I should think more about prioritizing this business. Sure, it'd be a juggling act with property management and plowing and still finding time to ski. Maybe I could do it without turning it into a joyless profession. Do it without sacrificing one of my few escapes.

Yes. That's definitely something I should think about. Not today though. Today, I'm thinking about what I have with Ronnie and the night I have planned. It's awesome seeing her let go more and just go with the flow.

We have a real connection with each other. I can feel it. We have a relationship, out in the open. I can feel that she wants me the same way. These last two weeks, I've felt the darkness and depression I've been so used to being replaced only with the drive to keep her in my life. I've loved her secretly for so long.

With the knives finally finished, I can think about the night ahead, the days ahead. Ronni will be in town four more nights, leaving Friday. I'm picking her up tonight after she has dinner with Collin and Lizzy, and she's going to spend the night with me on my pretreat and plow run. I'm glad we've got a few more nights to sort some things out.

I've gotten so used to doing these rides alone, well with Rex really, that the idea of taking her out is weirdly exciting. It's like I get to give her a real peek into a part of my life no one else gets to see. So many nights I've seen a fox, a moose, even the rare stray wolf, or seen the stars in a clear night sky and wanted to share it with someone, only to be reminded that I'm alone.

Part of me always thought it was crazy that I was so head over heels for her most of my life. For someone that I had no clue whether they felt the same way about me. Now, after diving in so deep with her, I feel like I love her even more. I always knew she cared about everyone in her life and that she was passionate about skiing, cooking, and her job. And none of that has changed over these last few years since I last saw her. But being so close now and with her so much, I see just how much she opens her heart up, how much she's willing to do for others without anything in return.

I'd gladly spend the rest of my life being there for her, letting her have someone to lean on for a change. I'm determined to do anything I can to keep her in my life forever.

She's the one for me.

She's always been the one.

The only one.

Chapter 40

Veronica
PDA

C ollin's low voice hums, "Fuck me, that feels *so good*."
"Ugh I needed this. I've been *so tight*." Lizzy's voice is muffled by her pillow, but I can still hear her whimper.

They're too much.

"For fuck's sake guys, I love you both but I'm trying to enjoy my massage and it sounds like you're reliving your cowboy encounter. Can you tone it down a notch?"

I can feel the masseuse's hands pause for a brief second and I think I hear him try to choke back a laugh. I turn my head on the massage table to judge Lizzy's reaction. She's still looking down into the headrest of her massage table but manages to lift an arm and give me the middle finger. The other two masseuses shake their heads and are grinning but don't stop working.

I can see Collin though and he's shaking his head too. "Look *lil sis*, if Tanner and you are going to subject us to constant PDA, then you're just going to have to suck it up. Lizzy and I are buds now."

"Hell yeah, Collin. You tell her." Even with her head still buried in the massage table, her sassiness comes through loud and clear.

Maybe booking a three person massage wasn't the most relaxing idea? There are six of us in this small, dimly lit room with rainforest sounds playing in the background and it's definitely making for an interesting vibe. Either way, I'm glad to get some alone time with these two. I've spent most of the last week and a half trying to enjoy every second I can with Tanner and feel bad that I haven't had as much time with them as I had planned. Even if this new unholy alliance of Collin and Lizzy is a terrifying force to be reckoned with.

"Well, I'm glad to see you've moved on from your fears about Collin hitting on you," I tease, still enjoying the hands working on my back. They aren't as big and strong, or as magical, as Tanner's, but this still feels great.

"Whatever, V. So did I get this right? Your date tonight is going out for late night coffees and then riding along with your *boyfriend* in his snow plow all night?" Lizzy finally turns her head on her table, looking over at me.

Ok, when she puts it like that, it doesn't sound that romantic or exciting I guess. But I can tell Tanner really wants to do this and I'm excited to get another peek into his life here in Jackson. And frankly, I'm enjoying these little mundane things with him. Small glimpses into his daily life.

"Yeah, that's exactly it. You got it right." I press my lips together, realizing I can't really shrug laying face down on a massage table. "I'm looking forward to it though. I just want to take advantage of all the time I have left here on this trip."

She smiles at me, closing her eyes when they roll back into her head while her masseuse works on her shoulders. "Yeah. So, have you guys talked about the whole long distance thing?"

Ugh. Why does everyone need to keep asking this? But I get it, they want to know and I'd be curious too. I mean it does feel crazy, but it also just feels *right*. I look back down into the headrest, not wanting to look either of them in the eye as I answer.

"We've talked a bit. Not in a ton of detail yet. We've still got a few nights in town to talk more. But it's serious. We know we both want to make this work long term. It's just a matter of how. And speaking of trips." I pause for a moment, thinking of what Tanner and I talked about the other night. "I sort of invited to Tanner to Utah next month on our Aspen Valley trip."

I can hear Lizzy sigh and almost see the expression in her voice. Here comes some condescending or sarcastic quip.

"That will be awesome. Especially if it means I get chill, relaxed Veronica. Oh and maybe I can meet his brother." She lets out a laugh and I know she'd be winking at me if we were facing each other. "But seriously, I hope it works. You deserve to be this happy all the time. You guys are amazing together already. I can't believe how much more confident and relaxed you've been the last week and a half. I'm putting my money on you two figuring it out."

My head jerks up, surprising the masseuse. Lizzy is rarely this serious and it feels weird to hear it. I wish I could see her expression, but her face is still resting in the massage table nook.

"Thanks. It does feel pretty great. But for the record, Clay is a grumpy asshole and even Tanner would tell you that." She's right though. I do deserve this. For once, everything is going great. I feel amazing. I just want this feeling to last forever.

Does that make me delusional? Even if it does, I don't really care at this point honestly.

Lizzy laughs. "Really. I'd take this version of you any day. You said fuck it, let's take the day off from skiing and booked us a last minute spa day? Three weeks ago, I couldn't imagine you changing our plans like that. Love this for you."

I hear Collin move and look to see him prop himself up on his elbows, facing me now. His expression is oddly serious. "Look, sis. I know I've been giving you guys shit about PDA. But I've always kind of known deep down that he was in love with you. Maybe I blocked it out, maybe I ignored it. But I remember the way his voice would change if I mentioned you or the way he'd follow you around like a puppy dog. Looking back now, so much more makes sense."

I look over. He shakes his head, reaching down for his water bottle on the floor and taking a drink.

"Fuck me, it's hot in here." He wipes the sweat from his brow and puts the water bottle back down. "But really sis, he will do anything for you. If there's one thing Tanner is, it's loyal. In fact, you probably have his loyalty to me, as a friend, to blame for him waiting this long to ever tell you how he feels."

He lays back down and lets out a low groan as the masseuse starts to work again.

"Well thanks for all this *girl talk.* I think this is going to end up being a great girls trip after all. Glad you two are here, really."

I try to relax again and enjoy the last twenty minutes of our massage. My legs are beat from all of the skiing and it feels amazing being able to stop and just lay here. I did need this. But maybe not as much as I would have three weeks ago.

Does it feel great? Yes.

Is it great to hang out with Collin and Lizzy? Yes.

Three weeks ago, I was completely burnt out and any physical relief would have sounded amazing and otherworldly. I would have begged for a massage at that point. But now, I find myself relaxed, my constant anxiety and accompanying physical stress practically gone. I find myself thinking about how much I want Tanner's hands on me. Thinking about the man that's been giving my body nearly endless pleasure, like he's making up for lost time. I'm thinking about how much I just want to see Tanner tonight. The man that's reminded me I'm so much stronger than I give myself credit for.

Hearing Collin and Lizzy be so optimistic is such a validation, a much welcomed one, of what's already been running through my mind.

This is real.

This isn't just in my head. I am this happy for once and I deserve it.

Chapter 41

Tanner
Toy Barn

"So, what's it like having a *real* coworker for a change?" Ronni looks at me from the passenger side of my truck. She's scratching Rex's head as he sits between us on the bench seat. He's clearly chosen her over me, that little traitor. Can't blame him though. He's always liked her.

"Is that a question for me or him? He's gotten way too used to spending these nights alone with me. So either way, he's probably just as excited about having the extra company as I am." I wink, scratching Rex's head between his ears, our fingers brushing against each other's.

I hear a little giggle, her lips barely parted in a smile, before she answers.

"Well, I still don't speak Rex like you yet. So thanks for answering for both of you," she says, smiling as she looks back at me. "So who's crazy mansions do we get to see tonight? Come on, you spoiled me already by showing me Tommy freaking Jacob's place the other night. You're going to have to tell me about them all."

"Hmm, alright. We'll save the best for last," I say, flicking my eyebrows up at her. "You'll just have to wait."

We stop at the Cowgirl Coffee drive thru for some caffeine, part of my usual routine before we make my rounds. She takes her usual large iced honey badger, still ordering an extra shot of espresso even at 8:00 PM.

"That's… *a lot*," I say, laughing at her as she takes the first big gulp of her drink. "I'm like twice the size of you and even I don't know if I could handle that much caffeine this late at night. I only got a medium and no extra shot."

She smirks back at me, shrugging her shoulders, eyebrows raised. "I don't think you'll be complaining if I'm up all night with you."

I feel myself holding my breath for just a second, my thighs clenching together. "Fair enough. I can't argue with that logic."

I lean over Rex, curled up between us, kissing her before we start making my rounds. I can taste her sweet, spicy coffee on her lips.

It's funny, as long as she's been coming here to visit her grandparents, there are still places all over town she's never seen. I love giving her an even more behind the scenes tour of a place she already knows so well.

Our first stop is a condo complex behind Target. I've always thought this place was weird, but I'm dying to see if I'm the only one that picks up on it.

"Wait, how many units are in this complex?" she asks, looking around the parking lot, eyes wide.

"There are twenty units, ten in that building and ten in the other," I say, already knowing she's seeing what I've always thought was bizarre.

"Ok. So twenty units. And there are like, nine or ten Honda Elements in this parking lot?" Her jaw is still hanging down as she looks around counting the old toaster shaped SUVs, pointing a finger at each one as she goes.

"Yep. Exactly. It's weird as fuck, right? Like, are they all friends? Did one of them own one and the others were like *oh hey that's dope?*" I look at her, so glad she appreciates the weirdness of this parking lot as much as I do.

Next, we head to a small secluded neighborhood running along Flat Creek, with charming old cabins near the base of Snow Queen resort, Jackson's other ski area. Her face is glued to the window. She looks like an excited kid watching all the little cabins go by, nestled carefully back in the trees. Since it's still about a week or so after New Year's, their lights are still up and they look like gingerbread houses. I love her reaction, showing her a place that she wouldn't have had a reason to visit before.

"I had no idea this little neighborhood was here. It's so cute!" she says, still looking out the passenger window.

"Roll down the window and listen," I say, pulling into my turn around spot at the end of the road.

She turns her head so her ear is now facing the open window outside into the dark. I see the edges of her lips curl up into a smile.

"Is that… Flat Creek? Are those rapids?" Her voice is excited, almost giddy.

"Yep, sure are. This spot doesn't freeze up in the winter, so the river still runs hard."

She closes her eyes and keeps her ear turned outside to listen. "It's so peaceful, so relaxing. A real life, natural white noise machine."

If her eyes were open, she could see me nodding. I love these spots where nature collides with civilization and nature still wins out.

We head back towards Teton Village and Moose Wilson Road to tackle some of the bigger private drives and access roads, before finally getting to my favorite ones, usually my last stops.

"Oh my god, what's that up there?" She points ahead excitedly, her voice almost squealing. In front of us is a gated street, with ornate stone columns supporting a wrought iron gate with an elk pattern formed into the metal. Behind the gate is a long evergreen lined road, showing no signs of what lies beyond.

"This is my *second* favorite," I say. "It's a large ranch. Super private and backs up to the river."

There's a stunned look on her face. "This is *one* house? One property?"

I laugh a little, my head nodding. "Well, sort of. It's one property, one owner. But he's got his main house, a guesthouse, a caretaker's house, a horse barn, and a toy barn."

The look on her face only shows more dismay. "How is this only your *second* favorite?"

"You'll just have to wait and see," I say, pressing the code to open the gate for the private drive.

We head down the road, passing their toy barn first.

"So what's a *toy barn* exactly?" She asks, her eyes glued to the fancy barn as we continue down the road.

"That's where they keep their ATV's, side by sides, snowmobiles, dirt bikes, you name it."

She shakes her head in disbelief. "This place had to be tens of millions, right?"

"Yeah… but I can't blame the guy. He actually lives here year round. He built the new main house as a place to retire and have his family come visit him. It used to be a big ranch but they've let nature take back over most of the land. He enjoys every second of this place though. I have no idea what it'd be like to have that much money, but if I did, this is what I'd want. Well, as long as I had someone like you to share it with."

That last part gets me a smile. God, I love her smile.

"You know, maybe you could get a place like this one day. Take on a partner with the property management company and have more time for knives, get in some fancy restaurants. Get your name out there."

I laugh shaking my head. "My knives are expensive but I think it'd take a couple lifetimes for me to make enough to afford a place like this."

She playfully jabs my shoulder. "You know what I mean, *Tanner*. You're good at what you do, all of it. I know you could grow both of your businesses and be great at it, if you wanted to."

Something warm stirs in my heart and I can feel the corners of my eyes tighten. "Thank you, Ronni. No one ever takes me seriously like you do. So thank you, thank you for seeing me as someone besides that goofy, carefree kid everyone still thinks I am."

"You don't have to thank me," she says as she squeezes my hand. "I'm glad I can be there for you, however you need me."

A smirk takes over my face as we drive down the road.

"But what you said, *if I wanted to*, I've thought about that... a lot. I'd love to grow the businesses. I *know* I could do it, I've just never seen the point in it before though. The other day, though, Giselle even asked me if I would consider it. I have been thinking about it more and more. So it means a lot that you think I could too."

The playful look on her face is gone and taken over by a more serious one. "I'm proud of you, Tanner. We're proud of you, because I know Collin is too. You work hard, don't think that people don't see that. And you're fearless when you set your mind to something. Whether it's running your own businesses or skiing off a cliff, when you want something, you commit. Hard. Not many people can say that about themselves."

I don't know why her words cut through me like they do. I believe everything she's saying. I know what I can do. I'm confident in myself. But hearing it from someone else, that someone really sees me, especially her, means so much.

We continue down the drive past the caretaker's house, which is now just an *extra* guesthouse, the other barn, and finally reach the main house and the other guesthouse. Her eyes go wide when we reach them.

"Jesus, this place is nuts," she says, taking in the massive complex in front of her.

"Well, you haven't seen my favorite part of it," I say, turning to drive down a path between the main house and guesthouse.

It takes us down towards the river, to the edge of a clearing in the trees. I throw the truck in park, turning off the engine but leaving the lights on.

She gives me a questioning look. There's still a smile on her face, but I can tell she's wondering why we're here.

"Is this your secret make out spot?" she asks, taking a sip of her coffee, grinning at me.

A quick laugh escapes my closed lips. "Nope. Never brought anyone here besides Rex."

"So then why are we here?" I watch her take another drink of her coffee, looking out at the clearing and then back to me.

"It's where I like to come and think. We're far from any of the developed parts of town or the village." I stop to look at her, my hand running over her cheek before I point up towards the sky. "If you look up, you can still see stars on a clear night. The owner and his family don't come down here very often, so I see a lot of wildlife too."

I can hear myself exhale. I do love coming to this spot. But with Ronni here, it's surreal. I can tell I'd be fine to open up more too. There's so much I've thought of here, in this spot, over the years. I've been sad, missing Collin, my family, and her. I've dreamt of what it would be like to be with her right here in this clearing.

And now, I'm finally sitting here with her, wanting to tell her all of it. But I know there's only so much time before she has to go back and we have so much to figure out.

"Hey." She's looking back at me, her eyes asking me to keep going. "What's going on in that head of yours?"

"Geez," I snort. "You really do see right through me now."

She nods at me and I can tell she's hoping I'll open up more. I watch her as she looks at Rex, scratching his head between us.

"I've always dreamt about sharing these nights with you. I've thought about you coming out with me on these runs, what life would be like if you were here all the time. And I don't think there's anything more in the world I could want than a life with you."

"I sense there's a *but*?" she asks, her face still close to mine, her eyebrows raised in anticipation of what's on my mind.

I sigh, looking down at the steering wheel and then to Rex, putting my hand on him to try and stay calm.

"I just… I don't want you to feel like you have to give up your life in Ohio because of me. I've never felt like I was good enough, worthy enough, for someone like you to do something like that for me. I know it's crazy to think that so soon, but what we have, it just feels so right and I want it to last forever. I don't know what I need to do. I just know I'll do anything for you."

She puts her other hand on mine, cupping it in both of hers now, her soft fingers stroking the back of it. I can hear her inhale deeply, getting ready to say something.

"Tanner. I love you. So, so much." Her eyes are sparkling, begging me to trust her and I do. "We will figure it out. Just please, keep fighting for it. You're not alone, in life or in this. I can't picture a life without you either now. It could be here, Dayton, a mix of both, whatever it looks like, we'll figure it out. Together."

Hearing her say that is like a weight lifted off my chest. "Thanks, Ronni. I love you too. I promise I will fight for this. Let's make the most of the next few nights and work on everything else."

She smiles back at me, but I can tell she's thinking about something. "Why are you so afraid to do that, Tanner? To open up and share? You're good at doing it with me."

That is not the question I was expecting. Not at all. One I've avoided thinking about for a decade. I can feel my body go rigid just thinking about the answer. But for her, I want to do this. I lower my head, closing my eyes, almost afraid to look back at her. The silence lingers for what feels like ages before I finally speak.

"It's not that I'm afraid to open up and share my feelings, Ronni. That's not it." I start, taking comfort in how she's holding my hand.

"Well maybe at first it was. It's easier to share the fun stuff, the happy things though. I've gotten so much better about that. It's the unpleasant stuff, sharing the things that are upsetting me, my burdens."

Her voice is soft and soothing. "Why don't you want to share those? I get you don't want to tell just anyone, but you have people who care about you and love you. You can talk to them."

I feel her hand gripping mine tighter. "That's exactly what I am afraid of. Back when my parents first moved to Salt Lake with Grace and Clay, it was supposed to be temporary while they were in school. But after Grace graduated and got a job and stayed there, they had all built a life there."

I open my eyes and look at her. Her eyes are locked on to me, watching me. "What's that have to do with sharing the bad stuff, telling people how you feel?"

I close my eyes again, taking in a deep breath. "Because that's the last conversation I had with my mom. She called to tell me that they were going to stay there, move there permanently. I had always hoped that they were going to come back. I was so upset, it already felt so lonely here. I didn't hold back. I told her I was upset about it. She was so excited to tell me and I took that away from her. We were both mad at each other."

I look back at her, rubbing the bit of moisture from the corner of my eye with the back of my forearm. "Neither of us wanted to give in. Dad finally got me to agree to call her after work a few weeks later. But before I was even done with work that night, I got a call from dad.

It was the night of the accident. She… she was gone and there was nothing I could do to take it back."

A few stray tears runs down from her beautiful hazel eyes. Her voice is almost a whisper. "Tanner. I… I had no idea. Does anyone know this? I'm so sorry."

"Dad does. But that's it." My heart is pounding. I've never shared this with anyone else and it feels good to get it off my chest, even if the pain of reliving those feelings is almost unbearable. "But since then, I've just wanted to keep my own problems, my own shit, to myself. I don't want to burden anyone else. I don't want my problems to be something that comes between me and the people I love and care about."

I take in her face, her eyes, the way she's looking at me. There's no judgement, no pity. Just compassion. "Tanner. I'm so sorry you felt like that was your fault, like you had to carry that around alone. I can't imagine it. But that doesn't mean you have to keep punishing yourself either. You were both adults. People make mistakes."

"That doesn't change how it feels. I'm terrified of that happening again, of driving someone else I love away," I say through clenched teeth.

She grabs my chin, tilting it up, forcing me to look into her eyes. "You need to forgive yourself and let yourself feel safe enough to tell people how you really feel, the good and the bad. It's not going to end badly every time. Sure it might be unpleasant when you tell someone something they don't want to hear, but you keep coming back to them.

You come back to each other when you love someone. If you're worried about us, I'm not naive enough to think we won't have bad days. But trust that I'm going to keep loving you. Just keep fighting for it, keep coming back to each other. Promise me that."

Her words put my mind at ease. She's right. And for her, I'll do whatever it takes. "I will always come back to you, Ronni. Always."

I lean over Rex, hugging her, savoring the way she rests her head on my shoulders and the smell of her hair. It feels like I can exhale finally after holding in a breath for ages.

We sit here for a few more minutes watching the snow fall around us. I finally notice some movement on the edges of the clearing, the reason I came down here in the first place.

"Ronni, look," I whisper, pointing to the river's edge.

"What? I don't see anything," she says, her eyes scanning the area I pointed out.

Before I say anything else, she notices the brush rustling, snow falling off some low pines. A cow moose comes out of the brush, shaking the snow off her back, walking into the clearing.

"Oh my god," she whispers, clutching my hand. "I always forget how big they are."

"Just wait." I put my finger to my lips, gesturing to be quiet before pointing back to the edge of the clearing.

The moose scans the clearing, seeing us. Finally, she looks back to the pines, letting out a low grunt. An older calf pokes its way out of the brush, catching up with its mother.

I look to Ronni, she's fixated on the mother and calf making their way across the clearing, before stopping in front of a bush to graze.

"I forgot how this place really is on the edge of wilderness," she says, breaking the silence. "I can see why this is your favorite of the places you help take care of. It's beautiful."

I run my fingers through her hair. She's right about one thing.

"Well, it's definitely beautiful. But it's still not my *favorite* place here."

She gives me a curious look. "Shit. I forgot you said it's your *second* favorite. What could be better than this?"

I shrug, my eyebrows raised. "Honestly, it's a no brainer. I'm surprised you haven't figured it out already. I guess you'll just have to wait and see. Only one more stop tonight."

"Ugh. You just love surprises," she says, her voice pretending to be annoyed as she presses her lips together into a line, trying to hide a smile and failing. She's so cute when she does that.

Chapter 42

Veronica
So talented

After leaving the giant ranch, we head back toward Teton Village. Tanner takes the truck down a familiar side road past an old dive bar and I finally realize where we're going.

I palm my face and roll my eyes at him. "Ok, you were right. I should have guessed *this* would be your favorite place that you have to take care of."

I look down the familiar driveway as we pull up to Tanner's cabin, our final stop of the night.

"You know I've always loved this place," he says, opening the door to let Rex hop out. "But I always thought it was missing something to be perfect. Now I know for sure that it was you that I needed here."

God damnit, he's adorable when he does stuff like this.

We head into the cabin and despite the relaxing day at the spa and my iced coffee, I'm still tired. Tanner wants to stay up and watch the weather forecast to see what's in store for our ski day tomorrow, part of his nightly routine.

Watching the weather and hoping for a pow day together might seem like it should be a boring way to wind down the day, but here in this cabin, with Tanner, it's everything I could ever ask for. I'm already in my flannel pajama shorts and my Teal Tigers crop top. Tanner's in grey sweats, no shirt. He runs hot and sleeps without a shirt and I'm certainly not ever going to complain about that.

I curl up next to him, feeling his warm skin. My head is on his shoulder, one hand splayed across his chest, running my fingers through his chest hair. Looking at the coffee table, I can see my phone light up. Tanner, seemingly never missing a beat, catches my eyes lingering on it.

"You going to check that?" he asks skeptically.

I smirk, not moving my head from his shoulder. "Nope. I'm not even going to open the message. I already know it's Jeff and I don't care. I don't even know why he's awake this late back home. Whatever it is, I'm sure he can figure it out." Jeff isn't going to be my problem tonight.

His chest rises and falls with his laugh. "Good. That's the spirit. I'm glad you're having so much fun out here. Speaking of fun. It's looking like it's gonna be a banner day on the slopes tomorrow. You ready to shred some fresh pow?" he asks, still watching the TV, his arm wrapped around me twirling my hair in his fingers.

"I'm always ready, you don't have to ask me. Just hope Collin and Lizzy are up for the task. They've been slowing down the last few days," I say, chuckling a bit.

"Yeah, they clearly don't have the endurance," Tanner says, eyeing me carefully now. "I think they aren't doing enough *cardio*."

"Hmm. I've been enjoying all of our *cardio* lately." Looking into Tanner's eyes is something I could never get tired of. His hooded gaze now drifts down to my crop top, the bottom edges of my breasts showing.

"Fuck me," he says, as he cups one of my breasts. "This fucking shirt is going to be my undoing."

The touch of his strong, calloused hands on my breasts sends a chill through me. I want him so much, always. I see the outline of his erection through his sweat pants and run a hand over his length, feeling how hard he is.

"No, greedy girl," he says, pulling my hand off and placing it back on his chest. "Hands to yourself."

Fuck. Is he really going to hold out on me?

He shimmies his sweats down and grabs his cock in his other hand, slowly working his shaft. It is so fucking hot watching him work his pulsing cock.

"Tanner, I want you so bad," I say, reaching for him.

"No. No touching," he says again, grinning at me now. "You can watch. I've jacked off thinking about you in a crop top so many times, it's your turn to sit back and watch."

As he says that, he lets go of my breast, slowly running his hand down my stomach, until he's trailing his fingers along the waistband of my shorts.

"You said you want me so bad? So if I reach in here, I'm going to find a tight, wet little pussy, right?" His eyes lustful as his grin grows.

I bite my lip and nod. Fuck. I want to feel him, any part of him, so bad.

"Good girl," he says. "Good fucking girl."

His eyes leave mine, looking at his own hand as he lowers it into my shorts. The touch of his fingers on my throbbing clit makes my whole body tense and arch off the couch. I look down at his hands. Watching him stroke his cock in one hand, while the other is playing with my clit is so erotic. I can hear his breathing get heavier and faster, watching him thrust his hips into his own hand.

Fuck. It's already so hot watching him jack off. It's so intimate, so raw. It's like he's letting me see behind the curtain into himself more. It's even hotter knowing he's working himself that hard while looking at my body. It's like my own private porn, just for me, except he's fingering me at the same time and it feels so damn good.

"God, Tanner," I moan into his shoulder, my eyes still watching his hands. "Your hands are so talented. Are you going to jerk us both off?"

His fingers spread my lips open, and he runs them through my slick slit. He teases my pussy, letting a finger linger on my wet opening. He won't let me touch him with my hands, so I'll have to settle for thrusting and grinding myself into him. I rock my hips forward, wanting him to do more with his fingers.

He obliges, always able to read what my body needs, sliding one in me, his thumb now running up and down my clit. I drape my leg over his thigh, pulling our bodies closer, side by side.

"Fuck, Tanner," I say, my words mixed with my heavy panting. "I'm gonna come if you keep doing that."

"This?" he says, as his thumb moves faster and his finger plunges into me deeper and curls in a beckoning motion.

I bite into his shoulder, feeling my orgasm coming. I don't know how he can make my body do as he pleases, as I want, so easily. I look back towards his other hand, fisting the shaft of his cock faster and faster as my own breathing quickens.

"Yes. That. Keep doing that." I rock my hips forward, pressing my self into his hand.

"Good," he grunts. "I want to feel you squeeze when we both come." He adds a second finger, stretching and filling me more.

Watching his hands work, pleasing both of us in unison, puts me over the edge. I squeeze my thighs together as I come, grasping his hand between my legs. My teeth dig deeper into the muscular flesh of his shoulder and my fingernails dig into his chest, pulling his hair.

"Fuck," he moans, as my grip tightens around his fingers. I watch in awe as he keeps stroking himself, harder and harder as he comes, his fingers still in me. His body lets go furiously, a wild grunt escaping him as rope after rope of his release lands on his flexed abs, almost reaching the tiger head on his chest. Fuck, it's so hot to actually see him let go like that. He grabs a tissue off the coffee table, wiping himself off before pulling me further onto his chest and lying down.

He rests his cheek on my head, holding me tight. I find myself lying here on the couch with him again, my body in physical bliss and I'm ready to fall asleep.

It just feels perfect, like home.

Chapter 43

Veronica
Princeton Mills

I've only woken up next to Tanner at his cabin a handful of times, but it feels like something I could get used to, something that I want to be my new normal. The dim morning light is starting to peek through the thin curtains of his bedroom, the light streaming across the bed as a gentle reminder to wake up. I roll over, watching him sleep on his side, facing me. The way the light casts tiny little shadows across his muscular body is breathtaking.

His bed is cozy. It's exactly what you'd dream a bed in a mountain cabin should be with soft flannel sheets, a red and black plaid pattern. I sink further into the bed, never wanting to leave, feeling like I could lay here next to Tanner forever.

I look over at my phone on the nightstand as I hear it buzz, ruining a perfect moment. I see Jeff's name flash on the screen. I'm jolted to my feet when I realize it's not a text message or app ping. It's an incoming call. He's calling me and it's still only 9:00 AM back in Ohio.

"Shit shit shit." I stand up, heading to the other side of the bedroom. I look back at Tanner still in bed, but sitting up now with a worried look across his sleepy face.

I answer the call, terrified of what might be coming my way. I can feel my pulse quickening, sweat on my forehead, the warning signs of an impending full blown panic attack all rearing their head.

"What are you doing right now, Veronica?" Jeff asks, his tone more curt than usual.

"Morning, Jeff. Just waking up. It's still early out here," I reply.

"I just got off the phone with Princeton Mills. Remember the last design we worked on with them for their instant coffees and teas? When we consolidated their branding and did that press release?" he asks.

"Yeah. Of course, why?" I'm not sure where he's going with this. It has nothing to do with Earth SnaX and that's about all I've been working on lately.

"It's a fucking shit show. Somehow all the print plates for their packaging are wrong and they don't match anything in the press release. It's halted their production and they can't ship anything. I need to go there and see what happened and help smooth this out," Jeff continues, his rushed breathing audible through the phone.

A sense of dread washes over me. Princeton is our single largest and oldest client. Anything they ask for, they get, no questions asked. I see Tanner out of the corner of my eye, heading my way. I can tell he knows this isn't good.

"So, how can I help? What do you need?" I ask, hoping for the best.

"I need you to come back, tonight or first thing tomorrow morning. I can't lead the Earth SnaX presentation tomorrow afternoon. I'll be at the plant to see how this got messed up for Princeton and doing damage control," he says, flatly, as if this is a normal, reasonable request.

"What? I'm on vacation, Jeff. Why can't they reschedule? Can we not do it over video?" I'm in disbelief. This guy never stops asking for more and more.

"Veronica. They're already flying in from Oregon. I talked to Cindy this morning and they already boarded their last connecting flight. They get into Dayton tonight. The best I could do was get the presentation moved to later in the afternoon tomorrow. Hopefully you can get back by then. We'll cover your flight change costs." Flight costs? He's calling to upend my whole vacation and that's what he thinks I'm worried about?

"Ok, Jeff. I'll let you know when I change my flights." I manage to reply, feeling completely defeated.

"Good. I'll see you in the office when I'm back on Thursday," he replies, before promptly hanging up.

My head is spinning.

Fuck. Fuck. Fuck.

I have to get to the condo and pack. I have to call the airline and change my flight. I have to go back through the entire presentation again. I've been in such a blissful bubble here I haven't even thought about it in days.

I rush to the side of the bed, putting my clothes on in a flurry, looking around for anything else I brought over.

As I'm getting dressed, I feel Tanner's hand on my lower back.

"Ronni," he says, his voice straining to stay calm. "Talk to me. What's happening? What's wrong?"

"I can't, Tanner. I have to go pack. I have to leave," I say, rushing to the living room to grab my overnight bag with my change of clothes.

"What do you mean you have to go? You're just going to leave?" he asks, struggling to get his jeans on, trying not to trip over following me around as I frantically try to find my things in the cabin.

I stop for a second, looking back at him. His eyes are tortured and worried. He's still shirtless and I desperately want to touch his chest and sink my head into him and feel his warmth. But if I do, I know I'll never pull myself off of him to leave.

"Yes. My boss needs me there. We can't reschedule this presentation and I'm the only one who can do it." My heart pounding in my throat as I start to spiral, thinking about what the next twenty-four hours are going to be like.

"You're kidding, right? That's bullshit," he says, his voice now unable to hide his disapproval. "They can't just cancel your vacation and make you come back. Don't they get that people have a life outside of work?"

"Please, I don't have time for this right now. Can you just take me back to the condo? I need to pack, like right now." I can barely contain my emotions. I can feel my legs shaking, my hands trembling. "Please, Tanner. I need to go back."

I can see his body language soften. He heads to the kitchen to grab his keys before throwing a jacket on over his bare chest. Even now, drifting into a full blown nightmare, the way his body moves, his muscles work, is poetry in motion.

"Let's go," he barks. Rex looks at us with concern as Tanner leads me out the front door, pulling the cabin door shut behind us.

The ride to the condo is silent. I've spent practically every hour I could with Tanner for nearly two weeks and now *he's silent,* almost unreadable. It's hard to tell, but I think his expression drifts from what looks like concern, to anger, to near tears. His jaw is clenched and his teeth are digging into his lower lip. His knuckles are white, his hands are grasping the steering wheel so tight.

When he puts the truck in park at the condo, I reach to open my door, but am caught by his hand on my elbow. He slides his hand down my arm to hold my hand, stopping me from leaving.

"Ronni," he practically whispers, his voice softer and more restrained. "You don't have to do this. You don't have to go back. Just stay here. We will figure it out, remember? Can we please just take a beat and talk this out?"

The pleading look in his eyes nearly shatters my heart. But I can't do this. I have to go. My mind is a frantic mess.

"I'm sorry, Tanner. This is the real world, business doesn't wait. There are consequences for delays. I can't just say *fuck it* and abandon them, not right now. There are expectations we have to meet. Not all of us live in a fairy tale like you, just saying screw it and doing whatever we want, whenever we want." I look down at my boots, unable to look him in the eyes, afraid that if I do, I won't be able to leave.

"Then don't go," he says, his voice now jagged and harsh. "That's a shitty way to live, constantly in fear of losing a shitty job that makes you miserable anyways. They're counting on you to rollover and give in, to be a sucker. And they aren't going to reward you for it either. It's not worth it. Stop wasting your life on something that brings you down like that place does. You don't need that, and they don't deserve you. Just quit. Fuck them."

"Excuse me! A shitty job? Wasting my life? What would you know about building a career, Tanner?" I can feel my fists clench as I pull my hand away from his. "I worked really fucking hard, Tanner, to make a career for myself. I've spent over a decade to get where I am and I'm fucking good at it. I should have known you wouldn't get it. You never take anything seriously, you don't even have a real job. Grow up already."

I wince as I hear the words come out of my own mouth. Shit, that was harsh. I didn't mean that, but it's too late.

"You're right. Maybe I should grow up and be more like you. Give up on the things I've always wanted, *like you*," he says, his hands trembling.

"I'm sorry, Tanner. I can't do this right now," I say, reaching to open the door again and starting to step out of the truck. "I have to go. I have to focus on my job. I have to get ready to leave."

"Wait, Ronni! Please don't le-." His voice is cut off as I slam the door behind me.

Fuck. What did I just do?

I practically run away from the truck towards the door to the mudroom, afraid to look back, not wanting him to see the tears running down my face. But I have to do this. I've spent most of my adult life trying to make this career into what I want. I can't just waste it now. I need to show them how serious and committed I am.

I rush into the condo, streaking past Collin and Lizzy at the dining room table having breakfast. Throwing my bag down in the bunk-room, I'm sobbing, but I don't care. I have to pack and call the airline.

I grab my suitcase, throwing it on the bottom bunk, haphazardly throwing everything of mine I can see into it. I can feel the sweat running down my forehead as my panicked breathing fills my ears. I notice Collin and Lizzy standing in the doorway, throwing me off just a second before I continue furiously packing anything of mine I can find.

Fuck me. My heart is being torn apart by fighting factions within me. Hopeful Veronica wants to stay and fight for Tanner and a life with him. I told him he could trust me. I can't hurt him, not with how much he's opened up to me, how much of himself he's given me. Practical Veronica is mad at herself for thinking this could work without having a real plan instead of just living in the moment. Career Veronica is panicking, desperate to do what she thinks is expected of her.

"Hey. What's wrong? What happened?" Collin says, trying to stay calm but obviously concerned by the look on his face.

"Jeff. He called. He needs me at the meeting. I have to go," I say, barely able to form sentences between sobs. I can feel my knees trembling and I try not to completely break down.

"What are you talking about, V?" Lizzy asks, resting a hand on my shoulder trying to calm me.

"He has an emergency at Princeton and has to go. Earth SnaX is already on their way from Oregon. We can't reschedule tomorrow's presentation. I have to go give it." I struggle to get the words out still, my chest heaving as I stop packing for a second to look at them.

"Fuck. Are you ok? Wait, where's Chap?" Collin asks, sensing there's more wrong than just the mess with work.

"I don't know," I sob, the words almost indistinguishable. "He didn't want me to go and we argued about it. He said my career was stupid, I was wasting my life. I got mad and I told him he needed to grow up."

Hearing my own words out loud, I'm terrified and angry. He hurt me, insulted me, but I hurt him too I'm sure. I want to fix it and make this pain go away, but I have to leave. He's probably angry at me.

No. Oh no. I think back to what he told me the night before about his mom, that wound he opened wide to share with me. The one I just poured salt right into. I told him he could say what's on his mind, even when it's bad and I just threw it back into his face. "Collin. I fucked up. I hurt him."

I explain what Tanner told me the night before about his mom. Collin and Lizzy are dead silent for what feels like forever, Collin visibly shaken.

But what can I even do? I don't have enough time to fix this. I have obligations back at work to take care of. This is my chance to finally make it where I want to go at Fischer, to push my career where I've been trying to take it for so long. To show them that I'm committed and have what it takes. I have to do this. How can he not get that?

My thoughts start to overwhelm me. My mind is spinning, my heart feels like it's going to break or burst through my chest, whatever gives out first. I fall to my knees, leaning over the bottom bunk on my elbows, sobbing into my hands.

"Hey hey hey, lil sis," Collin hushes. "Everything's gonna be fine. I promise. We'll get through this. What can I do to help?" Collin drops to the ground on his knees with me, holding me tight. I feel my breathing start to slow, his hug acting like a security blanket trying to ground me.

"I don't know what to do," I cry into his shoulder as Lizzy joins the group hug on the bedroom floor.

"Hey girl, we got you. You can trust us, it's going to be ok," she says, looking at Collin, both of them nodding. "Collin, go find Chap." She's calm with no sign of her snarky sassy self. It's eerie but oddly reassuring to hear her this way, empathetic for a change. My brain can't shake her words though, *trust us*. Tanner's voice is in the back of my head, telling me I can trust him, trust Collin and Lizzy. Fuck, I miss him already.

She looks back to me. "I'll get you packed. Go ahead and call the airline, ok?"

"Thanks guys," I sniffle as the tears slow to a trickle.

Collin gets up and leaves the room, I assume to go find Tanner. As we hear the door close, Lizzy looks at me.

"What happened with Tanner?" Her voice is still that unfamiliar calm and compassionate tone.

"I told you, we fought. I don't know why I was ever dumb enough to think this dream could last. I mean I was living in a fantasy, right? I knew he'd eventually be his old self, never serious," I say, still angry at what he said before. "He said my job was shitty and not worth all of this."

She frowns, "Is that all he said? I've only known him for like a week, not nearly as long as Collin and you, but I don't think *Tanner Chapman* has a mean bone in that ridiculous body of his."

I feel the corner of my mouth lift, thinking about Tanner.

"No, that's not all he said," I say, wiping the waning tears from my eyes. "He said they don't deserve me and that I don't need them in my life."

She pauses for a moment, before putting both hands on my shoulders, looking me in the eyes.

"Look girl. I love working with you, seriously that place would suck without you there. But like, he's not wrong. You hate that place and it sucks seeing you miserable. I've always heard you talk about being out here, like it's some magical escape, always thinking you were just embellishing and exaggerating about how great it is."

She stops for a moment, and I see a small glimmering tear in one of her eyes that she promptly wipes away. My own crying has stopped. Damn. Who knew Lizzy could be this comforting.

"Ugh. You're gonna make me ruin my makeup," She sniffles. "But after seeing you here, and seeing you *with him*, I can't picture you anywhere else. And I certainly don't want to imagine you back in Dayton at Fischer, not after knowing what a happy, excited Veronica is like."

We both laugh, hugging each other tightly again, before I break the silence.

"I'm still mad at him," I say, wiping my runny nose. "And I still have to leave for this fucking meeting."

"I know, V. I know. Don't worry about Tanner right now. Let Collin handle him. Focus on the presentation. We'll figure out the rest," Lizzy says, standing back up. "Now come on, we gotta get you a new flight, packed, and cleaned up. I won't allow you to be the weird sloppy lady in first class."

Chapter 44

Tanner
Your Move

My morning plow runs are a blur of anger and fear. After rushing through them and trying to calm myself down, I finally get back to the cabin. I can feel myself unraveling and I can't sit or stand still. I don't even bother going inside and I just start to walk down my driveway towards the road. I can feel the snow crunching under my boots with each step. I look around and my eyes strain, the bright white snow reflecting the light from the rising sun.

Before I realize it, my muscle memory has taken me to the dive bar off Moose Wilson Road, around the corner from the cabin. It's later in the morning, but they have a kitchen and serve food for the locals trying to get a bite to eat before hitting the slopes.

I grab my usual stool, finally calm enough to sit down at least. Benjamin stands at the far end of the bar cleaning while Alexis, the other bartender, brings me a beer. I typically come here on days I'm not skiing for lunch and a beer after my morning plow runs. I nod to her before she walks off, looking at the sweating bottle in front of me without touching it.

I thought about ordering breakfast, but my stomach is in knots and the thought of food makes me nauseous right now. I can feel my legs trembling, my foot tapping away at the bottom rung of the barstool. My mind is racing.

My heart feels like its trying to claw it's way out of my chest, tearing apart everything inside me on its way out. I feel like I'm either going to throw up or stroke out.

I think I just fucked up everything I've worked so hard for. I finally had everything I've ever wanted and I just needed to keep working for it.

Why did I have to say that to her? Why couldn't I have just helped her stay calm and say we'll see each other when you're back again soon, let's get you ready for your presentation? She trusted me and I let her down, not knowing what she needed. I should have just kept my feelings fucking buried.

That's what happens.

When I share too much, shit just fucking blows up.

Fuck.

I watch the veins in my forearm straining as my hand grips the bottle. The fingers on my other hand are buried in my hair and I can feel my scalp burn as they clench into a fist.

I'm sitting here fighting the urge to scream. If I fucked everything up… if I hurt her…

"Tanner," a voice from the entrance calls, stopping my thoughts in their tracks.

Shit. It's Collin. My heart flips hearing him call me that. He never calls me *Tanner*.

This is the thing I feared the most. The thought of hurting her *and* him. Losing both of them is what always kept me from ever trying to pursue Ronni until these last couple of weeks.

I never fucking deserved her and now I deserve whatever is coming next. I'm the one that crossed the line with my friends.

I raise a hand, gesturing for him to come over. To my surprise, he calmly sits down on the stool next to me.

"How'd you find me?" I ask, almost afraid to look at him.

"Well, your truck is at your cabin and you weren't there and there's like, only one place you walk to from your cabin," he says, raising a finger to Alexis, asking for a beer. "Also, you know you're a dumbass, right?" he says, the corner of his mouth lifting before taking a sip of his beer before punching me in the shoulder. A small laugh escapes my closed mouth.

Thank god. At least he's not *that* angry. But still, I wish he would have just left me alone.

"Tell me something I don't know," I say, finally taking a swig of my own beer.

"So, bro," he says, taking another sip. "Are you alright?"

That is not what I expected him to say. I expected a *what the hell is wrong with you*. I expected a lecture about upsetting his sister. But not that. Not asking if I'm alright.

"I'm fine." I grunt the words, not really thrilled about talking.

Collin exhales an exhausted, irritated sigh. "You're fine? Really? I swear to god dude. You can't keep doing this."

I set my beer down on the bar and turn to face him as I grind my teeth together. "Doing what, Collin?"

He exhales slowly, his jaw tight. "Veronica told me about your mom…" He pauses and his throat bobs as he swallows. "I can't even imagine. I'm sorry you felt like you had to carry that alone."

Jesus. This is not how I thought my day would go. I thought I'd be waking up in bed next to the naked woman of my dreams. I did not think I'd be in a bar breaking down and talking about my dead mom.

He looks back at me, his jaw loosening and eyes softening. "But still. You know I love you dude, but you can't just constantly put up this wall all the time and bottle shit up. You need to talk things out. You need to accept help and not be such a stubborn ass. Don't be like your shithead, grumpy ass brother."

I muster a laugh and turn away, looking back down at my hands on the bar. "She said the same thing." My voice is practically a whisper. Damnit. That's exactly what she told me.

"No shit, Tanner. She said that because she's right. You need to let people help you and actually talk out whatever you're going through. It's not healthy or good to go through life like you are man. We love you too much to let you do that. I can't believe you've been carrying *that* around for so long." His expression is still unusually soft and concerned, one I can barely remember seeing him have over the years. "That's why I fucking call you in the middle of the night when you're out driving the plow. But we can only do so much. We can't force you to talk things out. You need to try too. We care about you. So please, try."

Damnit. Have I been fucking up this bad for that long that everyone knows I've been unhappy and lonely? Just last week, Collin tried to get me to open up on the chairlift but I deflected and said I was fine. He was worried and he did try. And my grandparents. Apparently they've been able to read me forever. Maybe the walls I was putting up weren't as good as I thought and more people than I realized could see through. A knot grows in my stomach at the thought that people might have been trying to help me and were there for me and I was just too stubborn or oblivious to see it.

"Ok, Collin. I'll try," I mange to say, sincerely meaning it. Maybe if I had been better about opening up all along, things would be different.

"Good," he says. "It's about time. Just don't share too much mushy shit with me *all the time*."

A smile creeps on to my face, but I'm still a mess right now. "But what's the point, Collin? I already fucked up and she's going back to Ohio. This won't change anything now. I wasted my shot."

"Damn, ok. You really are a dumbass. You've clearly never been in a real relationship." he says, smiling at me as if he knows something I don't.

"Umm, ok? Then fill me in, Mr. Know It All." Now I'm dying to know what he has to say.

"Look, Chap. You did fuck up. But neither of you were wrong, you're just idiots that got upset and didn't communicate. That's not the end of the world."

A sense of hope starts to creep back in my head. Can I actually fix this?

"And this isn't your fault dude. The only ones to blame are that shit hole of a company and shit bag of a boss she works for. You two make each other better. I've never seen either of you this happy and that's saying a lot. So. I think you can still fix this. I'll help, but what's your move?"

"I want to go see her. I want to hold her. I just want to go to the condo and stop her. I don't want her to go," I say, desperate to erase the last three hours.

His eyes fall to the ground. "Yeah, that's probably not where I would start. She's in full blown panic mode now. She's got a one track mind and that's all about this fucking presentation back at the office. She's flying to SLC this afternoon and getting the first flight out tomorrow so she can make this client meeting."

"Fuck. What the hell am I going to do?" I feel like I'm losing her, like she's slipping through my fingers.

"Look, I know what she's like when this happens. Remember, I'm her twin after all," he says, peeling at the label on his beer, letting out a laugh. "We can do everything in the world to try and tell her to stop, relax, it'll be fine. But when her anxiety is that bad and gets to this point, there's only so much we can do. We're just along for the ride.

We can do everything to help avoid stressors and prevent it, but when it happens, we just gotta help her get through it."

"So what, I should just do *nothing*?" I look at Collin, trying to hide my irritation.

"Um, yeah. Exactly, sort of. For now, at least. If you try to convince her to stay right now, she's just going to get frustrated and feel like you're in her way, like you're not listening to her." I watch him as he takes a deep breath, like he's remembering something from their past.

"I know it sucks, but sometimes that's how it is dude. She's called me or come to my place absolutely panicking so many times over the years. Back in college it would be about exams. Then when she graduated it would be big work projects, interviews for promotions, you name it." Collin looks at me, taking another sip of his beer now. "It's hard to reason with her sometimes. In her mind the only thing that matters is crossing this thing off her list so the stress and anxiety go away with it. And I know all I want to do, all I'm sure you wanted to do, is try to fix it for her or rationalize with her. But really, she just needs you to listen and you need to ask her what she needs to get through this. It may not make sense to you, but that's sort of just how it is. And once she gets through this, she'll be ready to listen."

I take a minute to think about what he's saying, spinning my beer bottle in my hand. I didn't handle this great. I should have listened more. I should have just been there for her, however she needed me. Not try and talk her out of what she felt she needed to do, but just be there and support her decision.

While I replay the argument in my head, wishing I could get a chance to go back and get a do-over. I feel Collin's hand rest on my shoulder.

"Seriously, stop beating yourself up." He pauses again, shaking his head now as he mumbles under his breath. "I can't believe I'm gonna fucking compare my sister to skiing, but here we are I guess… Dude, remember the first time we skied Corbett's as kids? The conditions were perfect and we were feeling it. There was no way we weren't gonna do it."

He looks at me, expecting a response. I'm not sure if it's the one he wants though. What I do remember about that day is Collin was being a little bitch and was afraid to go down the steep rocky chute. Ronni didn't miss the chance to show up her brother and took the shot into the couloir while I was still egging Collin on to finally go.

My fucking Ronni. God I can't believe I fucked this up.

"Ok. So what?" I look at him, still not sure what he's getting at.

"Geez. I'm really going to have to spell it out for you then. My point is, this is your chance. Everything is lined up for you. You just have to let go, get out of your damn head, and send it Chap."

Fuck me. He's right. I need to stop moping around and make things happen.

"You know, you're actually pretty good at this motivational shit, Collin," I say, feeling the tension in my jaw slowly fade away.

"Yeah, no shit. Right? That's half my job. So really, what are you thinking about doing?" He looks at me with a curious smile.

"I think I've only got one choice then really. But I'm also gonna need a favor. Or two." I look at Collin, his eyebrow now raised, as he spins in his barstool to face me.

"Well now I'm the curious one," he says. The smile on his face is the one I've known since we were boys, the one we both make when we're about to do something dumb as hell, but fun.

"You ever driven a plow?" I ask, my expression matching his. Yep. This is gonna be crazy and dumb, that's for sure.

"Are you serious? You know I haven't but I've always wanted to!" He's practically jumping out of his stool, grabbing both of my shoulders.

"So, you're in?" I laugh at his reaction. "Just please don't crash it or hit one of my clients' houses, ok?"

"I'll do my best." He shrugs. "But what's the other favor?"

Chapter 45

Veronica
Earth SnaX

I managed to book the only remaining flight out today from Jackson to Salt Lake, leaving just after lunch. I'll have to stay in Salt Lake overnight, but it means I can take the first flight in the morning and get to the office in time.

Collin and Lizzy help me load my bags before taking me to the airport. I should get into Dayton just before lunch tomorrow and be able to go straight to the office. I'll just have to settle on wearing the most professional thing I packed on the trip. Good thing Earth SnaX is pretty casual.

At the airport, the mood is somber. We stop at the curb outside the terminal, and Collin and Lizzy get out with me. Collin goes around to unload my bags from the hatch of his SUV.

"You got this, girl. Go crush it. They'll have to remember this the next time you're up for that director promotion," Lizzy says, before leaning in for a hug.

I feign a smile, the best I can do. "Thanks. I sure hope so."

When I pull back from her hug, I find myself looking through the crowd outside the terminal. I realize I'm looking for that tall, handsome man I've fallen in love with.

"Hey, sis," Collin says, watching my eyes scan the crowd. "Just go kill your presentation. *Tanner* will be fine, I'll talk to him again."

His words make my heart sink. Do I still want him? Does he still want me? He didn't come to say goodbye. And can we still make this work? He still lives here in Wyoming and I'm going back to Ohio, to the real world. I feel myself starting to frown as my head sags.

"V. Stop it. Everything's going to be fine," Collin says, pulling me into a comforting bear hug. "I love you, sis. Have a good flight."

I feel Lizzy join in the hug. As I walk into the airport, I realize I don't know where I'd be without these two. But still, I find myself peering over my shoulder, looking back for *him*. It's been hours now and I still haven't heard from him.

My mind is consumed with going back over every detail of the presentation. I'm hellbent on killing it, my own personal fuck you to Jeff. By the time Wednesday morning comes around, I feel like my pre-vacation self.

I stayed up all night in my hotel room, reviewing each slide, time after time, prepping for this afternoon's presentation. Right on schedule, I arrive at the office by 11:30 AM, just enough time to grab lunch and run to the bathroom and check my hair. I'd love to do more than just check it, but I realized last night, at the hotel, that Lizzy forgot most of my toiletries when she was helping me pack. As soon as I realized, I placed an order for some backup items, already scheduled for delivery to my house.

Oh well.

I finish checking my makeup before heading to the conference room. Ok. Back on track, Veronica. You've got this.

Being back in the office feels surreal, like a cruel joke. Only twenty-four hours ago I was enjoying every minute in Wyoming, with Tanner, being outside, with friends, relaxed and having fun. Now I'm back in this old dated office building in suburban Ohio and it just feels foreign.

To his credit, Jeff had arranged for the Earth SnaX team to spend the morning with our R&D team, followed by lunch with our sales team, leaving marketing for last. But even with the time to prep last night and today, I'm still an anxious bundle of nerves. Before I head into the conference room, I stop to fill my water bottle to try and take care of my dry mouth. That's when I feel my phone buzz.

Jeff knows it's only ten minutes until we're scheduled to start. He should also know I can't change anything in the presentation at this point. When I look at my phone though, my heart sinks down to my stomach and immediately bounces back into my throat.

Tanner: Hey Ronni. I'd say good luck in the presentation today, but you don't need it. You'll kick ass. I know it. We'll talk soon. Love you.

I touch the screen as if running my fingers over his words will bring me closer to him. My heart slowly works its way back into its normal home in my chest as I hear his words, in his voice, in the back of my mind. Even over a thousand miles away, he can make me relax and feel confident in my own skin like no one else can. The thought of talking to him soon is enough to help me push through with the rest of the day, this presentation.

As I finally go into the conference room, I'm surrounded by familiar faces from Fischer. One face catches me by surprise though, Cindy. Shit, I totally forgot she wanted to talk when I was back from vacation. I wonder if she realizes I'm back early.

Alright. It's go time. Let's send it.

Two hours laters and I'm spent. Emotionally, mentally, physically. The presentation and pitch are done. It went amazing, at least I think so. I went through the material without even having to look back at the screen, knowing my transitions, talking points, everything by heart. Earth SnaX had some good questions, but I had better answers. I just wish Jeff would have been here to appreciate it. You're welcome, dude. Not only did I save your ass, again, but I blew it out of the water.

After the presentation, I head towards the water fountain to refill my water bottle when Cindy leaves the conference room and finds me.

"Hey, Veronica, that was great," she says. "We're really excited about the new packaging line."

"Thanks, Cindy," I say, feeling a small sense of vindication for all of my work. I'm relieved that Jeff couldn't take credit for my hard work and effort to make this entire presentation even happen.

"How was vacation? I'm sorry they called you to come back early. I know that must have been hard," she says, a bit of remorse in her voice. It's oddly heartwarming to hear that from someone in her position. I can't think of the last time Jeff was this nice or considerate.

"It was good. I wish I was still there though," I say, trying my best to not look like the last twenty-four hours have been a disaster.

"Well, I'm sure you're exhausted," she says, checking her watch. "But hey, when you're rested, give me a call. I had a project I was thinking you'd be able to help with and after that presentation, I'm positive you're just the person for it."

I'm still curious what this project is and why Jeff hasn't mentioned it, but she's right. I'm exhausted and just want to crawl into bed and get some sleep.

"Sounds good. Thanks for thinking of me, Cindy. Looking forward to hearing all about it. I know you are flying back tonight, so let's chat Monday." I shake her hand and say goodbye to some of the other Earth SnaX team before heading home.

When I finally get to my house, it feels just as surreal as the office. I drop my checked bag and carry on bag on the coffee table. Even just walking through my house, I feel out of place. I've lived here since moving out of my last apartment years ago, but there just aren't any real memories here. I've never even brought home a date. It just doesn't feel like *home*, like something is missing, like I don't belong here.

I'm drained, emotionally and physically a wreck. I head to the bedroom to pass out. I just need to sleep, get my head straight, and get back on with my life.

Chapter 46

Tanner
Another Night with Me

"Seriously, bud. I don't know how you got so lucky to spend most of your nights with me. But we have to stop making a habit of lonely nights."

I look at Rex in the passenger seat, as I drive through the snow, our usual nightly routine, the radio low in the background.

"I know, Rex. It's way more fun when she's here and you get to sit in the middle. You'll just have to settle for another night with me."

Driving through the snow, looking at the snowbanks along the side of the road, my mind is a mess. Before the last couple weeks, my mind always drifted through a bitter cycle of loneliness, depression, and anger.

The last two weeks though, I've felt *alive*. I've felt happy. I've felt hopeful. These last couple of weeks have been the best time of my life.

I always knew I loved her, but I never realized how much she would make me feel whole, how much she'd push me to open up and be the best version of myself. She understands me.

I still feel alive now, even with her back in Ohio. She lit a fire in my cold dark heart. But now I feel desperate, a driving need to get what we had back. To feel whole again, forever.

I need to fix this, to make things right. I hurt Ronni, the one thing I never wanted to do, and now all I can think about is fixing it. I promised her she could trust me, that I'd keep fighting for this. But I keep going back to what she said back at the cabin after our dinner at Gloria's.

> *It's your turn to trust me. I might have a bad day, I might panic, you're not always going to be able to fix everything for me. But trust that I'm going to keep loving you. Just keep fighting for it.*

I look over at Rex, he's staring right back at me. It's like he finally knows what I'm thinking.

"I know Rex, we've got a lot of work to do tonight. It's time to fight."

Chapter 47

Ronni
Full. Send.

Thursday morning comes and I'm back in the office. I grab a coffee from the cafeteria, again feeling like being here is some kind of cruel joke. The coffee sucks too, certainly not an iced honey badger.

As I walk through the building towards my cubicle, I remember that Lizzy isn't here to stop and talk with. Ugh I miss her. I miss Collin too. And Tanner. I wonder what they're doing back in Wyoming. My heart aches wishing I was there.

Lizzy is still flying home tomorrow and Collin is driving home over the weekend. And Tanner… I hope he's ok. I'd give anything to talk to him right now but I don't know if he would even want to hear from me. He texted me yesterday before the presentation and said we'd talk soon, but I haven't heard from him since. I told him to *trust me* and I just panicked and left, so I sort of get it. But still, I miss him.

I sit at my cubicle and try to get my head focused back on work. Since the presentation went well, I have a few things I need to start working on to finalize everything we went over yesterday and send it back to Earth SnaX. Then we can get their final approval before the new packaging goes into production. Hopefully it's not the same fiasco as Princeton Mills.

Not even ten minutes later, an unwelcome, albeit familiar nasally voice gets my attention away from my computer.

"Veronica," Jeff says. "I heard the presentation went well yesterday."

I spin around in my chair. I eye Jeff carefully, trying to hide the irritation, no, utter disdain I feel for him right now. He interrupted my perfect vacation, my perfect time with Tanner, and brought me crashing down and back here.

He's about as nondescript and dry as a person can get. Mid-fifties, a little overweight, receding hairline, wearing khakis, worn brown leather shoes, and a light blue golf polo. Basically, he's the picture you'd expect to see next to *Boomer Manager* if it were in a dictionary.

"Yeah, they loved it," I say proudly. "Just working on the next steps now for them to approve these drafts and get it into final production."

"Great," he says curtly, setting his coffee on my desk and leaning against the cubicle wall.

"So is there anything else I can help with since I'm back from vacation early?" I ask, my irritation starting to show, wishing he would just walk away. I'm still exhausted and just want to get through the day in one piece. Can he just go already?

"Nope, not really," he says. "Glad you're back. That could have been a disaster. We'll have to think twice about it the next time you want to take that much time off."

"You know, I had that trip planned for months. We could have scheduled the presentation for when I was going to be in town so I could give it, like I originally suggested." I bury my thoughts, not saying everything I want to out loud. Seriously Jeff, if you would have just listened to me months ago, this mess could have been avoided. It was your lack of planning that became my emergency.

"Well, glad it worked out. I need you here. We still need to be more careful next time with planning time off," he says, grabbing his coffee.

This fucking guy. Instead of thanking me for covering for him, he's haranguing me about my vacation and about taking time off in the future. What is his fucking deal? The. Fucking. Audacity.

"Well, if I'm so essential, maybe you should have thought about that when you turned me down for the director role for the third time." The words come rushing out of me, catching me off guard. But I'm not even sorry. It's true.

"You know that's not how things work, Veronica," he says, his tone matching my own irritation.

"Then how do they work, Jeff? I've been the top performer on this team for years. I've covered for you so many times. I've put together most of the work you've taken credit for. So yeah, tell me what I need to do. Enlighten me, please."

I feel the flood gates open, years of angst pouring out of me. In the back of my head, I hear Tanner's voice.

Stop wasting your life on something that brings you down... They don't deserve you...

Fuck, why does he always have to be right? I wasn't ready to hear those words when he said them, but after being back here, I know he was right. I don't need this. I still don't know exactly what I need in my life, but it's absolutely not *this*.

I look at Jeff, his eyes wide, a vein throbbing in his forehead as he opens his mouth, like a fish gasping for air, to start to say something.

Nope, hold that thought, Jeff.

Fuck it. Let's do it, Ronni.

Full. Send.

"Jeff, you know what, don't even bother telling me what I need to do to convince you I'm worthy of being director. I quit."

I quit.

Those two words.

I don't think I've ever felt more satisfied, more alive, more relieved, by saying two simple words before.

Is this what Tanner feels like all the time, just letting go and doing what he wants?

The stunned look on Jeff's face brings an eager grin to my own. Fuck, that felt so good.

I stand up, grabbing my bag and a couple things off my desk.

"It's been real, Jeff," I say, as I turn around and walk towards the exit, down the long drab hallway.

I've walked down this hallway thousands of times over the years. I remember the starry eyed Veronica that first came here, the dreams she had, how excited she was to be here. That girl feels so foreign now, her dreams no longer my own. Walking down this hallway now, all I can think about is how I don't want those things any more.

I want to be happy. I want time for the people I love. I want time to do the things I love.

The thought takes my mind back to something else Tanner said when we were arguing.

Maybe I should grow up and be more like you. Give up on the things I've always wanted, like you.

In the moment, I thought he was saying he should just give up *like me*. But now, thinking about all the things I want, I realize he meant *give up me*. Give up what he's wanted the most in life.

No Tanner, you were right. Please don't give up. Please keep fighting.

My heart stings at the thought of him being that hurt, feeling like he should give up hope.

Fuck. I can't wait to never see this toxic place again. I walk out the doors into the cool winter air with the warm sun on my face, feeling like a new me.

Chapter 48

Ronni
The Stowaways

I flop down on my couch, exhaling as the events of the last two days flash through my mind like a slideshow. Forty-eight hours ago, I was the happiest I've ever been in my life. I was in Jackson, waking up with the man of my dreams, living in a cocoon of security, sheltered from the stresses of my life.

Now, I'm back in the midwest. I crushed my presentation I left it all for, only to quit the job I've worked at for pretty much my entire adult life.

Fuck, Ronni. You really did it, you really channeled your inner Tanner Chapman.

I feel an unhinged smile forming on my face. I still have no idea what I'm going to do next, but for once, the uncertainty is welcome. I think... I'm actually excited about the unknown. I can start fresh, do what I want, on my own terms.

As I try to calm my nerves, I look at my large checked bag on the coffee table in front of me. It's been such a whirlwind. I'm normally the type to unpack the second I get back, but now I've been home for a day and still haven't stopped long enough to unpack and do laundry.

I unzip my checked roller bag. I let out a small sigh. Lizzy did a shitty job packing for me, it's a mess. She didn't even bother to use my packing cubes to keep stuff organized.

After pulling out a few things, my heart stops.

There's a roll of beautiful brown leather, held shut by a small leather tie wrapped around it. I run my fingers down it, feeling the smooth leather, my fingers trembling as they reach the horseshoe with a TC branded into it.

I unfurl the roll on the couch cushion next to me. My hand involuntarily jumps to cover my gaping mouth as I fight back tears.

There are two knives tucked into their pockets in the roll. At first, all I can see are the handles. The handles are a gorgeous, translucent resin, tinted teal. Floating in the teal resin of the handles are dried cayenne peppers, honeycombs, pieces of cinnamon sticks, and coffee beans.

I pull the larger knife from the roll, holding it out in front of me, admiring the way the handle fits perfectly into my hand. It's a long, K-tipped blade chef's knife. The Damascus steel blade is flawless, the alternating layers of light and dark steel look like tiger stripes. I place it back in its pocket, pulling the smaller one out to admire it.

As I pull it out, a note tucked behind the smaller one falls out. My heart is pounding. I've been so laser focused the last day and a half that I haven't texted or called Tanner back. Well that, and I've been afraid to.

I realize I'm holding my breath as I open the note.

Ronni,

I know you always said you'd like a set of your own. I made these just for you. I hope these are to your liking. I think they're the most beautiful ones I've ever made. Fitting for you the most beautiful, kind, strong person I know.

When I made these, I used some of Starlight's old horseshoes I found in the barn. I always remembered how happy you were when Grandpa would let you ride her. I hope you can think about being happy like that whenever you use these...

And I'm sorry. I'm sorry I said what I did. I'm sorry I didn't come to the airport. I never wanted to hurt you. I've loved you as long as I can remember and always will. I hope you can find a way to still trust me and forgive me.

Love,

Tanner

I stare at the note, watching a tear land on it, pooling over his handwriting before it runs down to my fingers.

I need to leave. I need to be with him.

I can feel the tears streaming down my face now.

I grab my phone to call Collin. He picks up on the first ring. Thank god.

"Hey lil sis, you doing ok? How was the presentation?" he asks, surprisingly calm.

I rush around the house in a flurry, grabbing things to throw back into my bag. "I'm coming back. I need to be back in Wyoming. I need to see Tanner."

"Woah. Hold up. Slow down. What happened?" I can hear the concern in his voice, as I try to fight back the tears.

"I quit. I killed the presentation yesterday, but today… I just couldn't fucking take it. I quit and walked out." I hear a brief chuckle before he talks again.

I think I hear Lizzy now in the background, asking what's going on before he replies smugly. "Well, it's about fucking time. I'm so proud of you."

"I'm looking at flights now. I'm going to come out. I can't stay here. I need to be there. I need to be with Tanner." I say.

"I take it you found the stowaways then?" His tone is so smug now, I can picture his shit eating grin.

"You little shit. I thought that was Lizzy. Can you pick me up at the airport today or tomorrow? If I can't get a flight, I'm just going to drive tonight. I just…" I can't fight back the tears. "I just need to be with him."

He pauses for a second before speaking. "V. Calm down. It's going to be ok. Get some rest today, we'll get you back out here. Please, just don't leave yet. You're exhausted and-"

Nope. Fuck this. I can't bear another second without him.

Screw flying, I'm leaving now.

I need to see him. I need to be with him. "I'm leaving Collin. I'll put you on speaker in the car."

I throw the knife roll into the open bag and hastily zip it shut. I walk out the door, locking it behind me before frantically rushing to my car in the driveway.

I throw the bag in my trunk before getting in the driver seat. God, I just want to be back in Wyoming. Back with him. Back in my safe place.

I start to back down my driveway when I look in my rearview mirror. God fucking damnit. Of course my delivery shows up now, blocking my driveway, parked practically inches from my car.

No one is fucking slowing me down from getting back to Tanner. No one.

I throw the door of my car open, trembling with rage ready to ruin this delivery driver's day if they don't get out of my way.

They're getting out of the delivery van, still behind their door as I step in their direction. Fuck. I can't wait to never see this toxic place again. I walk out the doors into the cool winter air with the warm sun on my face, feeling like a new me.

I feel my heart stop. My legs no longer working as the driver turns around.

It's not a delivery van. It's a Sprinter van. A slate gray Sprinter van.

It's *him*.

Here.

Over a thousand miles away from Jackson. In my driveway.

My rugged mountain of a man, Tanner.

"I'm sorry, Ronni. I just ha-," he starts to talk, Rex hopping out to be by his side.

I take the last hurried steps to him and collapse into his broad chest, holding him close. His scent, that familiar earthy leather and pine, surrounds me. His warmth, the sound of his heart beating in his chest, all of it making me feel safe and at home. I never want to let go of him again.

"Why did you come?" I manage to say through my sniffles, the tears slowing down. "How did you get here so fast?"

"I'm an idiot, Ronni. I'm sorry. I didn't mean to hurt you. I know you work hard, I know your career is important to you. I didn't mean to upset you or insult you. I hated seeing you like that though. I should have just been there to help you, however you needed it. I just need you to know that *I love you*. That I'll do anything to be with you. That I do trust you and you can trust that I'll always be here for you, that I'll always fight for us. Even it means driving twenty-four hours straight with Rex to come make sure you're ok."

His deep voice brings so much reassurance. It's only been two days since I last heard it and I still didn't realize how much I missed it.

"Well, I appreciate that Tanner. You're right, you were an ass," I say, one side of my mouth starting to form a smile as I sniffle. "But also, you were right about my job. I don't need that place. I don't need to keep things in my life that bring me down. I need the things that lift me up and make me better, like you."

"What are you saying?" he asks, tilting my face towards his, those evergreen forests peering into my soul with a questioning look.

"I quit today. Can we please just go back to Wyoming?"

Chapter 49

Tanner
Along for the Ride

Her hazel eyes are gorgeous, even with tears in them. I could stare into them and never get tired of the way they make me feel. Like she really can see me.

Looking into them now though, I've never been more surprised or impressed.

"Really? You quit?" I say, holding her cheek in my palm and I can feel my jaw slowly drop before I start to smile. I'm stunned, but I've also never been prouder of her. Even past the tears, I can see her confidence in herself growing.

"Yep. I went *full send.* Channeled my inner Tanner Chapman." Her tears are slowing to a trickle, a smile now trying to take root on her face. Fuck me, that smile. I missed it. I needed it. I drove twenty-four hours straight just hoping to see it again.

"Damn. I mean that's awesome. You're a badass. I guess I must have rubbed off on you more than I thought," I say, winking at her before kissing her. I exhale deeply. I can't believe how much I already missed her touch.

"You know, I was ready to live outside in your driveway, in the van, just to be close to you," I say, my voice low, holding my forehead to hers.

She pulls away, looking back up at me.

"Oh yeah? Not sure my neighbors would like that arrangement," she teases before wiping the last remaining tears out of her eyes.

I look back at the van. "Fair enough. But you're right, driving back to Wyoming with you sounds way better." The thought of being next to her, driving across the country for twenty-four hours sounds perfect right now. We have so much to talk about and I'll have to keep my hands on the wheel, off of her, which will be hard to do. But it will be worth it.

"So we're really doing this? Going back to Wyoming, together?"

I look into her hazel eyes, the little gold flecks sparkling back at me. I already know the answer but still can't believe this is really happening.

"Yes, please. I'm never leaving your side again. I'm along for the ride, wherever it takes us, as long as it's with you," she says, resting her head back on my chest. "So when can we leave?" She looks down at Rex then back to me. "I just want to go home, with you. So the sooner, the better."

Those words brand themselves on my heart.

Home, with you.

Home hasn't always felt *like home* for me in the past. But now, I don't know what's next. I just know for once in my life, whatever comes our way, I'll be happy having her by my side.

"Hey, wait," I say, a thought popping in my head. "Weren't you just on the phone?"

"Oh fuck! Collin!" We look back towards her car together, the driver door open only a few steps away from where we're standing.

"Collin, you're on speaker, if you're still there," Ronni says.

"Oh yeah, we're both still here. Didn't miss a word of *that*," Lizzy cackles. "So, are you guys going to hit the road? If you get your butts moving I'll get my flight changed and we can have a couple more days in Jackson together."

"Yes, that sounds perfect. See you soon. Love you guys. I'm hanging up now," Ronni says, grabbing her phone and making sure to finally hang up this time.

We go inside so she can finish packing, this time a little less hurried. It's the first time I've ever actually been to Ohio, much less her house. I'm guessing we'll come back again some other time to grab her car and other stuff, but for now she just wants to grab what she can fit in the van to take back to Wyoming. Who knows, maybe we can convince Collin and Lizzy to drive her car out with the rest of her stuff sometime and fly them back.

I can't stop laughing at her and shaking my head though. She just quit her job, in the middle of ski season and is going to have the foreseeable future off to enjoy the mountains in Wyoming. I'm almost jealous, actually.

I notice she's standing at her nightstand, looking down at some black silk bags in the drawer.

"What are those?" I wrap my arm around her, planting a kiss on her neck.

"Just my boyfriends before you." She turns to me, biting her finger tip. She runs her other hand across the front of my jeans. "I don't think I'll be needing them any more."

I crane my neck, bringing my mouth to hers, feeling it open as her tongue finds mine. I pull back, already feeling myself breathing heavy.

"Hey. Let's not be too crazy now. I'm not ashamed to say we could have some fun with those. And I think we have room to bring them along," I say with a wink.

She smirks back at me, raising one eyebrow.

"Ok. If you say so." Her voice is low and sultry and her fingers are still lingering on the front of my jeans. "Do we have time for a quickie? I've missed you and it would be a shame for you to finally make it to Ohio and not be able to say you got to fuck your girlfriend here."

Yep. I'm definitely hard now. I can already feel my cock straining against my my fly. Definitely wasn't part of today's plan but there's zero chance I'm saying no to her, *ever*.

"Take your pants off," I growl, already unzipping my fly and pulling my jeans off. "Now."

She eagerly obliges, pulling her pants down and kicking them to the side. She stands back on her toes, planting a kiss on my neck before looking into my eyes, a taunting smirk on her face. She reaches up to spin my black flat bill hat around. "Keep the hat on. I like it."

"Anything you want, Ronni." I grin before I turn her around and pull her into me, her ass now against my boxer briefs, teasing myself so bad. I get her on the bed and on her knees, facing the headboard. She pants as I kiss the back of her neck, running my hands up her thighs before I run my fingers along the fabric of her thong.

"I missed you, Tanner. I won't leave like that again, not letting you know where things stand. I love you." Her words shoot right to my heart, almost erasing the pain of the last two days.

"I love you too." I slide her thong down, leaving it at her knees. I press myself into her, my cock desperate to be out of my briefs as I grind it between her ass cheeks. I pull down my briefs and take them off.

I look to the side of the bedroom, to the mirror on the wall. We make eye contact in the mirror, each admiring the way our bodies fit together so perfectly, like they were made for each other. But the way she looks at me, the way *she sees me,* is something I'll never get tired of.

I run the back of my hand over her cheek before gently tucking the loose strands of her hair behind her ear. The way she closes her eyes and gently whimpers at my touch is pure music to my ears.

"Now, grab the headboard." I tell her, but don't even give her the chance before I grab her wrists and pin them on the headboard for her. The sight of her wrists and hands engulfed by my inked fingers makes my breath hitch.

Seeing the words *FULL SEND* spelled out in this moment, I can't think of another time in my life where just letting go and saying fuck it has given me so much. I was always so afraid of this one thing, letting my feelings for her be seen, out in the open, exposing myself.

I finally let go and here I am, with the love of my life and all she wants is me.

I look back into the mirror, addicted to the way she arches her back, pressing her ass against me, her body begging me to be inside her.

"I'm going to fucking remind your pussy that it's all mine. I'm going to make you come for me."

I run my cock up and down her slit and she's so wet and ready for me. The way her body wants me is intoxicating and unleashes something wild in me.

I rest the tip just inside her opening, teasing both of us. I lean forward kissing her neck as my hands reach for her hips. I run my fingers over her hip bones, pulling her tight against me.

"Please, Tanner. Fuck me. I want to feel you in me," she whimpers.

I crane my neck and whisper into her ear. "I will be, soon."

I leave one hand on her hip as the other runs down the front of her body to her clit. I spread her lips just enough to run a finger down to her opening and feeling the head of my cock in her, seeing just how wet she is. I bring the finger back to her clit and start running it over her swollen pleasure point in slow circles.

She moans and her body clenches, pressing herself further into me, driving my cock into her, past the tip now.

I ease in with slow thrusts, deeper and deeper each time, pulling her into me with my fingers still hooked on her hip bone. My other hand still teases her clit and she's rocking her ass back into me in rhythm with my thrusts.

"Fuck, Ronni. You feel so goddamn good. I'm not going to last very long like this." My voice is already fraying and I know it won't be long. I start running my finger over her clit faster and faster and can feel her walls start to tighten along my shaft.

"Good, because if you keep doing that I'm going to come so hard." Her words push me closer and closer and I start rocking my hips into her harder and harder.

I watch her nails dig into the fabric of her headboard as she moans and shudders. I feel her walls clench and flutter on my cock as she comes, muttering an inaudible swear into the headboard. The way she sighs and exhales in relief, her body still rocking with mine, feeling her ass against my hips with each thrust, pushes me over the edge. I feel myself let go, her walls tighten on my cock with each pulse of my release.

I grab her chin, turning her face to mine. I kiss her, our mouths open as we both gasp for air.

"I'm never going to stop fighting for us, Ronni. Never. I love you too fucking much." I press my forehead to hers, kissing her one more time.

After grabbing a shower and packing a few more things, we make one more pass through her house. I watch how she goes through the house, stopping to look at things here and there. Even though she might be back eventually to get what she needs if Collin or Lizzy can't help, I don't get the feeling that it's a hard or sad goodbye for her. She looks happy and excited, like she's welcoming the journey ahead and actually ok with not knowing exactly what's next.

After we finish loading up the van, we hit the road and spend the next twenty-four hours taking turns driving across the country with Rex, back to Jackson. Until the last day and a half, I've barely been more than five hours outside of Jackson, just occasionally visiting my family in Salt Lake. Now, I'm seeing new place after new place, listening to the radio, laughing, and talking about a future with Ronni.

Ronni, my forever dream woman.

As the drive wears on, it's my turn to drive across Eastern Wyoming on the final stretch before we get back. She sleeps in the passenger seat, head resting on a pillow against the window, Rex curled up at her feet. Even when she's sleeping, I can barely look away from her, stealing every glance I can while still watching the road.

I can't describe the feeling of hope, of optimism it brings me to be with her. She can make my day better just by smiling at me, grounding me in the present. She can read when I'm down and ask me what's wrong and be there to help. She fills a hole in my heart I was worried would be left open forever.

I fucking love this woman and I know I'll do anything for her.

Always.

Forever.

Chapter 50

Ronni
Home

T he bright sunlight reflecting off the snow covered ground sneaks through my eyelids, waking me up. Rex is asleep at my feet, acting like my own personal foot warmer. Tanner is still driving along, focused on the road. He's at ease, relaxed, a gentle smile on his always handsome face. His beard has started to fill back in but I can still clearly make out those dimples.

I could watch him like this all day. I try to stay still as long as I can, knowing if he realizes I'm awake he'll start talking to me, disturbing this magical little moment. I've learned that once you get him to open up, it's actually hard to keep him quiet.

"Well hello there, horny badger." His low voice breaks the silence. His eyes are still on the road, but I can see the side of his mouth lift into a smirk, deepening his dimple. "Hope you got some beauty rest. Not that you need it."

"Damnit. How'd you know I was awake?" I playfully punch him in the shoulder, trying not to move too much so I don't wake Rex up.

"You stopped snoring, so I figured you were up. Wait, you do know you snore, right? I have no idea how Collin sleeps on that top bunk with you down there sawing logs. Going to have to ask him how he does it, I guess," he says with a laugh. "It'll be totally worth it though."

The thought of going to bed with him every night and waking up with him each morning floods my head and makes my heart melt. I love the thought even more knowing that he's thinking about it too.

"Very funny, Tanner. I don't snore." I cross my arms, huffing and pouting in a way that would make Lizzy proud. I look down at Rex, realizing I moved enough to wake him up as he lets out a lazy yawn.

Tanner looks down at Rex before stealing a glance at me, flashing those green eyes. "You know he likes you, right? Like a lot."

"Well I like him too. But I love his dad even more." I grab Tanner's hand, squeezing it tightly. I never want to let go of it again. He is my forever person.

"I love you too," he says, his thumb rubbing the back of my hand in his.

Looking outside and down the road, I can just make out the Tetons, backlit by the sun setting behind them.

"So, it looks like we're near Jackson. How long of a shift did you take driving?"

"Oh, it's been about four hours. You zonked out pretty hard. I didn't want to wake you up. You're pretty when you sleep, *even if you snore.*" I see the corner of his mouth lift into a smirk again, one of his dimples peeking out.

"I do *not* snore, Tanner," I say, still in denial. "But thanks for driving so long. I can't wait to be back. What time do you think we'll get in?"

"Hmmm. I'd say about 6:30 PM or so. Should be back in time for dinner. You should call your brother and Lizzy. I know they'll want to see you and hear all about how you told Jeff to pound sand." He looks at me, grinning wide.

I told him the full story last night. He loved every second of the story and didn't even give me an *I told you so* lecture even though he was totally right about it. The way he looked at me when I told him, the awe and pride in his eyes, was more validation than I ever needed to know I did the right thing.

"Oh, Lizzy is going to love that story. It feels like so much has happened since they dropped me off at the airport. I can't wait to see them." I grin thinking about how she'll react when I give her all the details.

Tanner looks back over at me. "Yeah. I can't wait to see them either. Hopefully we can convince Collin to stay out in Wyoming for a bit longer. Two weeks just doesn't seem like enough time to spend together."

I'm still holding his hand, our fingers woven together. My thumb tracing the outline of the Tetons on his wrist, as we drive towards those very mountains outlined by the sunset ahead of us. I never want to let go of him. I think about the last time I ripped my hand from his, frantically running away because I was afraid to hear the truth about my job and come to terms with leaving it. It was barely three days ago, but it feels like a lifetime ago.

"We'll work on him. He can work remote for a bit I'm sure," I say, realizing Tanner hasn't been working for the last two days. "Hey wait, who's been managing the properties and driving the plow? We can't both be unemployed!" That question gets me a laugh, the boyish one I've known for years. The laugh that makes my heart flutter and brings out his dimples.

"Funny you mention that. Collin's been doing it. Apparently it's been a dream of his to drive a plow?" He's shaking his head and still laughing.

"Why am I not surprised," I say, palming my face. "You know, you guys would make a great team."

"That's not a bad idea at all, Ronni. We're definitely going to have to work on him," he says.

"So… *what's next*?" I used too hate this question. But now for the first time in a while, I don't have some grand detailed life plan and I'm perfectly ok with that.

It's simple now, just be with him.

That's all the plan I need.

"Right now? I just want to keep going and get us home," he says, eyes on the road but still smiling. "After that, we can do whatever you want."

I can feel his hand squeeze mine tighter when he says *home*.

I think about that word and the last two weeks. I've always thought of Jackson as this special place, a fairy tale escape. But now, I might actually get to call it home.

Home with Tanner, the man of my dreams. The man that grounds me. The man that I trust. The man that reminds me I'm strong. The man who pours his heart and love into me, giving me as much as I need. The man that I'm hopelessly in love with.

I look back to the road stretching out in front of us. With the sun setting behind the mountains, the sky is a beautiful collage of blues, purples, reds, and yellows. It's a view I've seen so many times, but now, with Tanner here, it's more magical. If I could live in this moment forever, I would.

I don't know everything that's in store for us. I know it won't always be easy. I just know that I want to be with Tanner. Always. I'd follow him anywhere. I don't care where we end up.

Home is wherever I'm with him.

He is my *home*.

Epilogue

Ronni
2 Months Later

After lunch, we get in line for the gondola. Tanner and I get in the car easily and watch as Collin and Lizzy stumble and fuss with their skis, failing to get on the same gondola with us. It almost looks like they're ignoring the help of the lifties. Somehow, even with all that practice two months ago in Jackson, Lizzy still hasn't figured it out here in Aspen Valley. Laughing, we look back at her and my brother. I see an amused look on her face and a shit eating grin on his. I must be seeing things because I swear I even see Lizzy wink.

I groan. "Those two. Always causing trouble." Across the gondola car, Tanner looks at me, his eyes that familiar, smoldering green. Somehow it never fails to make my stomach flutter and make my skin tingle.

"Oh no," I wave my hands in surrender. "No no no. Not again," I say, practically giggling. "We have no idea how long this gondola is and this one isn't nearly as tinted."

He laughs, but his gaze never leaves mine. It's been that way for the last two months since the *mudroom*. The two of us, his loving eyes always on me. And I've learned so much about myself since then.

Tanner and I have pushed each other to be the best versions of ourselves. He's helped me to focus more on the moment, to only worry about what I can actually control, and to keep learning to let go of the rest that I can't. I've pushed him to keep opening up, to stop bottling up his feelings, and to focus on what brings him joy, because I'll always be there for him.

Together, Tanner and I are learning we can both have what we've always wanted.

Jackson feels like home more than it ever has, for us both.

After our whirlwind drive *home* with Tanner, I put my house on the market. Collin took advantage of his ability to work remote and did the same. Now without mortgages in Ohio, we don't have to rent the condo any more and Collin is moving into it. He's going to keep his online clients, but he's taking on new clients at one of the local yoga studios from time to time.

Looking across the gondola, I can't help but feel my heart melt by the way this man makes me feel. He takes off his gloves and helmet, setting them neatly by his side before leaning across the gondola. I feel my cheeks flush as he smirks at me.

That smirk. Those dimples. He shows them more and more now and I make sure I never take them for granted. I feel like everyday he feels more comfortable about sharing his feelings instead of bottling things up. I've watched him become more focused, like a weight's been lifted off of him and he's free to focus on his property management company and making knives. With Collin's excitement about driving a plow, they plan to partner and grow that business.

He's even been dedicating more time and energy to his knives too. He seems so inspired to create. Now, instead of a case at the Eclectic Elk, he has a full wall dedicated to his work. Earlier this month, a chef at a big name restaurant in Seattle bought a set of his knives. He's working with Giselle to create a waitlist for custom pieces too.

Across from me, he lowers himself onto his knees, only pure worship in his eyes as the smirk leaves his face.

"I thought I just said we're not doing *that*, Tanner." I playfully raise an eyebrow at him. I can't believe I'm telling him *no*, but I've got to have *some* self control from time to time, as hard as that is around him.

"Ronni, I will always get on my knees for you. There's nothing you can do to stop me from loving you." His voice is gravel and strained. I've only seen him like this once before. That night in the mudroom when it looked like he was tormented about whether or not to kiss me. The night he finally leapt and we've never looked back.

And that's when my heart stops. He pulls a box from his pocket, one I've seen before. The velvet box I've kept my grandmother's engagement ring in all these years, hoping for my person to come into my life.

"Oh my god. Oh my god, Tanner." I gasp, my hands flying to my mouth. I can feel the tears already building in the corners of my eyes.

"Will you marry me, Ronni? I've been kicking myself for waiting this long to ask. But with you, I never want to waste another second that we could be together." His eyes stare deep into me, pleading yet confident, immediately grounding me the way he always does.

"Yes, Tanner. Yes!" I squeal through tears. "I love you so much."

"I love you too." He says, grinning wildly before leaning forward to kiss me like I'm the only thing in his world.

I still feel like I'm living in a fairy tale. He really was the missing puzzle piece in my life. With him by my side, it feels like the rest of my life has fallen neatly into place.

I have *my person.*

Someone that reminds me I'm strong and lifts me up. Someone that will take things off my plate without even being asked. Now I'm finally building my career to where I've always wanted. I'm surrounded by people that bring me up, make me better, and empower me to do more.

The first week back in Wyoming felt like the start of an entirely new chapter. I didn't know exactly what was next, but I was happy to be away from Fischer and looking for a fresh start. I still felt like I needed to close out that chapter of my life though, so I followed up with Cindy, as I had promised.

She was frankly not shocked that I left Fischer. As for the special project she wanted to talk about. Well, it was an offer to be the new Director of Marketing at Earth SnaX. One month into that job, and it already feels like I'm where I was always meant to be, like I found my professional home. I realized it wasn't the work that I hated, just the toxic environment that I was in and the people I was surrounded by.

And the best part about my job at Earth SnaX is that I work remotely, except for the occasional in person meetings I'll need to attend every few months.

Now I realize I needed the closure of going back to Dayton, to see just how much my life there was no longer what I wanted. Going back there, leaving the happy bliss of Jackson with Tanner, was the wake up call I needed. It made it that much easier to know I made the right choice to quit and do literally anything else besides stay at Fischer.

"I can't wait to get you back home and all to myself again," he says, his ever confident grin back. Those words, the thought of *home* with him, have never sounded better.

Instead of going into a dreary drab office five days a week, my new *commute* will be walk across the yard from the cabin to the old barn. After taking the job with Earth SnaX, Tanner started turning the loft of the old barn into a bright, airy, cheerful office for me. Instead of a worn gray cubicle with a view of a windowless hallway, I'll have a cozy room to myself with white shiplap walls and salvaged wood floors. Beyond the oversized picture window is going to be an incredible view, looking out over the yard and the mountains.

I look down at my hand now, staring at my Grandma's engagement ring on my finger, the one that my Grandpa had custom made for her, the one that I thought I would never find that *special someone* to wear it for. It's the perfect reminder of my grandparents' love for each other, their love of Wyoming and skiing, and now my love for Tanner.

Looking back into his eyes, my heart pounds. "I love you, and as good as that sounds, I'm pretty sure Lizzy will kill us if we go home early. She's been looking forward to this trip so much." I say, still grinning ear to ear. "But we've got a big comfy bed back at her condo we can put to use tonight." I wink at him, getting a gruff laugh in return.

"Alright, horny badger." He smirks and I can't help but giggle back at him. This man has my heart and it's so painfully obvious.

I have to admit that I can get a little distracted daydreaming about what our life will be like. I imagine looking out my office window into the yard to see Tanner playing with Rex, or listening to him work on knives in his shop. The feeling of warmth I get from picturing him smile out in the yard or hearing him use the forge, knowing he'll always be nearby, always there for me, is borderline overwhelming in the best of ways.

I know he would always say that Jackson isn't all fairy tales, but after living here now, with him, it feels like a dream come true. I can't imagine anywhere else I'd rather be. Building a life with this man in the mountains.

Acknowledgements and Notes

If you made it this far, thanks for reading my book. Seriously, getting feedback and hearing what people liked and didn't like was a huge part of what kept me writing this.

Doing this was a lot of fun and definitely a unique experience. I'm in my mid thirties and I haven't done any creative writing since I wrote a ten or so page short story in high school.

With the encouragement of my partner, I kept at it and had the first draft done in about 6 weeks. After a couple months of editing and toying with other ideas, I finally had a copy I felt was good enough to share with a few beta readers.

Their feedback was *immensely* helpful and I can't thank each of them enough. Between my beta readers and my partner (my alpha reader), the story and characters just kept getting better and better.

Flushing out these characters and their story was an exciting process and the more I dove into it, the more I enjoyed it. By the end of the book, I fell in love with the characters. Sharing their story has been something I've enjoyed so much and I hope you enjoyed it too.

And again, I can't say enough about my partner and our ski friends. I wrote this for them after sitting at an après ski bar when they said there wasn't enough good ski themed smut. You guys are the best.

About the Author

I grew up in and around the city of Cincinnati, Ohio, graduating with a degree in Engineering.

I'm an avid skier and traveler, spending almost all of my free time traveling and enjoying time outside, ideally in the mountains. More often than not, I'm with my partner and our fur babies.

There isn't much that brings me more excitement or joy than getting in a car and driving across the country and exploring. And besides, twenty-something hour long road trips means we have lots of time to cross plenty of wonderfully smutty romance novels off our TBR list. And who doesn't love that?